The
TABLETS
of
ARARAT

The

TABLETS

of

ARARAT

C.J. ILLINIK

kregel
PUBLICATIONS

Grand Rapids, MI 49501

The Tablets of Ararat

© 2002 by C. J. Illinik

Published by Kregel Publications, P.O. Box 2607, Grand Rapids, MI 49501.

For more information about Kregel Publications, visit our Web site: www.kregel.com.

Library of Congress Cataloging-in-Publication Data
Illinik, C. J. (Carol J.)
   The tablets of Ararat / C. J. Illinik
      p.   cm.
   1. Ararat, Mount (Turkey)—Fiction. 2. Women archaeologists—Fiction. 3. Americans—Turkey—Fiction. 4. Turkey—Fiction. I. Title.

PS3609.L57 T33   2002
813'.6—dc21

2001050853

ISBN   0-8254-2908-0

Printed in the United States of America

02 03 04 05 06 / 3 2 1

Acknowledgments

I wish to dedicate this volume to "Dr. Bob," my longtime husband and best friend, maker of meals, and critic of first drafts. To each of my children and their spouses, who read bits and pieces of *Tablets* over the years of its creation. To my dedicated reading committee, who gave their time to read and discuss the first draft: Mrs. Sue Meier, Mrs. Lorene Richardson, and Mrs. Marty Shepard. To Mrs. Betty Hochlowski, retired English and English literature teacher who read an early manuscript. To Dr. Gloria T. Randle, who performed the final forthright critique and who has, I hope, made me a better writer. And last, but certainly not least, to Mr. Steve Barclift, Kregel's managing editor, whose faith in *Tablets*, patience, and professional counsel has guided me throughout the publishing process.

PROLOGUE

Cappadocia Province, Turkey, 1969

Filthy head to toe, her entire body aching after a day excavating in the underground city's deep, seventh-level well, American archaeologist Arianna Arista was ready to return to the surface. The surface meant fresh air, natural light, and a panoramic view of the vast, rolling Cappadocian landscape. Underground, claustrophobic sandstone-hued tufa walls, ceilings, and floors surrounded her. She had worked long hours within her own little circle of illumination. At this level only lightless passages and rooms lay beyond.

She was about to put down her trowel when she heard a metallic "clink." Exchanging the trowel for a squirrel-hair watercolor brush, Arianna carefully whisked dirt from the object. When her efforts revealed blackened links of a silver chain, it took every ounce of willpower to restrain her hand. She wanted to recklessly attack debris hiding the artifact in its centuries-old burial. Brushing the last dust motes from it, she saw that she had unearthed an ornate Byzantine cross. Her fatigue immediately disappeared.

Cabochon rubies and emeralds embellished the tarnished silver. Where the arms joined, what appeared to be an asymmetric lump of amber contained what looked like a dragonfly.

Arianna rose to her feet and moved her excavation lantern closer, then she bent to scrutinize the ornament. Suddenly, bright metal flashed in the dim halo of light. On sweeping away the rest of the fine dust she uncovered a gold tablet inscribed with tiny cuneiform characters.

But something else lay beneath. Carefully sliding the tablet slightly to one side—without moving the cross and chain out of place—she whisked off more rubble, uncovering a second tablet.

Frowning, the archaeologist sat back on her haunches and

stared at the twin flat objects. Déjà vu tugged at her mind. Then she remembered. The artifacts she had just discovered looked identical to a mysterious tablet she had seen the previous year in the apartment of Turkey's chief archaeologist, Dr. Galip Yaldiz. Not even Dr. Yaldiz himself knew the tablet's origin.

But Arianna and Dr. Yaldiz's assistant, Halime, had their suspicions. If the original tablet, and now these additional two, were what she and Halime suspected, these relics were the find of the century.

PART 1

CHAPTER 1

Just Before the Great Flood

"Make tablets of clay," the Voice said.

Nūh sat up, instantly awake. For days he had experimented with ways to keep track of the animals and the feed the ark would carry. He had discarded palm leaves as writing surfaces, finding them too fragile when dry. To cut characters in stone was laborious and impossibly slow. Why had he not seen it before? The obvious, simple solution had been there all the time. No longer able to sleep, he rolled from his wife's warm side and stepped out of bed. Glancing down at Namaah, he saw that he had not disturbed her.

Still muscular and flat-bellied, though in his six hundredth year, Nūh easily hefted Namaah's bronze cook kettle to his shoulder. Clad only in a loincloth, he headed toward a shallow creek that drained the nearby marsh. A full moon shone behind the translucent canopy of mist that embraced the world, but no man, woman, or child had ever seen its face. Nor had they seen the sun. The air below the canopy remained perpetually subtropical, moist and temperate year round. The only crisp-edged shadows ever seen were those cast by fire.

Phosphorescent dew covered Nūh's skin and mantled the ground and the vegetation that brushed against his legs. His flowing hair and gray-streaked beard shimmered in the eerie silver glow as he strode to the place where the village women excavated clay. Blue-green slime oozed up between his toes, and once he almost fell when his bare foot slipped on the slick bank. Reaching a certain spot, Nūh squatted. With the edge of his palm, he scraped at a thin coat of algae to reveal the layer underneath. Scooping up a dab of the sticky clay, he tested it between his thumb and index finger. Though a stinking greenish-black when raw, the clay would bake to a rich reddish brown.

Nūh filled the kettle half full of the ooze and topped it with water. Leaving the vessel by the stream, he headed back to his house and bed.

By midmorning the next day, the clay had settled to the bottom of the pot. Nūh poured off the excess water, along with worms, insects, and bits of vegetation. After letting clean water trickle into the pot, he stirred the clay and water to a gelatinous soup, and again left it to settle by the stream.

"I need a piece of loosely woven cloth, about one cubit and two hands square," he told his wife.* "Will you weave me a piece like the one you made into a tunic last year for Ham?"

Namaah looked up from where she knelt at her grinding stone. "Must the cloth be newly woven?" she asked.

"No, but it must be strong."

Namaah stiffly arose, brushing flour from her work-calloused hands. Going to a gopher wood chest, she removed a folded tunic and held it out to Nūh. "Ham never liked it; he said it scratched."

Nūh nodded. "Sounds like our son Ham. But it is right for my use." Now he wouldn't have to wait for her to weave a new cloth; he could screen the clay immediately. "But, my love . . ." He hesitated. "I also need another large pot."

Feigning anger, Namaah frowned with one raised eyebrow, an expression Nūh especially adored in his wife. "Another? So, it was you who took my best cooking pot. I looked for it a while ago. And what new device are you creating for the great ship?" she teased, meanwhile pointing to a second pot.

He winked. "I can only say it is women's work." Before she could question him further, he was out the door.

Laughing, Namaah shouted after him. "Don't keep them long, or you'll not eat."

Grinning, Nūh hurried down the path.

It took Nūh nearly two weeks to prepare enough clay for his purpose. When it had reached the correct purity, viscosity, and

---

* A cubit is eighteen to twenty-two inches. A hand is four inches.

texture, he formed it into a ball, then mashed the ball into a crude rectangle the length of his forearm and the thickness of his palm. *This is what God plans for the babe, newly squeezed from its mother's womb. A man is merely a lump of clay that God molds throughout his life,* he mused.

He tried to lift the leathery slab, but it sagged over his wrists like a half-filled goatskin water bag. Judging it too wet, he laid it on the flat riverbank to dry. Later, when the slab had hardened, Nūh braced it in the crook of his left arm and tried to etch it with a sharpened twig, but the now brittle clay shattered. He threw down the pieces in disgust, his patience exhausted.

"Almighty God," Nūh shouted at the heavens, "You bid me make tablets of clay, but unfired the clay collapses or breaks." He flung his arms wide. "Yet fired, I would not be able to score it with a flint-tipped stylus."

His spirit its lowest since beginning the project, Nūh shuffled to the secluded glade beneath a lush umbrella of giant fern trees. Long ago, he had built a stone altar there. After centuries in the humid atmosphere—an atmosphere six times heavier than it would be in the twenty-first century A.D.—the structure was barely discernible. Massive roots had split the foundation rocks until the altar slumped and leaned. Velvety mosses in uncountable shades of green rounded the contours of the decaying, lichen-covered stones.

Nūh prostrated himself on the spongy ground. "Lord, how shall I finish the tablets?" he moaned.

No sonorous voice answered. But, as Nūh prayed, the sun briefly burned a hole through the swirling mist, and the brilliant ray struck a nearby pebble.

Nūh recoiled from the painful light. Blinking away the purple-black blotches that distorted his vision, he peered closer at the pebble and recognized that the stone was actually a gold nugget, about the size of his thumb. It was the first time he had seen the beautiful mineral in the glade, yet he had knelt there for centuries in supplication to Yahweh. As Nūh dug his fingers into the damp mulch to unearth the nugget, he uncovered an even larger one. Pure, malleable gold, just what he needed. God had again given him an answer.

The next afternoon, exhausted after a long morning applying the last coat of pitch to the ark's expansive deck, Nūh reclined on a knoll overlooking the plain where stood his home and the almost finished ship. He was nearly asleep, his eyes half closed. Nearby, a spindly-legged child tossed sticks at a lizard. As a new thought struck him, Nūh abruptly stood. *Truly I am getting old and forgetful.* "Charmak," he called to the child, "go to the great ship. Tell my son Japheth I wish to see him." He watched the boy run down the trail toward the ark.

Japheth soon hurried up the hill. "What is it, my father?" he panted.

Nūh lifted his eyes from the symbols he had been sketching in the dirt at his feet. "Japheth, tomorrow I want you and your wife to stop working on the ark. Instead, you are to go to the riverbank and gather much clay. Pile it on the damp skins I've laid by your mother's oven. Be sure to cover the clay with wet skins and cloths so it will not dry."

At his son's questioning look Nūh said, "I make tablets for a count of the animals and foods we take aboard."

Still puzzled, Japheth waited. When his father offered no further explanation, he went back to the ark to fetch his wife.

Nūh then sent for Ham and Shem. When they stood before him, he said, "I want you and your wives to go to the altar in the glade. Bring me all the gold you find there, and bring to me all the gold that belongs to you and your wives."

Surprised, Shem said, "I did not know the glade contained gold."

"God showed it to me only yesterday."

Shem shrugged. "My wife and I had planned to trade our gold for food anyway; gold cannot be eaten, can it?" Shem laughed and nudged Ham, who scowled and drew back.

"As always, you are logical, my son. True, we cannot eat the gold, but it is to go with us in another form."

"Must we give *everything?*" Ham growled. "My wife will not want to give up the things of her dowry."

"God has a better use for the gold." Nūh gripped Ham's shoulder and affectionately shook it. "Surely you can persuade my daughter-in-law to part with her trinkets."

Ham slid his shoulder from under Nūh's caress. "I will try, but she will not like it," he complained, and turned away.

As Ham followed Shem down the path, Nūh cried after them, "Even with the gold you both bring me, I will not have enough. And I sense time is running out." He mumbled the last under his breath.

The tablets measured a span wide by a cubit long and a finger thick.[*] Thirty of them lay drying between damp reed mats on the stream's sandy bank. They were ready to fire, but Nūh could produce neither a high enough nor a steady enough temperature in his wife's bread oven. When the first three tablets cooled too rapidly and shattered, he tried something else. Digging a pit, he lined it with straw and put a layer of heavy slate at the bottom of the hole. He arranged a pair of tablets on the slate. Together, he and Namaah packed the pit with straw mixed with cattle dung, then topped the mix with additional straw.

Plucking a coal from the cook fire with a pair of wet sticks, Nūh touched it to the straw. Flames roared into the sky, forcing the curious onlookers, who had gathered to torment him, to retreat.

"You would do better to set fire to that foolish ship," shouted one. "Yes, and let its ashes float on the wind—it will never float on water," hooted another. The crowd laughed in appreciation of the joke.

Nūh ignored them; he was used to their jeering and knew they would soon lose interest and leave. Letting the flames gradually die, he kept the temperature in the crude kiln as even as possible. At the end of three days, he eagerly removed

---

[*] About eight inches wide, eighteen inches long, and three-quarters inch thick.

the ash from the pit. Gingerly, he retrieved the two scorched tablets. Both had shrunk, and were slightly warped, but both were whole. Despite his weariness from the long vigil at the kiln, he felt like dancing.

Before baking the rest of the tablets, Nūh pounded a nugget of pure gold into a foil the thickness of his thumbnail. He then formed the foil around the fired tablet, but, when he tried to press characters into it, the gold sheet slipped beneath the stylus and ripped.

Discouraged to the point of giving up, Nūh put his head in his hands. *How can I attach the gold to the clay?* he silently pleaded. Suddenly, coming from the tree above his head, a staccato tapping caught his attention. Startled, he looked up. A woodpecker rapidly darted its bill in and out of a hole. The bird's actions gave Nūh an idea. Boring a hole into one edge of an unfired, still-moist tablet with a sharpened stick, he twisted the stick until the hole was wider at the bottom than at the top. Holding the tablet at arms' length, he studied it. Satisfied, he continued boring holes until they lined all four edges.

Of the rest of the tablets, several cracked in two when fired. Others split when Nūh bored the holes too close to the edge, causing an unequal stress during heating or cooling. Some tablets were too warped to use. Of the thirty fired, twelve came out of the pit in perfect condition.

While the last tablets baked, Nūh carved a flat tablet-size tray of fire-hardened shittimwood and lined it with beeswax. He poured a layer of molten gold into the tray's bottom and quickly pressed a fired tablet into the liquefied metal. Lastly, he poured more liquid gold over the tablet, filling the holes around the edges and creating an even layer on every surface. When the gold hardened, its rodlike extensions into the holes prevented the sheath from slipping.

It did not surprise Nūh that God had provided enough gold to finish exactly twelve tablets—no more, no less.

CHAPTER 2

Some animals approached the ark in pairs. Others, especially those named "clean" by God, came in groups of seven. It was as though God guided them with phantom leads and halted them at that exact point where Nūh could note their arrival. Supernaturally tamed, they walked, crawled, and flew up the steep ramp. A member of Nūh's family met each pair at the top and led it to its proper cage, pen, or stall. It seemed to the humans that the beasts were in a trance, so docile were they.

Whether a lanky giraffe or a diminutive, parasitic insect lodged in the wrinkled hide of a rhinoceros, Nūh marked it on his tablet. He rendered the hieroglyphic characters on the tablet as tiny as his swollen fingers allowed, leaving scant space between the lines of writing. When his legs and feet ached too much to stand, one of his sons helped him.

As the last two creatures, a pair of dun-colored steppe horses, trotted toward him, a rumbling began in the eastern sky. As the first rain drop splashed on Nūh's face, he anxiously glanced upward. With practiced jabs of his stylus, he hurriedly impressed angular symbols that represented the horses into the soft gold. At his concluding stroke—the last notation on the last line of the twelfth and last tablet—the drops increased to a curtain of falling water.

Though he knew it came from God, the unfamiliar rain frightened Nūh. He was thoroughly drenched and ready to go into the ark and shelter, but he took the time to draw a crude hull at the bottom left corner of the twelfth tablet. Staring at the rectangular character, he chewed the end of his stylus, and thought, *it is not enough*. A gust of wind whipped stinging rain into his face and blurred his vision. Scrubbing the water from his eyes, he nodded, smiling, then slashed four diagonal marks above the box. "Rain on the ark," he explained to the duns who stood patiently at the ramp's base.

As the distant rumbling grew louder, the horses cocked their ears in that direction and restlessly pawed. Nūh jumped aside when the nervous stallion abruptly bolted forward. Slipping and falling on the wet, dung-slickened boards, the horse scrambled up the ramp.

With the last tablet firmly clasped under one arm, Nūh grabbed a fistful of tail hairs belonging to the mare before she could follow her mate. Letting her help him up the steep ramp, Nūh marveled that the spirited wild pony did not bite or kick at him.

Safely inside the ark, Nūh dropped the dun's matted black tail. Groaning, he stooped and laid the heavy tablet on the deck. The long hours of pressing a stylus into ceramic-backed metal had stiffened his fingers. The skin at their tips was raw, and his spine felt as quavery as the gel that encased freshly-laid tree frog eggs. His right hand bracing the small of his back, and flexing his other elbow that had supported the tablets, Nūh straightened and peered out at the rain-saturated terrain. The landscape appeared dismal and strange, with not a living thing in sight. None of the neighbors and relatives—they who had mocked him for two centuries while he built the ark—had come to bid his family farewell. Knowing they all would perish gave him no gratification, only profound grief. Tears streaked his cheeks. Seeing his agony, his wife put her arms around him and tenderly stroked the rain from his beard.

Suddenly, a bolt of lightning crackled through the sky and struck their abandoned house with a stupendous explosion. Nothing was left of the place where they had lived for centuries except steaming rubble.

Shaking with terror, the couple staggered backward, deeper into the ark. At that instant, the ark's massive door squealed and stirred with a life of its own. Slowly at first, but gaining momentum, it slid horizontally on fat-greased hardwood rollers until it slammed shut with a thunderous crash, sealing them in.

* * *

379 Days Later

"At last we can go out," Nūh joyously shouted, as he untied the gate to the goat pen. It had been over a year since his family had walked on firm land. They had grown ever more eager to disembark the ship since, months before, it had come to rest with a mighty crunching and final lurch. Only when a released dove had not returned did they begin to have hope. Now, at last, God had told them to turn the animals loose and leave.

"Shem, Japheth, Ham, open the door!" Nūh had to shout to be heard above the bedlam as the animals caught the smell of wet, fecund earth streaming through the opening.

"Free the beasts," he ordered. Liberated from their long confinement, the animals streamed down the ramp and swiftly scattered.

As soon as he was able, Nūh built a stone altar on a hill far below the ark, and dedicated it to Yahweh. Within the altar's base he imbedded the twelfth tablet, the one that had upon it his special signature that depicted rain falling on the ark.

* * *

Centuries passed. Earthquake, ice, and wind weakened, then destroyed, Nūh's altar. Alluvial drifts from the eroding Ararat massif gradually mounted eighteen feet of sand and gravel over it. Shielded within the pile of rock, the twelfth inventory tablet lay dented, but intact.

Early in the fourth century A.D. a volcano in a remote region of southwest Africa erupted and spewed its bowels into the stratosphere. For two years, a dense cloud girdled the world, causing freakish weather and spectacular sunsets throughout the northern hemisphere. A reduction of the average temperature brought on unseasonable cold in what someday would be called northern Europe, North America, Siberia, and Asia Minor. Thirty to forty feet of snow fell on the flanks of Ararat and its surrounding hills and plains. Mile-thick glaciers developed on the mountain.

Eventually, there came a summer when a high pressure cell of unusually humid air, spawned by the torrid Mediterranean sun, swept north and met the frigid temperatures over the Asian ranges. Resulting thermals created towering thunderheads, turgid with moisture. Tepid rains poured on Mt. Ararat for three weeks, rapidly melting the snow imprisoned in the perennial glaciers at the summit. Melt formed rivulets; rivulets became streams; streams turned into huge rivers plunging down the mountain.

One such torrent funneled into a narrow ravine that immediately compressed its head into a fifteen-foot-high bore. The speeding bore carried with it tons of rock, from cow-size boulders, to a fine grit that acted as an abrasive slurry. Crushing or grinding smooth everything in its path, the bore approached the little hill containing the remnants of Nūh's altar. The hill caused the great wave to crest suddenly, then dive and shovel into the earth. It stripped away all but a four-foot layer of aggregate and mud from above the buried tablet.

A winter creek formed alongside the altar site. Every year the creek expanded and resculpted its shallow bed. One particularly wet spring, a swift current cut away the creek's northern bank and gouged the twelfth tablet from the gravelly vault that had held it safe for hundreds of years. Though the small stream lacked the power to move the heavy tablet far, it managed to drag it downstream until it smashed into a jagged rock. The rock's sharp edge ripped the thin gold sheathing, the tablet cracked, and the corner with Nūh's personal mark broke off.

The main piece sank to the streambed and stayed there, but the capricious current picked up the lighter, triangular-shaped corner, bumping it fifty yards downstream. It came to rest on the south bank, wedged in a tangle of roots.

Chapter 3

Armenia, A.D. 1038

As night fell, a delicious odor awakened the old sow bear denned in a hollow tree deep in the forest. Lifting her head, she wove it back and forth as her twitching nose sought the direction from which came the wonderful smell. She was trembling and woozy; for most of the five months she had hibernated she had eaten little. With muffled squeaks, tiny triplet cubs slurped at her teats. When the sow's empty gut grumbled, she tentatively stretched muscles atrophied by lack of use and rose from her bed, dislodging the protesting cubs onto the den floor in a squealing, squirming heap. Butting through the packed snow that covered the den's opening, she crawled out.

The black bear could not see well in daylight. At night her vision was even worse, and the whither-deep snow made the going tough. Clumsy in her weakness, stopping periodically to rest, she was dragged onward by a taut leash of scent until she came to the clearing where the manimals had their den. At the forest edge she paused, foreleg lifted. With upward jerks of her head, her doglike nose explored the air.

No sound came from the sod-roofed hut, but a slender thread of smoke curled from the crumbling stone chimney. Dim light, seeping through thin cracks between the shutters of a single window, cast convoluted streaks on the snowdrift beneath.

The bear's ravenous state nullified her normal caution; she plowed across the clearing and circled the hovel. Snuffling at the door, she knew the delicious odor came from the other side, and she nosed the rough-hewn wood, testing its strength. When the door did not yield, she raked it with her claws, but that action produced nothing but deep scars in the wood. Finally, the bear stood on her hind legs and leaned her full weight against the planks. The boards refused to break or separate, but the leather straps that secured them tore loose. Door and bear plunged into the one-room dwelling in a cloud of dust and splintered wood.

Disoriented, its head skimming the rafters, the great beast swayed on hind legs, little pig eyes searching the room. Suddenly they focused on two manimals. A dreadful rumble emerged from deep within the bear's chest.

When the bear clawed at the hut door, Anna had just started to serve her son, Gregori, a bowl of steaming venison stew. At the scuffing on the door she froze in midstep by the cooking fire. Though alerted, she was not unduly alarmed; wild animals often scratched at the walls or door, even on the roof, and they soon left. But this time, before she had time to think, the bear had shattered the door and cannonballed into the small room.

Startled and off balance, Anna tottered and nearly fell. Boiling stew slopped onto her hand, causing her to drop the bowl. The pottery dish broke as it hit the floor and hot stew spattered the bear's tender nose.

Mad with pain, mouth wide open, yellowed fangs bared, the beast lunged at the woman. Anna screamed only once before the bear's huge jaws closed over her face, and the powerful canine teeth penetrated her skull, instantly killing her.

When the bear attacked his mother, Gregori scrambled to the far end of the room and hid behind the corner woodpile. The six-year-old's eyes were tightly shut against the carnage. Whimpering, he clutched his ears, trying to block out the horrible sounds of the bear mauling his mother's body.

Returning home after a long day of cutting wood, Gregori's father almost didn't hear his wife's cry in the snow-insulated forest. At her faint, agonized scream, he tore off the bundle of wood that had been strapped to his back and sped toward the hut as fast as his crude snowshoes allowed. Left behind, lashed to the bundle, was his razor-sharp ax. Thus, unarmed, he burst through the hut's doorway.

The bear heard the male manimal coming. Rising on her hind legs, she met him as he blundered into the hut. Too late,

Gregori's father remembered the ax. Before he had a chance to gather his wits, the bear enclosed him in her deadly embrace. Had he gone limp or feigned death, he might have lived, but he struggled and perished.

Gregori heard his father's dying gurgle and screamed. The sow turned from the man's body and stared at the spot where the hiding boy crouched. Filled with killing rage and determined to get to him, she loped to the woodpile and dug at the logs. It was more than Gregori could take. When he saw the bloody teeth so close, he fainted. As he did, the bear's claws hooked the cloth of his pant leg. In trying to drag him free, she tore open the calf of his left leg. Though the scimitarlike talons ripped skin, muscle, and ligaments, they missed the major blood vessels. Because Gregori did not move, and because the smell of cooked meat tempted her, the sow lumbered back to the spilled stew and began lapping at it.

As the blood from Gregori's terrible wound congealed, the coarse cloth of his pant leg fused with it and acted as a compress. That, and the icy weather, saved him from bleeding to death. The next morning two hunters from Artaxata stopped to visit their friend, Gregori's father. Instead, they found the mauled bodies of Gregori's parents and Gregori, who was out of his head and mute. The hunters bound the boy's wounds and buried the bodies. Not knowing what else to do with him, they took Gregori to the Armenian orphanage in Artaxata.

It was five years before Gregori spoke again.

Chapter 4

St. Jacob's Monastery, A.D. 1058

The monk, Gregori, hunched over a piece of fine parchment spread on his crude writing table. Unconsciously, he leaned closer to the small oil lamp in its wall niche in an attempt to absorb its warmth. The flame cast a dim light over most of the table's surface, but did little to penetrate the gloom within the monk's austere cell. The inadequate light caused Gregori to squint as he brushed the last strokes of *sinopis* onto the image's upper lip.[*]

That detail completed, Gregori dropped the brush on the table and thrust his clenched fists inside the roomy sleeves of his black wool robe. He shivered again and hugged himself. No matter what he did to circumvent it, the freezing winds blowing off Mount Ararat managed to penetrate his barren cell in the monastery, which stood on the mountain's side at an elevation of seven thousand feet. The month before, a thin layer of ice, formed by his breath during sleep, had coated the wall above his straw-filled sleeping pallet. In the weeks following, it had gradually thickened into a glossy sheet, like an inch-thick miniature glacier.

Gregori pushed the parchment aside. With his hands still in his sleeves he rested his arms on the table and pillowed his head on them. He had finished all but the last cartoon for a series of paintings commissioned by the Patriarch of Cappadocia.[†] The drawings had been in progress all winter, and the group portrait of the twelve apostles was all he had left to do. He looked forward to early summer when he would personally carry the cartoons to Cappadocia and render the large paint-

---
[*] red ocher
[†] A *cartoon* is the preliminary drawing or sketch for an artistic work.

ings in the monastery there. Dawn was nearing and he was fatigued from working all night. But with dawn would come Mass and then the daily chores. Sleep would have to wait.

Barely six inches more than five feet, the monk was nearly as broad as he was tall. The she-bear's attack had left him with a shortened left leg and a pronounced limp. Having spent most of his adult life bent over a drawing table, he had developed a slight stoop and was, by age twenty-six, rather plump. When another monk occasionally teased him about his increasing girth, Gregori laughed and patted his generous paunch and reminded the other that he, Gregori, was a tribute to God's abundance and living proof of the prolific goats and abundant gardens of Arghuri, the village that sustained the monks of St. Jacob's.

Gregori studied the Christ head on which he had been working. It pleased him; it was one of his better pieces. He had drawn an admonishing frown on the noble face and had extended the image's first two fingers of the clenched right hand in the classic benediction.

Over the years Gregori had become a respected religious artist, known for his fine murals and mosaics. His encaustic panels were in great demand.[*] At the request of Patriarchs and Metropolitans, he had traveled to execute commissions throughout the Byzantine world. His most famous work, a mural depicting Christ's agony at Gethsemane, covered a wall at Trebizond's St. Savas Church overlooking the Black Sea.

Gregori had sailed across the Black Sea three times: once north to Cherson and twice east to Thrace. He still carried a cherished souvenir from Constantinople. While strolling through a busy open-air market on a hot summer day, a shiny gold coin had caught his eye. Striding over to the booth displaying the coin, he bent to examine it. The seventh-century solidus was in fine condition, and the portraits of the emperor Heraclius and his son were still crisp.

---

[*] *Encaustic* is a process in which colored wax is infused into a surface with hot irons.

On a whim Gregori asked the Greek vendor the coin's price. It was of course too high for an impoverished monk, who had no business contemplating such a material purchase in the first place. Gregori turned away, but the clever Greek had sensed the Armenian's yearning. He called after Gregori, urging him to purchase the coin. Suddenly Gregori had an inspiration. He drew from his habit's seemingly bottomless sleeve the small roll of parchment and piece of grape vine charcoal he always carried.

Squatting in the dust before the booth, Gregori began a sketch of the shopkeeper. Soon, a marveling crowd had gathered around him. When the vain merchant heard the observers exclaiming over Gregori's work and saw the accurate likeness of himself magically materializing before his eyes, he offered to exchange the solidus for it. It was as Gregori had planned. The exchange was made, and Gregori walked away with the only luxury he ever purchased for himself.

Gregori had also made the grueling pilgrimage southeast to St. Catherine's, a sixth-century monastery at the foot of Mt. Sinai. It had been the first Byzantine monastery built. During his visit there, the monks showed Gregori an authentic document authored by Muhammad, the military-minded founder of Islam, in which Muhammad had declared St. Catherine's forever safe from his marauding armies. Legend has it that his horse, Boraq, ascended to heaven from there.

Asleep with his head on his arms, Gregori did not hear the pealing of bells that signaled Mass was about to begin. It was only when a monk passed his cell ringing a *semantron*, a wooden gong, that he roused. Gregori jumped to his feet, quickly rolled up the sheepskin parchment, and tucked it into a goat-hide quiver with the rest of the finished cartoons. He placed the quiver on a shelf that spanned the width of the cell. The shelf was an integral part of the stone wall and high enough to foil the most agile rat.

Before leaving for Mass, Gregori removed the leather sandals and long woolen stockings he wore when working in his cell. To a lesser man, the subfreezing temperature would have been intolerable, but Gregori was well padded. Slipping his bare feet into the sandals and lifting the cowl of his robe over his balding head, he hurried out.

Late again, God forgive me, he thought. "God, forgive me," he prayed aloud, all the while mentally castigating himself for his lassitude. He limped down the corridor as fast as he could with his hands clasped across his stomach and his head bowed.

The monks who had built St. Jacob's had constructed the outer door with stout cedar planks. Gregori struggled to open it against the wind. When he succeeded, the frosty air bit deep into his lungs, making him cough. Flat-footed and exceedingly cautious in the dim predawn light, he crossed the ice-coated cobblestones of the chapel courtyard. Snow-laced wind stung the exposed parts of his body. Despite his body's generous insulation, his teeth were chattering by the time he entered the chapel.

The Office of Preparation, the first part of the Mass, had just ended. Father Thaddeaus, the abbot, was emerging through the left door of the dividing iconostasis screen that shielded the prothesis where the sacred vessels of the Eucharist were prepared.

Their heads bowed, his brother monks did not glance up when Gregori entered, late as usual, but Gregori saw Father Thaddeaus lift a disapproving eyebrow. He sheepishly shuffled to an innocuous position behind the rest of the men so that they partially concealed him.

Father Thaddeaus often speculated about whether Gregori would ever do anything on time. The abbot had long ago resigned himself to the young man's perpetual tardiness.

Automatically beginning the Holy Liturgy, Thaddeaus continued to muse over Gregori, who was like a son to him. *He is devout, a hard worker,* thought the abbot, *and what an artist he is— certainly a credit to the church. Though he lives in a world apart from the rest of us, I will sorely miss him when he leaves for Cappadocia.*

CHAPTER 5

Gregori finished the complex drawing of the apostles by the end of March. He was eager to be off to Cappadocia and, as the weather mellowed in the following weeks, access to neighboring cities became possible. Caravans, following the ancient horse-trading route that ran south through the Caucasus, stopped at the modest town of Iğdir before continuing the lengthy journey to Constantinople.

It was in Iğdir that Gregori planned to join a certain camel train. His plans changed when, two nights before the morning of his scheduled departure from the monastery, the abbot's wizened aide rushed into Gregori's cell. Shaking Gregori awake, the aide said, "His Holiness requests your presence."

"What does His Holiness want with me this time of night?" Gregori sleepily asked, peering at the old monk's lined face, hazy in the dim light of the oil lamp he held.

"I am not sure. His Holiness has been irritable and pacing his room since the messenger came."

"What messenger?" Gregori threw back the bedcover and stumbled to his feet.

"He arrived shortly after midnight, riding a half-dead horse that looked to have traveled far and fast."

"The matter sounds serious. It will take me only a minute to don my habit," Gregori said, slipping his robe over his head.

In the black silence of morning's second hour, the monks' sandals softly hissed on the uneven rock floor. The lamp jerked at the feeble old monk's every step, causing the two men's shadows to crouch and leap along the rough wall as they hurried toward the abbot's private quarters.

The tall, emaciated Thaddeaus was physically the opposite of rotund Gregori. Years of study and meditation, and the stress of managing the remote monastery, had etched the abbot's pale face with a network of fine lines. His hair, and the beard that flowed nearly to his waist, were prematurely white. As a part of his vows, he had chosen a life of celibacy. From the time Gregori had arrived at St. Jacob's from the Artaxata orphanage, Thaddeaus had loved Gregori as the son he would never have.

Gregori had never seen the august abbot so disheveled, nor as nervous. The abbot's voice trembled with trepidation when he spoke. "You are to leave for Cappadocia right away."

Though the blood began pounding in his temples and his feet wanted to dance, Gregori tried not to show the excitement that threatened to make him lose all dignity.

"Immediately?" he asked. "I have not completed the last drawing."

"It can be finished in Cappadocia, can it not?"

"Yes, of course, but . . ." Gregori stammered and stopped, worried that the abbot might change his mind.

Thaddeaus turned his back so Gregori could not see his anxious frown. "I have just received word that Arp Arslan and his Seljuk Turks have taken Manzikert. They may be headed this way." He pressed the heel of his palm to his forehead and massaged the aching muscles above his eyes. "First thing tomorrow, you are to leave for Cappadocia. I am sending some holy relics, including the tablets, with you."

Gregori stiffened, now uneasy and no longer excited about the journey. "I am unworthy of such trust."

But the abbot continued as though he had not heard. "The roads are dangerous, and the attacks on travelers many. However, I cannot send guards with you," he added, increasing Gregori's dismay.

His stomach churning, Gregori tried again to discourage the abbot from assigning him such a responsibility. "I am too unimportant to carry holy treasures."

The abbot swung around, smiling. "That is the precise reason it will be safe with you. No one will suspect a poor artist, an artist who is also an even poorer monk. If they should ask, merely tell people you have been assigned to Cappadocia and are on your way there."

"What of St. Jacob's and the rest of the brothers? Of you?" Gregori asked, suddenly aware of their peril.

"I do not believe we need fear the Turks. I hear they are quite tolerant of religions other than their own, that they allow Christians to worship in peace," Thaddeaus consoled Gregori, not letting him see his apprehension.

Gregori was dubious. "That may be so, but it is rumored that nothing is safe from their greed, even sacred reliquaries."

Thaddeaus shook his head. "The Moslems cherish many of the same relics as we do, especially those that belong to the saints venerated by both religions. But I'm afraid the fate of other relics is to be melted down and made into baubles destined to adorn the Turkish princes and their concubines." He gave a deep sigh. "Yes, it is best to send certain ones from St. Jacob's to Cappadocia, and not chance their loss."

Gregori held his arms wide, glanced down at himself, and grimaced. "I assuredly do not look more than I am, but is it not too much of a risk to send holy relics with me alone?"

Thaddeaus placed his hands on Gregori's shoulders. "You see? You are the consummate humble man for the job. There is no doubting it. And I promise, every St. Jacob's monk will be praying for the relics' safety. God will protect you and them." The abbot crooked a finger at Gregori. "Come, let us choose what is to go."

Entering the chapel, they passed through the right door of the iconostasis screen and into the *diakonikon,* the room that held the monastery's sacred books and relics. By tradition, a monk of Gregori's lowly rank was not allowed to enter the room, and Gregori had never been in it. His curious eyes could not absorb enough.

The abbot waved at a stack of shelves filled with broken pottery and wooden utensils brought down from the ark of Noah. He picked up a dark wooden box and delicately brushed a thin layer of dust from the top. "I wish you could carry all that came from the ark, especially the cup in this container. Some say it belonged to Noah himself."

Gregori's mind had changed about the assignment. "Why

can I not take everything to safety?" he asked, chagrined that some precious items might be left behind. "St. Jacob's has many donkeys at its disposal."

Thaddeaus smiled down at the little monk and nodded. "If only that were possible, but the most valuable and important objects must go with you on one pack animal. More beasts would attract too much attention." The abbot opened the box he held and lifted a perfectly turned pottery cup from a padding of fine carded wool. "This cup is my favorite, and I naturally want it to go to Cappadocia. But because it bears no gold or jewels, I do not think the Seljuks would find it of interest, so it will remain here."

Awed, Gregori gently ran his fingertips along the cup's slightly chipped edge. "It should go."

"It cannot!" The abbot replaced the cup in its fleece nest and closed the box, then strode to the opposite end of the room. He opened one panel of a six-foot-tall triptych, a three-paneled screen.

Before following the abbot through the open panel, Gregori paused to study the triptych that was painted with lifelike scenes depicting Noah's flood.

"Come, Brother Gregori, we have no time to waste," the abbot urged.

Stepping through the open panel, Gregori gasped. On a shelf, standing against the wall and illuminating the whole room in reflected light, were two gold-sheathed tablets.

The two tablets had remained intact the many generations since Noah passed them down to his son, Shem. Their true history, and man's ability to read the ancient script, had long been lost. Nevertheless, the tablets were revered, having had, according to legend, something to do with Noah. Once a year, they were put on display and honored by an *Occasional Office,* a special service attended by the inhabitants of surrounding villages.

"These you will take," declared Abbot Thaddeaus to the stunned Gregori.

CHAPTER 6

Gregori's anticipation of his upcoming trip to Cappadocia was so great that he had slept only fitfully, rising two hours before dawn. For once, he was on time. Still, when he reached the monastery courtyard, he found that his brother monks had readied the two donkeys. Huddling close for warmth, they awaited him. In the torchlight, the frozen breath of men and beasts formed glowing clouds around their heads. Thick, glittering frost encrusted the donkeys' coats and the men's shoulders and cowls.

Gregori was tugging at the saddle donkey's girth when Father Thaddeaus approached. The abbot patted the donkey's neck, saying, "If you hurry to Iğdir you can catch the season's first caravan from Persia."

Sensing Gregori's misgiving, the abbot's arms embraced the stout little monk. "Be not afraid, my son; our prayers go with you. God will see you safely to your destination."

Gregori could feel the gaunt abbot trembling in the cold. "I am not afraid for myself, Your Holiness: God will protect me and that which I carry," Gregori assured him. "But I fear for St. Jacob's and the villages."

"Do not forget. We also are protected by God." Father Thaddeaus nudged Gregori toward the saddle. "Ah, but it is time. Go!"

As Gregori mounted, five villagers entered the monastery courtyard. Each man led a heavily loaded donkey. During the midwinter months, when the roads were impassable, the village women knitted warm sweaters, stockings, and other items from sheep wool and goat hair. Later, when the roads cleared, their men traded the handmade articles for locally unavailable items. These five would accompany Gregori as far as Iğdir, then west to Ağri, or north to Artaxata. The last thing Gregori heard, as they lined up and rode out, was the abbot calling, "Send me word of your safe arrival."

The little band was well along the narrow trail by the time the sun topped the low foothills. Though the air was sharp in their nostrils and the snow on Mt. Ararat's summit deep yet, tips of grass had begun to thrust through the lowland's winter-hardened soils. In another two weeks a blanket of emerald would cover the treeless pastures through which they passed. Summer pastures on the higher slopes would not bloom until the lower rims of the snow fields melted. Then, the sun's heat on the newly exposed ground would trigger life in the many species of seeds that slept below the surface.

When they had started that morning, the road was frozen. By noon, it had thawed, and the donkeys sank to their fetlocks in sticky muck. The season's first ravenous mosquitoes and tiny biting flies, which drew blood wherever they lit, plagued man and beast alike. Not wishing to let the insect pests have a chance to feast, the men stopped only to water the donkeys and adjust the saddle packs. When it was time to eat, they fished food from their pockets or saddlebags and ate on the move. They drank yogurt diluted with water from skin flasks.

The band reached Iğdir, where the abbot had arranged for Gregori to lodge with the priest of the Armenian church, at dusk. Two members of the band stayed with the animals and trade goods. The other three scattered to the homes of relatives or friends.

Again too excited to sleep despite the difficulties of the day's journey, Gregori rose an hour before sunrise. He was stiff and sore all over, and the many hours in the saddle had generated a painful blister on his left buttock. Rubbing a particularly sore spot, he looked down and saw that multiple bruises discolored the insides of his legs. Leaving the village men, Gregori repacked and saddled his two donkeys but did not mount, preferring to stay off the saddle as long as possible. Iğdir's streets were nearly deserted as he set out to find the Persian caravan. The barking of dogs and the clop-clopping of his donkeys' hooves were the only sounds that broke the silence. Leading the donkeys, he limped the breadth of Iğdir before he heard camel groans and men shouting. He followed the sounds to the *caravanserai* courtyard where the caravan was reassembling.

Everything was enveloped in a haze of dust-laden fog. Gregori made his way through the confusion of men and animals until he spotted a man—by his garb, a Syrian—standing on a kneeling camel's saddle. The man's nose was like a hawk's beak and his bellow that of a bull. Gregori stopped to watch, marveling at the way the Syrian brought harmony to the chaos with only his commanding voice.

"Is this the Persian caravan bound for Sebaste?" Gregori shouted up at him.

Appearing annoyed at the interruption, the Syrian's flashing eyes glared at him. "Thus, it is so."

"I am Gregori from St. Jacob's Monastery. My wish is to travel with you as far as Sebaste."

Immediately the Syrian's expression softened. As a young man he had sought refuge from bandits at St. Jacob's. He executed a slight bow. "I am in debt to St. Jacob's and its monks. It is an honor to have you join us, Father Gregori."

The Syrian pointed with his quirt to a quiet spot several meters from the worst of the bedlam. "Take your beasts over there. Stay until I come for you."

Gregori led his donkeys to the indicated place in a vacant merchant stall. From there he watched the reloading of plush Persian carpets and packets of Chinese silk wrapped in water-proofed skins. In Iğdir the caravan always added beautiful Armenian rugs and fancy embroideries.

The bad-tempered camels swung their heads back and forth, seeking a body (two-footed or four) at which to spit, or flesh in which to sink their yellow teeth. To Gregori, the melodious tinkling of their bridle bells did almost, but not quite, counter-act their ugly attitude.

Every camel was loaded with its maximum weight, then donkeys were brought up and packed with the surplus the camels could not carry. When the caravan was loaded and aligned,

Gregori counted more than seventy men, fifty-two camels, and twenty-eight donkeys, including his.

Not a bit of the rich mosaic of sound and sight escaped the artist monk's observant eyes and keen ears. He savored it all, locking the sights and sounds into his memory for future reference.

Suddenly, a troop of well-armed men, mounted on fast, light-footed Arabian horses, charged into the courtyard. *Why should a caravan carrying silk and rugs warrant such a powerful guard?* he wondered. Then, emerging from the shadows like something from a dream, carried upon the shoulders of four giant, dark-skinned men, a dazzling palanquin entered the courtyard.

Dawn's first rays reflected from the splendor of the sedan's inlaid silver and mother-of-pearl sides. Spun-gold tassels jiggled and swayed on the tightly closed drapes of the cab. A tall, grim-faced man wearing a red turban walked by its side. As the drapes moved, Gregori tried to see who rode within, but the passenger remained hidden. He had just absorbed the sight of the first palanquin when two more came into view, also beautiful but not as opulent.

When the palanquins entered the *caravanserai*, the Syrian immediately leaped from his perch on the camel's back and ran toward them. Before he reached them, however, two horse guards pranced up and accompanied him, keeping him between their dancing steeds. When the Syrian and the red-turbaned individual met, they bowed, then conversed while the horse-men watched from a few feet away. Gregori could not hear the conversation, but his curiosity was definitely piqued.

When the Syrian at last came and showed Gregori to his position in line, Gregori stiffly climbed into the saddle, gingerly settling his sore limbs. The caravan moved out as the sun streaked the eastern horizon and flamed on the golden cross at the tip of the Armenian church's spire. Heading west toward Erzincan and Sebaste, it would continue to Ancrya, but Gregori planned to wait at Sebaste until he could catch a southbound caravan.

As the day wore on, the frozen dew melted and evaporated from the road. Fine, choking dust, stirred by the hooves of the foremost animals, clogged Gregori's nose and throat. It deposited a uniform coat of reddish-tan on everything. Gregori coughed and spat grit from his lungs for half the morning, then finally imitated the other men. Buying a *kaffiyeh* from one of them, he wrapped it around his head in the nomad style so that it covered and protected his lower face.

When the sun was at its zenith and the heat its worst, the caravan stopped in a large grove of scraggly pines for an hour's respite. The palanquins and their guards drew to the side and remained aloof while the rest of the caravan members, including Gregori, sat in the sparse shade to eat. They ate a light meal of bread and white goat cheese, washing it down their dry throats with camels' milk. As he chewed, the monk kept his eyes on the palanquins, until he saw a veiled figure daintily step down from each sedan, disappear behind some boulders, then hurry back into seclusion. Though long robes and veils concealed their forms, Gregori saw by their walk that one woman was young, the other two much older.

The caravan spent the night outside a small mountain village, and the palanquins again isolated themselves from the main group. The drivers ordered the camels to kneel and looped rope around their knees so they could not rise. When the loads had been removed, so, too, were the ropes; then the camels were prodded to their feet and their front pasterns hobbled. The donkeys were hobbled in the same manner, the restraints allowing the lot to graze at will, but preventing them from wandering too far from camp during the night. Their chores finished, the men settled themselves on bundles of carpets thrown down in semicircles around the cooking fires.

Every bone and muscle aching, Gregori wished only to curl up and sleep. He was too weary to have an appetite, but he knew he must eat. He padded his saddle with a blanket for a seat and joined the circle of drivers. Though they invited him to dip his pieces of flat, unleavened bread into their pot of spicy lamb stew, they were reluctant to include him in their conversation. When he had eaten, Gregori sought out a private place where he performed his evening ritual of prayer and worship. Spiritually cleansed, he returned to the camp, spread his saddle pads into a makeshift mattress, and collapsed upon it. Even the hard ground was a luxury—it was flat, and it did not move. He immediately fell into dreamless sleep.

CHAPTER 7

Something made Gregori awaken with a start. He scrubbed the sleep from his eyes and looked up. The Syrian stood over him.

"Come, or we leave you here." The usually grim caravan leader smiled and added, "The tea in my samovar is cold. Drink what you wish. We begin soon." With that, the Syrian hurried back to his work.

Gregori had not heard the drivers arise half an hour earlier. He was chilled to the bone, having fallen asleep without first covering himself with the sheepskin robe that served as his blanket. Horrified to think he might be left behind, he quickly jumped up and limped off to relieve himself. That done, he barely had time to gulp down a glass of bitter tea, bolt a stale piece of bread from the meager rations he carried, and ready his donkeys.

Gregori headed to his place in line. In agony because of the giant blister on his left buttock, he rode gingerly, leaning to the right. As he passed the first palanquin, the curtains parted slightly.

"Father, I would speak with you," a youthful, feminine voice whispered in Latin.

Before Gregori could respond to the request, the caravan began to move. Seeing that Gregori was not in his appointed position, the Syrian shouted at him, prompting him to trot painfully to his proper place in line. As he rode, or walked, Gregori often thought of the woman in the palanquin, but he had no chance to speak with her that day, nor at any time during the rest of the week.

As the sun rose higher in the sky and the days lengthened, the caravan drove westward through strata of gypsum and lava that undulated like the convolutions of a human brain. The terrain, alternating between mountain and plateau, was rough, but the ancient, well-engineered Roman road they traveled eased their passage.

Normally walking them, the drivers often urged their animals into an easy jog. Man and beast welcomed the gait change that helped to break the deadly boredom of the long trek. Gregori's unconditioned body suffered appalling torment to begin with, but by the end of the first week, it had toughened to the point where he could begin to enjoy the scenery.

For six days the Aras River flowed beside them. Later, their companion river became the upper Euphrates. Though there were frequent rainstorms, and many water courses were at flood level, the well-organized caravan was delayed little.

When they stopped, Gregori sometimes glimpsed the veiled women, never one without another. From the beginning, he had judged it imprudent to solicit their acquaintance.

One day, a man—Gregori thought him a palanquin guard— rode up the line to the place where Gregori walked. Gregori now saw that this man was not a soldier but some sort of dignitary. He wore clothes woven of fine fabrics, the front of his turban bore a large turquoise, and semiprecious stones studded the scabbard encasing his sword. As the man reined in his fiery desert horse to draw up beside the monk, he said softly, "My lady wishes to speak with you."

Gregori noticed the affection in the man's voice when he mentioned his *lady*. "Thus she has said, but we have not yet had a chance to meet," the monk answered. "From where does your lady come?" he asked, hoping to satisfy his increasing curiosity about the mysterious occupant of the primary palanquin.

The elegant individual smiled and said, in fluent Greek, "We travel from Baghdad . . . my lady . . . and her grandmother." Lifting his eyes to the heavens, he added dryly, "Her grandmother has the disposition of a hyena and is not one with whom anyone should trifle."

Gregori had to laugh. "Perhaps your lady wishes to escape the hyena?"

"The two women are close. I can say no more; you must

speak to her yourself. She wishes you to come to her tent this nightfall."

"Tell her I shall come," Gregori said, turning his head to hide his enthusiasm.

The horseman did not seem eager to leave Gregori's company. As the two men talked, they found they had in common not only Greek, but that they could also converse in Latin. Both men knew a smattering of other languages as well. Gregori learned that the man's name was Michael and that he was a distant relation of an Eastern emperor. Saying he had been the Byzantine ambassador to Persia, Michael told Gregori, "When I sent word to Constantinople, I was sure the Seljuks under Malik Shah would overrun the rest of Persia, and I was called home."

Exceedingly shy and inexperienced when it came to women, Gregori had not yet the nerve to visit the palanquins, but from then on, hoping to learn more of the divans' occupants, he often walked or rode with Michael. Their lively conversations covered subjects as diverse as the grand mosaics in the great churches of Byzantium, and old Empress Theodora's death.

When the caravan came to Camacha, it divided. Some drivers turned north to the Black Sea port of Trebizond. The rest took the southern route to Sebaste. The southern route included a desolate stretch through a treacherous mountain pass. Only two minor settlements lay between the cutoff and the junction at Zara. The Syrian decided to take the southern road, telling Gregori he had guided many caravans on it without mishap.

The caravan continued to rest for a two-hour siesta at the hottest part of the day. To compensate for the shortened travel time, the Syrian extended the caravan's movement into the cool evening hours.

They were less than thirty-five miles from Sebaste, following a perilous trail deep within a rocky river gorge. Gregori swayed in the saddle, his chin on his chest, half asleep, confident in the sure tread of his mount. He occasionally lifted a listless hand to swat a persistent gnat or fly that sought more tender skin than that of a camel or donkey.

Suddenly, a tremendous cracking and rumbling roused Gregori from his lethargy. Explosive echoes reverberated from the canyon walls. Almost thrown from his jigging mount, Gregori glanced up as a hundred-foot-wide section of dirt and rock tore loose. It plummeted toward the helpless caravan strung along the narrow trail below.

Immediately, the panicked lead drivers whipped their donkeys into a frenzied run. The uncontrollable camels, positioned after them, stormed forward, overrunning the much smaller beasts. One agile donkey managed to scramble out of the way, but four others died when, knocked over the precipice edge, they plunged to the gorge's rocky floor, four hundred feet below. During their somersaulting, bouncing fall, their packs burst. Glorious, multihued rolls of silk unraveled, and the gossamer streamers regally floated upward on the strong thermal currents. It all looked like a brilliant but bizarre celebration of the catastrophe.

Gregori was trapped between the slide and the column's rear, half a mile behind. His was the last in a segment of donkeys attended by two drivers, who walked together ahead of their charges. Behind him came a dozen camels with two drivers. The slower palanquins and guards came last. As the avalanche came roaring at them, the donkeys in front of Gregori whirled around and galloped toward him. He had no other choice but to reverse his mount's direction. Retracing the course that he had just ridden, he raced to keep ahead of the frantic charge.

The men and animals at the end of the caravan—a mile behind the leaders, and around a curve in the trail—heard, but did not see, the avalanche, and they continued to move onward. Gregori found himself trapped between the backward stampeding donkeys and the approaching camels. Forced to maintain a choppy canter, his only hope was to keep his seat and not let his mount stumble and go down. His body violently pitched back and forth, but he somehow managed to stay in the saddle.

Praying that the horde would have room to get by, Gregori reined his donkey as near as possible to the canyon wall on his left. His pack donkey crowded against the tail of the saddle donkey, its white-ringed eyeballs bulging as it desperately tried to pass its mate.

Like a boulder-filled waterfall, the slide overtook two men at the front of Gregori's section, carrying them after their donkeys into the gorge. They hardly knew what hit them.

Michael had been riding ahead of Gregori when the slide started and the line stampeded. Michael's fear-crazed Arabian reared and bucked. Losing its footing, the horse toppled. Writhing and thrashing, trying to regain its feet, it crushed Michael. The Arabian slid tail first over the edge, carrying Michael to his death.

The slide had lasted less than three minutes. Great clouds of choking dust filled the gorge. As the dust settled, the stunned survivors tried to gather their wits.

It took a day and a half to treat the injured, with Gregori doing most of the doctoring. It took three days for the drivers to round up animals and repack displaced loads. In an act of mercy they cut the throats of two donkeys with broken legs, and a camel with a dislocated hip was also destroyed.

The undamaged goods at the bottom of the gorge were hauled up. As there was now too much baggage for the remaining animals to carry, the Syrian had the excess cached in natural caves, hoping it would be safe, until he could pick it up on his return trip to Syria the following year.

They could not retrieve the bodies of the two men entombed in the avalanche. His lips forming a silent prayer, Gregori stood in homage during the Moslem rites performed by a driver, who was also a Moslem holy man.

They buried Michael's mangled corpse in a shallow grave. Over it, Gregori erected a cairn, hauling each large rock himself. When he had finished, he performed an Orthodox funerary mass, while tears streaked his cheeks. Those drivers who heard Gregori could not help being touched. Before the landslide, they had scorned him; they considered him an unapproachable infidel priest. From then on, they treated him as a brother.

CHAPTER 8

On the morning of the fourth day after the slide, the reorganized caravan was ready to go on. During the preceding confusion, Gregori had often seen the women from a distance. He knew they were mourning, but he had not had time to talk with them. He was tightening his pack bindings when the tall, fair-haired commander of the palanquin guard rode up to him.

"My lady wishes to see you, Father. You are to come at once. She is in dire need of comfort," he added in halting Greek.

"I shall come immediately," Gregori said, delighted to finally meet the mysterious woman.

With much effort on the part of drivers and guards, a narrow path had been cleared across the avalanche. The two palanquins had been carried over it to rejoin the caravan remnant on the far side. As Gregori approached them, he saw that the formerly glorious sedans were filthy and battered. Three veiled women, who sat on nearby rocks, were dusty and subdued. As Gregori started briskly toward them, a guard blocked him with a muscular arm. The man's other hand rested on the handle of the scimitar at his waist.

"Let him come, Hussein, then leave us," the youngest of the women ordered. She beckoned to Gregori with a tilt of her chin. "I am sorry, Father. Hussein is very protective since my father's death four days past." She put a hand over her face and began to sob. One of the other women tried to gather her to her bosom, but the girl pulled away, saying to Gregori, "My grandmother vowed to have Hussein beheaded if he did not take me safely on to Constantinople.

"You must go also, Grandmother," the girl commanded. "Take Zahra with you."

Flapping like a crow in mourning clothes, the old woman rose from her rock and clawed at Gregori's sleeve. "You, infidel priest, leave us be. I demand it," she hissed through tooth-less gums.

Stamping a dainty foot that raised a puff of dust, the girl cried in Arabic, "You will not deter me from confession, Grandmother. Be gone."

The crone started to say more, but her granddaughter pointed a stern finger at the palanquins. Throwing a baleful glare over her shoulder at Gregori, the old woman scurried away.

The girl turned back to Gregori. "Forgive her. My father was a believer, but my mother's mother is a follower of Muhammad. It makes life difficult at times."

"I can see that it could," Gregori agreed.

"Thank you for coming, Father. I have not been to confession for many months. Being so recently near death, I feel I can no longer put it off."

"I am at your command, my lady," Gregori said, dropping his head to hide the sensation that surged through his body—a stirring that made him extremely uncomfortable.

The girl's eyes above her veil were pale golden brown with green flecks. Enchanting rings of indigo circled her pupils and the outer edges of the irises. They were the most beautiful eyes Gregori had ever seen. Mesmerized, he forced himself to look away.

"My mother died during the winter, and the avalanche has caused my beloved father to join her in heaven." The girl's voice broke and she sank to the ground, overwhelmed with grief. "My grandmother is old. If she dies, I shall be alone."

Gregori was confused. What was this about her father? Suddenly Gregori realized that the girl was Michael's daughter. Deeply affected, he knelt beside her. "I myself am an orphan," he said, "but long ago I learned that an orphan is never alone. We are all children of God, and He is with us always, wherever we are."

The girl reached out and innocently patted his hand. Her small hand lay pale and delicate upon his strong brown one. Again, a thrill shot through Gregori's body. It took all his willpower not to clasp her hand in his. At thirteen, when Thaddeaus had brought him to St. Jacob's Monastery, he had declared a life of celibacy. Perhaps it was because he had only been in the company of men since the bear had killed his mother and father that his vow had never been tested—until now. At twenty-six, this was the first time he knew what it was like to desire a woman. He wanted to put his cheek to the girl's, to hold her close in his arms.

With a shudder he withdrew his hand and stood. Consciously disciplining his mind against his lust, he said gruffly, "I will take your confession at once, if you wish." Then, fully aware that he would be disobeying the confession doctrine of his order, he asked anyway, "How are you called?"

Not discerning the priest's indiscretion, she answered, "My father christened me Najila."

Brilliant Eyes! A perfect name for her, Gregori thought.

Until he heard Najila's confession, so simple and pure, he had not realized she was a mere sixteen or seventeen. When it was over, he helped her to her feet. His hands trembled as his icy fingers encountered her warm ones. Her head came to just under his chin, and her billowing robes could not completely hide her lithe young figure. As they rose together, he whispered, "Remember, God is ever with you."

"I know, Father," she affirmed, as the fabulous eyes again gazed into his. "But pray for me."

"Always, until death overtakes me," Gregori promised, and knew it to be true.

* * *

The decimated caravan reached Sebaste without further incident. From there, it would continue east to Constantinople, but Gregori would leave it to go south.

As the caravan with the two palanquins prepared to depart, Gregori made a special visit to see Najila. He had spent much time with her since her confession, though they had never again touched. That he had fallen impossibly in love with her was obvious only to him. As he approached the palanquins, Gregori saw the caravan master talking to Najila and her grandmother, who were already seated in their vehicles. His spirits were dashed by the Syrian's intrusion. Still, he managed to cover his disappointment as he bid the women good-bye.

Afterward, the Syrian drew Gregori aside and warmly embraced him, kissing him on either cheek. "We have one God, you and I, and He has truly blessed us by saving our lives," the Syrian said. "And your presence, monk, has blessed our journey." He pressed a rather heavy packet into Gregori's hand. "The lady asked me to give this to you."

"I . . . I cannot . . ." Gregori stammered, but the Syrian executed a stiff, shallow bow and hurried off to other business.

Gregori examined the gift. Whatever the thing was, it was wrapped in a filmy blue veil shot with silver—the same veil Najila had worn before she donned mourning garb. He lifted the packet to his face and an essence of jasmine and sandalwood titillated his senses. Carefully untangling the veil, he unwrapped an ornate silver cross that spanned the breadth of his palm. The cross bore an enormous slab of amber. Preserved in the glowing amber, its body the length of the vertical arm and its lacy wings spread across the horizontal arm, was a primordial dragonfly.

Gregori pressed the silver cross to his breast. *Oh, Najila,* he silently cried from the depth of his heart, *if only my fate was to be forever with you.*

Chapter 9

Sebaste (the modern Sivas) was once a critical trade center on the north-south road that ran between the Black Sea ports of Amisus and Sinope, and the Mediterranean port city of Mallus. The important, northernmost east-west route, between Persia and Asia Minor's west coast, also passed through the busy city.

Sebaste boasted several fine churches and an unpretentious monastery. Gregori stayed at the monastery by night and toured the churches by day, where he studied the mosaics and paintings within their sanctified walls. Contaminated water and spoiled food had often made him ill during the four-hundred-mile trip from Iğdir. He had lost much weight and needed a rest, but he was impatient to continue to the Hidden Valley. Two weeks later, rejuvenated, flat-bellied, and as tough as a horse's tooth, he joined a camel caravan heading south to Caesarea.

Because there were fewer animals to manage, the small caravan moved faster than had the ponderous silk caravan.

Despite their two-week respite, Gregori's donkeys were gaunt and weak; it was all they could do to keep up with the long-striding camels. The pack donkey's ribs showed, and it soon developed oozing saddle sores on its withers. To ease the pressure on the poor beast, Gregori added padding and repeatedly adjusted the rack that held the heavy relics.

One time, Gregori fell asleep in the saddle, and the rein dropped from his relaxed fingers. His mount, half asleep itself, bumped the rear of the camel in front. The short-tempered brute lashed out and kicked the little donkey in the knee, breaking the donkey's leg. It was up to Gregory to destroy his faithful servant. Gregori walked from then on, leading the pack animal. He sighed with relief as the caravan entered the suburbs of Caesarea, the capitol of Cappadocia.

The Greeks had renamed Roman Caesarea *Kappadokia,* which meant Province of Good Horses, for its fertile grazing lands. It was in Caesarea that St. Paul baptized the household of Cornelius.* When the Turks came, they altered the name to *Kayseri.*

The ancient city contained a site especially revered by Armenians. Around the turn of the fourth century, their patron saint, Gregory the Illuminator, the saint for whom Gregori had been named, lived in Caesarea. Years before, Abbot Thaddeaus had told Gregori the story of the saint's life.

"Gregory the Illuminator, an Arsacid prince, was born at the end of the third century," Thaddeaus had explained to the young novice. "His father assassinated the Armenian king Khosrov while Prince Gregory was still a boy. He was about your age, Gregori."

"After King Khosrov's murder, Khosrov's followers threatened to kill the young prince, but Gregory sought refuge from their revenge by fleeing to Caesarea. There, orthodox priests instructed him in Christianity.

"Later, Prince Gregory returned to Armenia and tried to convert his boyhood companion, the powerful King Trdat (known by some as Tiridates III) to Christianity. Someone in the court revealed to King Trdat that Prince Gregory's father had assassinated Trdat's father. Trdat's love for his boyhood friend turned to hate, and he had Gregory tortured and imprisoned in a pit.

"Prince Gregory survived thirteen years in the hole, remaining alive because a pious widow brought him food. When King Trdat became sick and then went insane, the king's sisters persuaded him to release Prince Gregory. No sooner had Gregory been released than Trdat experienced a supernatural healing. Proclaiming his cure a miracle, the king accepted the Christian faith, and from then on promoted it throughout his kingdom— often too forcefully. He even made Prince Gregory his bishop,

---

*See Acts 10:17–48.

and, as old men, they went together to Constantine's court in Constantinople.

"By the way, Gregori, did you know," Thaddeaus had asked, "that the arm of John the Baptist reputedly was in Caesarea, and that Prince Gregory took it to Jerusalem?"

The story had fascinated Gregori and filled him with longing for adventure. "Someday I shall go to Caesarea and Jerusalem," he had vowed to the abbot. "Maybe I can see the Baptist's arm for myself."

"I believe you will, my son," Thaddeaus had said, laughing with pleasure at his ward's enthusiasm.

* * *

In Caesarea, Gregori waited in vain for someone who was heading toward the Hidden Valley. It was already late September, and the Anatolian Plain lay parched and denuded. In a few weeks, snow would fall at the higher elevations. Freezing temperatures would make the nights uncomfortable, if not dangerous. He decided he had to leave Caesarea alone, or not at all. Before starting, he spent two days fasting and praying for a safe journey.

It was good to be on the road again. He missed the camaraderie and protection of fellow travelers but not the appalling dust created by a long caravan. If he did not find a cheap place to stay the night, he tethered his donkey in some secluded spot and, wrapping his robe tightly around him, slept under a bush or in a cave. He often ate a solitary supper of cold unleavened bread, sometimes adding a handful of dates or raisins sold to him by a farmer. If fortunate, he purchased a cup of inferior wine or fermented goat milk to wash down the dry bread. His main regret was that he had too much time to think—too much time to think about Najila.

Only once did Gregori have reason to fear for the safety of the wealth in his charge. Approaching the outskirts of a sizeable village at dusk, he encountered five Mongol horsemen cantering toward him on shaggy steppe ponies. The steppe men wore their traditional fur caps that had side flaps to cover their ears in frigid weather. Strapped to each horse's side was a flexible pole with a noose at one end.

The riders were reeling drunk and in an ugly mood. Gregori quickly guided his donkey off the road to let them by. He stiffened with alarm as they skidded their steaming mounts to a stop and began to circle him. The hairs on the back of his neck crawled.

Gregori's lips moved in silent prayer. *Please Lord God in heaven, save Thy holy relics and Thy servant.* He then tried to communicate with the Mongols in Greek, Latin, and Armenian, signing with his hands, contorting his face to demonstrate his words. The riders only laughed at his efforts.

A man on a gray pony suddenly freed his long pole from its binding. In one smooth motion, he deftly settled the horsehide loop over Gregori's shoulders. Gregori expected to be yanked from his feet and dragged off, but the Mongol did not tighten the noose. He merely sat astride his sweating steed and glared at Gregori with slitted, bloodshot eyes. A thin smile twisted his cruel mouth.

Gregori was feeling desperate, when he had an idea. Offering up a silent prayer, he formed the universal drinker's sign—fingers curled, extended thumb jabbing at his mouth. Staggering within the confines of the loop, he pointed at himself, then puffed his cheeks and guffawed.

The monk looked so ridiculous that the Mongols started laughing. But they laughed with him, instead of at him. They good-naturedly imitated him, jesting and poking at each other with their poles. One man was soon knocked from his horse, or he simply passed out; Gregori wasn't sure which. The rest reined in their ponies, dismounted, and attempted to help the fallen man remount. Gregori slipped the neglected noose off. The inebriated men's fumbling was so comical, Gregori nearly forgot his own predicament. While they were tending their fallen comrade, he quietly led his donkey away.

At the nearby village inn, Gregori described the incident to the village chief, a giant man with a luxuriant, waxed moustache.

"Every year at this season, the Mongols come to sell their fine steppe mares to the Armenian horse breeders," the village chief explained. "But the Mongols spend too much time in this very inn after being paid. I sent them on their way before they had nothing left to take home," he chuckled. "I have dealt with them for years." His huge paw irreverently slapped Gregori's back. "They meant you no harm."

Chapter 10

For three hours, Gregori's aching arms had tugged the exhausted donkey along the deserted path that bisected a narrow valley between arid ridges. Every footfall raised fine dust, and he and his donkey were coated with it. He had to stop. Dropping the lead rope, he rubbed his strained elbows, then climbed the sloping bank to his right. The donkey stayed where Gregori left it, too jaded to nibble at the clump of shriveled grass five inches beneath its nose.

When he topped the low rise, Gregori had to clutch the branch of a stunted shrub to preserve his equilibrium. The blinding midday sun reflected from yellow-white volcanic ash on a scene to which no verbal description could do justice. "I've reached hell," he exclaimed aloud.

Tightening his hold on the branch with his right hand, his left shading his eyes, Gregori stared across a vast and starkly beautiful sunken plain. The plain stretched many miles in three directions. Tablelands, such as that upon which he stood, but misty and blued by distance, encircled the valley.

The most startling aspect of the vista lay a thousand feet below. Wind and rain had eroded compacted layers of hardened ash into hundreds of peculiar cone-shaped formations. Here and there, a single cap stone tilted perilously on a cone's peak. Other cones were topped by more than one flat stone. Most of the peculiar formations had window and door openings cut into their sides. Later, Gregori learned they were called fairy castles and often described as phallic symbols. Bounteous vineyards, heavy with bunches of ripening grapes, covered most of the bare land between the cones.

At first, Gregori did not see people. Squinting, he finally discerned tiny figures laboring among the vines. When he saw a steep, winding trail that led from the cliff top, near where he stood, he scrambled back down the ridge. Grabbing the donkey's lead rope, he headed for the trail.

When Gregori reached the valley floor, peasants surrounded him, bombarding him with questions in Greek, Armenian, and Latin. The valley's populace was already diverse, with many races and tongues, though visitors from outside were rare. Gregori tried to field every question, but a second question often interrupted him before he completely answered the first.

The boisterous and rapidly expanding throng guided Gregori into an area where the cones were larger and more profuse. Suddenly, a monk rounded a gigantic cone, stepping onto the path in front of Gregori. Shaking his head, the monk clucked his tongue sympathetically. "By the looks of you and your beast, you have traveled far. Welcome to the Hidden Valley."

Gregori looked down at his ragged, dust-covered habit and grinned. "But for God's mercy, I would not be here, praise His holy name." He affectionately thumped the side of his bony donkey, which didn't even flinch. "And this faithful beast has served me well, from St. Jacob's to Cappadocia—a long journey indeed." Gregori's shoulders slumped. "Thank our God above; it is over. I am terribly weary with travel."

The young monk gently clasped Gregori's arm. "After you wash and quench your thirst, I, myself, will take you to our abbot."

"Abbot Thaddeaus of St. Jacob's Monastery upon Mt. Ararat sends greetings," Gregori said to the Hidden Valley's abbot, Manuel. "He has sent me for two reasons: the first, to render the paintings you requested; the second, to place certain holy relics in your care. Abbot Thaddeaus thinks they will be safer here." Gregori described his precious cargo.

Manuel's face blanched. "Why were the tablets not sent to an *Eastern* Orthodox monastery, instead of to us? They say the Seljuk Turks have taken Manzikert and are heading west."

"I have not heard the latest news, but I know the Seljuk hordes move swiftly," Gregori responded. "Abbot Thaddeaus told me you will know the best place to hide the treasures of St. Jacob's. My coming to Cappadocia was providential, for I could then bring the tablets. Abbot Thaddeaus is unusual in that he believes the relics belong to all Armenians, not to one sect of our divided church."

"And no guards accompanied you?" the abbot murmured, incredulous. It was miraculous that the St. Jacob's monk and his precious consignment had arrived without mishap. Manuel did not say it, but he agreed with Thaddeus: the relics belonged to the entire church, divided or not.[*]

Abbot Manuel wasted no time in ordering a shrine created to house the priceless relics from the ark of Noah. To construct it, he simply directed the monks to hew an annex into the wall of an existing chapel.

The churches were literally carved out of ingneous rock. As a room was needed, it was sculpted into the solid, but workable *tufa,* the volcanic material common to the region. Supporting, or decorative, columns were left behind, not installed afterward. If an iconostasis, a dividing screen, was planned, it, too, was formed by the sculptors as they chipped away the negative space around it.

The process of creating the new room fascinated Gregori, and he watched every step. Learning how to use hand cutting tools, he became proficient enough to help the other monks. They worked swiftly, finishing the annex in four months. The ark relics, including the tablets, were immediately placed within it.

Gregori demonstrated such artistic knowledge and skill that when the job was done, the abbot asked him to restore an abandoned chapel. Manuel introduced Gregori to the old sanctuary on a freezing December morning. Even the weak light of their flickering oil lamps could not diminish the glory that once made the ancient chapel a renowned place of worship. But

---

[*] Segments of the Eastern Orthodox (the Byzantine) church could not agree on several ideologies. In 491 it split, one faction becoming the Holy Apostolic Church of Armenia, and the other the Latin-leaning Greek Orthodox. The Holy Apostolic Orthodox Church of Armenia still believes it was founded by the apostle Bartholomew and the apostle Thaddeus, one of the Seventy.

where vibrant religious paintings had covered its walls, the tufa now was cracked, the paint faded and peeling. Of some images, only colored flakes were yet visible.

Gregori's fingers traced the red, yellow, and ocher motifs. He realized the work was more primitive than in other chapels. "The artist who did these might have walked and talked with St. Gregory," he remarked to the abbot.

"It is believed they may be of his era," Manuel replied.

Gregori flattened his palm on the chipped paint, trying to feel the strokes used in the crude rendition of a kind of grouse, a bird still seen in abundance throughout the surrounding valleys. Remembering the stains in the cracks of his own flesh, Gregori wondered if red, yellow, and blue paint stained the pores and cracks of the ancient artist's hands in the same way.

He examined the slightly curved ceiling, which was almost too high to be seen in the dim light. In the very center, barely discernible, was a huge red cross. The cross incorporated a circle in each of its arms. Gregori knew the circles represented Christ and His four wounds. Smaller crosses, to either side of the main cross, represented the thieves who were crucified beside Jesus on Mount Calvary.

"The ceiling must be redone," Gregori said. "But," he added, pointing to a well-preserved wall painting hidden in a niche, "I will not touch this one in honor of the man who did it." The painting he indicated was of Christ, emerging from the Jordan River after his baptism by John. The beautiful work had been protected from the elements and was as fresh as the day it was painted.

As a youth, Gregori saw and admired Constantinople's massive St. Sophia Basilica, completed in the year 537 and consecrated in 563. He decided to remake the old chapel into a Lilliputian facsimile of the basilica. First, he supervised the raising of the ceiling and the carving of a concave dome. Within the dome, Gregori painted a stern-faced Jesus, after a ceiling mosaic he saw in a Greek church. He adorned the chapel's columns and arches with figures of lesser Bible characters and church dignitaries, including portraits of the abbots Manuel and Thaddeaus. It was when working on a portrait of the Virgin that Gregori's heart and soul ached. The Virgin's face became Najila's—Najila's mouth, Najila's beautiful eyes—tormenting him almost beyond bearing. Despite his efforts to create a more traditional portrait, nothing he tried would change it. And when it was done, and his work in that chapel ended, he returned again and again to look at "Najila."

Months later, as the two men reviewed this latest project, Gregori said to Manuel, "There are too many unadorned surfaces. It needs something else." That night, as he lay restlessly tossing, on the verge of sleep, it came to him. The next day he began to paint replicas of glazed tiles in geometric designs on every available space.

When Gregori completed the Tiled Chapel, as it was later christened, Abbot Manuel could dream up nothing more for him to do. Then Gregori showed the abbot the cartoons he drew at St. Jacob's.

"Exceptional!" Abbot Manuel exclaimed. "You will construct a chapel for them . . . over there." He pointed across the ravine to a sheer palisade of red-striped, creamy yellow tufa.

When the new chapel had been carved into the yellow cliff face, Gregori began to transfer his original cartoons to its walls and ceiling. Abbot Manuel eventually named it the "Blue Church," because of Gregori's rich blue background in a tableau of the apostles. While decorating the Blue Church, Gregori attracted a devout admirer.

Like Gregori, Movses was orphaned as a young child. The monastery adopted him at age four, after his parents died in the collapse of their cave home. Now twelve, Movses trailed Gregori as an unweaned puppy trails its mother. Gregori befriended the shy, introverted lad, who was so similar to himself as a boy.

The keen-eyed youngster intently studied all phases of the artistic process. He was ecstatic when Gregori allowed him to clean brushes and mix paint. The boy's heart threatened to explode with pride when Gregori recognized his considerable talent, trusting him to paint a lamb at the feet of a Jesus figure.

With Movses acting as his apprentice, Gregori finished the Chapel of the Apostles in a shorter period than expected. Small, full-length images of the apostles ringed his rendering of *Christ the Pantocrator*, Greek for the "Creator of All Things." On the half dome covering the apse, a blue-robed Virgin Mary embraced the baby Jesus. Brilliant New Testament scenes filled the rest of the chapel.

The authenticity of the apostles' faces was no accident; each was a portrait of a living person Gregori recruited from among the monks and local villagers. Movses modeled for a youthful Jesus preaching on the steps of Herod's great temple. The Hidden Valley monastery was not as austere as St. Jacob's, and Gregori was assigned many projects to beautify its innumerable chapels.

Gregori continued to teach his skills to Movses and to others who showed promise. Thriving on the work, except for his undying longing for Najila, he had never felt so fulfilled.

CHAPTER 11

Cappadocia, A.D. 1063

Gregori tried to imagine how Isaac must have felt when he realized his own father, Abraham, was about to sacrifice him. What was Isaac's expression at that very moment, the moment Abraham's freshly sharpened knife was poised above his throat? Was it terror? Unbelief? Trust? Or did he not know what was about to happen to him?

Gregori glared at his painting. No matter how he tried, he couldn't get it right. He threw down his brushes in disgust and stepped back to consider the problem. He was still studying the mural when Movses, now a full-fledged monk, raced into the cavern, huffing after his run up the steep hill.

"Arp Arslan and his Seljuks are on the move. Abbot Manuel wants everyone in the dining hall immediately," Movses panted.

Gregori stiffened. "The rumors are true, then. Quickly, let us go hear what he has to say."

Abbot Manuel, surrounded by a group of somber-faced monks, stood at the long narrow table carved out of the tufa floor where they ate their meals. Noting Movses and Gregori's entrance, the abbot merely nodded.

". . . and we have been advised to conceal all valuables belonging to the monastery," he was saying. "I know the Seljuk Turks are supposed to tolerate the practices of other religions, but they also covet their treasure," Abbot Manuel added, grimacing. "Go now. Gather up those items I have designated; prepare them for travel."

As the other monks filed out, the abbot called, "Brother Gregori and Brother Movses, please stay." Gregori and Movses stopped, and the abbot strode over to them. "I have a special assignment for you. Come to my quarters first thing tomorrow, and I will reveal my plan."

The next morning, when Gregori and Movses entered the abbot's cell, they found that, besides Abbot Manuel, a strange man awaited them. Both men appeared agitated and haggard, having spent the night on their knees praying.

Abbot Manuel introduced the stranger. "This is Brother Paul. He carries an urgent message, warning us the Seljuks are coming in this direction. He is to guide you and the monastery relics to a place of safety."

Gregori and Movses remained silent and subdued as the abbot outlined his plan. "There is a town south of here that is partially above ground and partially below in fortified caverns. You are to carry the tablets and other relics there. Brother Paul knows the country in between, thus enabling you to avoid the main roads where you might attract attention. Before you leave, dress as nomads; you must not be recognized as monks. Call yourselves simply Paul, Gregori, and Movses, and do not address one another as 'Brother.' When you arrive at your destination, Paul will take you to an Armenian priest who can be trusted."

Gregori nervously cleared his throat. "What then?"

"Tell him he is to hide the holy treasure we send him. He knows what to do."

* * *

The three men rode donkeys and led five heavily laden pack animals. Winding through the back country, shunning people when possible, they reached the town at dusk on the seventh day. Paul rapped on the door to the tiny hut. A tall and muscular man with a waist-long, jet-black beard opened it. Bread crumbs littered his beard and the front of his black robe. Thinking the three men wandering merchants, he frowned, saying, "You have nothing I need or want. You have interrupted my supper."

The big priest started to slam the door when Paul hastily explained, "We are monks of the Hidden Valley Monastery.

Because the Seljuks are heading west, we have brought the monastery wealth here, where it is safer. Our Abbot Manuel said you would know where to hide it."

The Armenian priest gasped and, glancing up and down the street, he whispered, "Bring everything inside. When you have done so, lead your donkeys to that field over there and free them. They'll not go far with such plentiful fodder. Tell no one why you are here."

The four men unloaded the heavy packs and carried them into the priest's hut. Little space was left for them to sit or stand, so they sat on the baggage.

"When the village slumbers, I will show you where to hide everything," the priest told them. "Meantime, join me in supper." He spread his hands, palms up. "I apologize for the meager fare."

"We have food and drink," Gregori said. "There is more than enough, if added to yours."

As the sounds outside gradually diminished, the priest cracked the door and scanned the street. "It is time," he hissed. Shutting the door, he dragged aside a sheepskin rug and lifted a trapdoor in the hut's dirt floor. Handing Movses a pair of digging tools, the priest lit three torches. Keeping one for himself, he distributed the others to Gregori and Paul. "Choose something of what you have brought and follow me," he said. Hoisting an immense bundle onto his broad shoulders, the priest descended a rickety wooden ladder and disappeared into the hole.

Gregori untied the pack that contained the two tablets and a massive gem-encrusted gold bowl. He and Movses selected the tablets, Paul the bowl. Encumbered by a torch and a heavy relic, each man tentatively made his way to the foot of the ladder, where the Armenian waited.

Gregori lost track of time as the Armenian led them down a series of claustrophobic tunnels and through huge, echoing caverns. Becoming completely disoriented as they penetrated deeper and deeper into the earth, he realized he could never retrace his steps in the intricate maze. They paused only for short rests or to relight a torch. It seemed they had wandered for hours when, finally, the Armenian priest dropped his burden and turned around to face the weary monks.

Raising his torch high above his head, Gregori saw they were in a gigantic cavern, larger than any of the others through which they had passed. It was so expansive, the light of their torches did not reach the cavern's limits. Giant stalagmites met equally huge stalactites to form columns that spanned the distance from ceiling to floor.

The Armenian pointed to a round excavation. "There is a swift-flowing river under this cave. Years ago, a well to it was begun, as you can see, but few people came this far into the caverns, and the village council decided not to finish it. Those who knew of it have either died or forgotten the well was ever here. I may be the only person who remembers where it is."

Setting his torch in a wall bracket, the priest removed greased goat hides and a hemp rope from his bundle. Instructing the monks to tightly wrap the tablets and bowl in the hides, he carefully lowered them into the well.

They continued their trips to the site until, two days later, every article was safely deposited in the well. When all were secure, Movses started to shovel tufa debris into the hole. Gregori put a restraining hand on the youth's arm.

"I have things of my own to add," he told Movses. Searching his sleeve cache, Gregori pulled out the leather pouch that bore the gold solidus he acquired in Athens, and the silver and amber cross Najila had given him. He withdrew the cross. Instantly, a vision of Najila's beautiful eyes floated in Gregori's mind. Sighing, he replaced the cross and, tying the pouch to the rope, lowered it into the dark pit.

Profoundly saddened by their completed task, Gregori and Movses returned to the Hidden Valley. Brother Paul remained at the village. Within the Cappadocian monastery's many cone chapels, the niches and shelves that once held precious objects were now empty. Every morning, the monks awakened fearing the Seljuks might come that day. Despite the threat, looming just beyond the eastern horizon, their faith in God and strict routine upheld them.

* * *

In 1064 the Seljuk Turks conquered Armenia, swarming throughout Anatolia and Cappadocia. A day came when a troop of Seljuks came to see the famous caves. The "craven images" offended the Moslems, and they sought to destroy the painted faces. Movses caught a band of them stoning Gregori's wonderful painting of the apostles. Though he was greatly outnumbered, Movses tried to halt the desecration, but he was savagely beaten and left for dead. Never regaining consciousness, he expired the next day.

Two years later, Brother Paul, at home in his village, perished after ingesting tainted meat.

The Armenian priest who had led them to the well died a natural death at a respectable age.

Abbot Manuel was killed at age seventy-six when the weakened floor of his cell collapsed, and he plunged thirty feet to the floor of the room below.

Still celibate at the Hidden Valley Monastery, Gregori lived to age ninety-five. Though he never again saw Najila, over the years, his fantasy image of her expanded. One winter, he contracted pneumonia and lay delirious with a high fever. Alone, except for a stone-deaf monk attendant, Gregori rambled on about a silver cross in a well. But the old monk could not hear him. When Gregori—the last of the five men who knew the tablets' hiding place—peacefully passed away in his sleep that night, the secret of the tablets died with him.

CHAPTER 12

June 20, 1840

Mount Ararat's twin peaks lay quietly . . . waiting. Always, in man's most ancient memory, Asia Minor's eastern region had trembled. The monks of St. Jacob's Monastery and the inhabitants of Arghuri, the wine-producing Armenian village below, accepted the quakes as unavoidable manifestations from God. They also had always accepted the existence of Noah's ark as fact. Some claimed to be Noah's descendants.

If several consecutive winters were mild and Mount Ararat's glaciers in retreat, the great ark's stern stood exposed, though the rest of its massive gopher wood hull remained firmly lodged in ice. It was then that the heartiest of St. Jacob's monks and villagers sometimes climbed the dangerous trail to the ark to search for artifacts.

By the nineteenth century, the monastery boasted the world's only collection of ark relics, including several of Noah's personal belongings. The old monk Tsefon's job, as caretaker of the relics, carried with it much work and responsibility, but daily contact with the priceless objects gave him joy beyond description.

Sighing with pleasure, Tsefon stroked a fragile clay goblet. The goblet was his favorite. *Father Noah might have touched this to his lips,* he thought every time he lifted the piece from its protective box. He remembered the old rumor that other goblets and relics had been taken from St. Jacob's and hidden. No one knew for sure if the story was true. He glanced up at the narrow slot in the wall that served as his cell's sole window. The sun had already dropped behind the highest peaks. It was almost time for vespers.

Tsefon reluctantly tucked the goblet into its polished ebony repository and hurried to the storeroom. After setting the box gently in its place on a shelf, he had just reached for an oil lamp when the Ararat massif flexed its colossal, snow-capped shoulders.

The earthquake loosened tons of rock and ice and started an avalanche that hurtled down the nine-thousand-foot-deep Ahora gash in Mt. Ararat's side. In its path lay both monastery and village. Both were ground to slush under the enveloping slide. More than a thousand beings perished almost instantly. On that day, only one hundred people, who were away from the area, survived.

Old Tsefon was among those who died first, vanishing beneath the storeroom's collapsing rock walls. Buried under tons of impenetrable debris, every ark relic then known to modern man disappeared with him.

PART 2

Chapter 13

Lesser Armenia, 1891

"Our father is unjust!" Ephraim Trajian shouted at his twin sister, Ylenah. The boy pounded his fist on the sweat-blackened wood of the plow handle. "I hate these tasks of a *köylü,* a common peasant." At age thirteen Ephraim's voice had started to change. To his dismay, the shout became a raven's croak.

"Be patient," Ylenah said, averting her head so her twin could not see her amused smile. "We will finish by sundown." She scanned the rock-strewn rows they had already turned. Their work was more than half done, but the uneven lines would vex their exacting father.

Fifty years before the twins' birth, their grandfather had crafted the same plow they now used. He had formed it from the thick fork of a hardwood branch, using the centuries-old "check mark" design favored by farmers throughout the world. Ephraim's strength was insufficient to fully control the awkward old plow and, whenever it struck a large rock, it bucked and swerved. Though Ylenah walked to the left of the spotted ox, firmly gripping its lead rope, it was impossible to guide the animal in a straight line. The furrows wriggled like the earth worms the plow infrequently exhumed. Normally, an older, more capable brother plowed the family field, but the adult men were away on a carpet-selling trip. Ephraim had been assigned the work in their stead.

"Blisters cover my hands, and my arms feel like they are tearing loose from my shoulders," Ephraim whined. "I will do no more." Coming to the end of the furrow, he yanked the ox to a halt. Ahead flowed the shallow winter creek that bordered the field. "I am thirsty, too," he complained, licking his lips.

Ylenah sighed and pointed to the line of severely pruned, knobby poplars on the other side of the creek. "Early this morning, I cached a jug of water over there."

"Bring it to me," Ephraim ordered.

Only because she was also thirsty did Ylenah obey her brother without comment. She waded into the creek as Ephraim unshackled the ox. The beast immediately lowered its head and began to crop the desiccated stalks that had been a lush green when snowmelt foamed in the creek.

Ephraim flopped on his back in the sparse, mottled shade of a poplar. Tearing off a bunch of dried grass, he swiped at the perspiration on his forehead, merely succeeding in smearing dirt and sweat into his eyes.

Ylenah retrieved a long-necked water jug from a hole among the protruding roots of a stunted tree and lifted it to her shoulder. Wading through the creek, she returned to where Ephraim lay. With a flourish, she bowed. "I grant your wish, my *lord.*" A generous measure of water sloshed over the jug's lip and splashed Ephraim.

Ephraim threw his arms across his face. "Stop! That is enough, Ylenah. Leave me some to drink." He sat up and rubbed his eyes, smearing his face with more mud. "If I have to plow another row, I will run off and join a caravan," he moaned.

Ylenah had heard it all before. "I hear the life of a camel driver is difficult."

"You hear gossip," Ephraim snorted. "What do women know of such things? If I were traveling with a caravan I would relish every minute. And I would see the world, too. But I will die of overwork before I go *anywhere.*" He grabbed the jug from Ylenah and tipped the heavy vessel to his mouth. Water streamed down his chin, over his chest, and down the neck of his shirt. "That feels good!" he said. Lifting the jug higher, he lavishly poured the cold liquid over his head.

Ylenah snatched at the jug. "You waste water, Ephraim. I have carried it a long way from the well."

"For me to bathe in," he jeered, and poured more on his head.

Wearied by her brother's endless grousing and rude behavior, Ylenah asked, "Must you always think only of yourself?"

Ephraim's black eyes mocked her. "A woman is to serve a man's needs, not to question him."

As twins, the youngest of fourteen children, they were closer to each other than to their siblings. All her life, Ylenah had tolerated Ephraim's idiosyncrasies. She said to him now, calmly, and without malice, "When you *are* a man, Ephraim, another woman will serve you, not I."

Feeling sorry for her twin, she had persuaded their elderly mother to let her leave the loom to help him plow. However, she had already made a decision: this was the last time she would risk the wrath of a strict father who did not approve of his pubescent daughter going into the countryside unchaperoned.

It often puzzled Ylenah that their father, now in his mid-seventies, seemed to grow wiser as she grew older.

The Trajian children attended school in a room within the Armenian church, but they learned practical skills outside of school. Ylenah became adept at the calculations required to weave complex carpet designs. Ephraim often accompanied their father and uncles on oriental carpet-, mohair-, or livestock-selling trips. By watching the negotiations, he learned the subtle manipulations of fingers in the palm of the hand necessary to trade with the Arabs.

In an arrangement between the adults of both families, children were usually betrothed before puberty. When she was eight, Ylenah's parents had promised her to her second cousin, Gabriel Kiroyan, nine years her senior.

No family had offered its daughter's hand in marriage to Ephraim. Overweight and lazy, he was neither handsome nor likable. His one asset was an infinitesimal inheritance, what remained after his brothers received their shares of their father's wealth.

Their mother had delivered Ephraim and Ylenah late in life, her thirteenth and last pregnancy. Most of her children died in infancy and, with no babies following the twins, she had bestowed upon them an inordinate amount of affection. Crippled by osteoporosis, in perpetual pain, she left the household chores to Nika and Ylenah, the sole survivors of six daughters.

Nika, a widow in her mid-twenties, was more like a second mother than a sister to the twins. Having no children of her own, she also doted on them, particularly Ephraim. Ephraim and his brothers, Ervand and Hakob, were the last remaining of eight sons.

Ephraim dreamed of a destiny other than the futile cultivation of his father's arid land. He hated farming and, even more, he disliked herding goats.

Ylenah's shout shook him from his reverie. "Get up. We have to finish; Nika will worry if we are not home for the evening meal."

"Nika worries too much." Ephraim scowled, rubbing more dirt into his eyes. "What our sister needs is another husband."

"If Nika married again and left our home, who would pamper you?"

Ephraim stretched and yawned. "Women are supposed to spoil their men."

Ylenah rolled her eyes and headed toward the hole from which she had taken the jug. Ephraim watched her deftly balance the jar on her head as she struggled through the creek and up the sandy bank. She stooped to replace the pot in the little cave, but instead knocked the pot against the hole's crumbling sides. When the opening collapsed, Ylenah began to vigorously clear away the dirt. Suddenly, she cried out. Jerking her hand from the hole, she put her finger in her mouth and sucked it.

Ephraim got up and splashed through the creek. He squatted beside his sister. "What is the matter with you now?"

"Something cut me."

Ylenah gingerly thrust her uninjured hand into the hollow. Groping, she retrieved a triangular object. "It is just a piece of old broken pot like the rest we have found around here."

Ephraim seized the shard from her. Spitting on it, he wiped it clean on his shirt. Two pairs of dark eyes widened at the dancing reflection of sun on bright metal.

"It is covered with gold!" Ylenah exclaimed.

"Can I not see it myself?" Ephraim snapped.

"It looks old. And," Ylenah pointed out, "there is writing on it."

Ephraim turned the shard over. "There is writing on the other side, too, but I can't read it."

Ylenah leaned closer to see better. "Our father will know what it is."

Ephraim quickly hid the shard behind his back.

"No one else is to see this," he hissed between clenched teeth.

"Why?" Ylenah asked, completely baffled by his attitude.

"If we tell our father, he will take it from us."

"Do not be a donkey, Ephraim. What would father want with an old piece of clay pot?"

His face three inches from his sister's, Ephraim warned her in a harsh whisper, "This has to be something else; pots aren't usually covered with gold." He grabbed Ylenah's wrist and squeezed until she squealed in pain. "You are not to tell him . . . not to tell a single person. Promise!"

"Let go; you are hurting me." Ylenah wrenched her arm free from Ephraim's grasp and lurched backward. Running toward the house, she shouted over her shoulder, "For that, you can handle the ox and plow by yourself."

Ephraim instantly regretted the loss of Ylenah's help. What made him act so? He was fond of his sister. Besides, he needed her to guide the ox.

"Come back, Ylenah. I did not mean to hurt you. We found it together. . . ." When Ylenah hesitated, Ephraim paused, not sure he really wanted to share their find. But, afraid Ylenah might tell, he continued, "It belongs to both of us. It is our secret."

Ylenah didn't turn.

"I know of an old owl nest where it will be safe. I will show you," Ephraim shouted at her stiff back.

Coerced again, Ylenah shrugged, turned, and retraced her steps to the spot where Ephraim waited by the most ancient of the gnarled poplar trees.

"Watch!" Holding the shard in his teeth, Ephraim shinnied up the twisted trunk to its broad fork. Bracing his body against a large branch, he precariously balanced on his toes. He stretched as tall as possible, and was barely able to shove the shard into the nest hole with his fingertips.

Ephraim's mouth skewed in a satisfied smirk. "No one . . ." he grunted, sliding down the trunk, "no one will ever find it there."

CHAPTER 14

In 1891, the Ittihad, or "Young Turk," movement formally organized in Geneva. Its leaders would prove to be the nemesis of the Armenians who lived in Asia Minor. The Armenians had long wanted an independent state of their own, and, during the First World War, some of them joined Russia in an alliance against Turkey. They believed that the Russians might be more sympathetic to their cause should Russia defeat the sultan. To make matters worse, the Kurds, lawless tribesmen who hoped for an independence of their own, allied with the Turks against the Armenians.

In retaliation, and though most Armenians were innocent of treachery, the Turkish government by the end of 1915 had ordered the deportation of the entire Armenian population—about 1.75 million—to Syria and Palestine. Houses and farms, occupied by Armenians for generations, were forcibly abandoned.

During their flight, an estimated six hundred thousand to 1 million men, women, and children died of starvation. Turkish soldiers and police killed hundreds more. Still, about one-third of the population escaped deportation. Of those that left Turkey, many eventually settled in the Soviet Union, Europe, and the Americas.

* * *

Lesser Armenia, 1895

Seventeen-year-old Ylenah and her cousin, Gabriel, had been married only three weeks. When they returned home, they planned to live temporarily with Ylenah's parents. After spending a glorious honeymoon in the Lake Van region, where they visited Gabriel's many relatives, the unsuspecting newlyweds arrived home the day after the raid.

Ylenah learned from Ephraim what befell their parents. The same afternoon the village was destroyed, the *çete*, a band of brigands, galloped onto the Trajian farm. As the band's leader trotted his horse through the well-tended garden, the elderly couple, startled, looked up from where they were hoeing weeds.

The leader reined his horse to a skidding stop in front of Ylenah's father. "We have come to relieve you of your wealth, old man," he shouted.

Before the twin's father had a chance to resist, and for no apparent reason, the leader ordered his *çete* to shoot the help-less old people, drag their bodies into the house, and set the ancestral home on fire. Ephraim had been working in his father's field. At first sight of the brigands he flung himself prostrate, and lay there the whole time, cowering with fear.

Ylenah stood in shock by the remains of her home. Holding her scarf over her nose to suppress the nauseating smell of burned flesh, she watched with horror as Gabriel waded through the rubble.

Her new husband stepped gingerly, using the end of a scorched hoe handle to probe the still-smoldering coals of the house. Suddenly, Gabriel stopped. He turned to look at Ylenah, his face contorted. "I have found your parents," he said.

Ylenah collapsed to the ground and began rocking back and forth. Her wails blended with the haunting ululations sound-ing from the distant village. Then, remembering her missing sister, she searched the landscape. "Where is Nika?" she screamed.

They found Nika huddled in a field to which she had fled—in vain. She had been shot and was hemorrhaging internally. Before she died of blood loss, Nika managed to tell Ylenah her story.

Four men forced her to perform unspeakable acts and re-peatedly raped her. When they finished, one of them shot her, saying that if dead, she could not bear witness against them.

* * *

Samsun, Turkey, 1912

The room was warm and cozy, yet Ylenah shivered. She dug her nails into her scalp and yanked her hair, as if mere pain could erase the appalling images. Finally, gaining control of her emotions, she lifted the iron pot of bubbling bulgur wheat off its hook and set it on the table. Trying to rid her mind of the awful memories, Ylenah deliberately shifted her attention to her five-year-old daughter.

Mariyam sat on the floor, cuddling the puppy that was now awake and chewing on the little girl's fingers.

"Come to me, Mariyam," Ylenah said, holding wide her arms.

Mariyam stared at her mother, puzzled by Ylenah's strangely tremulous voice.

"Come! Come!" Ylenah coaxed.

Reluctantly pushing the pup off her lap, Mariyam rose and ran to her mother.

"Such a big girl." Ylenah hugged the child and bent to kiss her cheek. "I will let nothing happen to you, *sevgilim*, my darling."

Mariyam frowned. There it was again, the allusion to some terrible event that took place before she was born, something that depressed and terrified her mother. Her parents had never discussed the massacres in front of her, though she heard them whispering about it late at night when she was supposed to be asleep.

Mariyam had Turkish playmates, and her parents had Turkish friends; but, young as she was, Mariyam (as did everyone in Samsun's Armenian quarter) felt the threat that enshrouded them like an enigmatic gray fog. To her, the murder of her grandparents was a scary fairytale—not real, not affecting her.

When her parents spoke of sailing to America, Mariyam was all ears. Now she leaned against Ylenah, her chin pressed into Ylenah's stomach. Heart-shaped face upturned, she asked, "When are we going to America?"

Ylenah's eyebrows arched. "How did you—?" Midsentence, she abruptly stopped and clamped a hand across Mariyam's mouth. "Hush! Someone is coming." She swung Mariyam protectively behind her. They waited, apprehensive, as the running footsteps approached.

Ylenah's shoulders slumped and she gasped with relief when she recognized Gabriel's familiar step on the stoop. Flinging open the door, before her husband caught his breath, she asked, "Is there anything new?" Gabriel nodded, but said nothing. He struggled out of his boots and dropped them next to the wall. When he sank onto the bench by the door, Ylenah spread her skirt to sit beside him. Mariyam wormed her way into a spot between them.

"It is not good news," Gabriel said. "The Italians bombarded the two forts that guard the Dardenelles, and the government closed the shipping lanes. No foreign vessels can get through. That ends my Greek firm's operation in Samsun. What is worse, I have been transferred to Smyrna."

"Do we have to go?" Ylenah groaned.

"I must," Gabriel answered, "but, because the Italian navy recently shelled Smyrna, you and Mariyam will be safer here."

"Never!" Ylenah protested. "Our family will remain together."

"When are we going?" Mariyam asked, excited by the prospect of adventure.

Gabriel caressed Mariyam's silky curls. When his gaze met that of his wife's over Mariyam's head, his eyes misted. "When we are ready, little one," he whispered in her ear.

"Tomorrow!" Mariyam shouted, hopping up and spinning in gleeful circles.

"Next week," her father corrected.

Next week? Gabriel's earthshaking announcement stunned Ylenah. How could she be ready to move to Smyrna so soon? In her mind, she instantly began to list the things she had to do. Gabriel, noncommunicative, had retreated into his own deep thoughts. They sat in brooding silence as the falling sun turned the Black Sea to red.

The bluff upon which Gabriel and Ylenah's modest home perched presented an ever changing view of the Black Sea, so unlike the arid, barren foothills of Eastern Anatolia. Ylenah never tired of watching the gulls soar on the thermal currents that rose from the rocky beach below the cliff. The birds' graceful, swooping flight exhilarated her, giving her a sense of freedom.

Once, Gabriel had caught her standing at the bluff's edge, her skirt and shawl billowing in the wind, her erect body and extended arms forming a cross. "What are you doing?" he exclaimed, grabbing her around the waist and drawing her away from the dangerous precipice.

"I am flying," she had said.

Ylenah now pivoted her head slightly until she could see her husband from the corner of her eye. She adored his profile, his thick black lashes, sculptured Semitic nose, and full, sensuous lips. She reached over and took his hand in hers. Stroking the long tapered fingers, she said softly, "You know that the Vartanians moved to Smyrna last year? In a letter to Yeghnar, the baker's wife, Eghia Vartanian said Smyrna has a lovely harbor and milder seasons."

Gabriel curled his fingers and wove them into his wife's. "I'm not sure Smyrna is safe; the Greeks and Turks do not get along, and the Greeks control Smyrna. If Greece and Turkey declare war, the Turks will want Smyrna's port."

"But in Smyrna, we should be able to find a ship to take us to Greece," Ylenah said, brightening.

Gabriel smiled. "That is my thought, also."

CHAPTER 15

Smyrna, Western Turkey, 1915

Ylenah carefully arranged another dolma in the shallow pan. It was Gabriel's birthday and *Yaprak Dolmasi* was his favorite dish. She had even added extra currants to the traditional Turkish recipe of grape leaves stuffed with spicy rice, pine nuts, currants, and a touch of mint. First checking the fire in the old iron stove, Ylenah slid the pan of dolmas to the place of lowest heat. Lifting a basket of golden Smyrna apricots from the floor, she carried them to the table upon which a small samovar steamed. She poured a glass of tea from the samovar and took a sip. Setting down the glass, she began to slice the perfectly ripened apricots in half. She was digging out a stone when Mariyam dashed in, breathless and full of news from school.

Mariyam's happy shout rang through the room. *"Merhaba, Anacığim!* Hello, dear Mama!" In the three years since leaving Samsun, she had grown a foot. The energetic eight-year-old was slim like her father, but she had Ylenah's fair skin and curly auburn hair.

Ylenah spent more than an hour, twice a week, hand washing, starching, and pressing the enormous white bow that tied back Mariyam's long curls. She did the same with the broad collar that spanned Mariyam's shoulders like a short shawl, the stark white of the collar relieving the somber black of her school uniform.

Mariyam spotted the apricots. *"Kayısı?* You are making *Kayısı,* apricot meringue?" she cried with pleasure, and snatched a plump, unpitted fruit from the basket. Ylenah grabbed her arm, stopping her in the middle of a twirl. "Change your clothes, then separate out three egg whites for me. The Vartanians are coming to your father's birthday dinner tonight, and I need your help."

"Evet, Anacığim," Mariyam said, planting a resounding kiss on Ylenah's cheek before she danced off to the screened alcove where she slept and kept her personal treasures.

Ylenah continued to methodically pit apricots until she heard an unusual commotion in the street outside the house. Frowning, she stopped and listened, the knife motionless in one hand, juice from the fruit dripping in the other. There was a rattling at the door, and Gabriel rushed in, home much sooner than usual.

"It is nice you could come home early for your birthday," Ylenah said, pleased. "What is happening outside?"

Gabriel plopped into the chair across from her. His fingers nervously drummed the table. "All of Smyrna is in an uproar. The French and English invaded Gallipoli, and the Italians have declared war on Austria-Hungary and Turkey. It seems treaties are made and broken, as though by children playing small games. The world has gone mad. I have heard," Gabriel continued, "from a very good source, that Sultan Muhammad V's government has been taken over."

"That useless *çamur,*" Ylenah snorted, adding water from the samovar to a glass of strong tea, which she then gave to him.[*]

"An apt description of our great sultan," Gabriel laughed. Then his expression sobered. "I have also heard something I find difficult to tell you, my love." He reached across the table and took Ylenah's hand in his. "The Ittihat Central Committee is vowing to exterminate every Armenian in Turkey.[†] To go east is not safe. Between us and Syria are the Kurds, and small bands of mercenaries scavenge the roads everywhere else."

Gabriel rubbed the tense muscles at the back of his neck. His haunted eyes searched her frightened ones. "The persecution has begun again. Before the Ittihat dogs descend upon us, we must leave Smyrna. We must leave Turkey."

---

[*] *Çamur* means dirt or slob.
[†] The *Ittihat Central Committee* refers to the Union and Progressive Party.

Recalling the massacres that occurred when they were newlyweds, chills caused the skin to quiver over Ylenah's spine and
lifted the tiny hairs at the base of her skull. "Where can we go?"

"At this point, I am not sure. Istanbul has become increasingly hostile to Armenians, as well as Greeks. And the Russians? I don't trust them any more than I do the Turks, though
more of our excitable young men are joining the Russian army
all the time."

"Why would they do that?"

"To fight the Turks."

Ylenah gasped. "Surely you are not considering joining the
Russians?"

"That would be a foolish move," Gabriel said, with a tight
smile. "I would never ally myself with them."

"That is as it should be," Ylenah said, relieved. Resuming
her slicing, she commented, "Anyway, Smyrna's powerful Greek
community will protect us."

Gabriel shook his head. "Hear me! The situation is much
worse this time. The Turks want the Greeks out of Asia Minor,
too, despite the treaty the two countries signed last year. If
things get really bad here, I don't think even the Greeks can
successfully resist the army Mustapha Kemal is putting together."
Gabriel stood, hitching his trousers. "It is best we go to Greece
as soon as possible. We will take only what we can personally
carry aboard a ship."

Throwing her knife on the table, Ylenah jumped up. She
began to pace the main room of their comfortable two-room
home at the northern edge of Smyrna. Gabriel had worked
hard to buy it. One by one she touched familiar objects. How
could she part with any of them? Tears filled her eyes so that
she could barely see the beautiful carpet—the best she had ever
made—that covered the packed mud floor. Of an ancient design, handed down by the women of her family, the colorful
rug had taken her three years to weave. Her gaze passed over
the fine cotton curtains; it drifted across the matching chair
covers and runners that, as a young girl, she had sewn for her

marriage chest. As she caressed the sturdy poplar table Gabriel had finished only last month, she choked back a sob. "Must we leave *everything* behind?"

Gabriel's voice trembled with anguish. "Most must stay." When Ylenah began to sob, he tried to comfort her. "They are mere *things*," he said softly. "Remember, Saint Matthew cautioned us not to store up for ourselves treasures on earth. In God's sight, our lives, and the way we live them, are more important than what we amass."

Ylenah gestured at the table and other fine furniture crafted by her husband. "But you have labored so," she cried. Gabriel drew her close. "We both have worked hard, but we are still young and strong; we can start over when we get to America."

"America?" Ylenah collapsed into a chair. "America? It is too much to think about right now. The Vartanians are coming to your birthday dinner and I am nowhere near ready."

"Ah, but wait, my Ylenah! There is good news amid the bad." Gabriel pulled a crumpled envelope from a pocket and removed a slip of paper. He waved the paper in the air in front of Ylenah. "Today this letter came from my uncle in America. He says if we get to Greece, he will send us money for the rest of the trip. He promises me a job in his shop." Gabriel leaned over Ylenah and gently brushed her lips with his. "First, we must get out of Turkey. There will be more slaughter. I sense it in my very soul."

Ylenah shuddered. "I will begin to pack tomorrow; I could never go through another massacre." Her face pale and pinched, she added, "First, we must celebrate your birthday."

CHAPTER 16

Gabriel tried for six weeks to buy passage on a ship to Greece—on any ship that would take them there—but a world in turmoil had interrupted trade in the Mediterranean and Aegean Seas. Few ships were crossing. Meanwhile, throughout Turkey, the persecution of Armenians was increasing.

Under the influence of German business interests, Turkey undertook the construction of a transcontinental railroad. Armenian men in their prime were rounded up and forced to work on it. Before Gabriel could arrange his family's escape to Greece, four soldiers came for him. The Turks also took the two Vartanian men. Ironically, they were shipped to Eastern Anatolia, to very near where Gabriel and Ylenah were born.

With her husband's support gone, Ylenah and Mariyam soon found themselves struggling to survive. Ylenah's small hoard of gold jewelry, the family "savings account," bankrolled them for two months. (She refused to give up a finely wrought gold necklace and ornate pendant, gifts from Gabriel on their recent twentieth anniversary.)

The first week in August, Ylenah was forced to sell their house. She and Mariyam moved to a ground-floor room in the crowded Armenian sector. At least they were near friends who supported one another through rough times. In fact, things went rather well—that is, until one terrible October day.

It had been hot and humid. To catch the cool evening breeze coming from the port, Ylenah and Mariyam sat outside, by the door, in the shade of a scrawny tree. They were embroidering scarves to sell in the main Smyrna bazaar. Ylenah had propped open the door to their tiny, windowless room, to cool it so they might sleep that night.

Suddenly, anguished screams came from the direction of Eghia Vartanian's house. Ylenah leaped to her feet, her heart racing. "Stay here!" she commanded. "I will see what it is all about."

When her mother didn't return in half an hour, Mariyam idly sauntered down to the Vartanian home. As she approached, she heard a great sobbing and wailing. One voice was her mother's. Mariyam hesitated in the gaping doorway, unable to see anything within the dark interior.

When Mariyam's shadow crossed her face, Ylenah looked up, her eyes red and wet with tears. Eghia lay in a faint on the floor.

Mariyam rushed to her mother. "What is wrong?"

"Your father and Mr. Vartanian are dead," Ylenah moaned. "They were working in a tunnel. It collapsed on them." Ylenah beat her breast, crying, "The railroad won't even send home their bodies."

* * *

Bitter and grieving, Ylenah vowed to leave Turkey as soon as possible. Her luck in purchasing tickets by conventional means was no better than Gabriel's had been. Finally, she went down to the harbor. Spotting a rusty Greek freighter, she talked her way aboard and sought the captain.

The portly, silver-haired Greek leaned back in his chair and examined the woman standing before him. "This is a freighter. We do not take passengers," he said, gently but firmly.

"My daughter and I seek passage to Greece."

"As does everyone these days," the captain sighed. Though she appeared gaunt and pale, Ylenah's courage and dignity impressed him. *She was once beautiful,* he observed. *The accent is not Greek, probably Armenian.*

"I wish I could help, but I remind you again, my ship does not carry passengers," he said, regretting his inability to aid her.

"I am willing to work for our passage. I am a good cook and a skilled launderer."

"Do you have relatives in Greece?" the captain asked.

Ylenah did not want to divulge her Armenian blood, nor

would she reveal that Greece was only a preliminary step in her effort to reach the United States of America. "Yes, a brother near Athens," she lied.

"You say you cook and launder? My cook does the ship's laundry, too." Laughing, he added, "Perhaps it would help his cooking if he did not have to wash dirty linen."

Ylenah clasped her hands tightly in front of her and breathed a silent prayer.

"You would have to sleep below with the men."

"A space could be screened," she said, thinking more of Mariyam's privacy than hers.

He rose to hold the cabin door open for her. "I must think about it. Come back tomorrow afternoon. I will let you know then what I have decided."

Ylenah headed home to tell Mariyam the good tidings with renewed hope in her heart. When she went back the next day, she was told that she and her daughter could sail on the Greek ship, working to pay their way.

Two days later, having sold what they could and given the rest away, Ylenah and Mariyam boarded the freighter with only what they could carry. Instead of being taken to the crowded crew quarters below decks, the first mate escorted them to a small cabin he had vacated just for them. Despite having to wash dirty linens every day and hang them wherever she could find room in a dry spot, Ylenah managed to enjoy the voyage. For the first time in months she felt they were safe.

CHAPTER 17

New York City, 1923

Ylenah stood at the tenement's small bedroom window and yanked at the tangles in her hair with a tortoise-shell comb. The comb had been her mother's, one of the few personal objects that remained of her life in Turkey. Shrill screeching coming from four stories below caught her attention.

Staring down into the narrow, trash-littered courtyard, Ylenah saw a man cuffing a skinny boy who screamed profanities. Enclosed on three sides by scarred and streaked brick walls rarely touched by sunlight, the courtyard teemed with humanity. Black was the predominant color. Men in black suits and hats rushed off to work. Women, wearing long black dresses and scarves, herded restless children clad in black school uniforms. Over all hovered the specter of poverty.

New York is too crowded, too noisy, and everywhere so dreary, Ylenah mused. Though she had worn widows' black since her precious Gabriel's death, her lip curled in distaste. She closed her eyes and leaned her head against the window frame. During the early morning hours of the fall season, the sun's glorious rays flooded the room. The rest of the year, the tall neighboring buildings shadowed its light. It was getting harder to remember the sweet air and vast golden hills of Eastern Anatolia.

Precious little chance I have to sit in the sun since I started working at the shop, she silently lamented. Pulling a hank of hair forward, she fanned the silver strands across her spread fingers. *Only forty-five and already my head is white.* She glanced at the cheap timepiece on her wrist—her first watch—purchased for seventy-five cents at a pawn shop when she received her third paycheck.

"Mariyam, are you ready? We must hurry."

"I'm making my lunch," Mariyam answered from the

combination kitchen and parlor, the second room in the two-room flat.

Ylenah slipped from the window sill and dropped the brush on the bed she shared with Mariyam. Lifting her enormous black purse and a black shawl from a hook on the closet door, she carried them to the other room.

Because that day she was going on a field trip with her senior class, Mariyam did not have on her somber school uniform. Instead, the seventeen-year-old wore the lemon-yellow cotton dress she had finished that week in sewing class. It had loose cap sleeves and a bodice that fitted her like the skin on a sausage. Her luxurious, naturally wavy hair, darker than Ylenah's ever had been but burnished with the same red highlights, hung to her waist in two heavy braids.

Looking at her daughter, Ylenah had to smile. *The figure of a Greek goddess. No wonder the men gawk.* She stepped up behind Mariyam. Reaching around Mariyam's tiny waist, she tweaked her belt until it loosened two holes. "Do not make your belt so tight; it makes your dress too short," Ylenah scolded.

"But, Mama—"

"Not another word, Mariyam. Do you want to embarrass me by dressing like one of those 'floppers'?"

"*Flapper,* Mama, not flopper. And my dress comes halfway to my shoes." Mariyam did a few steps of the new dance rage, the Black Bottom.

Ylenah was aghast. "When you do that, your knees show."

"You always exaggerate, Mama." Mariyam slowly spun around, trying to gracefully balance on one toe like her best friend, Leeza, who took ballet lessons.

"My knees don't show when I *pirouette.*" Losing her balance, Mariyam grabbed at the table.

"*Pirouette?*"

"It's French for 'spinning around.' Leeza taught it to me."

"Speak English, not French, Mariyam," Ylenah commanded, though Mariyam's English was flawless. From their first hour in America, Ylenah had forbidden Mariyam to use anything but the new language. Ylenah herself spoke Armenian, or Turkish, at home, and when with Armenian friends. At work it was the same; everyone was Armenian, and no English was heard in the shop.

Standing in front of the parlor's cracked mirror, Ylenah knotted her hair into a severe bun. Tying the shawl ends under her chin, she told Mariyam, "I do not want my daughter to look like those movie people."

Mariyam had persuaded her mother to accompany her to a film, Ylenah's first, a few weeks earlier. Ylenah had been scandalized by the movie, particularly by the suggestive content, and the short, sleeveless dresses worn by the actresses. She had refused to stay through to the end, forcing Mariyam to leave the movie house with her.

Mariyam persisted. "Everybody is wearing shorter dresses."

"The Orthodox and Jewish girls wear their skirts respectably long. I have seen them myself."

"But, Mama, they are the *only* ones who do. They look like old-fashioned peasants."

"*You* have good peasant blood. It is nothing to be ashamed of," Ylenah snapped.

Mariyam grimaced. "In America, to be called 'peasant' is an insult."

"If it is an insult, it is an insult to be ignored," Ylenah said, unsympathetically. "Come, it is time to go." She headed for the door, pausing to seize a freshly baked *choereg*, a breakfast roll, from the table. "You are too thin. Take this." She thrust the roll on top of Mariyam's newsprint-wrapped lunch. "We will not again speak of flopper dresses. I have decided."

Undaunted, Mariyam glanced at Ylenah's unrelenting back, then bloused her dress above her belt, shortening it another inch.

The *Çeyrek* lay on an elevated wooden platform, half hidden behind enormous ceiling-high racks hung with carpets of all sizes. The exquisite nineteenth-century *Çeyrek* had been woven in Hereke, a town near Istanbul. A million tiny knots per meter resulted in a smooth, lustrous surface. Besides being made of pure silk, the *Çeyrek's* uniqueness came from gold threads that enhanced its ornate flower-and-fruit motif. Owned by a prominent politician, it was in the shop to have minor moth damage repaired.

Ylenah worked overtime to finish the lovely *Çeyrek*. She sat, cross-legged, on a clean white cloth, spread to protect the valuable carpet. Her eyes a foot from the rug's surface, she concentrated on inserting a needle between two minuscule knots. The dim light by which she worked shone through a flyspecked, three-foot square window set high in the wall. A low-wattage, unshaded bulb, suspended from a ceiling beam, provided little added illumination.

Ylenah did not hear the soft footsteps approach. Suddenly, a hand slid over her shoulder and cupped her breast.

Lurching sideways from under the probing fingers, she leaped to her feet. Her face blushed as red as the carpet's stylized poppies.

"Stop!" she screamed. "How can you do such a thing, Uncle Sarkis?" It was the first time he had actually touched her.

At their first meeting, outside the United States custom's building on Ellis Island, Gabriel's uncle had eyed her in a frightening way. Since then, she had often caught him watching her while she worked. Lately, he had begun to crowd her when they were forced to work in tight quarters together, or he brushed against her when she stood at the wash basin. But never before had he dared such blatant, indecent, familiarity. Now she realized she should not have accepted money from him, not ever, not even for her and Mariyam's passage from Greece.

Sarkis bore no resemblance to her late husband. Gabriel had been tall, lean, and handsome; Sarkis was so short, his pockmarked face, with its huge, blue-veined nose, was barely level with hers. Grossly overweight, always dripping with sweat and stinking of garlic and rotting teeth, he smelled worse than a ram in rut.

"God curse you!" Ylenah snarled and jumped off the carpet platform. She quickly glanced around the shop. It was empty. No one had seen the incident. She walked swiftly away from Sarkis.

Sarkis followed her around the platform until he trapped her in a corner. "Can I not appreciate a beautiful widow who has too long been without a man?" he wheedled.

"Appreciate?" she cried, amazed at his impertinence. "You do more than 'appreciate.' Do not touch me so again."

"Be a good niece," Sarkis sniggered, "or you may have to look for other employment. Jobs are difficult to find if you are not a citizen of the United States."

It was true, she was not a citizen. Ylenah's throat filled with acid; she almost choked. Her voice icy, she hissed, "Touch me again, and your wife will know."

His eyes narrowed. "We will discuss this later, when you are more cooperative." Before he stomped off, he managed to give her arm a suggestive squeeze.

Shaken to her very soul, Ylenah collapsed on the *Çeyrek*. *God forgive me, but oh, how I hate Sarkis.*

That night, as they lay in the big bed, Ylenah asked Mariyam, "How would you like to go to California?"

More asleep than awake, Mariyam merely grunted. "Hmm?"

"There is much talk about an Armenian settlement in a place called Fresno," Ylenah continued.

"Is Fresno a big city like New York?" Mariyam asked, her interest slight.

"I don't think so. People say it is a place of many farms, lying in a great valley where much food is grown. They say the area is much like Eastern Anatolia."

Mariyam barely remembered her early childhood when they lived on Turkey's coast. Anatolia meant nothing to her. "What about school and my friends?" she grumbled. "I don't want to leave them."

"You will make new friends," Ylenah answered. She decided it was time to tell Mariyam about Sarkis. When she described the situation at work, Mariyam responded, "I would kill him, Mama."

"God does not want to hear that kind of talk. Nor do I want to hear it."

"What are you going to do, Mama?"

"The solution is for me to leave the shop and for us to leave New York."

"I suppose Fresno has a good school, too."

"I am sure there are many," Ylenah said with a smile.

"When are we leaving?"

"When we have enough money to buy train tickets," Ylenah answered. "If we are careful, we will have enough in three months. I'll write my cousins who live in Fresno; I have many questions to ask them."

Mariyam rolled over, her head propped on the heel of her palm. "Can you stand to be around Sarkis that long, Mama?"

Ylenah sighed. "I will have to."

To Ylenah's relief, after she threatened to tell his wife about his indiscretion, Sarkis avoided her. One day, a week later, Ylenah was late to work, having overslept. She rushed into the shop and found it silent. She heard no whir of sewing machines, no bubbling of dye vats. Her fellow employees stood in idle huddles, talking quietly. There was no sign of Sarkis. Bewildered, Ylenah asked the yarn dyer, "What has happened?"

"The wife of Sarkis died in her sleep last night. The police just left; they asked many questions."

"What was wrong with her?" Ylenah asked.

"It is a mystery. That is why the police questioned all of us," the woman said, obviously relishing the gossip.

Ylenah barely knew Sarkis' wife, but at times she had felt sorry for the obscure woman married to such a man. She had a dreadful thought. What if Sarkis killed his wife because of her threat to reveal his indecorous attention? If so, what was to prevent him from molesting her now? She could not quit her job yet; she did not have enough money for train tickets to Fresno. Despair sent her spirits to a new low.

For two weeks Sarkis left her alone. Then, one morning, he told her he was increasing her time at the shop to sixteen hours a day, six days a week. Though the long hours would be hard on her, Ylenah was ecstatic, as it meant more income toward the purchase price of train tickets. But the first day of her new schedule, she was dismayed to find that she was alone in the shop at dusk. Apparently, no one else had been asked to work overtime. It didn't take her long to discover why.

Ylenah stood between two room-size carpets hung on drying racks. She was examining a spot she had recently mended for shrinkage, when Sarkis squeezed into the narrow space. Before she could escape, he grabbed her and pulled her against his gross belly.

"We both are lonely, Ylenah. Marry me now," he rasped.

Ylenah desperately tried to fend him off. "It is too soon after your wife's death."

"I cannot wait; I want you now. We are not children; the ceremony can come later."

Furious, Ylenah found strength to tear away from his grasp. "I will never marry you, *kehle*. You bug." Her tough, work-hardened fists pounded his face until blood poured from his bulbous nose. Sarkis instantly released her. Thrusting his hands into his pockets, he frantically searched for something to stem the flow of blood. Ylenah ducked under the hanging carpets. Crawling across the wet concrete floor on hands and knees, she reached the last rack. She ran to the wall where her coat and purse hung. Holding a blood-saturated handkerchief to his nose, Sarkis lumbered after her. Just in time, Ylenah escaped out the shop door.

That night, Ylenah and Mariyam counted the coins and bills Ylenah had stuffed into an old stocking. There was barely enough for two train tickets.

"I can never return to the shop," Ylenah told Mariyam. "We must leave for Fresno immediately."

"The semester is over next week. Can we wait until then?" Mariyam asked, unhappy that the time to go had finally come.

"It will take me a week to get ready, but I will buy the tickets tomorrow. I'll sell my gold earrings to buy us food on the train."

* * *

The two tickets safely in her pocket, Ylenah walked to the pawnshop where she had purchased her watch. As her hand reached for the doorknob, an item in the shop window caught her attention. The flat triangle-shaped broach was a gold replica of an Egyptian pyramid. It reminded her of something she had seen long ago. As she bent to study the object, a sense of déjà vu tickled her mind. Then she remembered the gold-sheathed artifact that she and her twin brother, Ephraim, found when they were children. Ephraim! She hadn't heard from him in years. *Did he ever go back for it?* she wondered.

CHAPTER 18

March 1918

Ylenah's oldest brother, Ervand, drew the bedcover over his head. The dog barked again, this time more urgently. Snow and the house walls muffled the sound. Ervand threw off the cover and listened. Something was wrong. His old dog hardly ever barked anymore.

Every arthritic joint protested as Ervand disentangled himself from the bedclothes and struggled into his trousers and boots. After donning his shabby coat with the moth-eaten wolf-fur collar, he took a straw-tipped staff and shoved it into the fire pit's last remaining coals. When the straw caught and flamed into a torch, he gathered up his old musket from its corner, headed for the door, and stepped out into the night.

That afternoon, an atypical spring storm had deposited six inches of snow on top of the eight already on the ground. Ervand shivered as a blast of freezing air tightened the exposed skin of his face and hands. The older he got, the more he dreaded the Anatolian winters. He often wondered if it might have been better if he had not survived the massacres, had not been one of the few Armenians overlooked during the forced exile of his relatives and neighbors. "If only Ephraim had stayed home to work the land," he mumbled through chattering teeth. However, he was the first to admit that his younger brother had never been much help and never would have been much of a farmer.

Ervand stood in the biting wind, peering around through slitted lids. He saw nothing unusual. Suddenly, a muffled shot sounded from the direction of the goat enclosure, the pen next to the pile of boulders that marked the northeastern boundary of his land. The dog howled once, then was still. Ervand stared in the direction of the shot, but the icy wind caused his eyes to water. He scrubbed at them with his knuckles and stared harder. This time, he saw a faint flickering in the distance. Hesitating a mere beat, he extinguished the torch by driving it into the snow.

Shoulders hunched against the cold, Ervand started toward the mysterious fire. He did not see the dog's body until he stumbled over it, almost falling. Squatting over the dog, he gently caressed its still-warm head. His hand came away wet and sticky. Probing, his fingers found a gory hole between the eyes. "The shot of a marksman," he muttered.

Enraged at the loss of his best herd dog and longtime companion, Ervand no longer felt the cold. Keeping low in the cover of brush and boulders, he stealthily continued toward the strange campfire. When he reached the goat pen, he crouched down and cautiously peered around the boundary rock pile. Under the goat shed, on the far side of the pen, two men huddled by a small fire. Ervand saw that they wore tattered blankets over ragged Turkish army uniforms. Their two rifles were propped against the shed's back wall.

Renegade mercenaries, the worst kind. Ervand spat in the snow. He crouched lower. The eyes of the frightened ewe goats and their yearling kids glowed eerily as they restlessly milled in the enclosure. Ervand noticed a freshly slaughtered carcass dangling from the shed roof. Blood still dripped from it onto the snow.

At first, the mercenaries did not see Ervand. He came at them out of the dark like a frosty specter, his ancient musket wildly weaving as he tried to cover both intruders at once. Crazy with wrath, the Armenian shouted, "You killed my animals!" The mercenaries leaped for their rifles at the same moment he fired, but, instead of launching a bullet, Ervand's rusty musket barrel exploded. Shrapnel shredded his face, instantly blinding him. As he sank to his knees, screaming with pain, the taller mercenary shot him through the heart.

After vainly searching their victim for loot, then stripping the body, the mercenaries traced Ervand's tracks back to his house. They spent the rest of that night, and the following day, comfortably warm, sated with tender kid and dried fruits and vegetables from Ervand's abundant larder. When they finally left, they took with them all they could carry.

That Sunday, Ervand's closest friend, accompanied by another old friend, went to the farm to see why Ervand had failed to appear at the church. They found Ervand's home ransacked and, later, discovered his frozen body by the goat shed.

* * *

The four Turks—three standing, one sitting opposite Ephraim at the rickety table—watched intently as Ephraim studied the trictrac pieces in front of him. He reached out to make his move when a clatter of hooves broke his concentration. Hauling back on the reins of a sweaty mule, an elderly man galloped up to the tea house.

Annoyed at the interruption, Ephraim glared at the stranger, who dismounted and tied the mule to a tree. The man looked around. "I look for Ephraim Trajian. I have news for him."

"You ruin my game," Ephraim snorted. Throwing down his playing piece, he growled, "I am the one you seek, but I am now called Ephraim Cesur."

The old man coughed, struggling to regain his breath. "Your cousin has sent me to bring you home," he gasped. "Your brother Ervand is dead, murdered."

* * *

At age twenty-six and still a bachelor, Ephraim had courted a childless Turkish widow who was eight years older. The mismatched couple rode a burro nearly sixty miles to the province capital, Ağri, where they married. At the same time, Ephraim changed his surname to the Turkish *Cesur,* meaning valiant or courageous. The newlyweds returned home to the bride's humble mud and rock hut.

Ephraim refused to farm or barter rugs, as had the generations before him; he became a forger of brass and copper. Erecting a booth in his village, near Doğubayazit, the first town of significance west of the Persian border, his skill increased, as did his reputation and his clientele. At last he earned enough to lease a windowless room next to the village bakery. Though he had changed his name, his Turkish neighbors knew he was an infidel Armenian. Behind his back, they called him a braggart. They tolerated him because their wives sought his expertly crafted wares and because of his Moslem wife. Those same men, who antagonized other Armenians, left Ephraim in peace. Eventually, they even invited him to join their nightly trictrac games at the *çay* house.

* * *

Ephraim wasted no time mourning his brother. Instead, he immediately maneuvered to increase his fortune and status. He sold the family property to a cousin. With the money from the sale, he purchased a tiny plot at the edge of the village. On it, he built a tiny shop and a one-room dwelling. Ephraim and his wife used the larger room as a combined kitchen, eating, and sitting area. They slept in a small, curtained alcove off the main room. Ephraim's endomorphic physique broadened on his wife's excellent cooking.

A low wall of stone delineated the property line in back. Ephraim's wife tied her two milk goats in the corner, where the house and wall joined. A makeshift shed of branches and thatching (out of reach of the always hungry goats) protected the animals from the worst of the severe winter storms.

Ephraim had changed his name and location the same year Ylenah moved to Fresno. In the process they lost track of one another. His memory of the strange, gold-encased shard lay locked safely within a secret pocket of his subconscious. Long ago, the ambitious dreams of his youth had faded, like the summertime thunderheads that collect and swiftly evanesce above Mount Ararat.

Ephraim and his wife knew little about the Great War that

involved most of the civilized world's industrialized nations. When word reached their village that Turkey had allied itself with the powerful, but distant, Germany, Ephraim only shrugged, saying it did not affect him. The names of the enemy countries involved in the conflict meant little to him, except for Greece. His business came first, his son second. He merely tolerated his wife. Nothing else mattered. Nothing, that is, until the German came to the village.

CHAPTER 19

Constantinople, 1923

The gaunt Prussian with the shaved, skeletal head was in excellent humor. He lingered at his preferred table, in his favorite *lokanta,* near the main gate to the *Kapalî Çarşi,* the Covered Bazaar. That very morning, he, ex-Oberstleutnant Wilhelm von Leidenhoffer, had negotiated a covert, but extremely lucrative, sale. Stretching his long, thin legs under the small round table—until they protruded beyond its circumference—he laughed aloud as a frazzled waiter tripped over his crossed ankles, nearly spilling the loaded tray he carried.

Wilhelm's sale of the rare Artemis statue to a rich American had been a real *coup de maître,* a masterstroke. The ancient silver image, plundered years before from the unguarded ruins of ancient Ephesus, had been in the private collection of a wealthy Greek. Desperate for the cash to leave Turkey, the Greek surreptitiously notified an underground antiquity dealer that the figure was for sale. Von Leidenhoffer purchased it for a ridiculously small sum, then sold it to an American millionaire for a fine profit.

Since the end of the war, von Leidenhoffer supported himself by discreetly negotiating the trade, or sale, of certain valuable items among collectors scattered throughout the world. Such individuals willingly paid outrageous prices for Asia Minor's increasingly popular artifacts. Meanwhile, he could appropriate choice specimens for his own private collection.

Wilhelm's pale eyes, cold and gray, set in cavernous dark-ringed sockets, idly focused on the courtyard of the old mosque across the street, the Bayazit Çamii. Devout Moslem men washed their hands and feet five times a day in the fountain. Before entering the mosque to pray, they donned cotton slippers.

Von Leidenhoffer's thin lips lifted in a sneer. Though raised in a strict Lutheran family, he now despised anything having to do with religion. He had heard all the better-known New Testament Bible stories as a child, but rarely associated them with the names of the archeological sites he now looted: Ephesus, Pergamum, Sardis, and others. To him, Turkey was the domain of endless treasure. Why, just the day before, he had heard talk of Noah's ark.

Von Leidenhoffer started to lift the nearly empty glass of potent, licorice-flavored *raki*, but suddenly stopped, the glass halfway to his mouth. *The ark was supposed to have landed on Mount Ararat. Did it?*

He tried to remember the old Bible tale. *Mount Ararat, the 17,000-foot peak the Turks called Büyük Ağri Daği, Great Ararat Mountain. Ja, it has to be the same.* Greed suffused his expression. *If the story is true, there must be a vast treasure of relics somewhere on that mountain.* As he gulped down the remainder of the *raki*, his fingers tightened on the empty glass. It shattered under the pressure. Cursing, he wrapped his napkin around the cut in the web between his index finger and thumb.

With his undamaged hand, von Leidenhoffer wiggled a bony finger at the Turkish waiter. "*Tamam*," he said. "I have had enough." Tossing two coins on the flyspecked cloth, he leaned back in the spindly chair and began making plans for an immediate trip to eastern Turkey.

CHAPTER 20

It was while on a trading trip to Doğubayazit that Ephraim initially saw von Leidenhoffer. It was not only the rider, but also the fine bay mare the man rode that held Ephraim's attention. Even without his beautiful animal, the elegant horseman, in his German officer's cap and polished boots and spurs, stood out from the drab villagers like a silky Angora goat among fat-tailed sheep.

The rider reined in his lively Arabian mare and leaned down to speak with a *sucu*, a water vendor. Apparently, he had no interest in the water contained in an elaborate copper dispenser strapped to the vendor's back. Instead, the rider seemed to ask a multitude of questions. The *sucu* kept jerking his chin up, showing he did not understand. Curious, Ephraim moved closer.

"What is the best way to Ağri Daği?" The stranger spoke in fluent Turkish, but with an abominable accent.

No wonder the sucu *cannot understand him,* Ephraim scoffed. Never one to pass up a chance to make money, he stepped up to the horseman. "I can guide you to Büyük Ağri Daği," he offered. "I know the area well."

Wilhelm von Leidenhoffer straightened in his saddle and stared at Ephraim.

Ephraim almost shuddered. *His eyes are the color of dirty ice in a skull's empty sockets.*

"And how much must I pay you to guide me?" von Leidenhoffer asked in his atrocious accent.

Ephraim paused. If he asked too little, it would not profit him to close the shop. Setting too lofty a price might send the man and his assets away. "How many days do you wish me to guide you?" he ventured.

"It is for you to tell me," the horseman growled.

Spreading his arms wide in mock exasperation, Ephraim said, "I do not know where on the mountain you wish to go."

Von Leidenhoffer eyed Ephraim through slitted lids. "When your work is finished, we will decide what you have earned. *Peki?* Right?"

The man must think me a fool, thought Ephraim. But Ephraim desperately wanted the job. He hesitated only a moment, then dropped his chin on his chest and placed his right hand over his heart to show he agreed to von Leidenhoffer's proposition.

"It is settled. Come tomorrow morning to the *caravanserai,* the old inn. Ask for Oberstleutnant Wilhelm von Leidenhoffer." Wilhelm jabbed the mare with his spurs and she leapt forward into a canter. Ephraim watched, entranced, as horse and rider disappeared in the direction of the *caravanserai.*

That afternoon, Ephraim posted a notice on his shop saying that it would close for an indefinite length of time. At their evening meal, he told his wife he was leaving the next morning; he could be away several days, perhaps weeks.

"Where are you going? Why must you go for so long?" she asked.

"*Suş,* shut up, old woman," he snapped, and cursed her for prying. After years of emotional, often physical, abuse, Ephraim's wife knew better than to rebuke him. She ducked her head and went back to preparing the evening meal, asking herself for the thousandth time why she ever married him.

Before dawn the next morning, Ephraim walked to the ruined *caravanserai* that lay west of Doğubayazit. He passed through the ornate Seljuk entrance into the walled courtyard. By the light of several fires, he saw that von Leidenhoffer commanded a respectable entourage of six men and ten donkeys. Piles of baggage lay heaped about. Two large tents, one larger than the other, stood at the far end. The donkeys and the Arabian mare contentedly chomped hay in the now roofless side rooms that once housed travelers.

Ephraim sauntered over to the tents. The individual he had talked with in town was nowhere in sight, but a short, slender man, dressed in formal European clothes, sat on a camp stool in front of the larger tent. As Ephraim approached, the man whipped out a cloth from the back pocket of his black, high-collared coat. Bending over a pair of begrimed boots, he began to clean them.

"Von . . ." Ephraim could not remember the horseman's difficult German name. "Von . . . *Bey* asked me to come," he stammered in Armenian, then in Turkish.

"Oberstleutnant Wilhelm von Leidenhoffer," the valet corrected. Disdainfully examining Ephraim, he asked, "He is expecting you?"

"*Evet.*"

"I will tell Herr von Leidenhoffer you are here." The pompous valet disappeared through the tent fly.

Ephraim was listening to incomprehensible German coming from within the tent when there was a crash behind him. Ephraim spun around. A Turkish laborer had dropped a polished ebony box, and the box lid had sprung open. Ephraim's eyes popped as dozens of bright silver eating utensils spilled onto the dusty ground. A rotund man, garbed in a soiled white apron and lopsided chef's hat, waddled up screaming in volatile Greek at the hapless laborer. The laborer meekly gathered up the utensils. When the cook turned away, Ephraim noticed that the Turk's glare, directed at the Greek's back, was one of pure hatred. *All is not well here,* he thought.

The rest of the expedition consisted of tough-looking peasant types, men who looked like they could plow a full day and night straight. Ephraim's arms and legs twitched at the idea.

Von Leidenhoffer flung the tent fly aside. "*Güzel!* Good! You did come, after all. Are you mounted?"

At first, Ephraim did not know what the German meant. When he understood, he was ashamed and muttered, "No, I have no horse or ass."

The German sat on the box vacated by the valet and drew on a boot. "I have an extra beast you can use. We start when the animals are loaded." He pulled on the second boot. Standing, he stomped his feet to force them into the boots. "Come with me," he demanded. Slapping a swagger stick against his thigh, he strode toward the animal pens.

Under von Leidenhoffer's direction, the Turks loaded the baggage on seven donkeys. The cook, valet, and Ephraim hoisted themselves onto the backs of the three remaining donkeys.

Von Leidenhoffer sprang to the back of his mare. She pranced in place under a tight rein, her neck arched, her tail flagged high over her croup. As though an integral part of the animal, the German's gaunt frame flowed fluidly with the mare's every movement.

Ephraim ached with envy as he sat on the lethargic, lop-eared donkey.

As dawn glowed in the eastern sky, the small caravan wound its way down Doğubayazit's main street, once the ancient trade road from Persia to Constantinople. Every head turned to appraise the elegant mare and her stiff-backed, cavalry-trained rider. Sitting on his humble mount, Ephraim reddened when a trictrac playing friend called out to him as the caravan passed.

As they left the town and headed east, Wilhelm spurred the nervous mare into a collected canter, keeping her well ahead of the plodding donkeys until she had expended her excess energy. Then he trotted back to ride abreast of Ephraim.

Looking down at the Armenian on his scruffy little beast, von Leidenhoffer asked, "You know of the ark? Noah's ship?"

"There is a story of such a ship in the Bible, as well as in the Koran," Ephraim said, cautious because he did not yet want to reveal just how much he really knew about the ark.

Wilhelm pointed at the snow-covered massif looming from the plain. "Do *you* believe the ark is somewhere up there?"

"My own grandfather saw it himself. It was long ago, in years when the snows were lighter," Ephraim boasted.

Von Leidenhoffer's eyes glittered. "I want to see the ark," he said. "Can you make it so?"

Ephraim shook his head. "This is not the season. There are many dangers—landslides, bandits, storms." Sniffing the slight breeze, he said, "There is already the smell of winter in the air." He waved a hand toward Ararat. "People caught on Ağri Daği in a bad storm die. Last year, two Englishmen froze to death near the top. It was even earlier in the year than now, but a terrible storm caught them. Their bodies remained on Ağri Daği until the ice released them the following summer." Ephraim's face bore no sign of emotion as he explained what had happened.

Ephraim didn't mention that the Turkish authorities had displayed the cadavers in the courtyard of the *caravanserai*. He shuddered when he recalled the stench.

Von Leidenhoffer's gaze reluctantly left the mountain and fixed on Ephraim. "It would not be wise to ascend Ağri Daği now," von Leidenhoffer said aloud, to himself, rather than to Ephraim. "Next year I shall come earlier."

Ephraim feared he was about to lose a fee, but he tried to hide his disappointment. "I can show you other things in less dangerous places—ancient altars and strange carvings on rocks."

Ephraim's statements refired von Leidenhoffer's imagination. "I am always seeking unusual souvenirs of a particular kind."

The German's sly reference to illicit artifacts did not deceive Ephraim; the Armenian was well aware of the international trade in them. Many tourists and opportunists came to the area in search of relics. Once he had even translated for a Belgian collector, but the young government in Turkey's new capital, Ankara, frowned on the exportation of ancient relics.

Ephraim hissed at a sudden recollection. He glanced quickly at von Leidenhoffer. The German had not noticed, but was again studying Ararat's snow-capped peak that mystically floated above the earth on a cushion of haze. Ephraim had remembered the gold-wrapped shard on which Ylenah had cut herself when they were children. A picture of the hole in the poplar tree was as clear in his head as if he had placed the shard within it the day before.

With the shard in mind, Ephraim decided to bait von Leidenhoffer. He assumed an expression of naïveté. "What souvenir would please you? A pretty clay pot or little statue? There are places where artifacts are in the ground like gravel in a riverbed," he purred.

A former army officer, used to command, Wilhelm was an experienced judge of human nature. He caught the avarice in Ephraim's voice. "My interests are many," he said, pretending to take the hook. "The most common articles, and usually the least valuable, are articles of clay. I would have to see them myself. That is how I will know if they have worth."

Ephraim nodded and said nothing more. First, he would have to retrieve the shard from the owl hole, then wait for the right moment to offer his treasure to the German—for a price, of course.

CHAPTER 21

They did not go far on the dusty Doğubayazit-Iğdir road that day. Ephraim pointed out two sites of ancient ruins, and Wilhelm stopped to explore them both. By early afternoon they had barely reached the barren hills at the base of Ağri Daği. Having found nothing lucrative, Wilhelm was in a foul mood. He called a halt for the night at a third ruin near land owned by Ephraim's family long before the persecutions began.

The Turks raised the largest tent for von Leidenhoffer and erected the smaller mess tent a short distance away. Ephraim saw with envy that the Greek would sleep in the cozy cooking shelter. Ephraim had naively left town without sleeping gear or provisions; he had only the smelly donkey pad for a pillow, and his coat to cover him. Too late, he realized his foolish oversight. Contemplating an uncomfortable night in the crisp fall air, he shivered. Then he had an inspiration; he would borrow warmer clothing and bedding from his cousin who lived a mere hour's ride from the encampment. The old owl nest, with its treasure, was close by.

Wilhelm von Leidenhoffer stood in front of his tent, legs widely braced and back arched, his eyes fixed on Ararat's inviolable pinnacles. A handsome Turkish meerschaum, carved with entwined tulips and wild roses, was clamped in the corner of his mouth. As Ephraim approached, he turned to face him.

Ephraim spoke first. "My relative has a farm a short distance from here. I will spend the night there and return by first light."

Wilhelm slowly removed the pipe from his mouth. His pale eyes measured Ephraim. Jabbing the pipe stem perilously close to Ephraim's face as enforcement, he ordered, "Be back before dawn. We must begin early and go farther than we did today. We will stop only to eat a light midday meal."

Ephraim bobbed his head, eager to be away. "I will be here. I tell you, I know the mountain's secrets like I know the fingers of my right hand." He knew of at least four more sites he was sure von Leidenhoffer would want to investigate.

Ephraim heaved his corpulent body onto the old donkey's back. Brutally whipping its flanks with a freshly cut switch, he drove it at a fast trot toward his childhood home.

* * *

For years birds and weather had enlarged the owl hole, allowing rain and snow to penetrate the old poplar tree's heart. One fall, during a raging storm, a mighty gust snapped off the tree's top ten feet, exposing its vulnerable pith. In the following decades, the trunk gradually rotted and the shard dropped yet lower into the tree's crumbling base. Finally, after many years, the gold-sheathed corner lay buried beneath a thick layer of sand and mulch within a squat, insect-ravaged stump.

* * *

Ephraim reached the stream just before dark. He stared stupefied at the opposite bank. Where were the poplar trees? Dismounting, he slid down the two-foot high slope and sank to his ankles in sand and gravel. The donkey stood where he left it, its head hanging, bloody froth bubbling from its nostrils.

Stumbling through the rank trickle of water that puddled in the middle of the stream bed, Ephraim struggled to the place where the hardy poplars once stood. All that was left of the ancient tree line was an erratic row of rotted stumps. What had happened to the owl hole? Had the artifact washed away? His hysterical thoughts scrambled over one another like ants from a ravaged nest. A paranoid notion briefly whispered in his brain. Had his twin sister, Ylenah, come back to Turkey for the secret cache? Hardly! She had never been interested, and he did not even know if she were alive; they had not corresponded for years. "Why did I not remove it long ago?" he screamed at the wind.

He glanced at the western sky. The sun was disappearing behind the hills; he had to hurry. Frantically pacing the bank, he searched for signs of the owl-nest tree. When his foot caught on a protruding root, he tripped and almost fell. "Oh God, let me find it," he babbled.

A compacted scrap, containing the tiny bones of a rodent, caught his eye. It was the remains of an old owl pellet. This had to be the tree! Ephraim looked around for something with which to dig, but the peasants had scavenged every branch and twig for firewood.

Cursing, Ephraim waddled along the bank. He shouted triumphantly when he spotted a stout branch that had apparently been wedged into a pile of rock during the last flood surge. Yanking at the branch did not budge it. Desperately, his hands scrabbled at the rocks, dragging them away one by one. Finally he freed the branch, but not before shredding his fingernails and scraping raw his palms and fingers. He scurried back to the mound of pulverized bark and wood, his alarm increasing as the light rapidly faded.

Ephraim methodically sifted the debris. The end of the branch struck something solid. Shaking with anticipation, Ephraim dug into the mulch and pulled the object out. It was only a flat stone. Disgusted, he flung it to the ground.

He probed farther. Suddenly, the branch hit something that had a different feel and sound. Dropping to his knees, he carefully cleared away the mulch. Even though the light was nearly gone, he saw the glimmer of gold. He felt like crying, so absolute was his relief.

The stars lit Ephraim's way to his former home. As he had planned, his cousin, who had bought the land from Ephraim, insisted he stay the night. While Ephraim dined on pilaf and yogurt, his cousin and his cousin's wife prodded him for the latest news. He told them he had been hired as the guide for von Leidenhoffer's expedition, but did not tell them about the gold-sheathed artifact.

Exhausted, Ephraim collapsed on a makeshift bed in his

cousin's kitchen. In the privacy of their bedroom, the cousin and his wife discussed Ephraim's filthy condition. The wife said with disdain, "The Moslem woman does not properly care for my husband's cousin. He is as dirty as a wallowing ox."

"Then wash his clothes," answered her husband, wishing only to go to sleep.

"I will ask him if he wants me to wash them in the morning," she smugly replied.

Quietly, so as not to wake his cousins, Ephraim rose from his bed. Unable to sleep, he sat cross-legged by the dying fire. He cleaned and polished the golden artifact, taking particular care not to damage the inscriptions. When it shone to his satisfaction, he snuffed out the lamp and again reclined on the sleeping mat. He lay in the dark, fantasizing generous monies the German would pay him for his golden prize. At last, he fell asleep with visions of himself parading down the main street of his village on a fancy Arabian mare—better yet, a powerful stallion.

Ephraim rose before dawn, prepared to leave. He was downing a cup of *ayran,* yogurt thinned with water, when his cousin's wife said, "Let me wash your coat before you leave us." She started to remove the garment from Ephraim's shoulders.

Ephraim jerked back, fearing she would see the artifact tucked into the back of his sash. "I do not have time," he said. "But I must ask another favor." He turned to his cousin. "I need a donkey to replace mine. Also, a blanket and a warmer coat."

Though the cousin knew Ephraim's old donkey was near death, he spread his hands magnanimously, saying, "It is enough for you to ask. What is mine, is my cousin's."

"I will return the clothing and beast when the German has finished with me." Ephraim shrugged. "I do not know when that will be."

"It is of no matter. The donkey is yours as long as you need it," his cousin assured him.

CHAPTER 22

Again in Ephraim's possession, the shard resurrected poignant memories of his childhood, Ylenah, and the hated plow. A fleeting image of his sister leading the big ox touched his mind like the ephemeral brushing of a fledgling's down. He remembered how, when she cleared the little cave for the water jug, Ylenah had cut her finger on the broken edge of the shard.

Suddenly, a flock of birds whirred from the roadside shrubbery, causing the donkey to shy. The sharp-edged shard prodded Ephraim's spine, and Ylenah's image wafted away as a feather on the breeze.

* * *

The Turks were packing the camp's gear by the time Ephraim arrived. No one noticed he had exchanged Wilhelm's donkey for his cousin's beast. Uncertain whether to call out that he had returned or to drift aimlessly about the camp, he rode straight to von Leidenhoffer's tent and dismounted. Nervously shuffling his feet, Ephraim waited.

The German must have seen Ephraim's elongated shadow on the canvas, for he flung aside the flap and stooped in the opening. His pale snake eyes stared up at Ephraim. "I see you have returned. *Çok iyi,* very good. Have you eaten a morning meal?" When Ephraim lifted his chin, von Leidenhoffer gestured in the direction of the cook tent. "Tea should be ready. Tell Sol he is to feed you."

Von Leidenhoffer shouted across to the bustling cook, "Sol, I will eat now." He abruptly ducked into his tent and dropped the flap behind him. A scowl darkening his features, Ephraim lumbered over to eat.

Sol had rolled up the anterior wall of the cook tent. Despite the frigid fall morning, sweat gleamed on the Greek's fat red cheeks. Steam misted his round, rimless glasses. His sparse hair, parted in the middle, clung to the sides of his head, resembling flattened wings.

"Eh? What do you want?" Sol asked in heavily accented Turkish.

"He said you are to give me food and *çay*." Ephraim stood just inside the cook tent with his arms folded. "I will wait."

"*Herr* von Leidenhoffer, you mean." The cook did not attempt to hide his disapproval. It was below his station, as an esteemed member of the colonel's personal staff, to make tea for peasants. However, one should follow orders if one was to remain a part of that staff.

As a prisoner of the Germans and assigned to the colonel's private mess during the war, Sol had learned well the lesson of obedience. His father, a reputable chef in Sofia, had taught his son to cook at a young age. Soon after his capture, Sol was running the colonel's mess and creating exquisite dishes for the colonel's table. As Sol's reputation spread and word of von Leidenhoffer's gourmet repasts got around, von Leidenhoffer was the envy of every German officer in the sector. Following the war, each man went his separate way.

Three years later, von Leidenhoffer spied Sol shopping in the Constantinople spice bazaar. By then, the German ran a profitable business dealing in illegal antiquities. He could afford a cook, as well as the valet already in his employ. He asked the ex-prisoner to cook for him.

An aura of danger and excitement surrounded von Leidenhoffer. It had always fascinated Sol, and he could not resist the offer to be a part of that environment. Sending his wife and five children to her parents in Sofia, he left his job as cook at a second-rate *balîk lokanta*, a fish restaurant. Though his family rarely saw him, every month he sent the greater portion of his salary to Greece.

"Take a glass." Sol jerked an elbow at the huge ebony chest with polished brass fittings that contained Wilhelm's translucent porcelain dishes and silver utensils. Now, a dozen wasp-waisted glasses on a silver tray, and a bowl of course-grained, brownish sugar cubes, sat on the chest.

Ephraim took one of the tiny glasses, but rejected the sugar. He handed the glass to Sol for filling.

The cook poured black syrup into the glass from a teapot simmering on the top of a large brass samovar. To the half-filled glass he added boiling water out of a spigot sprouting from the samovar's fat midsection. Handing the filled glass to Ephraim, he wiped his hands on the soiled apron covering his paunch.

The cook tent was cozy and the source of delicious aromas. Ephraim stood appreciatively in the entrance, sipping his tea. He watched Sol place a wicker lap tray on the top of the teak box, then spread the tray with an embroidered linen cloth. On it, he laid a place setting for one, adding a plate of fresh rolls and a glass of thick, creamy *ayran*—more like buttermilk than water. A small saucer of bright pink rose-petal jam lent color to the breakfast tray.

Ephraim was outrageously hungry. When Sol added a thick slab of salty white *feta*, goat cheese, to the plate, Ephraim had to look away. It was plain the common help would be fed later.

When Sol carried the tray to von Leidenhoffer's tent, Ephraim followed as far as the campfire. Fuel was sparse in the area, so the fire was small. Ephraim stooped, set his glass on the ground, and extended his arms over the fire, turning his hands to warm them. He saw Sol pause before entering the German's tent, then go inside.

The Turkish laborers gradually assembled at the cook tent, where each man poured his own glass of thick tea syrup, diluted it with hot water from the samovar, then shuffled to the fire. Crouching close to the meager flames, their work-calloused hands wrapped around the hot glasses, the men drank. The only sound, beside the popping of wood, was the slurping of tea. The older Turks displayed only blackened remnants of teeth, rotted from years of sipping tea through sugar cubes. Ephraim's even, white teeth proved he did not have a sweet tooth.

They eyed him with rancor, but he pointedly ignored them. Even so, a man hunkered close to either side of him. Shoulder-to-shoulder, taking advantage of communal body heat, they all sought protection from the cold.

Before long, Sol carried three baskets from the cook tent and placed them on a baggage box he had positioned between the fire and the tent. Ephraim discovered that von Leidenhoffer fed his men surprisingly well, thus encouraging their loyalty. One basket held loaves of fresh unleavened bread, the second held fat bunches of multicolored grapes. Juicy red pomegranates filled the last.

Ephraim was ravenous, and the other men must have been just as hungry. Shoving and growling like dogs over a rabbit carcass, they quickly emptied the baskets. What the men did not stuff into their mouths they secreted in pockets or under their jackets. Besides chunks of bread, Ephraim thrust a pomegranate into his sleeve.

As the men crowded around the food, a giant Turk with a great curling moustache and massive shoulders deliberately bumped Ephraim. To keep from losing his balance and falling into the flames, Ephraim awkwardly hopped over the fire. Hot tea spilled from his glass, scalding his fingers.

Dropping the glass, Ephraim lunged for the man, who stood a good head taller and looked like he might have been a muscle-bound competitor in the annual Constantinople wrestling matches. Eager to see a good fight, the rest of the men cheered their champion. Suddenly, realizing he was a poor opponent for the fierce Turk, Ephraim backed off. His urge to fight instantly vanished. Still seething inside, he turned away and picked up his unbroken tea glass. Refilling it, he returned to his place by the fire, despite the sneers and hostile stares.

Like a big Anatolian wolf—assured of his alpha rank in the pack—the big Turk glared at Ephraim over the top of his tea glass. Ephraim feared the tension between them could only worsen.

Chapter 23

The wilderness border along the Aras River, between northern Persia and Turkey, was notorious for its lawlessness. Many luckless persons who ventured into the region died at the hand of bandits or simply disappeared. The expedition Turks from Constantinople often glanced out into the predawn darkness toward the mountain. They spoke little, and, when they did, it was in muted tones.

Grinning, Ephraim mumbled to himself in Armenian, "The cowardly *hamalar* are nervous."

The burly Turk sitting next to Ephraim heard only *"hamalar."* Sure the Armenian did not use "camels" in a complimentary way, he glowered. Seeing his reaction, Ephraim's lip curled. "Is it not so?" he goaded the big Turk. "Do not thoughts of Kurdish bandits make you wish to return to your warm home and soft wife in Constantinople?"

Growling deep within his chest, the Turk threw down his tea glass and reached for Ephraim's throat. But before his clawing fingers could close upon the Armenian's neck, von Leidenhoffer exploded from his tent, shouting, "It is time to go!"

His face livid, the big Turk reluctantly withdrew. "Son of a worthless donkey," he spat at Ephraim, "your fate is in my hands. Live each day as your last." He leaped to his feet and headed toward the pack animals.

Shaken, Ephraim remained in place. He finished his tea as the Turks tossed their empty glasses to Sol, who deftly caught them in his apron without chipping a one. Most of the men were still within hearing when, smacking a silver-headed crop against his thigh, von Leidenhoffer stomped up to the fire and stood over Ephraim.

"Thwack!" Von Leidenhoffer's crop hit Ephraim's boot. "Help load the animals. I pay you to work, not sit. *Şimdi!* Now!"

Ephraim flushed, biting his tongue. He ached to remind the

German that he had been hired as the guide, not as a laborer. He was furious; he had been humiliated in front of the Turks, but he dared not chance losing his place as guide. Red-faced, he went to pack his own donkey first.

Von Leidenhoffer marched restlessly to and fro, following the men about, barking orders as they worked. Though they barely understood von Leidenhoffer's rapid mix of German and heavily-accented Turkish commands, his convincing manner made his meaning clear; it didn't take them long to pull down the tents and pack the animals.

With decampment complete, the valet saddled the Arabian mare and brought her to von Leidenhoffer. Cupping his hands for the ex-officer's foot, he hoisted him to the mare's back. Immediately, the frisky mare bucked and jigged sideways, trying to take the bit in her teeth, but her skilled rider expertly controlled her.

Von Leidenhoffer pranced up to Ephraim, pulling the mare in with such a strong hand, she came up on her hind legs. Her flailing hooves barely missed the guide's head. Ephraim was familiar with donkeys, but he knew nothing about horses. He could not help himself. Terribly frightened, he recoiled from the slashing hooves so close to his face. Tripping over his own feet, he nearly fell. Von Leidenhoffer guffawed and someone else snickered behind Ephraim's back.

Ephraim spun around with murder in his heart. The huge Turk who had bumped him earlier at breakfast was walking away, laughing aloud. Not only had Ephraim made an enemy, he knew he had now lost even more face with the rest of the Turks. It was a bad omen.

"When they are ready, start for the mountain," von Leidenhoffer said, still smirking at Ephraim's reaction to the rearing horse. "I will join you when Hismet has worked off her morning joy." He whirled the spirited mare and headed her at a tightly collected canter toward Ağri Daği.

Ephraim watched as von Leidenhoffer rode off. Prancing, with her neck arched, Hismet was beautiful beyond description. Her ground-length tail flagged high over her back, and her silky black mane hung almost to her knees. Her luminous eyes and flaring nostrils were set wide in the refined, dished face unique to a hot-blooded, desert Arabian. Ephraim felt his chest constrict; a tenebrous curtain of envy half-blinded him. Though he had ridden donkeys all his life, he had never been astride a horse. He longed, with every fiber in his body, to be in von Leidenhoffer's boots and to have those boots firm in the mare's stirrups.

"One day I shall own an animal such as that," he whispered to himself. By selling the golden artifact to the German, he would obtain the unobtainable.

The majestic mountain loomed over its skirting of gently rolling, treeless hills. Its enormous size and the magnifying quality of crystal-clear air made it look closer than it really was. An early snow from two days before coated the higher pinnacles. Dawn tinted the vast glaciers blush pink until the mountain looked as though it glowed from within. But today, Ephraim was blind to the beauty of Ağri Daği, known to the Armenian people as *Massis,* Mother of the World. The golden artifact dominated his thoughts as he led the column of men and animals along the narrow, unpaved road. He expected to see von Leidenhoffer and the mare, but they were nowhere in sight.

As the sun rose, its rays reflected on wisps of powdery snow blowing from Ağri Daği's peaks, causing a smokelike halo to form around the summit. To Ephraim's consternation, von Leidenhoffer still had not reappeared. The western route closest to Mt. Ararat was arduous, often dwindling to a mere trail. Occasionally, it disappeared altogether, and Ephraim had to scout ahead for signs of it.

Ephraim knew that invisible eyes continually marked their progress. Twice he spotted horsemen watching them from a distance. As the sun peaked, von Leidenhoffer rejoined them. The now docile mare was white with dried sweat.

From the arctic north it came, born in the Barents Sea. A mere infant of a storm, slightly more than a broad-based squall, it slowly moved east-southeast to the North European Plain and on to the uplands of Central Russia. The jet stream carrying the storm divided over the Ural Mountains. Part of it veered due south, where it met a low-pressure strata of freezing air high above the Caucasus Range, and where it increased in strength and size.

Von Leidenhoffer poised the mare on a rise overlooking the trail. The atmosphere was hot and electric. Even the most docile animals had been hard to handle all day, and the men were also irritable. Examining the northeastern horizon, Wilhelm marveled at the deceptive beauty of the towering thunderheads that hid Ağri Daği's uppermost heights. He leaned forward in the saddle, searching the barren landscape for a place that might provide shelter from the upcoming storm. There was nothing in sight. He wheeled the mare on her heels and recklessly plunged down the rock-strewn slope.

Von Leidenhoffer rode up to Ephraim's side. "A storm is on its way." Ephraim waited for von Leidenhoffer's command to pitch camp. He said instead, "We will move on as fast as possible and try to outrun it."

"Mein Herr, the storms are very bad here," Ephraim warned him. "We should stop."

"There is no sheltered place in sight, and the tents will not stand in high wind. There may be a better place to stay farther on." Von Leidenhoffer wheeled the mare and trotted down the trail ahead of Ephraim. Ephraim clicked his tongue in disgust.

The day's long ride in the heat and dust had tired them all, including the animals. The men's normal vigilance diminished as they became engrossed in keeping the beasts together in the failing light and ever-increasing wind.

Just before dark, von Leidenhoffer galloped back down the trail. "Ahead there is a ravine bordered by a ridge on either side. We shall set up camp there."

At its entrance, the ravine was little more than the width of a horse. A hundred yards farther, it widened to an oblong basin that contained a willow-lined spring. The place would shield them from the worst of the storm.

Chapter 24

Wilhelm von Leidenhoffer sat alone in his tent, listlessly sorting through an array of artifacts that lay on a small folding table. He picked up a flat rock, the width of his hand, and squinted at the three crosses carved into its surface. Though storm clouds had covered the sun making the tent's interior too dim to see well, he was reluctant to light the lantern and use up precious oil. To better examine the piece, he rose and carried it to the tent opening. If the crosses were Sumarian, the rock was the single object of promise so far collected.

As Wilhelm stepped out, a blinding bolt of lightning streaked between the sky and the ridge above the camp. A deafening blast of thunder followed the lightning. Huge raindrops mixed with snow drummed on the tent canvas. He groaned and ducked back inside. The good weather was probably over and the expedition a failure. As the thunder rolled down the gorge, he screamed at the elements. "For now, I shall leave this godforsaken part of the world. But I will come again next year."

He had a sudden thought. *Godforsaken? What God? There is no God.* Wilhelm spat, sweeping the artifacts from the table and into a crate. The large stone with three crosses landed on a delicate shard, crushing the smaller segment to powder. Cursing, Wilhelm slammed the crate lid shut.

"Von Leidenhoffer, Bey?"

It was the *schwabe,* the cockroach, Ephraim. "What do you want?" Wilhelm shouted.

Hearing the German's angry tone, Ephraim hesitated before answering. He knew his timing was bad, but could he again garner the courage to approach von Leidenhoffer about the gold-encased artifact? The change in weather now made it urgent to return home before the snows began. Straightening his shoulders, Ephraim took a deep breath. "I have something that might interest you, von Leidenhoffer, Bey."

Wilhelm lifted the tent flap just enough to see the Armenian, who looked like a half-drowned village cur standing in the deluge. "Get yourself in." Wilhelm widened the entrance and stepped back to avoid the water dripping from Ephraim's clothing. He tossed a rag to Ephraim. "Use this to dry yourself. I do not need more *wasser* in here."

Ephraim pulled the saturated wool scarf from his head and shoulders, letting it fall to the floor. Shivering from cold and nerves, he wiped his face with the grimy rag.

Wilhelm sat on his cot, repacking the meerschaum. "Well, why is it necessary for you to come out in such a storm?"

Ephraim fished the shard from his pocket. "My sister and I found this as children when plowing our father's field. It is *çok eski*, very old. And it has value, very much value," he added, hopeful. The gold itself was precious—he knew that for sure—and the mysterious writing on it could increase the price.

Von Leidenhoffer reached for the triangular shard Ephraim held out to him. Though the shine of gold piqued his curiosity, the article did not look like an important archaeological find. He held it closer to the lantern for a more thorough inspection.

When Wilhelm saw the spidery characters on both sides, he was afraid Ephraim could hear the accelerating beat of his heart. *What do you fear, Wilhelm? The ignorant peasant knows nothing about ancient writing.* The German's eyes glittered. He bounced the artifact on his palm. "This broken little piece is not worth much. But where it came from, there could be more, yes? I would like to go to the place where you found it."

Ephraim noted the greed behind von Leidenhoffer's expressionless mask. *Ah, he is interested,* Ephraim thought with relish. His face also bland, he explained, "It is no longer my father's land. Long ago he sold it to the Turkish government."

That statement was an out-and-out lie. Ephraim did not want his cousin to know about the shard. Especially, he did not want von Leidenhoffer to learn the location of the field; the rest of the artifact might still be there. "You will have to seek permission to enter government land," he told Wilhelm. "But snow shall surely come before the Turks give an answer. The bureaucrats never hurry." Ephraim snorted a dry laugh. "They will not grant permission for you to return until next year. It is unfortunate, but you must wait."

Ephraim reached to take back the golden corner. *Your adventure is kaput, mein Herr,* he gloated inwardly, *but buy the thing from me first.* He audibly clicked his tongue against the roof of his mouth. "I must return to Doğubayazit and my shop before the trails are blocked by snow."

Von Leidenhoffer tightened his grip on the shard, keeping it from Ephraim. *Little pig, I do not need anyone to take me to the place. I will find it without you.* His voice oily, Wilhelm asked Ephraim, "How much do you want for this bit of nothing?"

Ephraim silently rejoiced. *He thinks he is the clever crow, but I am the hawk that takes him.* He named the price he had previously set, expecting the German to bargain. When von Leidenhoffer did not give a counter offer, Ephraim knew the object was far more valuable than he had originally believed.

Wordlessly, Wilhelm reached under the cot for the leather belt that held his purse. He pulled out a handful of coins from the wallet and counted out the amount Ephraim had quoted.

Ephraim then realized he could have asked for more, but it was too late; he had set his own trap. Reluctantly, he took the coins and dropped them into his pocket.

CHAPTER 25

The storm lasted five days. Icy rain drenched the men. It left the animals knee-deep in mud that clung like thick mucous. Water oozed through the walls of Sol and von Leidenhoffer's tents, saturating their contents. Neither Ephraim nor the Turkish personnel had the questionable luxury of a tent. Instead, they used whatever materials were handy to construct havens among the rocks. Ephraim searched until he discovered a man-sized hollow under an overhanging ledge. Employing his saddle pad for a bed, he stayed drier in his little cave than the Europeans in their tents.

No one left his protected location except to relieve himself, feed the animals, or dash to the dank cook tent to snatch a quick bite of food. Boredom, and the miserable conditions, caused tempers to flare and fights were frequent.

Ephraim dreaded contact with the other men. He particularly tried to avoid the burly Turk who had bumped him their first day out, but the man exhibited warped creativity in finding ingenious, sometimes cruel, ways to irritate. One morning when Ephraim went to feed his donkey, he found it lying on its side, half-submerged in mud. He thought the beast had perished, until its side heaved and Ephraim realized it was alive, though barely conscious. The donkey did not appear to be in pain, but no matter how Ephraim yanked its halter or wrung its tail, it refused to rise. Soaking wet and shivering, Ephraim finally gave up and fled to his dry cave.

By evening, the donkey had fully recovered. When his Turkish antagonist taunted him about his inability to keep a donkey from devouring hashish, Ephraim knew what had happened. Retaliation was out of the question. Outnumbering him four to one, he knew the Turks would unify against him. To end the harassment, perhaps even to survive, he would have to leave.

The next day, to everyone's relief, the clouds disappeared and the sun emerged. Ephraim immediately went to von Leidenhoffer. "The rain has stopped. It will soon snow and I must go home," Ephraim told him. "You and your men should return to Constantinople before the snow traps you. The bandits already know you are here," he slyly added.

After a brief face-saving haggle, von Leidenhoffer grunted, "You have failed to lead me to anything of significance, and you are not worth what I have paid you. Be gone!"

That night, Ephraim staked his cousin's donkey far from camp and from other animals that might call to his. While everyone slept, he slipped away on the donkey (which von Leidenhoffer still believed he owned) and sped for home.

Von Leidenhoffer chose to ignore Ephraim's warning about weather and robbers. The sky had turned blue and cloudless. There had been no sign of trouble. He decided the camp should dry out before they headed back to Doğubayazit. His men lazed in the sun or played intense games of trictrac. Drying pads, blankets, and miscellaneous garments lay draped across the boulders like clusters of brilliant flowers. The small valley looked as though spring had arrived.

The tent sides were propped open to let air circulate through them. Von Leidenhoffer sat on the teak chest in the entrance to his tent, the meerschaum firmly lodged in the corner of his mouth. As he cleaned his rifle, laying the parts upon packing cases, he hummed a Prussian march.

A lounging Turk first spotted the string of riders who surveyed the camp from the tall ridge that bordered the valley's west side. Von Leidenhoffer saw the mounted men at the same time. His fingers blurred as he frantically reassembled his gun. It was ready and loaded when fifteen men, riding single file, entered the valley.

A heavy-set Kurd rode at the head of the troop. He wore a red turban and was the only man holding a rifle. Von Leidenhoffer identified the weapon as an obsolete Russian model. Though old, it could be effective. Twin bandoleers crossed the leader's breast, and a broad red sash around his waist supported a wicked scimitar. His rugged men carried curved swords and daggers.

The bandit chief galloped up to von Leidenhoffer, skidding his shaggy steppe pony to a stop a bare two meters in front of the German. Von Leidenhoffer flinched when flying pebbles stung his skin. The rest of the band circled, ogling the camp and its occupants.

The chieftain's insolent stare met von Leidenhoffer's cool one. "You trespass in my territory. Why do you come here?" he asked, speaking Turkish.

Wilhelm waved his arm in a three-hundred-sixty-degree sweep that encompassed the surrounding hills. "I am Wilhelm von Leidenhoffer. I seek the ark, said to be on this mountain."

The Kurd curled his lip. "I, Aziz, have lived here all my life. I have never seen the ark."

Von Leidenhoffer's steady gaze didn't waver. "That does not mean it is not here," he said, keeping his voice calm. "One cannot see everything in a lifetime."

Aziz merely shrugged. His darting glance, thoroughly examining the camp, missed nothing. Taking in the German's expensive attire and modern gear, it casually paused on the shiny new rifle von Leidenhoffer loosely held at his side. The mind behind the fierce eyes calculated the gun's worth. Suddenly, Aziz saw von Leidenhoffer's beautiful, fine-boned Arabian mare grazing nearby. Unable to conceal his cupidity, he gasped. He pointed to the mare. "I wish to trade my strong horse for that wormy, undernourished nag."

"It is not possible," Von Leidenhoffer said through a sneer, lifting the end of his rifle ever so slightly. *Does the boor know I can kill him, and eliminate half his men, who have no firearms?*

The German's stiff-necked arrogance annoyed Aziz. "You have no choice," he snarled, spurring his horse uncomfortably close to von Leidenhoffer.

Von Leidenhoffer looked around for help. No Turk was in sight. Sol had vanished, and the valet's pale face peeked from behind a boulder. Von Leidenhoffer at last understood—he alone braved the Kurds.

Aziz motioned to von Leidenhoffer's tent. "My family lodge is poor. Surely a person of such ample property can spare one shelter."

"I will give you nothing." Von Leidenhoffer raised the muzzle six inches higher.

The Kurd smirked. "I would have your weapon, too." Without warning, Aziz savagely spurred his mount into von Leidenhoffer, knocking him down. The German's rifle flew through the air, bounced off a large rock, and landed beside it.

Von Leidenhoffer scrambled crabwise as he tried to reach the gun. His fingertips had just touched the polished stock when Aziz shot him in the back of the head. Von Leidenhoffer's body spasmed twice and lay still.

Aziz hauled on his mount's reins, positioning the nervous horse so that it straddled Wilhelm's spread-eagled corpse. He slid off and snatched up the German's weapon. Brandishing it above his head, Aziz fired into the air. He triumphantly shouted to his men, "This tent and the mare are mine. The rest belongs to you."

As one, the Kurds leapt from their horses to ransack the tents and equipment. Aziz stepped across von Leidenhoffer's legs and beckoned to one of his men. The man reluctantly ceased his looting and stood before his leader. Aziz handed him the reins to his steppe pony. "My horse is now yours, a reward for your loyalty." Beaming, the man bowed to Aziz and led the pony away.

Spotting von Leidenhoffer's smoldering pipe, still lying where it had fallen, Aziz picked up the meerschaum, stuck it in his mouth, and filled his lungs with smoke. Choking and hacking, he hurled the pipe to the rough ground. The delicate stem and handsome bowl shattered.

Aziz cursed and thrust his boot toe under von Leidenhoffer's body. *The infidel smoked the offal of dogs.* Rolling the body over, he rummaged in the corpse's pockets, where he found several coins and a gold commemorative watch bearing the Kaiser's image. These, he dropped into his own pocket. Exploring von Leidenhoffer's last pocket, he discovered the gold-sheathed artifact.

Born in Tabriz, the bandit chieftain, as a youth, had worked in his uncle's small shop. His uncle mainly dealt in fruits and vegetables, but he occasionally bought and sold artifacts brought in by the locals. Aziz wondered if what he held in his hand was such an object. It looked old; and those peculiar marks, what were they? He would show it to his uncle the next time he visited Tabriz.

Von Leidenhoffer's Turkish laborers had melted into the hills. The Kurds, intent on plunder, had no reason to chase them. Sol and the valet were not as fortunate; they sat back-to-back, their arms tied together, forced to watch Aziz strip their master's body and don his clothing.

Aziz galloped Hismet up and down the valley until streaks of lather whitened her sleek hide. Tears coursed the valet's cheeks, not for his dead master whom he had served, but for the mare he loved as his child.

When Aziz tired of displaying his skill as a horseman, he skidded Hismet to a halt near Sol and the valet. "And what do you sons of donkeys have for me?" he asked.

"We have only the clothes we wear," Sol whimpered in bad Turkish, made worse by his terror.

Angry disappointment flushed the bandit's face. "You say you have nothing to barter? That is untrue. You have humility." He jumped from the horse. Shoving the cringing servants to their knees, he pushed their faces to the earth with his foot. He stood over them while his men finished packing the expedition's donkeys with their spoils. Before riding off at the head of his whooping band, Aziz turned the two servants loose.

If it had not been for a random herder who searched for a lost goat, von Leidenhoffer's cook and valet might have died of exposure or starvation. The shepherd took them to his village where they stayed until spring.

Chapter 26

Ephraim reached Doğubayazit in one-third the time it had taken von Leidenhoffer's party to travel the same distance. First stripping the jaded donkey of its tack, he turned it loose in his wife's goat enclosure. "Feed and groom my cousin's donkey," he commanded. When their two boys asked where he had been, Ephraim smiled and jingled the coins in his pocket, saying he would soon bring home a surprise. Ignoring his wife's questions, he immediately went to find the horse trader. "I want to buy a good mare with desert blood," Ephraim told the trader.

The shrewd trader examined the man before him. *Too fat for a horseman,* he decided. *He has no muscle in his arms or shoulders, and his legs are too straight.* Categorizing the Armenian as an easy mark, he led Ephraim to a pasture filled with mares and yearlings. He extolled this or that animal while Ephraim looked over each one.

"That is the one I want," Ephraim said, pointing to a racy bay filly, the image of von Leidenhoffer's flashy mare.

"You have fine taste," the dealer said. "She is the best of my three-year-olds, and worth much."

Ephraim confirmed his choice. "It is she I must have."

The two men slowly approached the grazing filly, and the horse dealer gently looped a thong around her neck. "You can see she is gentle and well mannered," the dealer said. "I myself have ridden her. She gave me no trouble."

"What is her price?" Ephraim asked. He shuddered when the horse dealer named a figure that would take all but a few *piasters* of the money he had received from von Leidenhoffer. He really wanted the mare. "I can ride anything with four legs," he boasted. "I will give you half what you ask for her now, half when she has proven herself."

"You must give me the full price when you take her, and for

a few more *piasters*, she can be gentled so that even a small child can ride her."

"I wish to train her myself," Ephraim said, knowing he did not have the extra money to pay the dealer for the filly's schooling. Besides, he was especially eager to show her off to his trictrac-playing friends at the *çay* house. "It is as you wish, then; I will pay her full price today."

The dealer shrugged. "It is done," he said, thinking, *This foolish man will ruin a good animal or else kill himself.*

Ephraim decided to ride the filly home bareback, using a rope twisted into a figure eight and looped around her neck and nose for control. Unfortunately, in his enthusiasm, he did not recognize that a young, inexperienced horse is far different in spirit and temperament than a donkey.

The dealer restrained the filly by a low wall so Ephraim could awkwardly mount her. Ephraim's corpulent body landed hard on the young horse, and she flinched, but she was firmly held in place by the trader. Ephraim settled himself more comfortably on her spine. In doing so, he raked her tender ribs with his boot-shod feet. Yanking the rope from the horse dealer's grasp, the startled filly leaped forward to escape the predator on her back. Ephraim had nothing but a tenuous hold on the filly's silken mane. As she lurched forward, he flew over her tail. Somersaulting once, he hit the hard ground on his right hip. The last sound Ephraim heard, before he fainted, was a sickening crack as his pelvis splintered.

CHAPTER 27

Tabriz, Persia, 1932

Louis Beaudoin cursed the day his Parisian-trained chef left him for the austere kitchen of an English diplomat who promised a larger wage. He had neither the time nor the *savoir-faire* to cook for himself. He was especially annoyed because he had paid the chef's way to Syria. Worse yet, he was now forced to do his own grocery shopping, the task which presently occupied him.

A thin film of dust drifted in from the street outside, coating everything in the fruit-and-vegetable shop. Louis picked over the produce under the Kurdish proprietor's watchful eye. He selected a half kilo of favo beans and a shriveled onion, then pawed the bright display of fruit before adding a bunch of grapes and an orange. The grapes were *comme ci comme ça*, the orange, deplorable—it looked like it had come from Spain in a rowboat.

Louis carried his selection to the proprietor, who waited behind a flyspecked display case, his fingers idly playing with the beads of a scarred abacus. A glint of gold, shining through the case's clouded glass, caught the Frenchman's attention. Louis pointed to it. "Please, may I see the gold object in the case?" he asked.

The Kurd reached into the case and pulled out the thing. "My brother bought it in Turkey," he said. "It is rare and costly."

Louis lifted an eyebrow. "It is a mere piece of something. Where is the rest of it? *Whole*, it might have value and—"

"Yes, but there is writing on both sides," the Kurd interrupted. He turned the object back and forth so Louis could see the tiny characters impressed in the gold. "Someone who can read such marks may solve the mystery of this object."

Louis took a small magnifying glass from his pocket and examined the artifact. The symbols on it were different from anything he had seen in his thirteen-year experience as a Parisian museum curator. It might be worth further investigation; he might have time to research the writing while in his new position at the Peking Museum. Returning the glass to his pocket, he began negotiating for the fragment.

* * *

Peking, October 1936

Louis sat across from his good friend Zhu, a Chinese professor who spoke fluent French and who was a virtual wellspring of knowledge concerning Asian artifacts, knowledge that surpassed his own.

So far this day they had discussed nothing but Chiang Kai-shek's declaration of war on Japan. They had come to the conclusion that Japan was too small and too weak to invade the mainland.

Louis ordered another pot of tea and then pulled the gold-sheathed triangle from his pocket. "Here is something I purchased years ago. I'd forgotten I had it." He handed it to his friend and awaited his reaction.

"It looks ordinary enough," Zhu said. "The hieroglyphics are unfamiliar and look old. I do not think they are Sumarian." He turned it over. "Did it come from Persia? Excuse me, I forget it calls itself Iran now." He laughed, embarrassed by his mistake.

Louis laughed with him. "Who can keep up with world changes these days? No. It is not from Persia. I bought the piece in Tabriz in a disreputable little shop that sold fruits and vegetables. The Kurd who sold it to me said his brother bought it in Turkey. I never thought his story plausible. Why would a Kurd *buy* something like this? I think he just found it somewhere or stole it for the gold. That the gold was not stripped and melted down is a miracle."

"That is a most likely conclusion," Louis's friend agreed. "It is unfortunate you were not told the region of Turkey in which it was found. That would be of help." He laid it on the table between them. "May I keep it for a while? I think I have something that is similar."

"Of course. Keep it as long as you wish." Louis rose to go. "I never could make anything of it."

* * *

Peking, 1937

The shouting outside grew louder. Louis stopped his hurried packing. Stepping to the window, he looked down at the swarm of people in the street below. Chinese civilians normally dodged the Japanese patrols like a school of smelt threatened by sharks, even crossing to the other side of the street to avoid one. But an old woman, carrying a heavy yoke across her shoulders, was in trouble. She had not satisfactorily yielded to a pair of soldiers sauntering along the narrow street. As she passed them, she stumbled and her yoke struck one of them. Enraged, he slashed at her head with his rifle butt, knocking her down. As Louis watched, the noisy onlookers began to close around the Japanese. The soldiers threatened them with their rifles and they scattered, still shouting.

Yes, I must leave China, Louis thought. Standing in the doorway of the flat, he took a last look at what had been his home for four years. Hoisting his two travel-worn bags, he sighed and stepped out, shutting the door with a bang of finality.

Only later, on the ship out of Tientsin to Hong Kong, did Louis remember that he had not said good-bye to his friend Zhu, who still had the gold-sheathed artifact.

CHAPTER 28

Fresno, California, 1966

Coming from the hostile, crowded environment of New York City, Ylenah had immediately felt at home in California. Fresno's climate was so similar to that of Eastern Turkey that she could not recall any difference. Perhaps it had been colder in the winter, hotter in the summer. When she lived in Lesser Armenia, she had been a small child, and memories of such things tend to be forgotten by the young.

She and Mariyam had thrived in California. Their health improved with the warm sun and the abundance of fresh fruits and vegetables from the "market basket" of the United States. But her greatest satisfaction was being among her people. And now she was expecting the delight of her life, Mariyam's daughter Arianna. She hoped to see more of her favorite granddaughter now that Arianna at last had her Ph.D. in field archaeology. How she missed the girl when she was away at school, or when she was overseas on a dig.

Anticipating her visit, Ylenah parted the lace curtains covering the leaded glass window in the door. Just as she looked out, an old tan Volkswagen bug pulled up and parked on the other side of the street.

Ylenah studied her granddaughter as she climbed out of the car and crossed the street. Faded blue denim shorts and a revealing halter enhanced the girl's long, tanned legs and graceful figure.

As Arianna came down the front walk, Ylenah dropped the curtain and opened the door. When Arianna entered the old house, it seemed to Ylenah as though a bright light or a sweet bouquet of flowers had come into the musty, gloomy room.

Arianna was already twenty-eight and still unmarried. As far

THE TABLETS OF ARARAT

as Ylenah knew, there were no prospects, either. Ylenah shook her head.

"Is something wrong, Grandmother?" Arianna asked, mentally preparing herself for another critique of her choice of wearing apparel.

Instead, Ylenah wrapped her arms around her granddaughter and hugged her. The girl's firm young flesh felt warm and smooth, even through the long-sleeved black dress Ylenah always wore. "How can anything be wrong, Arianna, *sevinç*, my joy? You are here; I am too happy to see you." Ylenah's welcoming beam turned into a sorrowful pout as she added, "But I regret that I may be responsible for your many long absences from Fresno." A single tear slowly coursed down her lined cheek.

"How can you think you could possibly be responsible for my decisions?" Arianna followed her grandmother into the kitchen for the inevitable *çay* her grandmother always offered. "I'm doing what I've always planned to do. Besides, don't I come to see you as soon as I'm home again?"

Sniffing, Ylenah picked up the steaming teapot. "If I had not told you stories of the old country when you were a child, you would not have wished to explore it. You would have stayed in Fresno and made great-grandchildren for me with that nice young man."

Hiding a smile, Arianna lifted both sides of the drop-leaf table and latched them into place. As she took two teacups off the shelf and set them on the table, she said, "He was just a friend, Grandmother. Other than that, he meant nothing to me. I didn't love him."

Ylenah shot a stern look at Arianna, countering, "In the old days, parents chose a girl's husband. Love came later. Your mother, Mariyam, could find the right man for you."

Arianna had heard it all many times before, but she tilted her head and threw Ylenah an affectionate grin. "You loved Grandfather. You have often said so. Would you condemn me to a marriage without love?"

Ylenah poured tea, then set a plate of honeyed baklava, lib-

134

erally sprinkled with ground pistachio nuts, in front of Arianna. Taking up her cup, she shuffled to her pillowed rocker and settled with a mild groan. "Love grows with time, like . . ."—she had forgotten the allegory. "He was such a nice young man," she wistfully finished.

The two women talked for an hour before Arianna took Ylenah's tiny, heavily veined hand in hers. "I've come to tell you I'm leaving for Ankara in two weeks, Grandmother."

Snatching back her hand, Ylenah clasped her chest. "You cannot go back to Turkey," she gasped. "God protected you the first time. Now you wish to test Him once more?"

Arianna sighed. It was the same old thing—her grandmother's obsessive fear of the Turks.

Arianna tried to comfort Ylenah. "I'm not out to test God, or anyone for that matter. I'll be working directly for Turkish archaeologists this time. There is nothing to worry about."

"You must not tell them you are of enemy blood, that you are half Armenian and half Greek," Ylenah cried.

"I don't have to, grandmother. I am an American. That's what is on my passport and that's all anyone needs to know."

With that, Ylenah relaxed. She really was interested, and even a bit envious, of her granddaughter's exciting adventures. "Do you go to Ephesus this time?"

"Nope." Arianna leaned forward, her eyes glowing. "Several months ago, I read in an archaeological journal that a new underground city has been discovered in Cappadocia. I plan to join a team that's going to work there."

Cappadocia! Ylenah's eyes dimmed as she reminisced. "When I was a child, I heard stories about places in the ground where some of my people hid during the massacres."

"They're probably the same. Very little is known about those mysterious underground cities, except that at some time they were inhabited by Christians. I've wanted to explore them ever since I first heard about them from you. Now, I finally have a chance to . . ."

Arianna stopped in midsentence. Her grandmother's eyelids

had closed, and her chin was slowly sinking to her breast. She stood and gently helped Ylenah from her chair. "It's already dark; I'm sorry I came so late. Let's get you to bed."

Ylenah allowed herself to be led to the bedroom. "Come in the morning, yes?" she asked Arianna.

"I promise, I'll come before noon."

When her grandmother was cozily tucked into bed, Arianna fluffed the pillows around Ylenah's head. "Tell me the story of Aram and the wicked dervish again, or better yet, how you and Uncle Ephraim found the pottery covered in gold," she coaxed.

But Ylenah had already begun to softly snore.

PART 3

CHAPTER 29

Central California, 1965

When someone ridiculed his hometown of Bakersfield, Morgan McCauley would laugh and retort, "Yep, it's a quiet town because the tourists driving down old Highway 99 speed through as fast as possible—especially in the summer. We like it that way. And if they stop for a meal or gas and boost the economy before going on, that's even better."

Personally, he relished the San Joaquin Valley heat. Since the Korean War, he could hardly stand anything below seventy degrees Fahrenheit. The long, frigid march through Korea's northern mountains with the Seventh Marines had left him perpetually cold. His left foot lacked two toes, the result of frostbite contracted during the push toward the Yalu River.

Dug in with his unit at Koto-ri, he had dreamed of Bakersfield's sweltering September dog days. Korea's thirty-degrees-below-zero temperature made it hard to imagine, but imagination helped him to survive. It was while in Korea that he decided never again to live or work in a cold climate. So far, he had kept that vow.

Bakersfield's early morning hours were best for outdoor activities. The temperature was warm enough then to jog in shorts and a tank top, yet cool enough to stimulate the blood. Morgan had promised his vacationing neighbor that he would walk her female pup twice a day; he and the dog preferred going out then. By noon, the thermometer soared above one hundred. The average person could only tolerate it by immersing in a swimming pool or by staying inside an air-conditioned car or building. Though the temperature began to drop after dark, the streets and buildings radiated heat into the air for hours after the sun went down.

Tonight, at 10 P.M., the temperature remained in the upper nineties. The bottoms of Morgan's feet were thickly calloused from his going barefoot, but not even his tough soles could withstand the hot asphalt for more than a minute. Stepping to the curb edge, he wrapped the dog's chain lead around his wrist, then checked the traffic.

When it was safe, he yelled, "Let's go!" He and the dog dashed across the street to the park's freshly sprinkled lawn. Morgan had the six-month-old German shepherd sit on the wet grass while he checked its paws for trauma. Eager to explore the park's delicious smells, the pup wriggled impatiently and furiously thumped its tail. Finding no scorched pads, Morgan unsnapped the leash and the dog shot off.

Morgan found a dry spot under a tree and sat. Half aware of the German shepherd snuffling from tree to shrub to tree, his mind was preoccupied with the ad he had seen four days ago in the *Wall Street Journal.* Hong Kong University was seeking English-language teachers and a Management Techniques instructor. Morgan had grown increasingly restless since seeing the ad. His position as general manager for a heavy-equipment company in Oildale was at an impasse. The oil reserves in Taft and Oildale had petered out long before and with them went the area's chief revenue. The job now bored him to distraction. He craved a change, but employment at his level in the southern San Joaquin Valley was limited. At age thirty-four, having worked off and on most of his adult life in his hometown, he felt he was going nowhere. To make matters worse, only the week before, after a two-year engagement, his fiancée had suddenly announced her plan to marry someone else. There was nothing to keep him in Bakersfield.

He had spent two months in Hong Kong before returning home from Korea. The British, in their usual colonization zeal, constructed their own little enclave within the territory. They filled Hong Kong with reminders of home: London-type pubs, a turf race track, cricket fields, and English parks and gardens. But the swelling population of Chinese and other Asians kept the city uniquely different, thwarting British efforts to transform Hong Kong into an absolute copy of an English city.

Hong Kong's hodgepodge of cultures, its vigor, and the intrigues of international finance excited and fascinated Morgan. He vowed then he would someday return, after college. He felt that providence, or God (if there was a God), had put the ad in the paper to lure him back.

Morgan let the dog run for twenty minutes, then whistled. The pup galloped up to him and flopped flat on its belly, its tongue lolling and hind legs sprawled.

"No future, no wife, no life," Morgan muttered as he attached the leash. He took the puppy's head between his palms. Gently shaking it, he told the questioning brown eyes, "Guess I'll apply for the job, girl. Too bad I can't take you along."

Chapter 30

Peking, 1966

The Vietnam War continued to write its ineffectual chapters. Billy Graham conducted his Greater London Crusade, and Mao Tse-Tung issued his *Quotations from Chairman Mao.*

Except for having to read Mao Tse-Tung's little red book and the necessity to keep a low profile during the cultural purges, these events did not affect the Peking Museum's curator of ancient Chinese history. His priority was to find room in the museum to display artifacts from the recently discovered tomb of a Tang Dynasty princess. The museum did not have funds to buy new fixtures, so he ordered the repair of an old, damaged case he found in the basement storage room. A museum sweeper, known to have some woodworking knowledge, was assigned to fix it.

Though he would receive no extra pay, the impoverished sweeper rejoiced at the chance to gain status. Slipping off his straw sandals, he eagerly set to work. Alternately dragging and shoving the heavy, dust-covered case, he managed to get it to an open space where he could work. Squatting, he examined the cracked base and saw that, to get at the break, he would have to remove the bottom drawer. The sweeper pulled tentatively at the drawer handle, but the drawer refused to budge. When he applied more force, yanking the handle, the warped wood gave with a screech. The drawer shot out, landing on the sweeper's bare foot and spilling dozens of potsherds on the floor.

A cloud of dust clogged the sweeper's lungs as he danced on one foot, then the other, trying to ease the torment in his bruised toes. When the pain subsided and he could again breathe without coughing, he placed the drawer on a work table and bent to retrieve the scattered shards. He gasped as a flash of shining yellow amid the dull terra cotta fragments caught his eye.

The sweeper hesitated, his hand hovering above the hypnotic gold. How could it be that such a beautiful object lay among the dusty shards? No one had touched the old case in years. Surely its contents had been forgotten. He glanced toward the doorway. Seeing no one, he grabbed the artifact and thrust it inside his jacket.

On his way home that afternoon, the sweeper detoured to a certain shop, where he traded the golden artifact for a few coins and a new hammer. The shop owner straightaway contacted a reliable old friend, an enterprising Mongol who called himself Xu.

Though his bones had become frail and his flesh desiccated, the sixty-eight-year-old Xu had for years made the arduous journey south to Hong Kong. There he received the highest price for objects he smuggled out of mainland China. Once he had owned a cart, but since the Revolution, he traveled more anonymously, taking the bus on the long road south to Fatshan. In Fatshan, Xu's practice was to go directly to the farm of a distant cousin who would then drive him in his wheezing farm truck to Shekki, the port from which the ferry sailed to Hong Kong.

His age had taken its toll this trip, and Xu spent a night at a cheap inn in Shekki to recuperate. The next day he went to the shop of a fence with whom he had dealt for many years. To his horror, he learned that the man was dead. Xu stumbled to a shabby tea house. He was contemplating his bad luck over a cup of watery tea when the sound of two muffled voices, coming from the other side of a paper-thin wall, caught his attention.

"Chung Li is as big as an elephant," said one.

"Ah, that is so, but Chung Li is wealthy beyond an emperor's dream," replied the second man.

"A wealthy elephant that tramples all in its path," said the first, clapping a hand on the other's shoulder as they walked past Xu and out of the tea house.

Leaning against the seawall, Xu patiently watched the casino's green facade. He sat for more than two hours before his vigil paid off. Xu slowly rose as an enormous but impeccably dressed man extricated himself from a taxi and puffed up the steps to the entrance doors. There was no mistaking the famous Chung Li, Hong Kong's smuggling tzar.

Chung Li's luck at the casino had been bad all that week. He tried to curb his wrath to better concentrate on the cards spread across the green felt before him. He did not notice the old man who elbowed his way through the Saturday gamblers until Xu sidled up to the blackjack table and tugged at Chung Li's left arm.

Chung Li wrenched his arm from Xu's clutch and drew back in disgust. The old man smelled and his clothes were soiled rags. How had the peasant entered the casino? Xu clawed at Chung's arm again, and Chung saw that the long ragged fingernails were dark with grime. Someone would hear about this intrusion; someone would lose his job.

Seeing he had Chung's attention, Xu spoke in a raspy whisper. "I have something of value for you, Lord."

Chung Li recoiled from the fetid breath that whistled through the brown stumps of Xu's teeth. The smuggling tzar didn't catch Xu's next sentence, obliterated in the dissonance of laughing, moaning, chattering customers, and dealers calling bets and numbers. Chung raised a fat hand to beckon a security guard. Before help came, the claw hooked his sleeve again.

"I have something for you, my Lord." Xu quickly opened his threadbare jacket and brought forth a small parcel. Keeping the parcel out of sight between his body and the blackjack table, he removed the dirty wrapping paper.

Seeing the object that lay on Xu's palm, Chung Li dropped his arm, and his eyes narrowed speculatively. "I do not deal with beggars. Take it to Fong Kee in Shekki. It might be of interest to him." Chung Li turned back to the blackjack table.

At that moment, two security guards grabbed Xu by the arms and hustled him out of the casino. Disappointed, but not defeated, Xu immediately headed for the Shekki ferry and the mysterious Fong Kee.

When Chung Li's current blackjack game ended, he waddled

to a poker room in another part of the casino and up to a dealer. The dealer nodded as Chung Li hissed something into his ear; then the man hurried to a side door. Outside the casino, the dealer motioned to a man who waited with a bicycle propped against a tree. At the dealer's summons, the man leaped to his feet and wheeled the bicycle across the street. The dealer spoke a few words, and the cyclist sped off in the direction of the Shekki ferry.

CHAPTER 31

Due west of Hong Kong, near the west bank of the mouth of the Chu Kiang River (also known as the Canton or Pearl), lie the three islands of Macao. The main island is Macao. Its largest city, also called Macao, is at the east end of the island. To the south of the island group is the South China Sea. To the north and west lies mainland China.

An eon of silt-bearing waters created an ever-expanding delta through which the Chu Kiang cuts an undulating swath. Only the installation of a breakwater prevented the outer harbor of Macao from silting up.

Macao is a Portuguese overseas territory that technically belongs to China. Some of Macao's architecture betrays Portuguese influence: official buildings, some large homes, and the old Catholic churches. There is little else to remind a person of the Portuguese colonization; the overall flavor is Chinese. During the era of great sailing ships, Macao had a reputation as one of the world's most sinister ports. An exotic fleshpot in the old days, sailors from every seafaring land looked forward to shore leave there.

Recently, Macao's many casinos have made it obvious—even to the most naive tourist—that the city is a gambling mecca. Hidden behind the glitter is the graft and corruption that such an enterprise attracts. The casino patrons come from all nations and professions, but most are locally-based tourists, wealthy residents of Hong Kong, and Chinese nationals. Behind the facades of cute, hole-in-the-wall shops that are sandwiched between quaint tile-roofed buildings, an illicit trade in drugs and ancient Chinese archeological objects thrives.

CHAPTER 32

Kowloon, 1966

Kwan Mei expertly folded and stacked the tourist-rumpled silk scarves strewn helter-skelter on the table. Glancing at her watch, she groaned and shivered. Time to close, almost time for her meeting with Chung Li. Slide-show images of Chung Li's wandering hands and lust-filled eyes played with her mind, and her stomach heaved.

Swallowing back the bile scalding her throat, Kwan Mei locked the glass display case that held hand-carved images of jade, quartz, and semiprecious stone. Gathering up trays of rare coins and precious gems, she placed them in the back-room safe. No matter how often she saw them, the sparkle and color of the jewels almost always thrilled her. Tonight their beauty failed to do so. As it often happened, her employer had left early, leaving her in charge. She was glad he was not there to see her trembling hands and pallid cheeks.

Kwan Mei dropped the silk shades over the shop's ceiling-to-floor plate glass windows fronting Kowloon's busy Nathan Road. Setting the silent alarm system, she checked the store. Everything was secure for the night. Locking the shop door behind her, she left the Jade Lady and headed south.

Homeward-bound workers thronging Nathan Road dodged slower-moving, window-shopping tourists who had not yet settled into restaurants or caught transportation to their hotels. Often the way was blocked by a skeletal refugee from mainland China, begging for his or her destitute family that lived in a packing box hovel in some dismal side alley. Kwan Mei's church and other organizations did what they could to help, and Hong Kong was building housing as fast as it could, but the incoming tide of people fleeing Communist China overwhelmed everyone, including the system.

Kwan Mei crossed Nathan Road in the middle of the block between Jordan Road and Bowring Street. She paused on the center traffic island to wait for a break in the bumper-to-bumper line of cars. Spotting a break in traffic, she darted across and walked south another block before reaching the Shamrock Hotel and her rendezvous with Chung Li.

Though the Shamrock's entrance and lobby were brightly lit, the hotel was nearly unidentifiable amid the gaudy shop windows to either side. Before Mei could enter, a group of young Scandinavians disembarking a tour bus streamed into the old hotel. She slipped through the door after the last of them—a statuesque blond woman wearing a forest green backpack—had entered. Maneuvering through the small lobby cluttered with piles of baggage, she pressed the elevator "UP" button.

Kwan Mei did not understand why Chung Li always had her meet him at the rundown Shamrock. Surely he would prefer going to one of the luxury hotels recently built in Hong Kong or on the Kowloon Peninsula. But it was not for her to question Chung Li. He commanded; she obeyed. Her participation in the underground trade of antiques and artifacts riddled her with guilt. Fully aware that she was committing a great sin, even if her role in the operation was small, she continued to do it for the money. It was the only way she would ever earn enough for two passages to the United States. Sudden tears blurred her vision when she remembered how her scholarly father had survived the Japanese occupation only to be imprisoned and slaughtered during the Cultural Revolution. Now just she and her mother would go.

The Jade Lady's owner required that his salesgirls wear the traditional Chinese *cheongsam*, a body-clinging sheath split to midthigh. Today, a *cheongsam* of brocaded silk encased Kwan Mei's slender form. The pastel violet complemented her creamy skin and lustrous black, waist-length hair.

Kwan Mei's natural animation disappeared and her body unconsciously slumped as the elevator door glided open and she faced the crowded Shamrock dining room. The elevator doors slithered to a close as she stepped out and hesitated. Lithe as a spotted deer, an enticing vision to every man present, she appeared about to whirl and flee at the tiniest hint of danger.

She stood and searched the room. When she saw Chung Li, she clenched her teeth so hard her jaw ached, but she modestly bowed her head and lowered her eyes as she passed the maitre d'. It took enormous courage to approach Chung Li's table, half hidden behind an exquisite ebony screen. The six-foot-high antique, inlaid with figures of mother-of-pearl and red coral and set with jade and semiprecious stones, was enclosed in a glass case. Tiny white lights, hidden within the case frame, illuminated the screen so that it became a fairy-tale fantasy.

But sitting behind the beautiful screen, like a monstrous dragon in its lair, Chung leered as Kwan Mei silently walked up. His heavy jowls jiggling, he nodded toward the chair at his right. Instead of taking that one, Kwan Mei selected the chair at the opposite side of the table, in order to be as far from him as possible.

As he ate, Chung Li's eyes never left Kwan Mei. She sat silent while he deftly shoved vegetables and rice into his mouth with a set of gold and ivory chopsticks. It took all her willpower to remain in his presence, so repulsed was she, but her expression remained impassive as the smuggling lord feasted.

Though Chung must have known she hadn't had time to eat after leaving the Jade Lady, he offered her nothing as he ate course after course. She could not afford to order a meal for herself, even if she had dared to join him. She prayed he did not hear her stomach growl.

Nearly two hours passed before Chung Li finished eating. At last, snatching away the napkin that had been tucked around his fat neck, he tossed it on the table. His sweaty face gleamed like the silver-gray silk of the expensive Western-style suit he wore. Leaning back in his chair, he joined his hands across his bloated stomach and burped twice.

Reaching into his inside coat pocket, Chung Li pulled from

it a fat wallet. "Tonight you will meet Fong Kee at the number thirty-four machine." Chung thrust the wallet at Kwan Mei. "He will give you something in exchange for this. Bring the package here to me tomorrow night."

Chung flicked a ticket across the table. "For the Macao ferry. Go!" He dismissed her with a flutter of fat fingers.

When Kwan Mei picked up the wallet and ticket and started to leave, Chung Li grabbed her wrist. "Remember, be here tomorrow at this time. Then you will receive your reward." His smile was evil.

CHAPTER 33

Kwan Mei walked swiftly through the steel and glass ferry terminal. Boarding the ferry to Macao, she pushed to the front of the pleasure-seeking crowd and found a seat on a bench near a window. Within minutes, two elderly Caucasian women joined her. One woman wore glasses and the other had glasses dangling from a chain around her neck. Both ladies bubbled with excitement.

The dangling-glasses woman immediately leaned toward Kwan Mei, saying, "Hello, I'm Doris and this is Bernice. We're retired teachers from Missouri."

Kwan Mei was in no mood to carry on small talk. Pretending she didn't speak English, she smiled and shook her head. Doris smiled in response, then returned her attention to her companion.

To keep her mind from dwelling on the meeting with Fong Kee, Kwan Mei concentrated on the Americans' conversation. Educated in Hong Kong's British schools, at times she found it difficult to understand their Midwestern accent. The idioms particularly intrigued and puzzled her. Thus occupied, she temporarily forgot why she was making the trip to Macao, and the crossing quickly passed.

From the ferry dock Kwan Mei hurried to the big green casino and trotted up the building's broad staircase. Inside, she checked her coat and headed to the south slot room. Pausing in the doorway, she did not see Fong Kee among the machine players. As her gaze wandered over the room, it accidentally met that of a well-dressed, middle-aged man who boldly examined her from head to toe. His smile broadened knowingly when he saw she had noticed him. Kwan Mei flushed. How could he think such a thing of her? She coldly turned away.

It was uncommon for a young Chinese woman to go into a

casino unescorted unless she was a whore. Still, it angered and humiliated her that a man would think of her that way. Before taking the ferry, she had even gone home to change out of the *cheongsam* so as not to resemble a prostitute on the prowl. She now wore a demure navy-blue skirt and white blouse with navy purse and shoes to match. Her jewelry consisted of a modest lavender jadite pendant on a gold chain, tiny matching earrings, and a white jade ring on her right hand.

Hoping the pleasure-seeking man would not follow, Kwan Mei hurried to machine 34. It was unoccupied. She glanced over her shoulder. The leering man was nowhere to be seen. Neither was Fong Kee. To her left, at the far end of the row, already glassy-eyed with concentration, the two retired teachers methodically tugged handles of neighboring machines.

Kwan Mei rummaged in her purse for change; there was just enough to play five or six games. Chung Li's agent had to come soon if she were to catch the next boat back to Kowloon. It was already dusk outside, and it was not wise for a young, attractive woman to walk alone on the island's streets after nightfall.

Sliding a coin into the slot, Kwan Mei tugged the handle down and closed her eyes while the wheels spun to a stop. The resulting combination of fruit symbols netted her nothing. She sighed and put in another coin.

Fong Kee spotted Kwan Mei before she saw him. He didn't go to her immediately, but stood at the far end of the aisle and studied her. *A most desirable woman. Chung Li's woman. If she were not, . . . well . . .* It was dangerous to entertain such thoughts.

Fong Kee strode up to Kwan Mei and bowed. "*Joa san,* Kwan Mei. Your beauty delights these eyes. Chung Li does not often send you to Macao."

"*Joa san,* Fong Kee." Kwan Mei bowed her head so he could not see the hostility she felt. *Get Chung Li's package and leave,* she thought. From beneath lowered lids she hastily checked the nearby slot players. Everyone was intent on his or her machine. "You have a parcel for me," she said softly, determined to get away from him as soon as possible.

Fong Kee took hold of her arm. "Before we conduct business, Kwan Mei, we will have tea at my favorite tea house, the Green Cricket—a charming place." The Green Cricket was dark and intimate and far from the ferry terminal.

Kwan Mei knew she must not leave the casino with him. Thinking fast, she said, "I have to wait for the next ferry, but a cup of tea at the casino coffee shop would do fine—I have never been in there." Pulling her arm from his grasp she turned to leave.

"Ah, but the Green Cricket has the best tea in Macao, perhaps Hong Kong, too. You must also sample the special almond treat that no other shop in Macao can equal. Come, I will take you there." Again grasping her arm, Fong Kee tried to propel her to the casino exit. Kwan Mei yanked her arm free. "I must remain at the casino. I have a taxi coming for me," she lied, "and I do not wish to miss it." She headed in the direction of what she hoped was the coffee shop.

Kwan Mei's rebuff brought bright red splotches of irritation to Fong Kee's sallow cheeks, but he knew better than to cause a scene. Nevertheless, he was close beside her as her high heels clicked down the corridor toward the coffee shop.

Fong Kee frightened Kwan Mei. Though he had been suggestive at previous encounters, he had never before touched her. She dared not be alone with him. Picking a booth next to the waist-high wall that divided the café from the wide hallway, she slid into it. The only other customer in the room—a tall Caucasian male—sat at the counter.

Once before, at a similar meeting with Fong Kee, she had mentioned that she had never been to Canton, the city of his birth. To distract him, she asked about his childhood in Canton. But as if seeing through her ploy, he parried her questions with his own about *her* personal life.

Realizing she could not divert Fong Kee from his intent to make their relationship more intimate, she avoided looking at him. Feigning boredom, she assiduously scrutinized the elegant fashions in the display cases that lined the wall across the hall.

When her neck cramped from constantly turning her head to the left, she studied the café decorations, the hanging plants, and the waiter.

Fong Kee's rage spiraled.

CHAPTER 34

A fellow instructor, a "Brit," introduced Morgan to a young English woman, but after several dates with her, during which he found they had nothing in common, he lost interest. The novelty of living in Hong Kong had worn thin in less than six months. It was the end of the break between semesters, and he had spent the entire past weekend in Macao in an orgy of gambling and drinking. Suffering a blinding headache, he wanted only to be alone. Instead of risking his stomach's shaky condition on the ferry back to Hong Kong, he decided to have a cup of coffee, then find a room and stay the night.

As Morgan sipped his coffee, he idly spun the counter stool and scanned the cafe's interior. A slender, rat-faced Chinese man in a Western suit and a young Chinese woman entered. The woman's beauty stunned Morgan. Then he noticed the frightened expression on her face. Mildly curious, he carried his cup to a vacant table where he could watch the couple. *Probably a lover's spat, none of my affair,* Morgan thought. But he couldn't keep his eyes off the young woman.

* * *

The longer Kwan Mei ignored him, the greater Fong Kee's anger grew. He studied her profile, his eyes roving down her cheek to her neck and on to where the "V" of her blouse framed a tear-shaped jade pendant. He smirked and reached across the table. Making sure to first brush the hollow of Kwan Mei's throat, he lifted the pendant with the tip of his index finger. "Which lover gave you this valuable gem?" he purred.

Kwan Mei snatched the chain from his fingers. "It belonged to my father's sister. She gave it to me before she died."

Her whole body was shaking. Trembling, she fished Chung

Li's wallet from her purse. "Here is the money. Give me Chung Li's package."

Fong Kee sneered. "There is no hurry, Kwan Mei. I delight in your presence."

"Give me the object without delay," she almost screamed at him. "Chung Li will not like that you did not act promptly. And Chung Li does not tolerate improper advances to his favorite woman," she added, inwardly cringing as she said it.

Fong Kee paled at this last remark. Reluctantly, he pulled from under his jacket a small package wrapped in newspaper.

Kwan Mei narrowed her eyes. "Unwrap it. I have been told to see the object for myself before I give you the money."

Fong Kee slowly removed the paper from the parcel and handed a gold-sheathed, triangular-shaped object to her.

She briefly examined it, then slid the wallet across the table to him. "Give me the wrapping paper."

He shoved the paper at her. Rewrapping the artifact, she dropped it into her purse. She glanced at her watch, then drew in a sharp breath. It was almost time for the ferry to leave. She sprang from her chair. "Our business is over, Fong Kee. I must go."

Crazy with desire for her, Fong Kee jumped to his feet. Throwing some coins on the table, he grabbed Mei's arm. When she tried to pull away, he tightened his grip until she whimpered with pain. Forcing her ahead of him, he propelled her out of the coffee shop.

Kwan Mei's eyes frantically searched for help, but they were alone in the hall. "Chung Li expects me; I must go," she cried, struggling to free herself.

Fong Kee cruelly twisted her arm behind her back, wrenching her wrist and shoulder. She screamed from the pain.

Suddenly, like magic, the tall Caucasian appeared next to them. He spoke in a low, soft voice with an American accent. "Pardon me, but the lady doesn't want to go with you."

Though Fong Kee was of medium height, the American loomed over him. It was difficult to face down a man so much taller than he, but Fong Kee was not easily intimidated. He refused to release Kwan Mei's arm. He glared up at Morgan through slitted lids. "This is not your concern. Leave us."

Morgan only stepped closer, so close Fong Kee had to tilt back his head at an awkward angle to meet the penetrating scrutiny of the intense blue eyes. As Fong Kee's tension increased, his fingers dug into Kwan Mei's flesh. She uttered a tiny moan.

"Hurting her is not necessary." The American seized Fong's wrist in a powerful and painful hold.

Fong Kee cringed. The man had the iron grip of a trawler net-puller. Shaken from his momentary madness, Fong Kee released Kwan Mei. Besides, to persist could attract the attention of casino security, and security might report the incident to Chung Li.

Kwan Mei jumped away from Fong Kee to a safer position slightly behind the American. Her numbed arm hung uselessly at her side. She rubbed it with the other hand.

The American loosely rested his arm across Kwan Mei's shoulders. To Fong Kee, he said, "Maybe you should get out of here now, mister, before I call security."

Fong Kee muttered a flood of Chinese expletives. In English he hissed, "I will not forget you, American dog. If you take pleasure in your life, leave Macao."

Morgan's lip curled, and he raised a clenched fist. "Beat it, buster."

Fong Kee's eyes glittered with malice, but he turned his back and insolently swaggered toward the exit.

Morgan watched until Fong Kee was out of sight, then faced Kwan Mei. "I'm Morgan McCauley. My apologies for the ugly business with your friend."

Mei gave the handsome American a twisted smile. "Fong Kee is not a friend; I do not even like him." Still trying to rub the circulation back into her arm, she said, "Thank you for rescuing me, but you have offended him, of course, and he can be dangerous."

Morgan noted that she spoke a cultured, British-accented English with barely the hint of a Mandarin accent. Strangely, it pleased him the man was not her lover. "I don't easily frighten," he said. "Besides, I have the protection of the Hong Kong government. I teach at the university."

"They can do little to protect you, if Fong Kee sets out to harm you," Mei responded. "He is a vengeful man and has many influential acquaintances in Macao and Hong Kong." She gazed up into Morgan's sapphire eyes. In passing, she had noticed the light eyes of tourists when she waited on them, but she had never seen eyes so deep a blue.

Morgan grinned devilishly. "Fong Kee would not dare."

Remembering the rumors of Fong Kee's terrible deeds, Kwan Mei shivered.

"Would it be impolite of me to ask why he treated you like that?" Morgan asked gently.

"It is a private matter." A sudden feeling of shame contorted her face.

Morgan peered down at her. "Well, at least I can escort you to wherever you may be going."

She hesitated, then checked her watch. "I'm almost late for the last ferry to Hong Kong. Could you call a taxi for me?"

"I'm taking the ferry myself. We can go together—for your protection," he added, chuckling.

She normally discouraged such familiarity from a stranger, particularly from a person other than her own race. But this tall American with the gemlike eyes fascinated her. "For my protection, then." She smiled.

Morgan's headache had miraculously disappeared.

CHAPTER 35

The next day, before meeting Chung Li at the Shamrock, Kwan Mei purchased something to eat from a street vendor. Unbothered today by a gurgling stomach yet nauseated by the grotesque figure seated across the table from her, she again waited nearly two hours while Chung Li slurped and burped. Why did he ask her to come so early? Why not have her come after his meal? Was this some sort of subtle torture he enjoyed?

At last, Chung Li finished eating. "Did you accomplish the exchange in Macao?" His speech was low Mandarin with a country accent.

"Yes." Kwan Mei slid her large tote from the floor where she had laid it and started to open the bag.

Chung raised a fat hand to stop her; his small black eyes darted over the crowded dining room. "Do not display it here, foolish child," he grunted, rising from his chair. "Come, we will walk together to the service elevator." His huge shoulder made a barely perceptible move in the direction of a small elevator next to the restaurant's kitchen. "We will conduct our business on the way down."

Chung Li waddled out without leaving a tip or paying at the register. He did nod at the maître d' in passing, but Kwan Mei saw that the maître d's smile was stiff above his courteous bow. In the manner of women of her grandmother's era, Kwan Mei meekly followed two steps behind the smuggler lord.

When the elevator doors closed behind them, Chung Li pressed the STOP button to halt the cage's descent. He turned to face her. "The artifact, Kwan Mei. Let me see the insignificant object five hundred pounds purchased for me." He had spoken in cultured Oxfordian English.

Kwan Mei's mouth fell open; she had never heard Chung Li speak anything but course Mandarin. How could he . . . ?

"Come, come, you gape like a hooked fish," he barked.

Embarrassed that she had allowed him to shake her composure, Mei quickly fished in her shoulder bag. Retrieving the newspaper-wrapped package, she thrust it at him. "It was not easy to bring it through customs. I had it taped to my stomach, beneath my blouse." She gingerly touched her stomach. "The tape was painful."

"The hurt will not last, and I pay you well for the little damage to your lovely flesh." Mei shuddered as Chung Li's stare massaged her body. Finally, he looked away, and his pudgy fingers began to unwrap the package.

At first glance, except for its gold sheathing, the object was unremarkable. One side of the triangular-shaped slab—the long leg—was rough and jagged. Its remaining two edges were smooth and beveled. It looked as though it had been broken from a larger piece. Centuries of exposure to the elements and long burial underground had stained the fired terra cotta dark brown and black, but the sheathing gleamed in the elevator's dim light.

Chung Li let her see a small grimace of pleasure. "Perhaps this is of value, after all." He rewrapped the fragment and stuffed it into his briefcase. Reaching into an inside vest pocket, he pulled out a thick wallet and extracted an American twenty-dollar bill. "This is a guarantee of your silence, yes?"

"I want to again work for you," Mei said, praying that her disgust did not show.

"Then we understand each other." He moved closer and pressed a sweaty palm against her thigh, where the slit in the *cheongsam* exposed her skin.

Mei hesitated only a moment before she snapped the edge of her palm down in a fast judo chop.

Chung Li snatched away his hand. His eyes were mere slits as he rubbed his wrist on the silk fabric of his pant leg. "It is not wise to treat me so, Kwan Mei. I can do much for you." His stubby finger punched the DOWN button. The elevator doors opened and he motioned for Kwan Mei to go ahead. Following too close, he hissed in her ear. "I will see you again—soon."

Careful not to sound disrespectful in front of the lobby onlookers, Kwan Mei murmured over her shoulder, "As you wish," then hastened her step to lengthen the distance between them.

Kwan Mei was already through the entrance and out of sight before Chung Li had time to lumber to the sidewalk in front of the hotel. As he stepped to the curb, a late model Rolls-Royce drew up. A young Chinese man in full livery jumped out from behind the wheel and ran around the front of the car to open the back door.

The chauffeur, an illegal immigrant from mainland China, bowed low as Chung heaved his bulk into the luxurious sedan. Though Chung Li was a difficult boss and paid him a pittance, the driver stayed on. The powerful smuggler had threatened the man that at the slightest sign of disloyalty, he would turn him over to the Hong Kong authorities.

Chung Li spoke three words in the Hunan dialect, and the driver deftly swung the sleek silver car into the traffic's flow. Turning on the overhead light, Chung opened the briefcase and extracted the package Kwan Mei had given him. Without unwrapping the parcel, he leaned against the seat, closed his eyes, and hummed a tuneless refrain as he fondled the package.

The Rolls approached a luxury high-rise building at the eastern edge of Kowloon Peninsula. As the chauffeur drove into the underground parking facility, Chung Li quickly returned the package to the briefcase. "I will need you in the morning at ten." The driver nodded as Chung Li entered the elevator to his penthouse apartment.

His housekeeper had left for the day, and Chung Li preferred not to have anyone in the apartment at night, unless it was a woman from the pleasure house. This evening he was too tired to call for a companion. He dropped the briefcase on an intricately carved teak table in the entrance hall. Shuffling to the kitchen, he filled a saucepan from the tap and placed it on the stove to boil. He chose a delicate Ming Dynasty teapot from a cupboard and dropped a generous pinch of green tea leaves into it.

While the water heated, Chung Li stripped off his suit and

donned an embroidered silk smoking jacket and plain black slacks. Sighing with pleasure, he slipped his swollen feet into custom-made, mink-lined slippers. Only then did he retrieve his briefcase from the hall table. Carrying it to his favorite recliner, situated between ceiling-to-floor corner windows with a grand view of Victoria Harbor, he carefully set the case on an antique Italian side table. Before returning to the kitchen, he lovingly trailed his fingers along the black veins in the oval table's pink marble top.

The water came to a boil, and Chung Li filled the teapot. Arranging the pot, a saucer, and a cup on an enameled tray, he set everything on the Italian table. When he at last fell into his oversized recliner, the chair creaked and popped. Sighing, he opened the briefcase and removed the package. After adjusting the flexible neck of a high-wattage lamp in order to see better, he unwrapped the artifact.

Chung stared at the shard in his lap and pondered its intrinsic worth. He had the experienced antique dealer's innate ability to discern the authenticity of an artifact, but how could one estimate its value? If he separated the gold from the clay, he would reap only the price of the gold. The piece had to be more profitable unchanged. Would its ultimate worth be for it as is—only a part of the whole—or must it be complete, joined to its missing component or components? *It is like a piece in a tangram, a Chinese puzzle,* he thought. But the artifact was not Chinese, that he knew for sure.

Puffing out his fat cheeks, and with much effort, Chung Li got up from the recliner. Crossing the room to a handsome rosewood credenza, he took a magnifying glass from the top drawer of the chest. Holding the artifact under the light, he peered through the glass, turning and examining the shard from every angle.

Chung Li sensed that the piece was of enormous age. Impressed in the gold on both sides of the triangle were hundreds of tiny, odd-looking marks, some true hieroglyphics, some a kind of cuneiform. Not adept in ancient languages, he left identification and translation to those experts who hovered on the fringes of his smuggling operation. Suddenly, his attention focused on a boxlike figure with four diagonal lines above it. It was as though the author of the mysterious writing had added a postscript to the bottom of the piece. Or was it a signature? The object held him spellbound. If someone had been there to ask "Why?" he could not have answered.

As Chung Li meditated on the artifact, he stared at, but did not see, the harbor lights that shone like glittering jewels on the water. He knew his most difficult task was yet to come—to sell the object. But first he wanted to discover more about its origin, to explore the mystery without putting himself at risk, personally or financially. For the first time in a lengthy and lucrative career of nefarious ventures, Chung Li regretted his ignorance.

A pair of jet-black jadeite *jingluo* balls rested in an amethyst saucer on the Italian table. Chung Li's gluttony and his exertions in coping with the day's business had fatigued him. As the last flames of a brilliant sunset faded from the western sky, Chung Li picked up the polished orbs and began to roll them in the palm of his right hand. The *jingluo* balls soon soothed him into sleep; his chin sagged to his chest. The spheres slipped unnoticed from his limp fingers and rolled over his ponderous stomach down to the floor.

CHAPTER 36

Kwan Mei's excitement built as the hands of the clock neared closing time. She could barely finish her task of counting the day's receipts and straightening the merchandise for tomorrow. When a customer entered the shop, she looked up expectantly.

At last it was Morgan who pushed open the door. As he made his way toward her, Mei's hands trembled so much that she knocked over the T-shaped rack of silver bangles she was arranging. Bracelets flew everywhere. Merrily tinkling, one rolled under the glass display case and stopped at Morgan's feet. Sporting a mischievous grin, Morgan retrieved the bangle and, twirling it around his finger, carried it to her. He propped his elbow on the counter and whispered, "I think you dropped something."

The past two months had been divine. Since that day when Morgan accompanied her on the ferry from Macao to Hong Kong, they had seen a lot of each other, and her memory of Fong Kee's aggression was rapidly fading. The week following the incident in Macao, Morgan had escorted her home from her job every evening. As they spent even more time together, she introduced him to the finest Chinese restaurants. He wined and dined her in the famous Jimmy's Kitchen or took her to fancy hotel restaurants. The best hours were when they just walked and talked.

Still, as well as she thought she knew Morgan, when she took the bangle from him and their fingers touched, she flushed and had to duck her head. Mortified, she murmured a faint "Thank you."

While Morgan wandered through the shop, Kwan Mei finished tidying up, rearranging the stock, and locking the display cases and cabinets. Going to the back room to set the security system's master switch, she said loud enough for him to hear, "I will not be much longer."

Morgan's rapt attention was on a large elephant tusk that held within it the intricate carving of a miniature village, complete with fishing boats and fishermen.

"That's okay, no hurry," he called back to her.

Morgan's astonishing good looks and personality attracted many women, most of whom readily responded to his adept wooing. He usually achieved his goal to bed them by the second date; but, for some reason, he had not tried his usual tactics with Kwan Mei. He could hardly believe that she had twice managed to drag him to her mission church—and that he had gone willingly.

Mei stalled, fussing with a beaded sweater, draping it just so on its hanger. Conflicting thoughts fluttered in her mind like frightened finches. For weeks Morgan had tried to get her to come to his apartment for an "all-American meal." The dishes he described sounded exotic and delicious. Mei knew that he was good to her and was fun to be with. She wanted to trust him, but she was uneasy. Her previous dates had been with young men she met at church. Invariably, they would take her to their homes for a meal and for an introduction to their parents. Morgan's home was across the Pacific, and he was not even a Christian. Yet, after several refusals, she had finally agreed to tonight's intimate dinner at Morgan's flat near the Central District.

As they left the shop, she asked herself for the thousandth time if she should be going to his apartment alone without a chaperone.

When Morgan ushered Kwan Mei into his apartment, she gasped at the unexpected elegance of its furnishings. Morgan's deceased father, Brian McCauley, had owned three productive oil wells in Oildale, a small, dusty town outside Bakersfield, California. Morgan had invested his inheritance wisely, and the interest from it supplemented his modest salary at Hong Kong University and allowed him to live more than just comfortably. An exquisite three-foot-tall replica of a Ming vase and the cherry chest upon which it stood were the first objects a person saw on entering the apartment. Above the vase hung a very old silk-embroidered tapestry. The soft glowing colors of the vase were repeated in costly, handwoven Chinese carpets and in the wall color and drapes.

Donning a stained and ragged apron, Morgan immediately busied himself in the tiny kitchen. Though Mei tried to keep out of his way, he conscripted her to slice potatoes for French fries. The main course consisted of fat hamburgers grilled on his Japanese hibachi.

Giggling like children, Morgan and Mei took turns cranking the stiff handle of the old ice-cream maker. A dedicated "ice-creamaholic," Morgan could not bear the thought of doing without his favorite treat and had shipped his antique wooden ice-cream maker from the States. Finding rock salt had been a problem; he had spent most of his free time the first month in the country chasing it down. He finally found a supply at an ice house in Aberdeen, near the fishing village. It guaranteed him homemade ice cream whenever he had the craving.

After they finished their apple pie à la mode and cleared the dishes from the table, Morgan gently took Mei's hand. Leading her to his sitting room, he motioned toward the loveseat. She sat, and he lowered himself to the cushion beside her. When he reached toward her to draw her to him, she stiffened. Morgan halted his advance as if he had been slapped. To hide his irritation, he yawned and leaned back against the sofa's uncomfortable wooden arm. "Well, how did you like your first all-American meal?"

"It was very different."

"Did you *like* it?"

The food was too greasy, she thought. Not wanting to hurt his feelings, she looked around the apartment and changed the subject. "Your flat is very nice."

Morgan fought back a grin. He leaned forward, his face two inches from hers, and stared wide-eyed in mock ferocity. "You haven't answered my question. Did . . . you . . . *like* . . . the . . . dinner?"

She laughed and wrinkled her nose. "Not very much; it is the first time I have eaten cow meat." His smile disappeared. To soften her criticism of the meal, she added, "I liked the chocolate ice cream. That was quite good."

"Well, if you like chocolate ice cream, you're a woman after my own heart." He rose from the loveseat. Drawing a small box from his hip pocket, he said, "I have something for you—even if you don't like my cooking." Reaching for her hand, he pulled her to her feet. Still not opening or giving her the box, he asked, "Will you trade a kiss for it?"

Up to now, Morgan had only held Kwan Mei's hand or put his arm around her shoulders. Enfolding her in his arms, he bent and kissed her. His lips were soft and warm. She resisted a little at first, then not at all.

Kwan Mei slid her arms around Morgan's waist. She liked the smell of aftershave lotion that masked a hint of fresh, masculine perspiration. Nestled against his broad chest and encircled by his muscular arms, she felt secure. Soon, she was returning his ardor with equal passion.

Suddenly, Morgan drew back. "I can tell you liked that better than my hamburgers," he teased.

With a shy smile, Mei breathed, "I would like for you to do it again."

Morgan was suddenly serious. "First, I want you to take this." He handed her the small gray box.

When she opened his gift, Kwan Mei squealed with pleasure. "It matches my pendant." She lifted the lavender jade ring from the box. The oval stone shone a light translucent purple and was set in gold. Two rows of seed pearls circled the jade. Cupping the ring in one hand, the box in the other, and looking puzzled, she exclaimed, "Why do you give me such a precious object? I cannot accept it."

Morgan gently closed his huge hand over her small one that held the ring. "I want to marry you, Kwan Mei; I love you and I want you to be my wife." Gently uncurling her hand, he took the ring from her palm and slipped it onto her finger. "Take all the time you need to answer." Leading her to the door, he said, "I'll walk you home."

Morgan's proposal and declaration of his love took Kwan Mei by surprise. Her body had been giving her signals from his first touch, though before this evening she had not openly reacted. He was a good friend. The possibility of their marrying had never occurred to her, but the idea was delightful. She stood on her toes, reaching for another kiss.

Morgan groaned. "Come on, I'm taking you home—this instant." Following through was one of the most difficult decisions he had ever made.

CHAPTER 37

Kwan Mei was too excited to sleep on the night of Morgan's proposal. She wore the jade ring round the clock, touching it to her mouth whenever she remembered his kisses. The jade, warmed by her skin, was as smooth as his lips. But once her initial excitement lessened, she began to think more clearly. Their circumstance was far more complex than it appeared on the surface.

What would her mother think? She had met Morgan and liked him, but Morgan was a Caucasian, a foreigner, and worst of all, he was unsaved. Mei thought her mother might be persuaded to accept the first two conditions; but if her daughter chose to marry outside her faith, it would devastate her. Not too many years in the past, a female child was, more often than not, considered a useless burden, and an unwanted newborn baby girl was drowned or abandoned to the elements. It still occasionally happened. Why, only last week, had not the Hong Kong newspapers reported a rash of such murders in China's northernmost province? In the old days, Mei might have suffered the same fate. As a clearly treasured daughter, Kwan Mei did not want to make any big decision that might displease her mother.

It did not worry her that Morgan might ask her to quit her job, or take her to America, *Praise God.* But leave her mother behind? Never!

There was that other thing, too. She had not told Morgan about the darker side of her life. Before she could marry him, she must end her relationship with Chung Li. *I'll do it tomorrow,* she promised herself.

The next morning Kwan Mei left home early enough to stop by the Shamrock Hotel, where she left a message saying she would like to see Chung Li. She left the same message at a Ladder Street shop that sometimes fenced illicit objects for him.

Mei waited impatiently for an answer. Two days passed without a word. It was Friday before Chung Li's chauffeur came to the Jade Lady and delivered a note printed in neat Chinese. The note gave the address of Chung's apartment and instructed her to go there Sunday afternoon.

Kwan Mei told Morgan she could not see him Sunday because relatives were coming to her house and she had to be there to help her mother. It was yet another lie—another sin. Though sure of her salvation, she knew she was not pleasing God. Feeling guilty, she repeatedly recited Psalm 30:5: *"For his anger lasts only a moment, but his favor lasts a lifetime."* It never failed to comfort her.

Mei slowly ascended the hill that rose behind the Zoological and Botanical Gardens. Though she was high above Hong Kong Island's Central District, the heat was oppressive, made worse by the 83-percent humidity. By the time she reached Chung Li's apartment building, perspiration had molded her blouse to her skin. Tendrils of her sleek hair were glued to her cheeks and forehead.

She pressed the button marked "PENTHOUSE" and waited. At Chung Li's muffled inquiry that came from the screened speaker, she identified herself. A loud click signaled the lock's release and she entered a dimly-lit hall. At the hallway's far end was an elevator with a gilded wrought-iron gate. The modern lift carried her silently upward.

Chung's enormous mass filled the penthouse doorway. The gold-embroidered Mandarin coat of Chinese red that he wore only exaggerated his obesity. His small, pupilless eyes undressed her as he backed away from the door and motioned for her to enter. Trying to hide her fear, she squeezed by without touching him.

Chung Li pressed a meaty hand on her back and pushed her down the hall before him. "A beautiful young guest is an occasion for celebration," he mouthed.

Kwan Mei's stomach churned. Too late, she realized the dangerous situation she had let herself into. Terrified, she almost forgot her reason for coming. She had to tell him—tell him before she lost her nerve. Spinning to face the smuggling tzar, she nearly shouted, "Chung Li, I wish to end our agreement!"

"Perhaps you have found another benefactor?" The monstrous form oozed closer as onyx black eyes bored into hers.

Her entire body trembled. "I am working for no one else." She hesitated; then, bravely plunging on, she announced, "It is simply that I no longer wish to participate in illegal operations."

"Ah, Kwan Mei. I am saddened that you want to leave me." Palms together, Chung tapped his fingers. "With my guidance, you have a magnificent future." He opened wide his arms and waddled toward her. "I have much to teach you." The buzzard eyes fixed on the front of her blouse.

Suddenly, Kwan Mei was desperate to escape the fat dragon's lair. She scooted under his outstretched arms. Knowing she could not get past him where he stood because he was blocking the hall, she quickly scanned the room. Spotting a large recliner between two corner windows, she went to it and sat down. Holding herself primly erect on the seat's edge, she hoped to divert his attention from amorous advances and return to the conversation and to the matter at hand.

Undaunted, Chung Li moved in on her like a lumbering tank. Hovering over her, he grabbed her shoulders. When he lowered his jowls to nuzzle her neck, she cringed into the chair.

His weight crushed her. She was smothering. Rising bile threatened to strangle her.

Clawing at Chung Li's face, Mei screamed. Her flailing arm struck the pink marbled table beside the chair and something made a clicking sound. At the periphery of her vision she saw a pair of *jingluo* balls. Her fingers instinctively closed around one. At that same moment Chung Li lifted his head to see what she was doing.

Kwan Mei's reflex was automatic. With all her strength, she slammed the hard jade sphere into Chung Li's left temple.

Chung's body instantly went limp. As he slipped slightly down and to one side, his hand groped at Kwan Mei's neck. The fat fingers caught and snapped the jade pendant's chain.

Blood flowed from the crushed and rapidly bluing skin of Chung Li's temple. Blood dripped onto Kwan Mei's pale yellow skirt. Sobbing with horror, Mei struggled under the gross mass, shoving and pushing at it with both hands, but it was too heavy for her to move. Whimpering, her breath rasping from squashed lungs, she made one last effort to dislodge the dead weight of Chung Li's body. At last she wriggled free. Scrambling across the arm of the chair, she knocked over the pink marble table. The second *jingluo* ball, along with a gold-sheathed object, fell to the floor. Chung Li did not move.

Though dazed and shaken, Kwan Mei recognized the artifact she had received from Fong Kee in Macao. Hardly knowing what she was doing, she grabbed it from the floor and threw it into her purse. Then her only thought was to flee the penthouse.

CHAPTER 38

Hong Kong's midsummer humidity penetrated even into the modern, air-conditioned apartment. Sitting on the edge of his bed, Morgan pulled off his sweaty socks and tossed them and his reeking tennis shoes into a corner. His shorts and shirt followed. Scratching an itch beneath the waist elastic of his briefs, he headed for the kitchen.

He had overslept because of his night out on the town with Kwan Mei, and it had nearly made him late for the morning's match. His tennis game was stale; he had lost three easy sets out of five. Taking a tall glass from a cupboard, he opened the refrigerator and removed a pitcher of tea, dropped ice into the glass, and filled it.

Oh, for a scotch on the rocks, he ruminated. *Not good! Recovering alcoholics can't afford to think such thoughts.* Kwan Mei had persuaded him to stop drinking, and he had joined a Hong Kong AA chapter. He mentally chastised himself, then appeased his craving with two extra teaspoons of sugar.

For the first Sunday in weeks he did not have a date with Kwan Mei, and it annoyed him. A long afternoon loomed before him, lonesome and dull. Morgan snatched a ragged beach towel off the sink as he exited the kitchen and went to the sitting room. He spread the towel on the Tianjin carpet that lay in front of his stereo. Swigging a long drink of tea, he set the glass on a table and dropped to all fours. *Should've done this when it was cooler. Should've gotten up earlier and worked out before tennis.*

After performing one hundred pushups, Morgan lay flat on his back, hands behind his head. Since that significant day in Macao, when he had rescued Kwan Mei from Fong Kee's unwelcome advances, his mundane existence had changed immeasurably. The flowers had grown brighter, the sky bluer. Now he looked forward to every day. On the other hand, if Mei had not come into his life, he would not still be in Hong Kong's heat, teaching summer school. Instead, he would be surfing a pristine bay in Western Australia. However, one day without Kwan Mei and he was abysmally miserable.

Herb Alpert and the Tijuana Brass boomed from the stereo. At first, Morgan's bare toes tapped to the lively beat, but even the Latin rhythms could not prevent sleep. He had just begun to snore when staccato pounding on his door snapped him awake.

When Morgan flung open the door, a disheveled and hysterical Kwan Mei flew into his arms. Her momentum would have knocked him off balance, had he not braced his hip against the door frame. Clinging to him, her face jammed into his bare chest, Mei stammered broken sentences between gulps and sobs. "Ch-ch-chung Li is d-d-dead. He's D-DEAD!"

Morgan saw that Mei was near to collapsing. He picked her up. Kicking the door shut, he carried her inside and carefully laid her on the loveseat. Turning off the stereo, he knelt on the floor and took her ice-cold hand in his.

It was then that he noticed her skirt and blouse were stained with fresh blood.

"What the . . . What happened to you?"

But she couldn't speak.

Morgan's fingers tenderly brushed away her tears. "It's all right, hon. Everything will be fine. Just tell me what happened."

Kwan Mei turned her pallid face away from Morgan. "I killed Chung Li," she whispered.

"Whoa, wait a minute," Morgan snorted. "Who is Chung Li?"

"Everywhere . . . blood all over me . . ." Kwan Mei's sobs increased; her hands scrubbed at her skirt. "Look!" She stood so he could see the gore on her clothes.

Morgan's mind was racing. "I can't believe that you murdered someone, but if somebody is dead we must go to the constabulary."

Mei's features contorted with horror. She grabbed his arm, her nails digging painfully into his flesh. "No," she wailed. "The police cannot know. It would be in the papers. It would shame my mother."

He spoke to her gently, as he would have a child. "The police cannot know *what*? And *what* is bad enough to shame your mother, Mei?"

As she told Morgan the whole story, Kwan Mei suddenly remembered she still had the artifact. She took it out of her purse and handed it to him.

"This is what I purchased in Macao for Chung Li. I took it when . . . after I hit him." Agitated, Kwan Mei yanked at her bangs. "I do not know why I took it," she cried. "I do not want it." Her shoulders sagged, and the tears streamed down her cheeks.

Morgan briefly examined the gold-covered shard, then laid it on the couch. It interested him little; he was more concerned for Kwan Mei. He respected the law and knew he should immediately inform the authorities. But devotion to Mei overcame common sense, and he did nothing.

That night, Kwan Mei stayed in Morgan's apartment. They lay entwined in one another's arms on Morgan's bed, but he did not touch her otherwise.

Macabre nightmares tormented Kwan Mei all night and violent shudders racked her body. An image of Chung Li's bloated, blood-smeared face haunted her. Every restless move she made disturbed Morgan, who comforted her until she quieted. Neither of them got more than a few successive minutes of sound sleep.

The next morning, Morgan made a light breakfast of toast and tea, which neither of them tasted. Kwan Mei sat on a high stool, looking like a toddler in a high chair. "I have to go to the shop. I am needed there."

Morgan paced the kitchen. During the night he had done a lot of thinking. He knew what she must do. "Kwan Mei, you have to inform the law." He glanced at his watch. "I teach an eight o'clock class at the university this morning, or else I'd come with you. Promise you'll go to the police right away?"

"I cannot. I am afraid." She was adamant.

"If you won't go this morning, I'll pick you up when the Jade Lady closes. We'll go together." He leaned over and kissed the top of her head. "Okay?"

She meekly nodded, relieved at the postponement.

He kissed her lightly on the mouth. "I'll see you keep that promise." He was collecting his briefcase and papers. "It's time for me to leave. Here, wear my shop coat home. It should cover the blood. Can you get by your mother?"

"It is her day to shop in town. She will not see me."

"Well, don't forget to change."

How could she forget? The very smell of Chung Li's blood—now dried and stiffening the fabric of her skirt and blouse—perpetually reminded her.

CHAPTER 39

The afternoon of the same Sunday that Chung Li died, Fong Kee boarded the ferry to Hong Kong. He had with him a choice item he hoped to sell to Chung Li—an exquisite water buffalo cow and calf, carved from velvety blue gemstone-quality lapis lazuli. The bas-relief piece was among the finest he had ever seen, and he wanted to deliver it personally, if only to see the expression of delight on Chung Li's fat face.

Fong Kee arrived at Chung Li's apartment building only twenty minutes after Kwan Mei's desperate flight from the premises. He had never been to Chung Li's home; they normally rendezvoused at the Shamrock Hotel restaurant. However, this was a special occasion, and he was coming unannounced, without previous arrangement.

No one had entered or left the building since Mei's wild dash out. Fong Kee was only momentarily puzzled when he found the apartment-house street door wide open. Taking the lift to the penthouse, finding that door also ajar, he immediately knew something was amiss.

Fong rapped lightly on the penthouse doorjamb. When no one answered, he knocked again and then pushed the door completely open. Neither seeing nor hearing anything unusual, Fong Kee crept farther into the penthouse. Stopping in the middle of a long, dimly lit hallway, he called out, "Chung Li, it is I, Fong Kee. I have brought you something of great beauty and value."

Receiving no answer, Fong Kee walked to the end of the hall and entered the main room. An odd sight stopped him in his tracks. Chung Li knelt on the floor beside a chair, his head resting on the seat cushion and his face turned toward the windows.

Fong Kee politely shuffled his feet to attract Chung's attention. When there was no response, he cautiously approached the smuggling tzar, but Chung still did not move. Laying the package he carried on the floor, Fong gingerly touched Chung Li's left cheek, then pressed harder. The flesh was cold—too cold for life. Suddenly, the body slid from the chair and onto the floor. Only then did Fong see the terrible temple wound and rapidly congealing blood.

Fong Kee exhaled with a long hiss. The main source of his income, the fountain of his fortune, was dead. He balled his fists and reared back. Wheeling, he scanned the room, seeking a clue to his mentor's killer. His attention was caught by the magnificent opulence of the place, and a new emotion instantly defused his rage. Fong's eyes narrowed and a grimace resembling a smile bared his yellowed teeth. His trip to Hong Kong would be profitable after all.

After closing and locking the penthouse door, Fong quickly searched the rooms. With practiced expertise he filled two pillow cases with precious antiques and jewelry. Next, he turned his attention to Chung Li's body. He pushed and pulled at the huge corpse without budging it. Finally, by rocking it back and forth, he managed to roll it over.

The body was now on its side, and Chung's hands, which had been under his chest, were free. Fong Kee cackled with glee when he saw five costly rings on each hand. He stooped to pluck them from the body's right hand and discovered that the fingers were entangled in a gold box chain. He tried to disentangle the chain, but the dead hand clasped it in a grip of steel. It took all Fong Kee's strength to pry open the thick fingers. When he recognized Kwan Mei's jade pendant exposed on the corpse's palm, shock like a bolt of electricity jolted him.

Kwan Mei murdered Chung Li. Kwan Mei had rejected him for this fat pig? Furious, Fong kicked the dead leg. *The pig!* He kicked it again and again.

Finally, panting from exertion, he grabbed up the stuffed pillow cases and ran from the penthouse. By noon the next day, Fong Kee had put out a contract for Kwan Mei's assassination.

CHAPTER 40

Though the police had briefly detained Kwan Mei, Morgan, through his university and embassy contacts, arranged for her release in his custody. Every evening the rest of that week, Morgan walked Kwan Mei home from the Jade Lady. The police absolved her of all guilt when she convinced them that she had hit Chung Li in self-defense. Though she could not shake the image of Chung Li's leering face from her mind, she also could not overcome the remorse she felt at taking a life.

Walking home one night, Mei tried to explain to Morgan how she did feel. "Though Chung Li was an evil man, and the world is already improved without him, I should not have killed him. Good or bad, he was created by God." She started to sob.

Morgan threw his arms around her and drew her close. "Kwan Mei, you've got to stop blaming yourself for what happened. You should have told me about it before. I would have taken care of him for you."

"The Bible teaches that it is wrong to take a human life."

Morgan's mouth tightened. "Yeah? Well, it seems I've heard that a couple of times God had someone wipe out a whole town, even the children and animals."

Kwan Mei sighed. "That was different. The people in those towns did not believe in Him. That was how He punished them."

Morgan snorted. "I'm sorry, Mei, I can't go along with that kind of justice. Isn't God supposed to be merciful?"

"That is true, he is merciful. He sent Jesus to us—to save us!"

Morgan snorted. "'Jesus saves!' That's been plastered on signs up and down California's Highway 99 as long as I can remember. Jesus may have been a good man, but his followers made him into an idol. Hitler's followers thought *he* was pretty great, too."

Kwan Mei's heart nearly burst. "You compare Jesus and Hitler? What an awful thing you have said!" For the first time she and Morgan were discussing religion, and it was turning out badly. What more could she say? She started walking away to hide her distress.

Morgan caught Kwan Mei's elbow. Looking down, he saw her anguish. "I'm sorry, Mei. I admit I don't know much about the Bible. Maybe you'll get the chance to educate me after we're married," he said softly.

Kwan Mei didn't answer. It was all too much to comprehend: Chung Li's death, her love for Morgan, and her impending marriage to him. Now, on top of it all, she had to question the wisdom of bonding with an unbeliever. She was suddenly very tired. When they arrived at her flat, she entered it without kissing Morgan good-bye or asking him to come in.

Morgan stood outside Kwan Mei's door to see if she would reopen it. When she didn't, he thrust his hands in his pockets and headed home. Religion didn't matter. He would never understand all that nonsense about Jesus anyway. That he and Kwan Mei loved one another was enough.

* * *

Despite their disagreeable parting the night before, Morgan stopped to escort Mei home from the Jade Lady as usual. They were on their way to the police station to ask again about the necklace. For the sake of peace, she temporarily decided to forget the subject of religion. The loss of the pendant not only saddened her, it worried her; something wasn't quite right.

"Where can my jade pendant be, Morgan?" she asked. "The police say they did not find it in Chung Li's flat."

"One of the police officers must have liked it," was Morgan's cynical answer. "Let's hope they can tell us more tonight."

Leaving busy Nathan Road, they took a shortcut through a narrow alley lined with booths and small stores. The crowded lane forced them to walk single file. Morgan led Mei by the hand.

After ducking around a woman laundress carrying an enormous basket of clean clothes on her head, Morgan stopped in front of a display table full of T-shirts. Pulling Mei to his side, he laughed and pointed at a neon pink shirt sporting a caricature.

"I think that's supposed to be our new president, Lyndon Baines Johnson," he said, bending for a better look.

Mei raised her eyebrows. "Maybe it is Charles de Gaulle."

Morgan straightened. "The nose is too short for de Gaulle. However, it's a pretty bad image of whomever it's supposed to be," he joked, grinning down at her. He started to lead her away when she was shoved hard against him. Kwan Mei's tinkling laugh turned into a scream that ended in a gurgling cough, and she slumped against Morgan. He seized her arms to keep her from falling. It was then that he saw the stiletto in her back.

There was very little blood. Morgan knelt and carefully laid Kwan Mei on her side on the cement. There he cradled her head in his lap. Mei looked up at him and whispered, "Everything is so beautiful. . . ." She was not focusing on him, but on the ethereal beyond, an expression of glorious joy on her face.

"Don't just stand there, you dumb idiots. Get the police!" Morgan shouted at the stoic men and women encircling them.

Holding Mei close, Morgan gently rocked her. When the last spark of life faded from her eyes, an ecstatic smile remained on her lips.

A roaring started in his ears. The sound of voices dimmed and suddenly he was eighteen again.

Kern River Canyon, California, 1949

Morgan, his steady girl, MaryAnne, and Morgan's best friend, David, and David's girl, Caroline, were on their way to Lake Isabella, east of Bakersfield. Their high school graduation had taken place earlier that afternoon, and they now looked forward to an all-night celebration at the lake. The four teenagers were already mildly drunk on the smooth bourbon whiskey Morgan had stolen from his dad's liquor cabinet. A full bottle rolled to and fro over the floor behind the driver's seat.

Morgan's cherry-red Ford convertible was a graduation gift from his folks. The power of the car's custom engine, combined with potent whiskey, made Morgan feel invincible. He drove recklessly, his left hand on the wheel and his right arm around MaryAnne. Always a fast driver, Morgan pushed the Ford to its limit.

Their feet planted on the backseat, the second couple sat on the convertible's folded top, swaying as the car swayed. Giggling, they grabbed at each other whenever the car sped around a turn. Morgan knew the road well; he had been over it often, but never before with alcohol in his system.

Leaving Bakersfield, the highway first followed the Kern River along a broad meandering valley. As the river tumbled through the foothills of the Sierra range, it had cut a narrow, twisting gorge, and the road hugged the gorge's south wall.

They had just begun to sing the Bakersfield High School fight song—terribly off-key—when Morgan directed the convertible into a sharp, downhill curve. As an oncoming car rounded the curve, its lights momentarily blinded Morgan. The approaching vehicle seemed to head straight for them.

Alcohol-impaired reflexes and dulled judgment affected Morgan's reaction. He automatically jerked the wheel hard to the right. As he fought to gain control, the Ford sideswiped the rock escarpment. Morgan heard screams from the backseat, then only screeching tires. He finally managed to bring the convertible to a stop on the shoulder, almost two hundred feet down the road.

It took Morgan a minute or two to collect his wits. When he had gained them, he saw that MaryAnne lay unconscious half on, half off the seat next to him. Turning around to check on the other couple, he saw an empty backseat. Then he remembered the screams. He bolted from the convertible and ran uphill to the bend. When he stumbled over a shrub and fell, Morgan realized he had to have a flashlight. He jumped to his feet and returned to the car. MaryAnne had regained consciousness, and he straightened her on the seat. Grabbing a flashlight from the glove compartment, he headed back up the road.

Even with a flashlight to light his way, Morgan nearly tripped over David's date, Caroline. The girl had been thrown out of the car and onto the gravel shoulder. She was still alive, but her breathing was shallow and irregular. Morgan searched for David. Suddenly, he saw a heap in the middle of the road and ran to it. It was David.

Morgan fell to his knees beside his motionless friend. "Are you all right, David?" he shouted above the river's roar. But David only sighed and exhaled one last breath. The other car's occupants never knew that their wheel had glanced off David's head, breaking the boy's neck.

Passing out, Morgan collapsed across his best friend's chest.

* * *

And now he had lost another person he loved. Kwan Mei, too, was dead.

PART 4

CHAPTER 41

Ankara, Turkey, August 1967

Morgan strode across the tarmac between the big airliner and Ankara's Esenboğa Terminal. His layover in Rome had not rested him; it had disturbed him. Countless hippies swarmed through the city begging from the tourists. They loafed on the rims of the famous marble fountains, smoking reefers and tossing the butts into the water. They sprawled on the Spanish stairs, blocking traffic.

Rome reminded him of his recent visit to his alma mater, the University of California at Berkeley. The hippies there seemed the same—aimless, dirty, vacant-eyed. When he attended UC, the campus had been immaculately beautiful, the majestic fountains gloriously splashing, not dry, and the statues not yet marred with graffiti. The pointless desecration of both places angered him.

Doing a mental inventory of his belongings in preparation for the grueling Turkish customs inspection, Morgan barely noticed the fierce August heat. As he walked, he thrust his hand into his jacket's inside pocket—the one over his heart—and gently fingered the small velvet pouch. He did not intend to declare the pouch's precious item to Turkish customs officials; they might confiscate it as an illegal antiquity.

Morgan impatiently waited at the tail end of line number 2. Pungent Turkish tobacco smoke blued the Esenboğa customs shed's interior. Rubbing his bloodshot eyes and arching his back, he stretched luxuriously, then kneaded his spine with his clenched fist. Every bone and muscle ached from the long hours squeezed into economy-class seats that were much too cramped for a man six feet, three inches tall. Not only did he stand out because of his height; his sun-bleached blond hair glowed above the dark heads that surrounded him.

His thoughts went back to Kwan Mei. Her assassin had never been found. The day after they buried her, Morgan realized he had to leave Hong Kong. Every sight, every sound, and every smell reminded him of her. He finished the semester and told the university he would not be back. Preparing to sell his living-room sofa, he pulled off the cushions to clean under them. That was when he discovered the gold-sheathed shard Kwan Mei had dropped there on the night of Chung Li's death.

He had made her a promise then. *Somehow, I'll make your death mean something, Kwan Mei.* It was the shard that originally ignited his notion to seek work at an archaeological dig somewhere in Turkey.

Morgan now focused his attention on the uniformed Turk who efficiently slipped flattened palms through the layers of clothing and research materials in Morgan's luggage. When Morgan claimed he had nothing else to declare besides his camera and its accessories, the official waved him on.

The Israeli Six-Day War had begun that June. Many Turks sided with the Arabs and were hostile to Americans, but most were not. One of the latter, the passport inspector, gleamed a friendly smile.

"Merhaba, nasilsiniz?" "Hello, how are you?"

"Iyiyim, teşekkür ederim. Siz nasilsiniz?" "I'm fine, thank you. How are you?" His automatic response to the Turk's greeting surprised Morgan. How easily the language came back—the Turkish he had learned during his tour of duty in the mid-fifties.

His papers in order, Morgan left the air-conditioned customs shed. This time, the superheated outside air slammed into him like a physical blow. His ears had forgotten the cacophony of automobile horns blaring from the fleet of battered taxies that lined the curb outside the terminal.

To attract a fare, each driver stood in the street next to the driver's door, his right hand punching a discordant tattoo on the horn button. Morgan chose a blue-and-white 1951 Chevy, less battered than the rest of the old cars queued at the curb.

He and the driver agreed upon the fare to the Dedemon Hotel before the cabby started his engine.

The long ride from Esenboğa Airport to Ankara was hot and dusty. Morgan moved to the middle of the frayed seat to escape the sun's blistering rays streaming through the open window. Turkey's unique blend of aromas assailed his nostrils. They flooded his mind with nostalgic memories of conversations over demitasse cups filled with fragrant Turkish coffee and of endless glasses of potent Black Sea tea. Since Mei's death, he had not drunk anything stronger. Suddenly thirsty, his fingers curled unbidden, as if around a wasp-waisted tea glass.

The acrid stench of a burning animal carcass, mingling with the reek of human excrement, jolted him out of his reverie. Morgan closed his eyes and chuckled. It was good to be back.

* * *

The swamp cooler roared but did little to quench the stifling heat in the hotel room. Morgan turned it off and opened the window. Stripping to his shorts, he flung himself on top of the bedcovers and instantly fell asleep. He slept until dusk, when a brisk breeze, whistling through the window, tickled the hairs of his naked chest and awakened him. He lay in a kind of stupor, dreaming about Kwan Mei. His arms felt as though they encircled her yet. He yelled at the ceiling, "What kind of God are you? She loved you, yet you let her die."

But he knew Mei's death was not God's fault; it was his own. He blamed himself for letting it happen. Morgan groaned, his grief and guilt too much to bear.

Islam's call to evening worship, sounding from the loudspeakers of a neighboring mosque, brought him to the present. A stinging cold shower helped force away all but a faint, shadowy memory of Kwan Mei. Despite his long nap, his physiology was still out of sync with Ankara time. He wasn't a bit hungry. Every takeoff from an airport had been followed shortly by a meal or a snack, and the thought of more food was anathema to him.

While in transit and during part of his interlude in Rome, he had poured over three editions of Middle Eastern archaeology that he had ferreted out in London's used-books stores. He'd also managed to go over a third of the archaeological documents he'd gotten permission to copy at the British Museum. His weary eyes would not tolerate another printed word, and he didn't feel like studying anyway. Too restless to remain in his room, Morgan left the hotel to wander through Ankara's vaguely familiar streets.

Morgan's stature and fair coloring attracted some stares; most Turks merely gave him polite, curious looks. Ankara was, after all, the capitol of Turkey—a cosmopolitan city used to foreigners. However, the city felt different, less hostile, than it did when he was there before. *Probably because I'm no longer with the military,* he mused. It was true; he no longer resembled a member of the United States Armed Forces. Notably, his hair was too long, and, even if his pace was brisk, he had lost something of the snappy heel-to-toe step he had learned in basic training. His shoulders had developed a bit of a slouch, too.

He meandered up the hill toward the Çankaya Tea Garden. In the old days, though the Marine Corps frowned on such fraternization, he had spent many off-duty hours there dressed as a civilian. He had immensely enjoyed the interplay with students from Ankara University. It was an opportunity for them to practice their English, and he, his Turkish.

Morgan recognized the small *pasta* shop that fronted the tea garden and entered it. Selecting two chocolate-filled pastries from the display, he carried them through an arched doorway to the rear terrace overlooking a steep, brush-covered hillside.

Though the trees had grown, the tea garden hadn't changed much. Many new high-rise apartment buildings had sprouted on the hill since Morgan had been there. The taller structures interrupted the once-unobstructed view of Ankara. Highly polished pink-tinted cement, cast with multicolored marble chips, formed the terrace floor. A two-foot rock wall, topped with wrought-iron fencing, protected the garden's patrons without impeding their view. Japanese lanterns cast a romantic glow on the white wrought-iron, glass-topped tables and ice cream-parlor chairs.

Kwan Mei would have liked this, Morgan thought, the knife again turning in his heart. He chose a table at the terrace edge. In broken Turkish, liberally embellished with pantomime, he ordered the smallest samovar available. The white-coated waiter set it on the table alongside a tea glass. A tin saucer set on the glass held two cubes of rough-ground brownish sugar and a Lilliputian tin spoon.

Morgan patiently waited for the charcoal in the samovar to heat the water to his liking. When the belly of the samovar gurgled and steam issued from the vents, he removed the tea-pot from the top and poured a third of a glass of the syrupy tea. Replacing the teapot on top of the samovar, he held the child-sized glass under the samovar's spout, filling it the rest of the way with boiling water.

Preferring his tea sweet, Morgan plopped both sugar cubes into the glass, methodically stirring them with the tiny spoon until they dissolved. A brilliant red and purple sunset lingered in fading splendor above the dark blue-violet mountain ranges that ringed Ankara to the north and west. The fantasy of color-ful, twinkling lights in the city—nearly a thousand feet below—gave the scene a fairy-tale atmosphere.

Sipping his tea, Morgan sighed with contentment and stud-ied the tea garden's other patrons. A young Pakistani couple, two tables to his left, murmured softly to one another over a two-person samovar. Morgan compared the woman—in her frothy, coral-hued, silver-laced sari—to a bright and dainty but-terfly. The fine gold ring in one nostril enhanced her exotic charm.

Wearing customary black business suits, a pair of Turkish men sat at a table to Morgan's right. Their Turkish was far too rapid for him to pick up the nuances, but he understood the general meanings. *I'll have the language again in no time,* he thought, pleased.

Animated voices drew his attention to a party of six. Three of the men and one young woman—probably college students— looked to be in their late teens or early twenties. The second woman was older, probably in her late twenties or early thirties. A fourth man, silver-haired and distinguished-looking, appeared to be in his mid sixties. At first, Morgan thought they all were Turks. When he saw that the older woman wore 501 Levis, however, he immediately knew she was an American. He frowned at her lack of consideration for Turkey's cultural taboos. It was still not considered proper for a woman to wear pants in a public place.

Morgan felt ashamed for his countrywoman. Intrigued, nevertheless, he stared at her. She was tall and willowy, with a gorgeous face and figure, but her voice was too loud. Morgan clearly heard her every word, which was directed at the gray-haired man.

"My interest is in the people who might have inhabited Göreme hundreds of years before the monks did."

Göreme! Morgan straightened. He was planning to visit the area the next week. His abrupt movement caught the American woman's attention, and she swiveled around to examine him.

He gave her a lopsided grin. She threw him a brief, scathing glance, then turned back to the man to whom she had been speaking.

Morgan kept his eyes straight ahead from then on, though he continued to surreptitiously listen to the conversation at the other table.

The woman became more vehement. "I'm an experienced professional with a doctorate in archaeology; I am not a summer-vacation volunteer!" Her sandaled foot rapped the floor as she spoke. "I want to work full-time in Turkey, and I particularly want to work in Cappadocia." She almost shouted now.

There was an embarrassed hush in the tea garden. The younger Turks at her table stirred uncomfortably, but the older man seemed to take it in stride. Morgan heard him say, in perfect English, "Do not worry, Miss Arista. Tomorrow, come to my office. I will see what I can do for you."

"I'll be there. You can bet on it." The woman jumped from her chair and strode toward the arched exit. Morgan's last impression of her was of a ramrod-straight spine and a tantalizing swish of the hips as she stalked out.

The silver-haired Turk gestured good-naturedly to the young people remaining at his table. "Miss Arista is a fine archaeologist, but she is tired from a long flight."

It was after ten when Morgan returned to his room at the Dedemon Hotel. An image of the bad-tempered American woman persisted in annoying him, and it was after midnight before he fell asleep. The amplified call of the Mezuin in the nearby mosque awakened him at four, but this time he quickly returned to a dreamless slumber.

It was after eleven when Morgan awakened in the morning; he had slept through the scheduled breakfast in the hotel dining room. His body, saturated with airline food and topped with tea and rich pastries, felt bloated and sluggish. It would take at least a week for him to adjust to Middle East time. To make matters worse, he had not had a hard physical workout in over a month.

After a leisurely bath in the deep, claw-footed tub, he stood before a full-length chiffonier mirror and searched his body for signs of flab. He didn't like what he saw. Pinching the barest hint of love handles at his waistline, he growled at his reflection. "An assignment to a tough dig in Cappadocia would be just the ticket."

CHAPTER 42

Arianna Arista seethed as she returned to her friend Beverly's apartment. She was not getting anywhere with the Turkish red tape. Despite two days' tramping from agency to agency, she had only a work permit and a giant blister on each heel to show for it. It seemed that every official step required not just a set fee, but often additional *baksheesh*, the under-the-counter bribe Middle Easterners take for granted. Thus far, she had not found any employment, let alone something in her field. No work meant no permanent visa, and her modest hoard of savings was rapidly shrinking.

One of her stateside professors had recommended that she see Dr. Galip Yaldiz, an esteemed archaeologist and a professor at Ankara University. She desperately needed Dr. Yaldiz's connections at the Department of Antiquities; but last night at the tea garden, the great Yaldiz had treated her like she was a naive high school freshman.

Arianna remembered her grandmother Ylenah's warning not to reveal her Armenian and Greek ancestry to anyone. Had Dr. Yaldiz somehow guessed her background? Could he be hostile to someone having the blood of Turkey's traditional enemies? She shook her head, disgusted with herself for being foolish. How could anyone in Turkey possibly know? Besides, she was sure that her heritage would make no difference to a professional like Dr. Yaldiz.

"Dr. Yaldiz wasn't interested in me," Arianna told Beverly. "Why doesn't something go easily for a change?" she complained, as she creamed off makeup in front of the bathroom mirror. She scrubbed the coarse washcloth across her face, though a cosmetologist had once cautioned her that rough treatment of the delicate skin around the eyes would cause lines. Right now she couldn't care less about wrinkles. "I lost my cool and acted really stupid," she groaned.

Hearing the gloom in Arianna's voice, Beverly came in and leaned against the door frame. "Your system hasn't completely adjusted to the time change and you're still tired after the long flight from California. Things probably seem worse than they really are. In a couple of weeks you'll be comfortably settled and laughing about all this."

Taking her brush from the sink, Beverly began to vigorously stroke her luxurious copper hair. She taught fourth grade at the elementary school at Balgat, the American base. The week before Arianna arrived, Beverly had signed up for her third two-year hitch with the Dependent Schools.

Yanking at snarls, Beverly revealed her thoughts to Arianna. "I was amazed when you wrote you were coming to Turkey without the assurance of a job—that took nerve. I've never heard of a person entering on just a tourist visa, then merely walking in and obtaining permanent papers without a hassle. It's something of a miracle. I mean, getting your work permit so fast." Beverly gave her hair one last stroke and went back into the bedroom. "God had a hand in it, you know," she yelled over her shoulder.

No way! Arianna thought. She didn't buy the idea of supernatural intervention. Certainly God would not pay personal attention to her. Did she even believe in Him? She tolerated Beverly's sermons only because Beverly had been her best friend since the two of them were roommates at Scripps College.

Arianna came out of the bathroom drying her face on a thirsty Bursa towel. "I have the work permit because you sponsored me," she said. "And by the way, I forgot to tell you, I checked at the Tumpane Company. They have a clerk position open. They've scheduled me to take a typing test on Friday." Arianna shuddered. "The thought of it scares me to death; I haven't taken a typing test since ninth grade."

"You can practice on my portable, but the keys might be slightly closer together than on a standard. That could be a handicap."

"Do I have a choice? I'll *have* to practice," Arianna stated resolutely. "The test is given on an IBM Selectric, but I wish they used something else. I've rarely used a Selectric. If you're not accustomed to it, the moving ball can be a distraction."

Beverly began to peel the madras cloth spread from her bed. "How fast do you think you type now?"

"About fifty words per minute on a standard typewriter." Arianna shot Beverly a wry grin. "Fifty words with five to eight errors. No matter how hard I try, I simply cannot knock down the errors to three or fewer. Typing definitely isn't my forte."

Arianna sat on the rim of the bathtub and gingerly applied fresh Band-Aids to her blistered heels. "I received a Sixty-Word Certificate in junior high school, but that was ages ago." She pulled off her slip and bra. Sighing with relief, she said, "It feels good to get out of this harness." Slipping on her nightgown, she confessed, "I haven't typed much lately."

"You'll do fine." Beverly was already in bed, yawning. "I'll be praying for you." *And for your salvation,* she thought.

"You know I don't believe in that stuff. But go ahead if it makes you feel happy," Arianna murmured. In response, Beverly rolled her eyes and clucked. Ignoring Beverly's mother-hen fussing, Arianna crawled between the sheets on the camping cot, temporarily installed for her in Beverly's crowded little bedroom. "Are you going to read yourself to sleep tonight or shall I turn off the light?"

"After correcting essays for three hours, I'm too beat to read. Teaching fourth graders is harder than anything else I've done. I'm not sure I'd go for an elementary teaching credential if I had it to do over."

"You'd do it again, Bev. You're a natural with kids."

"Maybe. Especially if I knew I could remain in Turkey forever. It's wonderful to teach here. The Dependent School is so efficient compared to stateside schools. And the students are better behaved; they have to be. If some kid winds up in serious trouble—gets into drugs or commits a burglary, for instance—the whole family is sent home, bag and baggage. They're ousted even though the father may be a noncommissioned officer, a civilian attached to the embassy, or the reigning general."

Arianna snapped off the light. "I suppose I should've gone on for my credential, too, but I like archaeology too much. Besides, what demand is there for a teacher who has a major in the history of medieval art and a minor in potsherd archaeology?"

Beverly laughed. "I don't think there's much demand for that combination. What made you finally decide to come to Turkey, anyway? I was never able to persuade you to come over with me four years ago."

Arianna made no comment. Instead, she asked, "Did I ever tell you my mother's parents were born in Turkey?"

"I think so, but you told me a long time ago."

"I'm half Greek, half Armenian. My mother was born in what was called Little Armenia. My father was a Greek."

"So?" Beverly asked, stifling a yawn, trying hard to stay awake.

"My maternal grandparents were both Armenian. They had to flee their family home to save their lives." When Beverly didn't answer, Arianna punched her pillow into a more comfortable form and whispered into it, "If the Turks open a new site near where my grandparents were born, I want to be there, digging tools in hand."

Chapter 43

Arianna had already finished breakfast when Beverly scuffed into the kitchen, yawning. "Hi! How'd you sleep?" she asked Arianna.

"I'm not completely adjusted, though I feel much better this morning." Arianna watched while her friend scorched two bread slices in the toaster. Beverly preferred her food overdone, including steaks. Arianna was a medium-rare person. Besides religion, the cooking of food was the one thing on which they disagreed.

Beverly poured a cup of coffee from the pot Arianna had made, plopped down in the other chair at the table, and smeared precious butter on her blackened toast. Butter, unobtainable on the local economy, she had purchased at the Balgat base Air Force Exchange, better known as the AFEX. Finally, she spooned rose petal preserves on the toast. She had found the preserves—which both women adored—at a Turkish shop in the next block.

"What you mentioned last night just registered," she commented. "It isn't so much what you said, it's how you said it. In all the years we've been friends, I always thought you were full-blooded Greek. When you say you are half Armenian, you sound ashamed." Beverly's eyebrows lifted. "Are you? Why?"

Arianna's eyes looked as if translucent shades had dropped over them. She shook her head. "Of course not, I'm proud of my heritage. I've never really disclaimed it, only . . ." She stopped.

Beverly tasted her coffee. "Ouch! That's hot!" She took a tentative sip, then asked, "Why the big secret, then?"

Arianna chewed her lip. "When I was a child, my grandmother Ylenah told such horrible stories about how badly the Turks treated her family, I was afraid to reveal to anyone I was part Armenian."

"Are you still afraid?"

"Simply wary. I just feel it prudent not to advertise my background, especially while in Turkey—sort of like the Jews who escaped pogroms in different countries, you know? They changed their names and histories to protect themselves against further persecution."

"When did your grandparents immigrate to the States?" Beverly asked. "The Armenian persecution was a long time ago."

Arianna rose and began to pace. "My grandmother and mother left Turkey in the twenties. I never knew my grandfather. The Turks conscripted him to work on the railroad, and he died in a tunnel cave-in."

"Are you acquainted with other Armenians who were born in Turkey?"

"Of course. Fresno is an Armenian enclave. We even have our own restaurants and churches."

"Really? I've never been there," Beverly exclaimed, intrigued.

"My second cousin lives in Fresno. During World War I, she was eight when she and her mother walked across eastern Turkey and part of what is now Syria. The Turks had burned their village and killed the men and older boys. After raping the women, they sent them *and* the children into the countryside with nothing but their lives and the clothes they wore."

"How awful!"

Arianna shrugged. "It's a centuries-old story involving politics and treachery. I believe it began in early Byzantium. Another case portraying man's inhumanity to man. The Armenian massacres have been called 'attempted genocide.'"

"It's a piece of history I know nothing about," Beverly admitted.

"Few in our generation do, yet the massacres spanned more than two decades. One has to remember, however, that the Armenians killed, too. In fact, it was an Armenian who led the Russian army when it overran Turkish Armenia. Armenians died fighting on both sides in the conflict."

"It's quite a story. Now—under the circumstances—I think I understand your wish to keep your family history quiet. I don't think it's necessary, though."

"Maybe not." Arianna threw back her head, closed her eyes,

and sighed. "I used to dream these horrible nightmares in which a giant Turk chased me. He wore a red turban and carried a huge, bloodstained scimitar. I'd have the same nightmare whenever my mother and grandmother got on the subject of the massacres . . . usually during dinner or right before my bedtime. But I don't have the nightmares anymore. Though it was hard to come to Turkey the first time, I thoroughly enjoyed that summer working on the Ephesus dig. I no longer feared the Turks; and Halime, my Turkish counterpart, and I became good friends. We wrote until we lost contact. The address I have for her is in Istanbul, but my last letter came back. I'd like you to meet her."

Beverly shot Arianna a sly glance. "Did you ever tell Halime you're Greek and Armenian?"

Arianna winced. "No."

"Well, I'd love to meet her," Beverly mumbled through a mouthful of toast.

"I'll try to find her next month after I'm settled. It's true, Bev, my return to Turkey *is* partially due to your persistence. The letters describing your trips throughout Asia Minor were fascinating. Then, when I read the article on Cappadocia you sent me, I had to come."

While Arianna talked, Beverly rinsed the dishes. Drying her hands, she said smugly, "I knew if I recounted my trips to all those ancient archaeological sites, you couldn't resist coming."

"How could I resist? Turkey is an antiquity treasure house. By the way, are you aware of any new excavations, other than the Hittite digs?"

"I've heard there's something going on in Tarsus," Beverly commented. Still talking, she went into the bedroom. "There's an item in this month's USAID (the United States Agency for International Development) publication that might interest you. An underground city was recently discovered in Cappadocia, near Niğde."

"Cappadocia is where I want to go. I'll let Dr. Yaldiz know today," Arianna said. "Did I tell you he accused me of being another 'idealistic American girl who wanted to retrace the disgraceful crusades'? Those were his exact words. When he said it, I lost my temper and left."

"Oh, Arianna, you didn't explode again!"

"I did; I was an idiot. Dr. Yaldiz is one of the world's foremost archaeologists, and I bet I've made a rotten impression on him. He'll never put me on a team." Apparently realizing she had jeopardized her future in Turkey, Arianna struggled to control tears.

If Arianna knew Jesus and had the Holy Spirit's help, Beverly thought, *she could control her temper.* Aloud, she said, "Arianna, you can't just keep blowing your cool."

"I know. My stupid tantrum attracted the attention of everybody in the place, including a blond god-type sitting at the next table. They probably thought me the typical ugly American. I'm so embarrassed when I think about it."

Beverly reappeared, dabbing a cosmetic brush at her nose. "Well, you can't undo it. What did Dr. Yaldiz think of your résumé?"

"I didn't show it to him."

Arianna had expected to impress Dr. Yaldiz with her *curriculum vitae* that listed her wide experience at northern and southwestern American Indian sites. The résumé, impressive for someone her age, included not only her work in Ephesus with the University of Pennsylvania but also a summer in Italy on an Etruscan dig.

To rationalize her bad behavior, she wanted to believe Dr. Yaldiz had deliberately intimidated her. After all, he was prominent enough to deserve mention in *National Geographic* and several archaeological periodicals. She was a mere nobody. Yes, she was angry with Dr. Yaldiz; but she was even angrier at herself.

Beverly glanced at the wall clock and flinched. "I have to leave or I'll be late to school. This time, give Dr. Yaldiz your résumé. Tell him archaeology and Asia Minor's ancient history is more than a casual diversion for you." Leaning close to Arianna, Beverly purred, "But you'd better apologize first."

"I'll beg him to give me a job, even if I have to get on my knees."

"Good!"

Arianna's face twisted. "Still, I'm sure Dr. Yaldiz knows I'm Armenian. I've been told my Armenian grandmother looked like my twin when she was my age."

"Aw, stow it, Arianna," Beverly snorted. "Your name is Greek and there's nothing in your appearance to distinguish you from any other American. For that matter, with your dark-brown eyes and hair, you could be Turkish. Even your spectacular California tan blends in. Besides, if Dr. Yaldiz is as respected and professional as you say he is, he should be able to disregard inherent social prejudices."

Arianna had to laugh. "That was a schoolteacher's lecture if I ever heard one, Bev. But, yes, one would hope that a man of Dr. Yaldiz's stature would be above racism." She rose, stacking her dishes. "Guess I'm suffering from self-pity and, maybe, a bit of culture shock. This past week of fighting public officials has gotten to me."

Beverly grabbed the string bag filled with school materials she had stashed near the hall door. "Time to catch the *Big Blue*, the Air Force bus, to Balgat. See ya tonight." She blew a kiss to Arianna and bolted out the door.

As Arianna fastened the security chain, the Air Force bus, carrying Beverly, pulled away. Having eaten the bowl of bland boxed cereal with reconstituted milk, she craved something tangy. Returning to the kitchen, she explored the old refrigerator's interior. It contained no fresh fruit, so she chose an icy Frukos. Halime had introduced her to the lemon-lime soda in Ephesus.

Arianna carried the Frukos and her bulging briefcase to the little alcove off the kitchen that served as a work area. She set the juice and briefcase on Beverly's desk and examined the tiny apartment. Beverly had furnished it mostly with things she had purchased in Turkish shops, the refrigerator and stove being the exceptions. She had bought those from an Army couple leaving Turkey. She had also made end and coffee tables from brass trays set on concrete blocks. Well-polished brass and copper pots, each containing lush foliage, complemented Beverly's collection of delicate antique lace, which she had framed and hung.

I need a file cabinet to hold the paperwork I'm accumulating, but where would we put anything else? Arianna thought. The three-room apartment was comfortable for a single person, but too small to accommodate two. Beverly had squeezed the cot into her bedroom; otherwise, Arianna would have had to sleep on an aged and very lumpy couch.

Getting down to business, Arianna went over what she had accomplished since her arrival. She could not give the Turkish officials an excuse to send her home. Though she would do whatever was necessary to stay in Turkey, she felt she was far too valuable and experienced as an archaeologist to do clerical work for long. Field archaeology was her primary love. Somehow, some way, Dr. Yaldiz must be persuaded to hire her.

Chapter 44

Dr. Yaldiz's office lay hidden within the old downtown complex that contained Ankara's Ethnological and Archaeological Museums. When Arianna had been there earlier in the week, she had neither the time nor the desire to study the displays the museums held. Nor did she stop to examine them today. The complex near the train station had not been difficult to locate. Pinpointing Dr. Yaldiz was a different matter.

When she was a child, Arianna's grandmother, aunt, and mother had conversed in a mixture of Armenian and Turkish when they didn't want her to know what was being said. Nevertheless, she had picked up an extensive working vocabulary by the age of five, and her knowledge of spoken Turkish had markedly increased during her summer in Ephesus. However, as she had practically no experience with the written language, the museum directional signs were beyond her comprehension.

Members of the museum staff were eager to answer questions and to offer help, but Arianna's limited Turkish—tainted with Armenian, eastern provincial Turkish, and American accents—confused them.

Once Arianna was misdirected to a staff tea room. Expecting to see Dr. Yaldiz at last, she flung open the door and swept into the room. Five men, tea glasses frozen in various positions on the way to or from their mouths, stared at her. She hurriedly left after a flustered apology.

When she finally found Dr. Yaldiz's office in an annex off the ancient *caravanserai* that housed the modern Archaeological Museum, the door was locked.

Though she dreaded facing the great Dr. Yaldiz again, she knew it was necessary. This time, she was determined to give him her résumé and letters of recommendation first; she had to convince him he was not dealing with an emotional ding-a-ling.

I guess I want more than anything to work for him, she thought. *If he doesn't want me, I won't be choosy; I'll accept a place on any team that will have me.* She considered that for a moment, then spoke aloud to herself, "Any team in Cappadocia, that is."

* * *

Today, sure of her way, Arianna breezed past the kiosk that guarded the hallway to the museum annex.

"*Efendim!*"

Arianna ignored the guard's cry.

"*Efendim! Dur lütfen!*"

At the guard's polite but firm command to wait, Arianna swung around. Last time the kiosk had been vacant, and she had passed unchallenged.

"The person you wish to see?" the guard asked.

"I want to see Doctor Yaldiz."

"Doktor Yaldiz? A moment, please." The guard called, and a boy of about nine scurried from behind a tall exhibit case. As the lad stared up at Arianna, the guard grabbed his shoulder and gave him terse instructions in rapid Turkish.

His chest swelling visibly, the grinning youngster said in perfect English, "Madam will come with Abdulah." He beckoned to Arianna and danced down the hall. Grinning also, Arianna followed him.

The boy wore a tattered but clean T-shirt and patched black pants. He walked pigeon-toed, slapping the floor in sandals far too large for him. To keep the sandals on, his grimy toes clenched the tips. The child's hair was shorn to a mere quarter inch in length. His flattened skull showed that his peasant mother had bound him to a board when he was a baby.

Abdulah led Arianna along a dimly lit corridor that reeked of Turkish tobacco and the moldering detritus of age. The massive stone blocks in the corridor's walls and floor had been hand-cut and laid centuries ago. Jagged bands of dull light crept around ill-fitting doors. Twice they passed enigmatic rooms where light glowed through dusty transoms and projected distorted rectangles on the corridor's high ceiling.

This time, Dr. Yaldiz's door was open. Abdulah stepped aside, bowing with sober dignity. Arianna thanked him and entered the tiny reception room. The door to an inner office was also open, and she saw Dr. Yaldiz sitting at an enormous desk.

Smiling, Galip Yaldiz looked up from the paper he was reading. "Miss Arista, I am glad you are here." Indicating a battered, leather-padded chair in front of his desk, he spoke in unaccented British English. "Do sit, please." When Arianna had settled into the chair, he said, "I believe you have documents for me to see."

"I have a résumé and letters of recommendation." Arianna took the papers out of her briefcase and handed them to him. While she silently waited, Dr. Yaldiz leaned back in his chair to read. As he rapidly scanned the documents, unfathomable changes of expression swept across his face. Occasionally, he lifted his head and contemplated her through his thick, horn-rimmed glasses.

Although the scrutiny made her a bit uncomfortable, Arianna was more at ease than she had been at the tea garden. She covertly studied the archaeologist and his workplace. The starkness of the room surprised her; she did not think an office belonging to such a busy man could be so completely free of clutter. Her professors back home occupied faculty offices that resembled junk shops: tables and desks piled with artifacts; stacks of papers interspersed with the remains of lunches and half-emptied cups of coffee; and bookcases jammed with musty tomes, research materials, and everything else from dusty skulls to plant and animal fossils.

In contrast, Dr. Yaldiz's desk, large enough to seat six people, was nearly bare. It held a malachite writing set, a desk calendar, a copper ashtray full of stale cigarette butts, and an elegantly carved section of a small Corinthian capital. *A paperless paperweight?* Arianna wondered.

A framed photograph and the paper Dr. Yaldiz had been reading were the only other objects on the polished surface.

The desk sat between two ceiling-to-floor windows hung with plain beige drapes, called curtains in Turkey. They were open, exposing the ancient disintegrating brickwork of a neighboring building. The customary stern-faced photograph of Attatürk mounted on a large black felt panel was precisely centered behind the desk. A pedestal supporting a black bust of the hero stood in a corner. The single splash of color in the otherwise drab office was a beautiful antique Kelim carpet.

Arianna noticed that Dr. Yaldiz's hair and ample moustache were silver rather than gray. Deep lines radiated from the corners of his eyes, and he had the hint of a dimple in his left cheek—signs of a person who laughed a lot. She now saw that the "sneer" she had so scornfully described to Beverly was actually caused by a scar on his upper lip, half hidden by his moustache.

Flies buzzed around the room, intermittently ticking against the speckled windows. Dr. Yaldiz pulled a crumpled package from his pocket and offered her a Turkish cigarette. When she refused, he extracted one and lit it. The strong smoke threatened to make Arianna's already nervous stomach worse.

After twenty minutes, the archaeologist meticulously stacked Arianna's papers in a neat pile on his desk. He rose, walked over to a door to Arianna's right, and opened it, the hinges shrieking and scraping. He called in Turkish to someone beyond Arianna's view. Leaving the door open, Yaldiz returned to his chair.

A pretty Turkish woman sailed through the doorway. When she saw Arianna, she stopped dead, nearly losing the armload of books she carried.

"Arianna!"

Arianna bounced up and ran to the astonished woman. "Halime Ortman, I can't believe it! What on earth are you doing here? I thought you were in Istanbul."

They hugged and kissed on both cheeks. Almost in tears, Arianna tried to rub a lipstick imprint off Halime's cheek. Suddenly she remembered where she was. Fearing she had goofed again, she drew away from Halime and cautiously peeked at Dr. Yaldiz.

The archaeologist's eyes twinkled and the corners of his mouth twitched. Halime had often spoken of her friend Arianna to Galip, who was like a father to her. When Arianna first approached him, he had recognized her name. His feigned attitude had merely been a cover for the anticipation he felt—the anticipation of personally arranging a reunion between the two young women. He was pleased his plan had worked so well.

"Is Arianna going to come with us, Dr. Yaldiz?" Turning to Arianna, Halime cried, *"Are* you?"

Arianna looked at Galip. "That is exactly why I am in Turkey, Dr. Yaldiz. I hope to dig in Cappadocia."

Before Galip could respond, Halime said, "Arianna is the one you have sought—she is an expert in potsherd archaeology."

Delighted, Galip chuckled. "Yes, Halime *bayan,* I know of your friend, Miss Arista. She comes highly recommended."

Arianna held her breath.

"Halime will tell you about the team I am forming," Galip began. "It will be working at a site in the vicinity of Göreme. We are missing a potsherd expert, and it would please me," he glanced at Halime, "if you would join us."

As the two friends joyfully hugged, Galip checked his watch. "I am sure you ladies have much to discuss, and I have a meeting to attend." He extended a hand to Arianna. "I will see you tomorrow morning at ten o'clock. We can complete the necessary arrangements then."

A dazed and wordless Arianna shyly, but gratefully, shook Galip's hand. How could she have thought ill of this sweet man?

When the door closed after Dr. Yaldiz, Halime and Arianna compared notes. After returning to the States, Arianna had embarked on course work toward her Ph.D. at Berkeley. She sent Halime her new address. Meanwhile, Halime had become an assistant to Dr. Yaldiz and moved from Istanbul to Ankara. They had lost track of one another when the Istanbul post office neglected to forward Arianna's last letter, containing her change of address, to Ankara.

"Come with me to eat the midday meal," Halime suggested. "I usually go to a restaurant that has the best *donar kebap* in Ankara. It is on Attatürk Boulevard."

"You don't have to ask twice, Halime. You remember how I love *donar kebap*. It *is* my favorite Turkish dish; I've really missed it."

Halime locked the inner office door and the exuberant friends, arm-in-arm, dashed into the corridor.

CHAPTER 45

In his search for information on archaeological sites currently active in Turkey, Morgan first went to the United States Embassy. There, he was told that the embassy official who might help him was on vacation in southern Turkey. He was advised to try at TAA, the Turkish-American Association.

Morgan climbed the steps of the unimposing building on Attatürk Boulevard that housed TAA. The minute he entered the lobby, a delicious medley of spicy aromas assailed his nostrils. He had eaten a hearty breakfast at the hotel and was not yet hungry again, but out of curiosity he checked the menu posted next to the TAA restaurant entrance. The prices were more reasonable than any he had seen thus far, and he mentally filed the fact for future reference.

Behind a counter to the right of the main door, an attractive woman in her twenties clacked on an ancient Underwood. She had seen Morgan enter, but when he headed toward the restaurant, she continued to type, her eyes on her work.

Morgan strode to the counter. "Hi!"

The woman started, exclaiming something in Turkish. Her fingers fluttered for a moment over the keyboard before she looked up. *"Efendim?"*

Morgan flashed her his best smile in return. "Excuse me, please; is there anyone here who has information on current archaeological digs?"

She gave him a blank stare. "Pardon, I do not speak good English."

Morgan almost laughed aloud, marveling that the receptionist at the Turkish-American Association didn't know English. When the woman realized they could not communicate, she came from behind the counter, led Morgan outside, and pointed to the building which housed the offices of USAID.

He had more success at USAID. Encountering a man who

happened to be descending the entrance steps, Morgan asked, "Can you tell me where I can obtain information on active archaeological digs in Turkey?"

"I can't help you, myself," said the man, "but I know someone who can. You need to see Dr. Galip Yaldiz."

Morgan took out a notebook and pen. "Where can I locate him?"

The man turned and headed back toward the USAID entrance. He held open the door, saying, "Come up to my office. Dr. Yaldiz is hard to find. I can show you on a map of Ankara better than I can tell you." As they climbed the stairs of the building, the USAID official asked, "Are you new to Turkey?"

"I was here years ago." Morgan did not mention his tour as a Marine attached to the U.S. Embassy.

The man thrust forth a hand. "By the way, I'm Robert Keller. And you are . . . ?"

Morgan met the man's firm handclasp. "Morgan McCauley. I'm trying to find a position on an archaeological team—I'd appreciate any lead."

Keller shook his head. "It may be difficult getting on a team . . . when you're already in the country, I mean. However, if anybody can help you, it's Galip Yaldiz. He's the head honcho in Turkish archaeology."

Thanks to the map drawn by Robert Keller, Morgan easily found Dr. Yaldiz's office. He had just turned to enter the office door when Arianna and Halime crashed into him.

Morgan's breath whooshed from his lungs. As he stumbled backward, he automatically wrapped his arms around both young women, partially to keep his balance and partially to keep them all from falling.

Arianna's briefcase flew from her hand as she slammed into Morgan. Her recovery was immediate, and she backed quickly away. It was then that she recognized the man she had seen at the tea garden. "Why don't you watch where you're going?" she snapped. Standing on one leg, she rubbed the ankle of the other.

Unlike Arianna, Halime did not escape with a mere bruised

ankle. Her head had rammed into Morgan's rib cage. When her jaws snapped shut at the impact, her upper front teeth had pierced her bottom lip. Now she bent over, moaning, her hands covering her mouth. Blood oozed from between her fingers and dripped on the floor.

"Oh Halime, you're bleeding," Arianna cried. "Look what you did!" she shouted at Morgan.

"Hey, I'm really sorry," Morgan stammered. He removed a clean handkerchief from his pocket and offered it to Halime. "I didn't see you coming."

Halime gratefully accepted Morgan's handkerchief and pressed it to her face. Tears streaked her mascara.

"Let me look at that." Morgan stooped and carefully lifted the bloody handkerchief. To his dismay, he noted two crescent-shaped incisions in Halime's lip, and the lip had already begun to swell.

"Halime, do you know where there is a first-aid kit?" Arianna asked. Halime shakily indicated Dr. Yaldiz's inner office. She tried to walk, but her legs wobbled and she lurched against the door frame. Morgan and Arianna each grabbed an arm to support her.

"Don't just stand there; *do* something. Help me get her into the office," Arianna growled at Morgan.

Morgan recognized Arianna as the shrewish female from the tea garden. His jaw muscle bulged and twitched, and a sarcastic retort came to mind. Controlling an urge to lash out at Arianna, he gently grasped Halime's elbow and guided her to a chair in the reception room.

Arianna stood, hands on hips, scrutinizing the room. "Where's the first-aid kit?"

With her free hand, Halime took a key from her purse and gave it to Arianna, who unlocked the inner office door so they could enter. Motioning to another door, Halime fell into one of the chairs by Galip's desk. Opening the door, Arianna discovered a space no larger than a walk-in closet. If Dr. Yaldiz's office exhibited ultimate order, this dark closet represented its antithesis.

"Halime, I can't see anything in here." Arianna called. "Where's the kit?"

Halime lisped, "It is in the cabinet on the left."

Arianna noisily rummaged in the cluttered cabinet and finally emerged carrying a small, military-green box. Pushing Morgan aside, she opened the box to reveal dingy cotton, a yellowed roll of gauze, and a roll of adhesive tape. There were no plastic bandages. The kit did contain a nearly empty bottle of denatured alcohol.

Arianna saturated a piece of cotton. "I think it would hurt less if you applied the alcohol yourself." When Halime nodded, Arianna gave her the cotton.

While Halime dabbed tentatively at her lip, Arianna formed a crude bandage from the gauze and tape. "This isn't a sterile compress, but it should stop the bleeding." She handed Halime a wad of cotton encased in gauze. "Hold it in place."

His collision with the two lovely young women had momentarily put Morgan off guard. His reluctance to ignore Arianna's rudeness was out of character; it was his habit to take control of a situation. *It's time I did so,* he decided. He squatted down in front of Halime. "We had better get you to a doctor."

Halime's face was visibly puffing beneath the bandage. Though the bleeding had slowed, it threatened to saturate Arianna's compress.

"It is all right," came Halime's muffled croak.

Morgan straightened. "She should see a doctor," he flatly stated to Arianna.

"I'm with you there," Arianna agreed. She asked Halime, "Is there a doctor within walking distance?"

Halime nodded, and Morgan helped her to her feet. "I'll take you to him," he said.

Scowling at Morgan, Arianna took Halime's other arm. "*We* will take you to the doctor," she hissed.

CHAPTER 46

Following Halime's directions, the tall American and the two women slowly walked the block to the Turkish doctor's office.

Morgan and Arianna waited while the doctor examined Halime's lip in the reception room. Neither of them understood the doctor's rapid Turkish. Through it all, Halime struggled to translate unfamiliar terminology. "The doctor says I have to have a . . . thread . . . he must sew . . . you know?"

"Uh-huh," Morgan said, nodding. "I thought it might require stitches."

After Halime was taken away for surgery, Morgan and Arianna sat across from each other on the waiting room's hard benches. The silence thickened by the minute. Arianna studied a Turkish periodical; Morgan unabashedly studied Arianna.

Morgan's curiosity finally got the best of him.

"Where's your home?"

"California."

Morgan grinned. "Ah, I should have known you were a California girl. You've got that California aura about you. I should know; I was born in Bakersfield, the city people drive through as fast as possible."

He saw that he had aroused Arianna's interest.

"Oh? I'm from Fresno." The whisper of a smile flitted across her face. "The tourists go through *there* pretty fast, too."

"You have a slight accent; I can't quite classify it." He must have said the wrong thing, because she frowned and refocused on the magazine in her lap.

Morgan tried again. "I didn't mean to be nosy. I guessed you were from the States, but I couldn't pin down the area."

He sounded so contrite that Arianna looked up—straight into his spectacular lavender-blue eyes. A thrill coursed her body. *What eyes! He's the handsomest man I've ever seen.*

"It's all right," she said in a small voice. "I guess all this, coming on top of a week of futility, made me lose my cool."

"How long have you been in Turkey?"

"A little over two weeks."

Morgan suddenly realized that Arianna was experiencing the frustration and fatigue of the first month of settling in a foreign country. "That certainly explains it," he said.

Confused, Arianna asked, "Explains what?"

"It's not important," he said. *It explains your rotten attitude,* he thought. He selected a fat book from the table and apathetically flipped the pages. It was in Turkish, and there were no pictures to give him a clue to the book's contents. He dropped it on the table and leaned back. Pretending to doze, he watched Arianna under half-closed lids.

Arianna knew Morgan was not asleep. She darted furtive glances at him. He did not seem to be in the American military—his hair was too long. Nor did he look like an archaeologist, if there was such a thing as a stereotypical archaeologist. What had he wanted at Dr. Yaldiz's office anyway? She had to admit that this strong, yet gentle and astonishingly attractive man intrigued her.

When Halime reappeared on the arm of the doctor, Morgan and Arianna jumped to their feet. A neat dressing covered Halime's wound, and her eyes sparkled with humor as well as pain. "I think we will lunch another day," she mumbled to Arianna. A fragile smile curved the side of her mouth that was not anesthetized and bandaged.

Arianna carefully hugged her. "It's a date, Halime. I'll have the doctor call a taxi and make sure you get home."

Halime raised a hand in protest. "The doctor called for a taxi. I will be fine."

Arianna insisted, "I'll go home with you."

Halime knew Arianna well enough from when they had worked together in Ephesus not to argue when Arianna made up her mind to do something. Her shoulders rose in an assenting shrug. "I would like that."

Morgan felt he had been relegated to the back burner. *Deservedly so,* he mused. But before he wasted time meeting with Dr. Yaldiz, he needed to ask Halime a question. He followed the two women to the street.

"Miss Halime, is Dr. Yaldiz conducting any digs in Turkey this year?"

Halime began to speak, but Arianna hushed her and answered for her. "It's Miss Ortman, Halime Ortman. And the answer to your question is yes. There is one starting in Cappadocia."

Exhilarated because of Arianna's confirmation of a new excavation, Morgan grinned and performed a brief mocking bow. "Thank you for telling me, Miss Fresno. Maybe I'll see you there."

"Maybe. Maybe not."

Later, eating a lonely lunch, Arianna mulled over the morning's events. The image of Morgan's deeply tanned face haunted her—those wonderful cobalt eyes, framed by heavy dark brows; his unruly hair, the color of sun-bleached oats. It suddenly occurred to her that she hadn't even learned his name.

CHAPTER 47

Later that day Arianna left Halime at her door, then she took the taxi on to the school at Balgat Air Base. Beverly had a faculty meeting after school and would not be leaving the base until the meeting was over. Arianna could not wait until Bev arrived home to tell her the good news about her reunion with Halime.

After paying the taxi driver, Arianna walked across the school parking lot to Beverly's car. Laying her briefcase on the hood, she leaned against the fender and scanned the parking lot. There was only one other car, in which a young woman sat behind the wheel reading.

When Beverly still hadn't come out after half an hour, Arianna walked over to the other car. The woman saw her coming and rolled down her window.

"Is the faculty meeting over?" Arianna asked.

"It ended some time ago. I brought my son back to the school for a conference with his teacher, Miss Smith." She peered at her watch in the waning light. "His conference should be over any minute."

"Thanks, I'm waiting for Miss Smith myself. I'm going inside, though; the wind is becoming chilly."

Smiling, the woman reached across the seat and unlocked her passenger door. "If you wish, you can wait in my car."

"Thanks, but I'm new to Ankara. I haven't been in the school yet, and I'd like to see it. What number is Miss Smith's room?"

"Room eleven."

"Thanks again. Bye."

Arianna found her way in the darkened building to Beverly's classroom. She peeked through the glass at the top of the door. Beverly was talking with a chubby, curly-haired boy. Not wanting to interrupt the counseling session, Arianna stayed outside the door and watched the interaction between teacher and student.

Beverly sat on a student desk holding her grade book on her lap. The boy sat at a desk across the aisle. Despite the closed door, Arianna clearly heard what they said.

"Something has been bothering you, Richie, and it has affected your work. Can you tell me what it is?" Beverly cocked her head and patiently waited for an answer.

Richie squirmed in his seat, defiantly looking out the window. "Nuthin's botherin' me."

"If you don't have a problem, then why have your grades dropped?" Beverly scanned the grade book. "You've neglected every subject except art."

"I-I-I like art, Miss Smith," Richie stuttered. "I don't care about any of that other garbage."

"You're really a good drawer and painter. Would you believe me, Richie, if I told you bits of the 'other garbage' will help you the rest of your life, even if you become a professional architect or artist?"

The child squirmed in the seat, his left foot swinging in small arcs. "Fractions won't help me draw."

"Oh? Tell me, how do you find a point two-thirds of the way across a sheet of drawing paper without using a ruler?"

Richie dropped his eyes. "I'd just guess."

Beverly nodded. "Perhaps you *could* guess. Let me ask you a harder question, then. What if a man wants to cut a door in a wall of his house and he hires you to draw the plans? The door has to be exactly two-thirds of the distance from one corner of the wall to the opposite corner."

"I'd measure it; I'd find out how many feet it was."

"You still have to figure two-thirds of the total wall length."

"I wouldn't do it," Richie declared.

"Then you wouldn't be paid."

Richie twisted around and hung over the back of his seat. "I don't care if I don't get paid, I just want to draw."

Beverly hid a smile behind her hand. "How do you get the nice clothes you wear, Richie?"

He looked down at the front of his colorful new sweater.

Stretching it out for Beverly to see the design of stylized rein-deer marching across its front, he said, "My dad bought this for me."

"I doubt you would have such a beautiful sweater if your dad didn't get paid."

"My dad's in the Air Force."

Beverly got up and gently guided Richie toward the door. "And isn't your dad paid by the United States government for whatever he does?"

"Yes."

"Well, ask him if he ever uses any of the 'garbage' he learned in school."

The boy suddenly stopped and looked up at her. "How *do* you find two-thirds of the way across a piece of paper?"

She patted Richie on the head and gently prodded him out the door. "I'll tell you tomorrow. Meanwhile, study those fractions. Promise?"

"I guess." Richie barely glanced at Arianna as he dashed past.

Arianna and Beverly watched the boy scamper down the hall. "You have a real knack with kids, Bev," Arianna said. Beverly pulled Arianna into the classroom and closed the door. "He's a bright boy, but all he wants to do is draw—in his notebook, in the textbooks, on his desk, on everything. He'll come along, if I can just redirect that enthusiasm to include the basics." She went to her desk and gathered up papers she had to correct that night. "What are you doing here, anyway?"

Arianna sat on the corner of a desk. "I have great news. Let's go to dinner somewhere, and I'll tell you. I'll buy."

"You're on. I'm starving for fresh, crisp lettuce, and a glass of ice-cold, honest-to-goodness milk. I hate the reconstituted stuff we get at the AFEX. The noncommissioned officer's club has a better cook and the best food, but I'm not a member there; we'll have to go to the officer's club."

Beverly parked her compact sedan in front of the United States Officers' Club on Cankaya Hill. It was Arianna's first visit to the club. The place wasn't large but the dining room had a fair-sized dance floor. As they entered, she heard the din of slot machines.

Arianna ordered roast chicken and pilaf from the copious menu. Beverly decided, "I'll have the pork chops with a green salad and baked potato." When the Turkish waiter left, Beverly turned to Arianna. "The officers' club rarely has pork chops. Here and the NCO Club are the only places where you'll find pork of any kind. Sometimes I have a terrible craving for it."

Arianna leaned forward. "I saw Halime today."

Beverly reared back in surprise. "No kidding! I thought you said she was in Istanbul."

"I did; that's what I believed." Arianna related the events at Dr. Yaldiz's office.

"Do you think you'll be working with Halime again?" Beverly asked.

"Could be—I sure hope so. Halime is Dr. Yaldiz's assistant. I might work with her, *if* I'm hired, and *if* he sends both of us to the same place."

They ate in silence until Beverly asked, "In what part of Turkey was Halime born?"

"I've never told you her story, have I? She was born right here in Ankara. She's the direct descendant of a concubine."

"Really?"

"Yes, but kind of keep it to yourself. Halime doesn't really mind people knowing; she just doesn't want it to be the subject of crass discussion."

"My lips are sealed," Beverly promised.

"Halime can trace her ancestry to Bulgaria, where the Ottoman Turks ruled five hundred years after their conquest in 1393. In 1876 the Ottomans abducted Halime's great-great-grandmother from her Christian parents when she was still a child. They took her to Istanbul and the harem of Sultan Abdul Aziz."

"Didn't Abdul Hamid II have the throne in 1876?" Beverly interjected.

"True. However, two other men ruled the same year. Abdul

Aziz was the first. He was deposed in May. Murad V, who immediately succeeded Aziz, was himself deposed in August. Abdul Hamid II succeeded *him*." Arianna laughed. "It was a rough year for sultans."

"It was a great era," Beverly, the history buff, said. "The Ottomans proclaimed a new constitution; Renoir painted *Le Moulin de la Galette* . . ."

". . . and Schliemann excavated Mycenae," Arianna, the archaeologist, finished. "Probably the most significant event—one which changed the world—was Alexander Graham Bell's invention of the telephone. Anyway," Arianna continued, "Halime said her great-great-grandmother became a favorite of Sultan Abdul Hamid II. At seventeen, she had a son by him. Six years later, at twenty-three, she had a daughter, Halime's great-grandmother.

"At first Halime's great-great-grandmother successfully evaded the rivalries and intrigues of the harem. However, her son, a prince and heir to the throne, was the target of harem jealousy. Because of it, she continually had to guard against his and her assassination. A mother with a son on the throne wielded almost as much power as the son."

Beverly interrupted Arianna's narrative. "We have to leave. It's getting late and I have to be at school at seven in the morning."

At their apartment, the two friends donned pajamas and robes, then flopped into chairs with their feet propped on ottomans. Beverly had been enthralled by Halime's biography, and she forgot about correcting papers and getting up early. She begged Arianna to tell her more of Halime's fascinating story.

"I want to hear more."

Arianna complied. "Her great-great-grandmother's precautions were in vain; the prince was strangled in his sleep when he was ten. The sultan's reaction to the loss of his favorite's son was to condemn to death a half dozen women who were suspected of fomenting the murder. He had the women tied into sacks weighted with stones, then had them tossed into the Bosporus."

Beverly shuddered. "The waterfront terrace at the Seraglio Palace is said to be where women who lost favor with the sultans were drowned."

Arianna yawned and stretched. "Uh-huh, but that method of execution did not originate with Sultan Abdul Ahmed II. It had often occurred in past regimes when the reigning sultan grew too old to control his harem." She laughed. "The *good* ol' days."

"It's good those days have ended." Beverly cleared her throat. "I'm awfully dry. Want to split a Frukos?"

"Sure." Arianna stretched and yawned. "I'm beat. After I drink it, I'm going to bed."

Beverly's loud protest sounded from the kitchen. "Not before you tell me the story's ending." She re-entered the parlor carrying two glasses. She handed one to Arianna. "So what happened to the great-great-grandmother and her daughter, Halime's great-grandmother?"

Arianna took a long sip of the refreshing drink. "Sultan Hamid assured the two women they could live out their lives in their own compartments within the harem. He gave the great-great-grandmother authority over the harem, a position she held until she died. Halime's great-grandmother stayed in the harem until the last sultan, Mohammad VI, deserted Istanbul and went into exile."

"What happened to them then?"

"At the collapse of the Ottoman Empire and the abolishment of harems, the sultan's wives and concubines scattered. Halime said some drifted to their native lands and others fled to Paris, London, or the United States. Several remained in Turkey. Accompanied by an elderly eunuch servant, Halime's great-grandmother went to a Black Sea village where the eunuch's cousin had a home. She had managed to save a few jewels she inherited from her mother; she lived modestly for a year while the eunuch sold the jewelry for her piece by piece.

When the eunuch suddenly died, she was left alone and unprotected for the first time in her life. She found a mentor in a kindly Turkish merchant whose wife had died the previous year.

"The merchant eventually asked her to marry him. She had exhausted her cache of jewels and, rather than starve, she accepted his proposal. Halime's grandmother, Aydogan, was born the following year.

"At eighteen, Aydogan married Halime's grandfather, an Istanbul attorney who had come to the village to investigate a property dispute. The newlyweds moved to Ankara and had Halime's mother. Like Attatürk, Halime's grandfather was a progressive man who believed in equality for women. Halime's grandmother is still alive. She must be about seventy-nine now.

"Has Halime known Dr. Yaldiz long?"

"Since she was a toddler. Her grandfather was a close friend of Dr. Yaldiz. It was Dr. Yaldiz who talked Halime's grandfather into sending her to England for a graduate degree after she finished at Istanbul University. Halime also worked as a translator for the British Museum. That's why she speaks fluent English."

Beverly sighed. "What a romantic story."

"Halime doesn't think so."

Beverly got up and headed toward the bedroom. "Is Halime a Moslem?"

Arianna trailed Beverly, turning off the lights. "She comes from a Moslem home, but she rarely talks religion. I do know that she's quite liberated; she wears miniskirts."

"Halime sounds like someone I'd like. When may I meet her, Arianna?"

"I'll see her tomorrow. I'll ask if we can all have dinner when her lip is healed."

"It should be fun. I'm looking forward to it."

CHAPTER 48

Instead of returning to Dr. Yaldiz's office that same afternoon, Morgan decided to go early the following morning. He found Galip alone in his office. The archaeologist had left the inner door open in order to see anyone who came in. Morgan hesitated on the threshold.

When Galip saw Morgan, he stood to welcome him. At six feet, Yaldiz was taller than most Turks. "Come in," he said in his own language. "May I help you?"

"My name is Morgan McCauley," Morgan replied in English. "I'm trying to find a Dr. Galip Yaldiz. The people at USAID referred me to him."

After leaving the Turkish Army, Galip had earned his Ph.D. at the University of Pennsylvania. Like Halime, he spoke excellent English, only with an American accent. Scrutinizing Morgan, he said in English, "I am Galip Yaldiz. You are from the United States?"

"I'm from California." It seemed to Morgan that every foreigner he met had heard of and admired California.

Yaldiz smiled. "Ah, yes, a swimming pool in every garden."

Morgan laughed. "Not quite. My family didn't have a pool. I swam at the park plunge." At Dr. Yaldiz's puzzled expression, he added, "A plunge is a large public swimming pool."

"Ah." Galip thrust out a hand. "Please have a seat."

They shook and Morgan took the chair in front of Galip's pristine desk.

"How may I help you, Mr. McCauley?"

Morgan came right to the point. "I want to volunteer for a field team."

"Most of our teams consist of students and amateur volunteers who don't get paid. I am interested to hear about you. Shall we talk over tea?" Galip held his hands out, palms up. "Unfortunately, I don't make tea as well as my assistant, Miss

Ortman." He stared at his wristwatch, commenting half under his breath, "I do not know where she is; she did not return from lunch yesterday."

Morgan groaned. "It may be my fault, sir."

Dr. Yaldiz raised both eyebrows. "Yes? How is that so?"

"I was here yesterday. As I started to enter your outer door, Miss Ortman, and another woman, an American, ran into me. Miss Ortman's head hit my chest pretty hard, and she bit her lip; she had to have stitches." Morgan explained in detail what had happened, ending with, "She went straight home from the doctor's office."

Just then, Dr. Yaldiz's eyes refocused on something beyond Morgan. Morgan swung around as Halime and Arianna entered the office. Halime had removed the cumbersome bandage from her mouth. Her lip was puffed and discolored. The ends of six black threads stuck out where the doctor had stitched the wound. Despite Morgan's genuine remorse, it briefly amused him that the stitches resembled stiff, week-old whiskers grown askew.

Galip jumped from his chair and came around from behind his desk. Bending over Halime, he peered at her damaged lip with fatherly concern. Speaking in English for the benefit of the Americans, he admonished, "Halime, you should not be here today."

"It is only my mouth, Doctor Yaldiz, and I have much to do," Halime lisped. In Turkish, she added, "It is of no consequence—an accident; the man feels very bad."

The archaeologist asked softly, "Do you feel strong enough to make *çay?*"

"*Tabii,* of course," Halime answered and left the room.

Arianna remembered enough Turkish to understand the gist of their conversation. "I'll help," she said, following Halime out the door.

Dr. Yaldiz turned to Morgan with a satisfied smile. "They are as sisters who reunite after many years."

"I'm afraid I spoiled it," Morgan lamented.

"I do not believe so. Do you not see their happiness? Halime is healthy and young; she will heal. Her beauty is not harmed." He smiled and nodded toward the giggles erupting from the other room. "I am sure the ladies have forgiven you."

Morgan did not think Halime was a person who carried a grudge. About Arianna he wasn't sure, nor did it matter. He decided to get right to the point. "Dr. Yaldiz, I'd really like to work in Turkey. Do you have anything going?"

"You are the second American in two days to ask me the same question. Miss Arista was the first."

"Miss Arista?"

"Arianna Arista, Halime's American friend who is in the other room with her." Galip took a crumpled package from his pocket and held it out to Morgan.

"No thanks, I don't smoke."

Galip tapped out a cigarette and lit it. When a cloud of rank smoke swirled around his head, he asked Morgan, "Are you an archaeologist?"

"I'm only an amateur, though I've pursued the field of archaeology all my life. My résumé will show that I dug a summer in Mexico and was in Peru as staff photographer. And I am financially independent," Morgan shrewdly added, inwardly chuckling. An offer of free, skilled labor was what every money-starved team director in the world yearned to hear.

To conceal his interest, Galip gazed at the ceiling and nonchalantly puffed on his cigarette. The fingers of his left hand drummed the desk. He blew out an impressive cloud before he said, "Our teams employ Turkish peasants from the local villages to do the heavy labor; their families depend on their wages." Galip leaned forward across his desk to grind his cigarette in the copper ashtray that was already overflowing with butts and ashes. "Do you have a university degree, Mr. McCauley?"

Morgan handed Galip his packet of papers. "My B.A. degree is in business education, with a major in management and a minor in economics. I switched to archaeology for my master's degree. I've also done graduate work in photography."

"It is an interesting combination, Mr. McCauley. Why did you come to Turkey?"

Morgan struggled to verbalize the sincerity of his love of Turkey without seeming maudlin. "I was in the United States Marines attached to the U.S. Embassy from 1953 to 1955. During my tour, I was intrigued by what I saw of Turkey, and I saw a lot. I like the Turkish people. You might say I consider Turkey my second home."

McCauley's honest reply gratified Galip. While attending the University of Pennsylvania, Galip had been dismayed at the average American's ignorance of world affairs. Few knew any Turkish history, except a little about Alexander the Great and something of the Crusades. Most believed that the crusaders were saints, which they were not. He had also discovered that the male students held highly romanticized ideas regarding sultans and harems. Some of them even prodded him for details of harem life—as if he knew. He soon realized his interrogators had gained most of their "knowledge" from Hollywood films.

"Do you speak any Turkish?" Galip asked Morgan.

"A little; I had to go to language school when I was here before. The longer I'm back in Turkey, the easier it is to communicate."

"That is usually so." The archaeologist thumbed through Morgan's papers, noting that Morgan had spent four years in the Marines. *Maalesef,* unfortunately. Having a military background might hinder Mr. McCauley in obtaining the necessary permits; Turkey was touchy about foreign ex-military. But the team badly needed a photographer.

While Galip read his résumé, Morgan's eyes moved to the photograph on the desk. The shorter man in the photo was fat and swarthy. He recognized the second image as a youthful Galip Yaldiz. So, Yaldiz had been in the Turkish army? Would it help or hurt his own cause?

After fifteen minutes, Galip tucked the papers into a neat pile. His manner revealed nothing conclusive, though he declared, "Tomorrow afternoon I will let you know what I have decided."

Morgan's spirits plummeted; he had hoped for a firm commitment right away. Before he could respond, Halime entered the room carrying a stained teapot, çay glasses, and spoons on a tripod tray. Arianna followed with a bowl of sugar cubes.

Intending to leave, Morgan started to rise from his chair.

Galip stopped him. "Mr. McCauley, please stay and have çay."

Without hesitation, Morgan sat. "Thanks, I'd like to."

Halime placed the tray on a corner of the desk. While she poured tea into the glasses, Arianna passed the spoons and sugar. As Morgan chose two lumps, she stared down at him, saying, "We haven't been properly introduced. I'm Arianna Arista. What do they call you? Mac?"

"Never 'Mac.' Everyone calls me *Morgan!*" he said, deliberately letting Arianna hear a trace of irritation in his voice.

Dr. Yaldiz plopped four cubes of sugar into his tea. As he slowly stirred the viscous liquid, he watched the subtle tension between the two Americans, and wondered if they could work together. He knew the two women could; they had proved that long ago. Their cooperative effort would be an asset to the Cappadocian team. In fact, he had half finished a letter to the University of Pennsylvania asking for help in locating Arianna when she had miraculously walked into his office.

The day before, to oversee laborers, Galip had signed Refah Bayles, a young archaeologist from Kayseri. Before hiring McCauley, Galip decided, he would await Refah's assessment of the tall American, and Refah was due in the office any minute.

Chapter 49

While drinking his tea, Galip weighed Morgan and Arianna's individual qualifications.

McCauley has an adequate, though not illustrious, résumé—too little archaeology, perhaps. Miss Arista has had far more experience than McCauley. Still, the man is financially independent, has managerial credits, and is a photographer.

The phone suddenly rang, interrupting Galip's reverie. He snatched up the receiver and listened, scowling. Then his expression softened. When he hung up, he said, "That was my team accountant. He has a serious case of hepatitis and is in the hospital; he cannot join us this season." Galip's piercing gray eyes peered into Morgan's blue ones. "Do you know accounting?"

Morgan felt a surge of anticipation. "I've had four years of it. Actually, I've taught all levels of accounting, including corporate accounting at Hong Kong University."

"Do you know inventory procedures?"

"Yes sir, retailing was a part of the university's management curriculum. When I first went into the Marines, I held the rank of storekeeper and dealt with inventories every day."

"*Çok güzel!* Very good!" Dr. Yaldiz clasped his hands, and a broad grin widened his luxurious mustache. "Allah blesses me, Mr. McCauley. The Cappadocia team needs an accountant *and* a photographer, and you can fit both positions. Does such an arrangement suit you?"

Morgan could not believe his luck. Or was it luck? The phone call seemed too coincidental. It was almost providence, if one believed in fate. He could barely cover his boyish excitement. "It would be a privilege to join your team, Dr. Yaldiz. When do I start?"

"Work is not officially scheduled to begin until late next spring."

Morgan's enthusiasm fell as flat as a road-kill hare.

Arianna abruptly looked away, trying to hide the tears that threatened to embarrass her. Dr. Yaldiz had said nothing about hiring her, but this McCauley character walks in, and he is accepted on the spot. The acetylene torch of envy flamed in her chest.

"However, in two weeks we survey the site in preparation for next year," Galip continued. "We stay there two weeks, perhaps more, if the weather is agreeable."

At that moment, a Turk in his late twenties entered the room. Halime's indrawn breath was heard only by Morgan, who sat near where she stood.

"Ah, Refah Bey, good morning," Dr. Yaldiz warmly greeted the newcomer.

Refah looked around and exclaimed, "Arianna! It is nice to see you." He went over and shook both her hands at once.

"It's been a long time since I've listened to you play at Ephesus, Refah," Arianna said. "I can't wait to hear you again."

Refah turned to Halime and bowed. "And Miss Ortman can dance to my music." He flushed when Halime averted her head and murmured, "It is not possible."

Galip remembered the many splendid evenings after a hard day on a site when Refah played old Turkish folk tunes on his *saz*, an ancient stringed instrument that resembled a long-necked banjo. Halime often danced or sang to the sometimes lively, sometimes haunting, melodies. He always looked forward to seeing the two perform. Once, he believed that Refah and Halime were ready to marry. However, Halime had not mentioned Refah since she and Refah had left Ephesus. Plainly, he had been wrong.

To cover an obviously awkward situation, Galip hurriedly introduced Refah to Morgan, saying, "Refah, Arianna, and Halime were at Ephesus. They are as a family, no?"

And I'm the outsider, Morgan thought, a bit uncomfortable at the idea.

"Refah Bayles. Morgan McCauley." Galip continued the introductions. "Refah Bey is my chief archaeologist."

Morgan stood a head taller than Refah, but the handsome young man was muscular and fit, and he had an affable and honest face. Morgan was immediately drawn to him.

"As you already know, Mr. McCauley, Miss Ortman is my administrative assistant," Galip said. "Halime Bayan, you and Mr. McCauley will temporarily work together. You can tutor him in Turkish law." Galip chuckled. "Help him cut our red tape, you know?" Halime nodded, agreeing to the arrangement.

Dr. Yaldiz then gestured to Arianna. "Miss Arista is our anthropologist in charge of the survey."

Arianna nearly lost it, almost shrieking with relief and joy. She retained her dignity in the nick of time by merely displaying a reserved smile.

Galip inspected his watch, then rose from his chair. "I must leave now; I have a meeting at the Department of Antiquities." He flipped the pages of his desk calendar. "Let us meet here at two o'clock tomorrow afternoon. Afterward, I invite you all to dinner at Gençlik Park."

I love this country, Morgan and Arianna thought simultaneously. Though they thought alike, they left Dr. Yaldiz's office separately without saying good-bye to one another.

Refah waited in the room a few more minutes, hoping to speak to Halime, but she had disappeared, retreating to the ladies' room. She stayed there until she was sure Refah had gone.

When it came to relationships, the Cappadocian team was off to a shaky beginning.

CHAPTER 50

Arianna was ecstatic when Dr. Yaldiz had told her that work would begin at a location somewhere in the well-excavated Hidden Valley. To go to a new site was more than she had hoped. Now, at last, they were on their way to Niğde. The 1941 Cadillac, a white limousine modified into a *dolmuş*, a taxi that follows a designated route, once had belonged to the Saudi Arabian Embassy. The big Fisher body floated over the rough macadam highway, its big shocks absorbing the worst potholes and bumps. Refah sat in the front seat, next to the Turkish driver. Arianna and Halime sat in the second seat. Morgan stretched his long legs across the rear.

Unfortunately, the Cadillac's air conditioning did not function. They had started the trip in the cool of early morning. By noon the heat had become insufferable. Near Ankara, the over-grazed earth lay scorched and arid, resembling California's San Joaquin Valley in midsummer. After they passed Tuz Gölü, a dry salt lake seventy miles in length lying southeast of Ankara, the ground was more fertile. Here the grain was at its peak, and the harvest had already begun. Mammoth threshers, as many as three abreast, gashed wide swathes on the gently rolling, golden hills.

"Those machines are like the ones I've seen in photographs taken sixty years ago. Farmers used them in America's Midwest, prior to the dust bowl catastrophe," Morgan commented.

Refah had to shout over the noise coming through his open window. "They are old Lend-Lease machines; they serve our farmers well."

The powerful dolmuş tore down the road, the driver pressing the accelerator nearly to the floor. Propped in a corner, Morgan soon slept. Refah also dozed, his chin on his chest. Halime, who had made the trip many times, concentrated on her embroidery.

Arianna was fascinated by the swiftly passing scenery. She pivoted in her seat to lengthen her glimpse of a small boy and a cream-colored ox. The boy rhythmically flicked a stick at the ox's flanks, urging the beast to circle the post to which it was tethered. As it trod the stalks, the ox's hard hooves loosened the grain. A group of brightly clad women flipped meter-wide wicker trays, tossing the crushed debris into the wind. In this way, in a centuries-old process, they separated seed from chaff.

In other fields peasant women flayed the wheat, gathered it into large bundles, then packed the bundles onto sad-eyed donkeys. The legs and flop-eared head of a loaded animal were all that showed under the huge mound.

"The women's skirts have such beautiful, vibrant prints," Arianna observed aloud.

"Some wear the *şalvar,* or pantaloons," Halime said.

Arianna plucked at her blouse. "How can they bear wearing so many clothes in this heat? I'm miserable in my sleeveless blouse and light cotton skirt, and those women have to be wearing three layers."

The Cadillac lurched across a deep pothole, awakening Refah and Morgan in time for them to hear Arianna's last sentence. Refah jerked upright. Scrubbing his thumbs at his eyes, he laughed, saying, "Their clothes stop the sun and the weeds, do you know?"

Refah's remark puzzled Arianna. "I understand how layers of clothing can stop foxtails, but how can they stop heat?"

Refah laughed again. "Not the hot; Turkish men desire soft, pale women." He turned around and winked at Morgan. "Even the peasant woman does not choose to become brown and withered like a fried *kertenkele.*"

"What's a *kertenkele?*" Morgan asked, still drowsy.

"It is what you call in English, a l-e-e-sard."

"A lee sard?" Morgan frowned, then the corners of his mouth twitched. "Oh, a *lizard.*" He was unable to stifle a loud guffaw. "I knew a few lizardlike girls back home," he boomed. "A few prunes, also."

Suddenly, Arianna recalled driving on Highway 99 through the San Joaquin Valley and seeing thousands of flats of wrinkled prunes and raisins drying under the intense sun. She suspected Morgan was needling her, but she would not give him the satisfaction of a retort. Every summer during her teens, to further tan her naturally tawny skin, she had slathered her hide with iodine-spiked baby oil, then baked for hours in the sun. Hearing Refah and Morgan, she wished she were as fair all over as she was in the places shielded from the sun.

Spotting Arianna's dour face, Morgan whispered with diabolic glee, *"Gotcha!"*

Clearly hearing his whisper, Arianna gritted her teeth, suppressing a stinging retort. She closed her eyes and pretended to sleep; the scenery had lost its appeal. She said no more the rest of the journey.

Sensing he had gone too far, Morgan's competitive spirit waned. *I shouldn't tease her; her skin, her hair, her face—everything—is perfect. It's her rotten attitude that needs adjusting.*

It was late when they reached the Niğde motel, which served as temporary team headquarters. Until Dr. Yaldiz arrived they had nothing to do except unpack and recover from the long, steamy drive. The four of them ate supper together in the motel's pleasant, air-conditioned dining room. They had eaten nothing but fruit, bread, and cheese all day. The superb *kuzu-dolmasi*—stuffed and roasted lamb—was especially tasty, even to Morgan, who ordinarily did not care for it.

Morgan was tempted to order a bottle of red Kavak, a smooth dry wine produced at Ankara's Kavaklidere winery. It had been his favorite when he was stationed at the embassy in Ankara. Refah and Halime, practicing Moslems who drank no alcoholic beverages, ordered bottles of Frukos, as did Morgan and Arianna. Their conversation over dinner was undemanding and trivial.

They were eating a late breakfast on the motel's terrace when Galip Yaldiz swung his dusty Anadolu into a vacant parking space. He had left Ankara shortly after midnight to escape the worst heat. Turkey's rugged highways and barely negotiable, rural graveled roads had aged Galip's practically new Turkish-made car until it looked like a battered junker. As the archaeologist stepped out of the Anadolu and stretched, Morgan and Refah went to help him unload.

Arianna remembered that Halime had been abnormally quiet the day before and noted that she was still withdrawn this morning. "You're not your usual cheerful self. Are you ill?" she asked. It distressed Arianna to see the haunted look in Halime's eyes. When Halime didn't answer, she leaned closer. "Something *is* the matter. Can you tell me?"

Halime's hand flew to her mouth, and she shook her head.

"I'm sorry, I didn't mean to pry," Arianna quickly apologized. Much could have happened to Halime in the months they were out of contact, and she did not feel she had the right to delve deeper into her friend's private life.

Halime ruefully smiled at Arianna. "It is not important. I promise, I will tell you someday."

But as Arianna turned to watch the men unload the car, Halime's smile disappeared. It was replaced by a sorrowful expression that evaporated as Morgan approached carrying an armload of shovels and hoes. He set the tools on the terrazzo saying, "Dr. Yaldiz promised we're going to the site as soon as he's eaten. Better get ready, you two."

"Finally!" Arianna crowed. Jumping up, she ran toward the room she and Halime shared. Halime slowly followed.

Two years earlier, a young Turkish businessman, while hiking among the tufa cliffs, had accidentally discovered a new underground city not far from the Hidden Valley. So enamored of his find was he that he vowed to spend the rest of his days searching Cappadocia for more caverns. It was to his last discovery that the team was headed.

It was too late in the year to begin any major excavation; the real work would commence the following spring. The top three levels of the labyrinth were already cleared and wired for electricity and recently opened to tourists. Access to the lower four levels was available only by special permit.

It was the survey team's main job to select the area, or areas, where the entire team would work the next year. Meanwhile, Refah would canvas the local villages for laborers who anticipated regular employment with the archaeological teams that came from everywhere in the world. The hourly pay was far better than the villagers could make otherwise, and there were often bonuses of cash or goods. Such employment was profitable and prestigious, and it relieved the boredom of small-town life. There were more applicants than there were jobs available.

To begin with, Galip kept Halime and Morgan busy planning strategy at the motel base. Later, he sent Morgan to Arianna with instructions for her to take him to photograph the areas she and Halime would eventually grid.

Morgan found Arianna in a small chamber carved in the hard volcanic stone. Since the episode had occurred, he regretted his sarcasm on the drive from Ankara. Stepping to Arianna's side, he slipped an arm around her slender waist. He asked softly, "How's the measuring going?"

"Don't!" Arianna jerked away, rapidly rewinding the tape. "Let's keep things strictly business, okay?" she snapped.

Morgan threw up his hands. "If that's the way you want it."

"That's the way I want it."

CHAPTER 51

In the weeks that followed, whenever Morgan accompanied Arianna, he was careful to keep his distance. Gradually, her hostility lessened until they reached a tolerable working relationship.

Not trusting the local camera shop—located within a bakery—to develop his photographs, Morgan constructed a makeshift darkroom in his own quarters. When he was not at the underground city or immersed in paperwork, he processed film.

Halime often assisted him, but Arianna avoided Morgan's room entirely.

"I'm going up top, Halime. My spine is killing me." Arianna stiffly arose from where she and Halime sat cross-legged on the rock floor. For the past week they had been graphing—by lantern light—the fourth level's infrastructure.

Halime blinked tired, red-rimmed eyes. "We have almost finished." She squinted up at Arianna. "I will go with you."

Ten minutes later, near the entrance to the underground city, Arianna found a shady spot and sat down on the hard ground near the huge white tent where the team ate and relaxed. Leaning against a boulder, she opened the bottle of iced Frukos she had taken from the cooler.

No more than five minutes had passed when she suddenly heard the sound of hooves clattering on stone. She couldn't help herself; she started laughing at the ludicrous sight of Morgan astride a donkey.

Back in Niğde, Morgan had completed his assignment early. Instead of waiting for motorized transportation to the field site (which occurred only if a dolmuş happened to be heading in the right direction at the right time), he had rented a donkey. His lanky, six-foot, three-inch frame was much too tall for the tiny animal; if he did not draw up his feet, his toes dragged in the dirt. Though Morgan slumped in the saddle, his shoulders towered above the donkey's ears. He swayed precariously when he awkwardly tried to shift his weight from the more vulnerable portions of his anatomy.

Arianna barely stifled her giggles as Morgan stopped the grateful donkey at an ancient grapevine, dismounted, and tied the frayed lead rope to the stump. Groaning, he settled beside her.

"I shouldn't have ridden this far. I'm so sore, I can barely move," he complained.

"The sight of you trotting over the hill on that scruffy little thing made my day. I feel awfully sorry for the donkey," she snickered.

It was pleasant to see Arianna drop her guard and have fun, even at his expense. "It was a crazy idea," he moaned. "*You* may not be sorry for me, but someone up *there* must be." He blew a kiss to the sky. "The owner in Niğde said he'll fetch the wretched thing, so at least I don't have to ride it back." Looking around, he asked, "Where's Halime?"

"She's in the tent." Arianna lay back against the rock and closed her burning lids. "By the way, the graphs are nearly done. Halime and I work well together."

"Is Halime always so gloomy?" Morgan asked, risking Arianna's ire by breaking his agreement to discuss business only.

At first Morgan's comment vexed Arianna, but she realized he was the one person with whom she could talk freely about her own concern for Halime. "It's not like her to act this way. I know something is upsetting her, but she won't tell me what."

Morgan added an observation. "It seems she's particularly paranoid when Refah is around. I can't figure her out; he's a really decent guy."

What Morgan said surprised Arianna; she hadn't noticed anything unusual between Halime and Refah. "Did you know Refah and Halime are somehow related?"

"No. I didn't."

"They seemed close in Ephesus. In fact, every time Refah

played his *saz*, Halime danced for him. I tried to get them to perform for us here. Refah is willing, but Halime seems reluctant."

"I've noticed."

"He's incredible. His Turkish and Greek folk songs are so haunting, I cry every time I hear them." Arianna forgot her reserve and turned excitedly toward Morgan. "He absolutely has to play for us before we return to Ankara next week. Maybe if you ask Halime, she'll dance." Arianna suggestively wiggled her eyebrows. "She does a very seductive belly dance."

Feigning lust, Morgan breathed heavily. "Ah, I can scarcely wait."

Arianna decided to reveal something Halime had told her in Ephesus. "Halime's heritage is special. The Turks captured her great-great-grandmother in Bulgaria when she was only eight and took her to the sultan's harem."

"Halime is the great-great-granddaughter of a concubine?"

"Yes, and she said her great-grandmother was born in the harem of Sultan Abdul II."

It hadn't occurred to Morgan that descendants of harem women might be living in modern times. "Do you mean that old rogue, Sultan Abdul II, is Halime's great-great-grandfather?"

"From what Halime says."

The history fascinated Morgan. He wanted to hear more, but Halime was walking toward them. "I wonder if her great-great-grandmother was as beautiful as Halime?" he whispered to Arianna. Glancing at his watch, he stood and stretched.

Arianna was aware she had said enough already—Halime would be horrified. "Don't let Halime know I told you," she hissed. "She doesn't want people to know." She raised her voice as Halime approached. "And Morgan, if you're looking for Dr. Yaldiz, he's down in the fifth level at the Graveyard Number 3 site."

"Thanks," Morgan said as he limped off, waving at Halime with one hand and rubbing his tailbone with the other.

Later, as she lay in bed, Arianna's mind replayed their

conversation. She remembered how Morgan had admired Halime's looks; hadn't he even implied she was beautiful? For some reason, the thought irritated her.

The next day, Arianna and Halime remained at the motel to compile their notes and maps. By a previous agreement with the management, they were able to spread their papers on a large table in a corner of the restaurant. The waiter brought them tea and left.

Arianna ceased writing and thoughtfully clicked the pencil on her teeth. "Halime, when are you and Refah going to perform for us?"

Halime bit her lip. "I cannot."

"Why, Halime? Refah's playing is wonderful, and you are marvelous. I've looked forward to seeing you both perform again."

Halime tilted up her chin and clicked her tongue. "It is not possible."

"You've been unhappy since we arrived in Cappadocia, and the others are beginning to talk. I'm worried about you." Arianna leaned across the table and patted her friend's hand. "Can I help?"

Arianna's unexpected sympathy weakened Halime's defenses. "It is Refah," she blurted.

"Refah? Has Refah done something wrong?"

"He has done nothing."

"Are you afraid he's *going* to?"

Halime looked away. "Refah and I were betrothed as children by our parents. He says we have waited too long to marry."

Halime's announcement stunned Arianna. It took her a moment to answer. "I knew you two were somehow related, and I presumed you were just good friends."

"Refah and I always planned to marry. When we were at Ephesus, he told me he did not want me to pursue my career. I begged him to change his mind; he would not. When I came to Ankara to work for Dr. Yaldiz, I told Refah we could *never* marry." Halime shrugged. "He still does not believe me."

Shocked, Arianna gawked at Halime. "They are still betrothing children? It's so old-fashioned. If your parents arranged for you and Refah to wed, how did they react when you called it off?"

"They were not pleased. Our mothers are first cousins, and it was their wish from the time Refah and I were born for us to marry."

"Didn't Attatürk outlaw arranged marriages decades ago?"

"Kemal Attatürk was heroic, and he created laws to liberate Turkish women." Halime twirled the three gold bangles on her wrist. "But people do not always do what their leaders ask, do they?"

At that point in their conversation, a middle-aged village woman passed the terrace. Two heavy, five-gallon cans filled with water swung from her shoulder yoke. A brightly-colored scarf, securely tucked along her cheek, hid the lower half of her face.

Halime pointed her chin in the woman's direction. "See, Arianna, the *köylü*, the peasant, wears a veil in public, though Attatürk's law forbids it." She stared down at the paper she had been writing. "When we were children, Refah was my friend. When I danced for him in Ephesus, he became not just a friend, as when we were children; he became . . . too affectionate. He wanted more," she confessed, blushing.

"Aside from his wanting you to quit your job and become a mere housewife," Arianna sighed, "Refah has the best qualities; he's intelligent, steady, gentle, kind, has a good sense of humor, and he *is* quite handsome. What more could you ask?"

"I agree with you, Arianna. Refah is a very good man, but we are as brother and sister. I cannot marry my brother."

CHAPTER 52

During the third week of the month-long Moslem celebration called Ramadan, Galip called a halt to all work at the underground city. The Turkish laborers were more than willing to stay on the job, but tempers flared and energy levels dropped during the difficult month of fasting when no food was consumed between sunrise and sunset. Each day, as soon as the sun sank beneath the horizon, the feasting began; it often lasted beyond midnight. The next morning, the apathetic workers did manage to drag themselves out of bed and to the dig, but productivity suffered.

"Is the survey finished?" Galip asked Halime. He hunched over a makeshift table—a plank propped on two chair backs—in the motel room that served as the team office.

Halime stood opposite him, her face pale, dark shadows ringing her eyes. The past weeks had been difficult, not only because of Ramadan but because of the tension between her and Refah. Fatigue had made her listless and depressed.

"Arianna and I have the last section to do, but it will take us no more than two days," she told Galip.

"That is good. We will leave for Ankara when you complete it."

Halime was relieved the season had ended. She was eager to go home to her parents, her own bed, and her mother's cooking. Yet, despite her mixed feelings regarding him, she knew she would miss Refah.

Refah would spend the winter at his family home in Kayseri, the capital of Cappadocia, located eighty-three miles northeast of Nevşehir. Weather permitting, he would periodically return to Niğde to study life within the local villages. By investigating the contemporary population he hoped to find clues to the culture of the ancient people who created the underground cities.

Galip always spent his off season teaching at Ankara University, and Halime continued as his assistant and secretary after she returned from her break at home.

The Tumpane Company had not found clerical help, so Arianna again applied for a position there. She barely passed the typing test, but Tumpane quickly hired her.

By pooling their incomes, Beverly and Arianna could afford a larger place. Morgan helped them move to a three-bedroom apartment. They asked Halime to live with them, but her father would not hear of it.

"I can't believe that Halime, at twenty-six, is still under the thumb of her father," Arianna exclaimed as she and Beverly ate their first meal in the new flat. "I thought she was liberated." Both Americans had been on their own since their late teens.

Beverly gestured with her fork. "That's just the way it is in Turkey. Attatürk eased the laws that held Turkish women in bondage, but centuries-old habits don't immediately change. The women have it worse in other Moslem countries—Saudi Arabia, for instance."

"I suppose," Arianna said, "but it would have been fun having Halime live with us."

"If her father adheres to an old-fashioned ideology, she pretty much has to go along with it."

"I do think Halime needs to be more independent," Arianna mused. "She seemed unusually depressed that last week at the dig. Being on her own might help."

Morgan, who never had cared for hotel living, also set out to find an apartment. After a two-week search, he found a delightful efficiency penthouse atop a new apartment building on Çankaya Hill. The penthouse had a large fireplace, and a fabulous bird's-eye view of the city. The place was Bauhaus sleek and suited Morgan's austere taste. When his shipment of personal effects at last arrived by boat in Istanbul, Morgan went to retrieve his belongings—and had his first encounter with *Beyanname.*

Required by Turkish law, a *Beyanname* was the customs document that listed a foreigner's personal belongings. Unless an item was sold to another foreigner currently living in Turkey, then whatever came into the country with someone had to go out with that same someone when he or she left Turkey for good. If two parties, not Turkish, wanted to buy, sell, or exchange an item on a *Beyanname*, it involved complicated manipulations, starting at a customs office.

As long as Morgan stayed in Turkey on an extended visitor's permit, a *Beyanname* was not required. Once he became a permanent resident, he had to have one. *Beyanname* was a nuisance, a red-tape rat race, but it helped to stabilize the Turkish trade balance and, therefore, its economy.

Morgan scheduled a skiing trip to Switzerland for the first week of December. Until then he was content to spend most of his evenings in the penthouse by himself. At dusk he never tired of watching the jeweled lights of Ankara blinking a thousand feet below. Now, as he listened to his vast collection of classical music on the stereo, he felt like a contented, well-fed African lion surveying his domain high atop a *kopje*. It was a time of self-healing. The memory of Kwan Mei's death gradually slipped into a back pocket of his mind, securely buttoned up and only occasionally coming out when he chose to release it. But solitude soon became old.

He enjoyed cooking, but it was no fun to cook only for himself. One evening, having had enough isolation, he decided to throw a dinner party. The next day he purposefully strode down the hill to Arianna and Beverly's apartment. No one was home, so he left a note on the door inviting them for dinner on Saturday of the following week. From there he went to Dr. Yaldiz's office, intending to invite Halime also.

When she saw Morgan, Halime greeted him with impetuous enthusiasm. "Morgan Bey, it is very good to see you." She wanted to clasp his hand, but she didn't dare; it was not proper. Halime's color was becomingly high, and she had outlined her eyes with mascara or Kohl in the exotic Egyptian manner popular with young Turkish women.

Suddenly something in Halime's expression reminded Morgan of Kwan Mei. The affable expression on his face shriveled to a scowl. He instantly changed his mind; he could not ask her to his dinner party. Knowing very well Dr. Yaldiz was at the university teaching a class and unavailable, he asked, in a voice as cold as ice, if Galip was in.

Though Morgan's unexplained change of attitude astonished Halime, she calmly answered, "Dr. Yaldiz will be in his office tomorrow."

"I'll come back when he's here," Morgan growled and abruptly left.

Perplexed by Morgan's hostile response, Halime asked herself, "I wonder what that was about?"

CHAPTER 53

Striding down the gloomy hallway from Dr. Yaldiz's office, Morgan began to regret his decision to not invite Halime to dinner. He hesitated once, almost returning to the office, but his vulnerability, whenever he was reminded of Kwan Mei, irritated him. No! It embarrassed him. Instead of going back to apologize, to explain his rude behavior to Halime, he continued down the corridor.

Calling a taxi, Morgan decided, *I have to get away more often. It's time to see some of Turkey, but that takes a car.* He spent the rest of that day and most of the next pinning want ads for a good used car on every public bulletin board. He left them at all the U.S. base facilities, at USAID, and at the Turkish-American Association.

Thursday morning, Morgan walked to the Kavaklidere Winery to get wine for the dinner. He could now drink a glass of wine without craving more, and he drank nothing stronger. He'd still not had a response to his ad. While he stood at the winery's tasting-room counter sampling Kavaklidere's famous Kîmîz, another man entered. Morgan nodded to the balding, middle-aged American. His physique reminded Morgan of the appellation *Mr. Five-by-five.*

The two men silently swirled and sniffed the contents of their glasses, then quaffed down the rest of their samples. The other man spoke first. "I've been assigned to Vietnam. Afraid I won't be able to find stuff as good there," he lamented.

Morgan set his glass on the counter. "Are you planning to take some Turkish wine with you? I've heard it doesn't travel well," he said as the white-coated winery representative filled his glass halfway with Özel, a red wine he had not yet tasted.

"Yeah, I've heard the same thing, but I'm taking a couple of bottles anyway. Wish I could take my car, too, but it's not allowed."

Morgan's ears perked. "What make is it?"

"It's a '65 Mercedes Benz. Bought 'er in Germany two years ago; drove 'er into Turkey. Always meant to take a Mercedes back to the States. I thought Turkey would be my last so-called *hardship* post. Should've known better." The man shoved his glass out for more wine.

"How much do you want for the car?" Morgan cautiously asked.

"Look at it first, then I'll name you a figure—that is, if you're serious."

After test driving the silver sedan, Morgan knew the vehicle was worth the price quoted. Money wasn't a problem, but knowing the USAID employee was desperate, Morgan haggled until the man came down fifteen hundred dollars.

The rotund man knew all about the *Beyanname* procedure and helped Morgan through it. Dealing with a fellow American simplified the process. If a Turk had bought the car, both he and the Turk would have had to drive it across the border and transact the deal there. Then the Turk would have had to re-cross the border with it. In comparison, a deal between two Americans was straightforward. A transfer to Morgan's *Beyanname* meant that both men had only to meet at the main customs office in downtown Ankara. Because of the other man's schedule, Morgan had to wait until the end of the following week before the car finally belonged to him.

* * *

Morgan was glad that he had invited Halime as well as Arianna and Beverly to dinner after all. His Italian lasagna would have been easy to make in the States. In Turkey, where beef was rare and pork virtually nonexistent, the creation of such fare became a real challenge. He searched Ankara for two days. When he discovered he could not buy the meat he wanted, he substituted a fatty, ground mutton for the beef. He spiced a portion of the mutton to replicate pork sausage. The ploy worked well, and the three women raved over his innovation.

Morgan hadn't yet finished furnishing the penthouse in the Danish Modern he preferred. He had ordered a sofa and chair at a furniture store in the Maltepe district, but they hadn't yet arrived from Denmark. They ate dinner picnic style, sitting on striped goat hair rugs that Morgan had spread on the floor in front of his picture windows.

As night fell, the apartment chilled, and Morgan lit a roaring fire in the huge fireplace. They talked softly over their wine while watching the sun drop out of sight behind the distant mountain ranges. The last of its rays cast a purplish glow over everything on Çankaya Hill, but a thousand feet below—where Ankara's lights merrily twinkled in the crisp October air—it was already dark. The evening's camaraderie did more to draw Morgan and Arianna together in a single night than had their many weeks spent in Cappadocia. Amused, Halime rarely interrupted them, and quietly observed the relationship's development.

"You have a wonderful view, Morgan. I wouldn't get anything done; I'd always be looking out a window," Arianna mused, her voice wistful.

Morgan nodded. "It's the chief reason I rented up here, but the super fireplace was a factor also. I'd build a fire every night, if I could."

"If you could?" Arianna looked puzzled.

Beverly explained in her Georgian drawl, "People in Ankara have to conserve wood. There is very little available."

Morgan didn't always know how to take Arianna's friend. They were a mismatched pair, and Beverly often rubbed him the wrong way. He wondered how Arianna put up with her preaching.

Immediately on the defensive, Morgan retorted, "I light only small fires." Gazing into the cozy flames, he recalled the ragged, barelegged child he had seen the day before, and his beautiful fire lost its luster.

He had been on his way home after visiting the Attatürk Memorial when he saw a tow-headed moppet picking through a pile of trash in a vacant lot. She was searching for scraps of paper and wood. As he walked by, she looked up with a sunny smile, revealing a gap where two baby teeth had fallen out. A light snow had fallen the night before, and he was wearing not only a heavy winter coat, but also a muffler and fur-lined gloves. The little girl's frail body, clad in a thin cotton dress and her tiny sockless feet in oversized sandals, pained him. He vowed he would not build another fire that winter unless the electricity was off and a fire his only source of heat. He vowed that someday, when he knew more about Turkey's charitable organizations, he would look into a way to help children like that.

Retreating from the uncomfortable subject of poverty, he announced, "I bought a car. I'll get it next week."

"That's terrific. What kind?" Arianna asked.

"A 1965 Mercedes Benz."

Arianna's eyes glowed with appreciation.

Beverly leaned forward. "It must have cost a fortune. Where did you ever find it?"

"It belonged to a guy at USAID. I met him at the Kavaklidere Winery when I was buying tonight's wine. He bought the car new in Germany, but he's been transferred to Vietnam and can't take it with him."

"Why didn't he ship it home?" It baffled Arianna that someone would so willingly sacrifice such a prize.

"He doesn't have a stateside home. He's single and a career man; home has always been overseas."

"The less one has, the easier it is to transfer to somewhere else in the world," Beverly said. "That's why I don't want a car. It's just extra baggage, especially if it is on *Beyanname*." She peered at Morgan. "Are you having any *Beyanname* trouble?"

"Nope, it's all taken care of. Dr. Yaldiz helped me get my work permit, and I'm now officially a part of his permanent team, not a temporary guest of the country."

"Congratulations!" Arianna and Beverly exclaimed.

But Arianna was not as happy for Morgan as she pretended. She wished she could devote all of *her* time to archaeology. It rankled that Morgan, not a true archaeologist, was now a member of the permanent team, while she, the professional, had to work as a mere clerk to make ends meet.

"And what will *you* be doing for Dr. Yaldiz?" she asked Morgan.

Morgan's eyes narrowed at her sarcastic tone. "Number one, I will be soliciting funds all over the world. Number two, I'll be handling the logistics and organization of the dig while Refah is in Kayseri. My main job is to free Dr. Yaldiz for less mundane duties. Does that satisfactorily answer your question, Miss Arista?"

Arianna was a bit taken back by his curtness—but not humbled. "Well, be sure you do a good job for Dr. Yaldiz. He deserves the best." She tossed her head, daring Morgan to disagree.

Sensing a change in the atmosphere, Beverly decided it was time to leave. "We should go; I have to be up early tomorrow for church."

"I'll go with you." At that particular moment, Arianna had a sudden urge to attend a service, though she didn't know why; it was just a feeling that inexplicably stirred deep within her.

"To church?"

"Of course."

Astonished that Arianna would willingly attend church, Beverly almost "whooped!" Instead, she covered her open mouth with her hand as if stifling a yawn. "That would be great," she said, trying to sound nonchalant.

Arianna had never shown an interest in religion. Though Beverly regularly went to church while the two were roommates in college, Arianna had always refused to go with her. Beverly had given up asking long ago. Now, she hardly dared to believe her ears.

The next morning, Beverly knocked on Arianna's door. "Time to get up if you're going to church with me."

Arianna's muffled reply was slow in coming. "Yeah, uh, I'm too tired this morning. I'll go another time." The urge she had felt the night before had disappeared.

Beverly's pleasure and anticipation shriveled. "Are you sure? You still have time to get ready."

"Go on without me, Bev. I really want to sleep."

"Maybe next time." Sad and disappointed, Beverly turned away.

Two weeks later, Arianna and Beverly prepared dinner for Morgan. As soon as he came through the door, they noticed the twinkle in his eye. He soon divulged the reason. "You already know that I plan to be in Europe the rest of the winter. If you two are staying in Turkey, would you like to use my car until I return?"

Drive around in a nearly new Mercedes Benz? What a silly question! As they happily accepted Morgan's generous offer, Arianna and Beverly had all they could do to keep their expressions dead serious. Then both of them squealed with delight. Running to Morgan—Arianna knocking over a glass of Frukos in the process—both young women hugged him, until he begged for mercy.

PART 5

CHAPTER 54

The colder the winter, the thicker was the bituminous coal smoke that blanketed Ankara's valley like a murky brown sea. The denser the smog, the more difficult it was to breathe. Beverly and Arianna's apartment lay atop Çankaya Hill in the purer atmosphere a thousand feet above the city. When they did not have to go to work or run an errand, they traveled away from Ankara or simply stayed home. During the coldest days, when inversions held the city in sooty bondage, they looked down from the apartment windows and saw only a billowing, nicotine-colored lake. Every year, the smog crept higher up Çankaya Hill. Vehicles descending Attatürk Boulevard plunged into the thick smog like planes into a dark storm cloud.

With no television to entertain them, Arianna and Beverly joined a multiethnic group of jigsaw fanatics. Membership in the club included a puzzle exchange. The two friends always had a card table set up with a colorful puzzle in some stage of completion. This particular Saturday afternoon they poked at a scene of the Swiss Alps, complete with chalet, tawny cows, and dirndl-skirted shepherdess. As she picked through the loose pieces, Beverly casually asked, "Why don't you come to church with me this evening? An Armenian woman is speaking. You might like to hear her."

On more than one occasion, Beverly had unsuccessfully tried to get Arianna to go with her to the Sunday church service the Baptist missionary held in the United States Embassy basement. As Beverly knew it would, the word "Armenian" caught her friend's attention.

Saying nothing, Arianna stared at Beverly for a moment. Her expression completely blank, she deliberately set another jigsaw piece into the dirndl skirt.

Careful to choose the right words, Beverly continued. "This is Olga's first day back at church since she contracted pneumonia last fall. She almost died. It's a wonder she made it; she's over ninety."

Arianna picked up another jigsaw piece and slowly turned it in her fingers. "Do you know what her talk's about?"

"Her personal story, I think. Something about the expulsion of the Armenians from Turkey."

Arianna's stomach lurched; she really didn't want to hear about it again. Yet she shouldn't miss the chance to learn more of her roots. Quietly she said, "My grandmother used to tell me stories. I don't have anything else to do. I guess going with you is better than sitting home alone."

"Some of us are going to the *pasta* shop on Attatürk Boulevard after the service. You'll come to that, too, won't you?"

Arianna finally smiled. "You win! I love Turkish pastries, and you know I can't resist Turkish chocolate chip ice cream. That shop has the best of both. I'll come."

The young missionary's strong arm supported tiny, skeletal Olga Hazarian Diaz as she limped to the front of the room. She had turned ninety-five that same month. Deep lines crosshatched the ashen skin of her face, and she was so stooped that it was difficult for her to meet the gaze of the taller people with whom she spoke.

The congregation's rustling and murmuring ceased when Olga's rasping voice permeated the room. For most of those present, the old Armenian woman's heavily accented speech was difficult to understand. For Arianna, it was like listening to Ylenah. Soon, she became oblivious to everything but the unfolding tale, so horribly similar to the one she had heard during her childhood.

"I was born in 1871 in Little Armenia," Olga began. "It is now a part of Turkey. I lived there under the last three Ottoman sultans. When Abdul Hamid II ordered my people, the provincial Armenians, massacred in 1890, I was nineteen. The soldiers murdered my husband and two sons. They raped me. If I had not had to live for my little daughter, I would have killed myself. Those who were left, the women and small children, were forced to go to Russia or Syria. I decided to go to Armenian Russia, where I had distant relatives. My daughter and I walked. Sometimes I carried her. We begged rides in peasant carts. All the time, we starved."

Olga stopped speaking. A dry cough racked her frail body, and the pastor rushed out of the room for a cup of water. Olga took a sip, then, smiling weakly at her audience, continued.

"We believed we were safe with my relatives, but Czar Nicholas II of Russia was almost as bad as the Turks. He closed many Armenian schools, libraries, and cultural centers, and even stole property that belonged to the church. He also stole the home of my relatives. We Armenians were not free in our own country."

"When things got better in Turkey, my daughter and I returned to Little Armenia. There I met my second husband, a Spanish rug dealer who came to my village to buy carpets. He took us to his home in Constantinople where we were married."

"The Armenians still wanted their independence from Turkey, and they caused the Turkish government much trouble. In 1915, a group called The Young Turks decided to kill all the Armenians or drive them out of the country. My younger brother and his family, who lived in another village and had survived the first massacre, were driven from their home. To this day, I do not know what happened to them." Olga lifted both trembling hands heavenward. "If they are dead, I will soon see them."

Shining through her tale of terror and persecution was the old woman's deep-seated belief and trust in God. She said it was terribly difficult at first, but, long ago, she had forgiven the soldiers who had murdered her family and raped her; she had forgiven the enemy as Jesus commanded in Matthew 6:14–15.

Arianna struggled to understand. "I could never have forgiven them," she hissed behind her hand to Beverly.

Later, Beverly introduced Arianna to Olga. Leaning on her cane, the old woman twisted her head up and sideways like a bird to appraise Arianna. Jet black eyes smoldered from bluish-purple hollows and a faint smile stretched the corners of the withered lips.

"My dear, you remind me of myself when I was your age." Shaking her head, she looked down at Arianna's ringless fingers. "By your age I had married twice and had five children." Youthful passion momentarily glimmered in the dark eyes.

Revealing nothing about herself, Arianna made polite small talk. After the horrifying experiences she had just heard Olga Diaz relate, she was even more resolved to keep her background to herself.

The group that gathered after church, besides Beverly and Arianna, included a German couple connected to the German Embassy, a marine from Alabama who was stationed at the U.S. Embassy, and a young Lebanese connected to the World Bank. Arianna abandoned hope of having her favorite ice cream when the rest decided to go to a *donar kebap* shop instead of the pastry shop. However, she relished *donar kebap* almost as much as the ice cream.

As they waited for their food, Arianna examined her table companions, trying to detect the common denominator that made them friends. Though the group had astonishingly diverse backgrounds and rarely saw each other outside of church, they seemed empathetic to one another. An aura of joy and peace surrounded them; laughter came readily. Beverly had always been a part of that same ambience, but Arianna had never given it much thought. She had always taken her friend for granted.

The marine and the Lebanese were debating Scripture. They had to shout to be heard above the cafe's blaring Turkish folk music. The marine leaned across the table and shouted something to the Lebanese. The Lebanese grinned at the marine. Waving his arms, he gave the table a resounding thump, then shouted something back. They continued to josh each other until heaping plates of *donar kebap* were placed before them.

Well, that wasn't exactly a churchy-quiet discussion, Arianna thought, amused. She watched the others at the table. The elderly Germans were quieter, but they were obviously enjoying themselves. Arianna discovered that the man and wife had advanced university degrees and the marine a mere high school education, but they discussed a variety of subjects as equals. She envied their camaraderie, their warm intimacy. What was their bond? She couldn't quite pin it down. Whatever it was, she knew she lacked its substance.

When those at the table discussed the Bible passages Olga Hazarian Diaz had quoted about forgiving and loving enemies, Arianna had nothing to offer. Though she followed the sometimes heated exchange with interest, she was isolated by ignorance. Inexplicably, tears filled her eyes. She turned her head so the others could not see. For the first time in her life, she wanted to know more about God and the Scriptures. The hunger was suddenly very intense.

When Beverly and Arianna returned to their apartment, Arianna put pride aside and asked Beverly if she could borrow her Bible.

Inwardly Beverly rejoiced, but she hid her pleasure from Arianna. Taking two books from her bookcase, she held them out. "I have these two Bibles, besides the one I take to church. One is a King James Version, the other a *Living Bible.* You can borrow either one, or both, if you want to. The Living Bible is easier to understand, though." She paused. "On second thought, you can keep the LB." Placing the King James Bible back on its shelf, she said, "If you need to use this, it will be here."

Arianna took the *Living Bible,* handling it as if it might bite. "Where do I begin?"

An old hand at evangelizing, Beverly knew her friend's life was on the verge of monumental change. "Start with the book of John. It's the third book in the New Testament. Read John 3:16–18 first. Here, I'll show you where it is." Beverly thumbed pages until she reached the passage, then handed the open Bible back to Arianna. "Read the rest of John, too. If you have any questions, just ask."

From then on, Arianna read the Bible every night. At first,

she rarely went to church, and Beverly didn't press her. But the more Arianna read, the more questions she formed. Over the weeks, she developed a tremendous thirst for spiritual knowledge and began to attend both Sunday school and church regularly. Soon, she was participating in the after-service group discussions as well.

Arianna was surprised to discover the important role Asia Minor played in the establishment of the early Christian church. She was familiar with the physical remnants of it—remnants of interest to the archaeologist—but she had given little thought to the lives of the people who had created those things. Now the work in Cappadocia began to have new meaning, one far beyond her professional perspective.

The U.S. Air Force sponsored a library in Ankara that had a fine collection of books on Asia Minor and, in particular, books on Byzantium. Arianna spent nearly all her free time at the library reading or poring over the books she took home. She refused to date, even when the handsome marine asked her out. The only way in which a man interrupted her concentration was when Morgan's image crept unbidden into her mind. It happened too often to suit her. Suddenly, she missed him.

CHAPTER 55

Ankara, Turkey, 1968

Late in March, Galip held a briefing for the team at his Ankara apartment. All but Morgan and Refah were already in Ankara. Refah had driven in from Niğde the night before the meeting.

Morgan had flown into Esenboğa from Switzerland that morning but hadn't had a chance to retrieve his Mercedes from Beverly and Arianna. His muscles were stiff from the flight, so to loosen up he walked to the briefing instead of hiring a taxi. He was the last to arrive, a half hour after everyone else. Climbing the steps to Galip's apartment, he noticed a man standing in the shadows but paid no further attention to him.

"It's great to see you all again," Morgan greeted them with a wide grin.

Arianna noticed he looked tanned and fit—even more handsome than she remembered. When their gazes suddenly meshed, her heart rate increased and she self-consciously folded her arms over her chest. Though she felt the heat rise up her neck and into her face, she managed to keep her expression blank when she spoke. "You look healthy enough. How was the skiing?"

"The skiing was great everywhere." Hearing Arianna's flat tone, Morgan, a bit annoyed, wondered, *What's eating her now?* He tossed his coat over the back of the only empty chair, across the room from Arianna, and fell into the seat with a sigh. Since leaving Turkey, he had skied several famous resorts, spending two or three days at each. However, the last two weeks, he had loafed in the Canary Islands, absorbing the sun. By then, he was eager to get back to Turkey. And, he had to admit, he missed the vocal sparring with Arianna, though she could be a pain at times.

On the Swiss Air flight to Ankara, Morgan had time to reflect on his life. With his inheritance, he had plenty of money; he was free to do what he wanted to do. *Then why isn't it enough?* he had asked himself. He had no confidant, no one to cherish. *I suppose I need a woman, a woman who is more than a one-night stand.* The thought had come unbidden. But he knew he was not yet ready for a serious relationship; Kwan Mei's memory was still too fresh.

"The skiing couldn't have been better," Morgan told Refah, "but since Korea I can't stand much cold. I had to go to the Canaries to thaw." Casting a roguish glance in Arianna's direction, Morgan said loud enough for her to hear, "You should have been there; those islands are made for romance. Might have warmed you up a bit." For once, Arianna had no ready retort. Morgan's sarcasm hurt more deeply than she ever would have expected. Why did she let him get to her like that?

Her attention was then drawn to Dr. Yaldiz, who was answering questions about the room's furnishings, proudly pointing out the exquisite lace and embroidered doilies and runners his wife had made when she was a girl. At that moment, Galip's wife entered the room accompanied by Halime. Halime carried a tray with two small pitchers and a stack of folded cloths. The two women poured a little rose water onto each person's hands and offered a hot scented towel to dry them. Finally, the team members were brought tea or coffee and rich honey-soaked baklava liberally sprinkled with bright green, finely ground pistachio nuts.

Morgan had settled into an overstuffed chair in a dark corner of the room, where he could observe the others without being in the limelight himself.

Feeling apologetic for her lack of warmth earlier, Arianna carried her refreshments over and perched on the arm of Morgan's chair. "Bev and I enjoyed your Mercedes. It was super of you to leave it with us."

"Did you get a chance to go anywhere?"

"We made one trip to Istanbul, but bad weather kept us close to home most of the time. We did a lot of running around in Ankara though."

"I haven't had a chance to see much of Ankara yet," Morgan said. "How about showing me around before we leave for Niğde?"

Arianna nodded. "But you drive. I detest driving in the city. And you buy lunch."

"I have to drive and buy, too?"

"Of course. Isn't that a proper date?" Laughing, Arianna left him to join Halime on the other side of the room.

The affable encounter with Arianna was a pleasant surprise. A *date,* she had said. How was he to take her comment? Morgan reflected on it as he half listened to Galip outline the coming season's work.

Galip closed the meeting two hours later. When Morgan rose to leave, a button on the left sleeve of his jacket caught in the chair arm's lace doily. The doily flipped off onto the floor, and Morgan stooped to pick it up. As he straightened, a yellow gleam reflecting from a large object in the cabinet next to the chair caught his eye. Curious, he bent closer to examine the gleam's source. When he saw what shone so brilliantly in the dim light, his face blanched with shock.

Galip noticed Morgan staring at the cabinet. The American, frozen in position, was shaking his head in disbelief. He jumped when Galip seized his shoulder in a friendly grip. "I see, Morgan McCauley, that you admire my mysterious golden tablet."

Unaware that Morgan had been struck dumb, Galip continued. "I found it many years ago. No one has yet deciphered the writing on it. Perhaps one day, yes?"

"A corner is missing," Morgan managed to finally mumble.

Galip shrugged. "Unfortunately, yes, but I do not think there is much lost, a few characters, perhaps. One would hope those are unimportant."

Morgan turned slowly around and faced the archaeologist. "It seems impossible, Dr. Yaldiz, but I may have the missing corner."

Chapter 56

Galip clasped Morgan's arm with an iron grip. "Where . . . how . . . did you acquire this piece you say is the missing corner to my relic?"

"I got it in Hong Kong." Morgan choked back what was nearly a sob, then hoarsely whispered, "A friend left it with me."

Galip was incredulous. "How in the name of Allah did it get from Turkey to Hong Kong?"

"It's a long story." Morgan could say no more about how he obtained the corner; the memory of Kwan Mei was still too painful. Yet his curiosity had been aroused. "How did you come by your piece?" he asked Galip.

"That, too, is a long story," was Galip's answer.

The two men were caught, each in his own time capsule. The room and other team members ceased to exist as Galip remembered. . . .

* * *

Near Mount Ararat, 1922

Treeless, rock-strewn hills surrounded the mountain Westerners call "Ararat." The barren slopes sent quivering heat waves skyward. Vegetation that did grow lay in low, withered tufts. Perched on a scorched boulder, an agitated lizard, the single visible life form, jerked its body up and down.

Born in the port city of Tekirdağ, Galip suffered intensely in eastern Anatolia's dry heat. He longed for home—to smell the tang of moist salt air, to plunge into the refreshing waters of the Marmara Sea. He tugged at his army cap, squinting to protect his sensitive gray-green eyes from the sun's glare. Pulling a rag from his pants pocket, he wiped his nose and coughed. To add to his misery, an allergy to the ever-blowing dust caused him to wheeze day and night.

Galip Yaldiz's partner, Tuhaf Cesur, threw his rifle to the ground and flopped into the boulder's sparse shade. The alarmed lizard scurried off.

"It is too hot to walk," Tuhaf whined. His dark brown eyes, tawny skin, and Semitic nose betrayed his Eastern Turkey ancestry while Galip, with his light eyes and fair skin, could have passed for a central European. The two men, one tall and slim, the other short and plump, represented but a small portion of Asia Minor's amalgam of race and culture.

Galip removed his cap to wipe perspiration from his forehead. Unhooking his canteen from his belt, he started to lift it for a drink, then stopped and shook it. Only a few drops were left; he had indulged his thirst too often during the morning. Vowing to wait for another sip of water, he reattached the canteen. With no other shade to shield him from the burning sun, he reluctantly squatted alongside Tuhaf, whom he detested.

Galip still felt sick when he remembered last year's slaughter of the Armenians. Tuhaf's constant boasting of his participation in the incident grated. Being ordered to patrol with the vulgar, bloodthirsty soldier was almost more than Galip could endure.

"Bokdan dağbaşi! What a foul wilderness!" Tuhaf hoisted his left leg and twisted the ankle from side to side. "My feet are sore," he complained. He swept the back of a sweaty hand across his thin lips, leaving a streak of saliva and dirt on his chin.

Galip had to agree with Tuhaf; the area was a wasteland. His gaze drifted to Büyük Ağri Daği, Great Ararat Mountain, thrusting its huge bulk from the desolate, eroded plain. The shimmering heat haze blended with the opalescent ice of its high-altitude glaciers, blurring the mountain's definition. The jagged Ahora Gorge gouged a gigantic black rip in its side.

Tuhaf shook his canteen. "It is empty," he informed Galip. He licked his cracked lips. "Do you have water?"

"No!" Galip had no sympathy for Tuhaf, who guzzled down his entire water ration in the first two hours of every patrol, then predictably demanded more from anyone with him. They would not reach the little stream that marked their turning point for another hour. Galip tried not to dwell on the thought of a long, cool drink. It only served to exacerbate his thirst.

Galip coughed and spat. "We must go on before we evaporate and become dust ourselves."

The two young soldiers gathered up their obsolete rifles, for which they had twelve rounds of outdated ammunition between them. As they started down the narrow track, Galip wondered, *Why does anyone need to patrol the godforsaken road at all? And why do I have to be paired with Tuhaf, a Communist boor?*

Since its inception, the Red Army had moved through the southeastern part of Russia driving town by town toward the Turkish border. The sultan had sent Galip's unit to prevent the Reds from entering Turkey, and to maintain law and order in the Mount Ararat region. Communist sympathizers had infiltrated the *erat*, the Turkish military. It hadn't taken long for the eternally disgruntled and egotistical Tuhaf to join their cause. Tuhaf tried to indoctrinate Galip with his Marxist philosophy, but gave up when Galip, who was a head taller and in far better condition, threatened to thrash him.

A typical bully, Tuhaf was not only a coward but had a vicious lust for blood. Whenever he could, he hunted small birds and animals for the sheer pleasure of extinguishing life. Tuhaf's fondest diversion, however, was hunting the most exciting animal on earth—man.

Galip would always regret his own part in the destruction of the Armenian village. Ordered to do so by his senior officers, he had helped to round up the men and older boys who were ultimately shot—but not by him. And, yes, he looted and burned, but he had not violated the women. From then on, he tried to avoid those who had taken part in it.

Tuhaf boasted of his odious deeds because he knew it irritated Galip. Now, as they approached the stream where they would break for lunch, Tuhaf launched into another of his lurid tales.

Galip had heard enough. "*Suş!* Shut up, or I'll put a bullet through your mouth, you son of a donkey."

Tuhaf glared at Galip, his face contorting with rage at the insult. He stuck the end of his rifle barrel under Galip's nose. Galip saw Tuhaf's knuckles whiten as his finger tightened on the trigger. He knew Tuhaf could fire at the slightest provocation, but Galip pushed the rifle away. Turning his back, he walked toward the poplars that lined the stream.

Trembling with anger, Tuhaf lowered the rifle. He would bide his time. When it was right, Galip would pay for the affront.

Though not profoundly religious, Galip was a Sunni Moslem and a spiritual man who believed in the one God, Allah, Creator of the world and all upon it. He did not enjoy the company of men who relished the idle killing of God-given life, but he had to follow orders or face a firing squad or hang.

Galip's abhorrence of intentional slaughter had begun while he was a boy of eight. His father had taken him to the mountain range that edged the Black Sea to hunt deer, but the hunt was a dismal failure. Whenever Galip had a deer in his gun sight, his finger refused to pull the trigger.

His father did not punish him, but he never again asked Galip to accompany him on a hunting trip, and neither of them again discussed the incident. Galip suspected his father thought him less a man for it. The father had always wanted his son to follow in his own profession as a doctor. As a result of Galip's attitude toward hunting, he mistakenly thought Galip couldn't stand the sight of bleeding flesh. Therefore, he gave up his dream of a medical career for his son.

By the time Galip reached his late teens, the political climate of Turkey had changed, and the social, political, and economic systems had become chaotic. In 1918, Mustapha Kemal, later known as "Attatürk, Father of the Turks," declared Turkey a new republic.

Mohammad VI, the last of a series of decadent sultans, stepped down from the throne under pressure. In 1922, Turkey officially became a republic, and Attatürk became president.

When Galip, idealistic at eighteen, insisted on joining the new Turkish Army, his father worried that his son would come to shame. However, Galip soon proved he could kill in the line of duty, which somewhat puzzled but pacified his father.

No longer eager to fight, Galip yearned to leave the army. His tour of duty ended in a month, and he would go home to Tekirdağ.

Galip and Tuhaf had reached the stream at that lazy hour of a sweltering day when animals, including humans, enjoyed a nap. The underground water table provided enough water year round for the moisture-seeking roots of the poplars and willows that ringed the tiny oasis. But at this season, the stream was only a stagnant trickle.

The stream had shifted many times over the centuries. Once, during a particularly severe storm, it had overflowed its banks and dug a new bed, the length of a soccer field away from the original cut. Later, the stream gradually worked its way back to where the large piece of Noah's twelfth golden tablet, the tablet missing the corner with Noah's personal mark, lay buried. Decades of erosion further stripped layers from over the tablet until it was hidden by a mere centimeter of sand and gravel.

Galip and Tuhaf settled under separate willows on the stream's bank. After he had eaten, Galip lay on his back with his hands pillowing his head. No matter how he wriggled his body around, he couldn't get comfortable. He sat up and examined the spot where he had been lying. Something just under the surface poked his back. Using both hands, he brushed aside gravel and sand. He immediately realized he had uncovered something gold. Before he could stop himself, he cried, "Praise be to Allah!"

Galip's loud exclamation awakened Tuhaf, who growled, "What is wrong with you? Why do you shout so?" But when Tuhaf saw Galip on his hands and knees frantically digging into the bank with his bare hands, he scrambled over to see what Galip was doing.

Both men gasped when Galip worked free a large tablet that looked to be *solid* gold. Galip carried it to the stream and rinsed off the age-old coating that dulled it. When he made out strange symbols pressed into the metal, he clutched the tablet to his breast. "I don't know what this is, but it is surely ancient."

Eyes glittering, Tuhaf stroked the tablet. "Is it gold throughout?"

Galip turned the tablet. "It is only covered with it," he said, his voice catching. He rubbed a finger along the broken edge. "See? The *çömlek,* the pottery, shows underneath where a corner is missing." He traced the delicate impressions. "Who could have inscribed such remarkable characters?"

Galip opened his tunic and tucked the heavy tablet inside. "It may have been washed down from the Ahora Monastery when the earthquake and landslide destroyed it in 1840. I must take it home for my father to see."

Tuhaf had seen only the yellow shine of gold; it was all that mattered; he had to have it. Tuhaf gritted his teeth. He would make sure Galip's father would never set eyes on it.

That night, and three more, Galip slept with the tablet at his side under the covers. During the day, he left it at post headquarters with an officer he trusted—an old friend of his father's. Neither Galip nor Tuhaf mentioned the find to anyone else.

Four nights later, as Galip soundly slept flat on his back, something bumped against his cot, awakening him. His eyelids flew open. Reflecting in the moonlight that shone through the window, a knife blade slashed toward his chest. Galip yelled and threw up a protective arm, parrying the hand holding the knife. His swift reaction saved him from serious injury; the knife merely penetrated skin and muscle and glanced off a rib. Despite the agony of his wound, Galip grabbed the knife-wielding arm and forced it toward the direction of his assailant's face. A man screamed, and the knife clattered to the floor. Groaning, Galip curled his body around the excruciating torture in his chest and arm.

The noise had awakened others. There was the sound of a scuffle next to Galip's cot as three men pinned a fourth to the floor. Grunting with pain, Galip rolled to his side. Someone held a lantern close to the pinned man. Tuhaf's glittering black eyes bored hatefully into his.

One side of Tuhaf's face had been badly gashed. Vile curses spewed from his mouth's bloody orifice. Even when they took him away, struggling against the ropes that bound him, Tuhaf did not reveal why he had attacked Galip. When questioned, Galip reported only that he and Tuhaf had disagreed on something.

CHAPTER 57

Tekirdağ, Turkey, 1922

Ascribing his injury to a troop training maneuver, Galip walked into his parent's home in Tekirdağ with his chest still sore. He unpacked his duffel and presented the golden tablet to his father. The unexpected gift overwhelmed the older man. Nothing in his extensive collection of antiquities was as impressive as the golden tablet, nor would prove to be such an enigma. With tears in his eyes, Galip's father embraced his son for the first time in many years.

It had taken Galip's father a lifetime to gather his fine collection of artifacts, which had stimulated Galip's own interest in ancient history at an early age. As a very young child, Galip's favorite piece in his father's collection had been a diminutive statuette carved from cream-colored soapstone. Though the voluptuous fertility goddess was headless, Galip incorporated it into his childhood play as a doll. Such idols were common finds in Turkey, and his father did not mind his son playing with the already damaged piece. It was the beginning of Galip's love for antiquities, and the love for his childhood plaything expanded to an interest in the ancient inhabitants of Asia Minor. Finding the mysterious gold-sheathed tablet had been the deciding factor in Galip's choice to become an archaeologist.

Galip's parents sat fascinated as Galip related how he had discovered the tablet. Galip asked his father, "Could it have washed down from the old Ahora Monastery?"

Galip's father had paused, deep in thought. "Yes, I do believe it could have come from the monastery. But if it is not from Ahora, it may be worth only the gold it contains."

At that time, Turkey was in turmoil, and its new government, under Kemal Attatürk, was in the process of reorganization. Galip's father thought it best to keep quiet about the tablet, and he cautioned Galip to do the same. Four months later the officer in Galip's former unit, the man who was a friend of Galip's father, sent a letter. In it, he mentioned that Galip's assailant, Tuhaf, was serving a long prison sentence for his attack on Galip. Galip was then forced to reveal to his father how he had really been injured, but it did not affect their new, closer relationship.

When his father died, Galip inherited the family collection of artifacts, including the tablet. Many of Galip's contemporaries saw the tablet displayed in Galip's living-room cabinet. Few theorized, and none guessed, the tablet's true origin.

After World War II, Galip sent a photograph of the tablet to a famous German cryptographer. The man, who was old and feeble by then, declared the writing a combination of hieroglyphics and an ancient form of Aramaic, which Galip had already surmised. What it was beyond that, the cryptographer could not say. He suggested that Galip send the actual tablet to him for intensive tests and study.

Before Galip could make up his mind whether or not to risk shipping the tablet to Germany, the old cryptographer died. Galip decided not to pursue the tablet's origin any further.

* * *

Now, with trembling fingers, Galip fished a ring of keys from his pocket, chose a key, and unlocked the cabinet. He had to use both hands to remove the unwieldy tablet. Holding it tightly against his chest, Galip turned to face Morgan and the rest of the team, which had gathered around the two men. The archaeologist's body seemed to increase in stature. He stood with his head thrown back. The harsh light from the room's single lamp illuminated his face, enhancing his prominent cheekbones and aquiline nose.

Dr. Yaldiz reminded Arianna of a carving—one depicting the Hititte war god that she had seen in the Ankara museum. The seven-and-a-half-foot stone image had been rendered in bas-relief. Its left arm was thrust forward and bent, its right hand held a club, or ritual object, against its chest. Neither Arianna nor Galip could have imagined that over three thousand years before, a remote ancestor of Galip's had sculpted the relief.

Galip's voice cracked when he asked Morgan, "Is the corner piece here in Turkey?"

"It's at my place," Morgan choked out.

Galip peered at his watch. "It is very late, but I *must* see it . . . try to fit the two pieces together."

Morgan nodded. "I'll drive you to the penthouse, Dr. Yaldiz. I'm as anxious as you are to see if they match."

"Let me have the Mercedes' keys," Morgan said to Arianna. "I'll drop you off on the way."

Handing the heavy tablet over to Morgan, Galip left to get his coat.

Arianna drew closer to Morgan. "I heard just bits and pieces of your conversation with Dr. Yaldiz." She ran her hand over the smooth gold. As her fingers gently traced the ancient inscriptions, her hand accidentally brushed Morgan's.

Despite his preoccupation with the tablet, Morgan warmed at her touch. "I may have the missing piece at the penthouse. I'll let you know what happens tomorrow," he said, heading toward the door as Galip rushed up buttoning his coat.

"But, I . . ." Arianna started to protest.

"Tomorrow!" Morgan repeated. He turned to Refah and Halime. "How about you two? Need a ride home?"

"I'll call a taxi for Refah and Halime," Galip said, moving toward the telephone.

Refah intervened. "Please, Dr. Yaldiz, there is no need to call for one. I myself will see that Halime arrives safely at her home. It is but a short walk from here."

Smiling, Galip replaced the receiver. "*Evet, daha iyi,* that is a good suggestion, Refah Bey."

Halime grimaced. She'd rather not be alone with Refah, but there was no way she could gracefully decline his offer. Yet, she had to admit, lately she had often welcomed his company. They had so much in common, so much to talk about. As children, they had been very close; she remembered racing Refah with warped hoops made of twisted grape vines, remembered constructing miniature villages of clay and straw. She was still smiling wistfully at the recollection as he held out her jacket.

* * *

Morgan dropped Arianna at her apartment, then drove on with Dr. Yaldiz. To protect the tablet, Galip had swaddled it in a thick Turkish towel. Deep in thought, the archaeologist cuddled the precious bundle in his arms. He was afraid to believe Morgan really had the missing corner. *If they are two parts of the same whole,* he mused, *it is an amazing coincidence.*

When they arrived at his apartment, Morgan immediately went to the night stand by his bed to fetch the cloisonné box that contained the corner. Meanwhile, Galip unwrapped the tablet and laid it on Morgan's coffee table. He watched, teeth bared and lids half closed, as Morgan reentered the room, opened the box, and removed an object wrapped in jade-green silk.

Balancing the silk-enshrouded object on his flattened palm, Morgan stated in a somber voice, "I hesitate to show this to you; if the pieces don't match, both of us will be terribly disappointed."

Galip squelched his urge to rudely snatch the packet from Morgan. Instead, he bellowed, *"Çabuk!* Hurry! Let us see if the two are one!"

Morgan carefully removed the triangular-shaped shard from its silk shroud and laid it on the coffee table beside Galip's tablet.

Galip's rapidly indrawn breath whistled through his teeth. Even without fitting the two pieces together, the match was obvious. He reverently leaned down and positioned the triangular shard into the very corner from which it had been torn thousands of years earlier.

Galip decided the two pieces of the tablet should temporarily remain as they were—the large piece with him, and the corner with Morgan. During the rest of winter, he attempted to decipher the tablet's mysterious characters on his piece. Twice, when experts in interpreting Hittite cuneiform happened to be in Istanbul, he took drawn copies of a few of the characters to them. The philologists were equally puzzled and demanded to see the originals. But Galip would not exhibit them. He did not want the tablet publicized until its authenticity had been proven. Once others knew about the artifact, Galip believed it would no longer be secure in his and Morgan's possession. As spring and the date to begin work on the Cappadocian dig approached, Galip decided to better protect the tablet pieces.

Morgan initially rebelled at relinquishing his last memento of Kwan Mei. Lately, though, it had not seemed as important to him. Galip finally persuaded Morgan to let him put it, along with the larger portion, into the museum vault.

Occasionally, Galip would remove the tablet pieces from the vault and take them to his office for contemplation. Sitting at his desk, he would fit the two pieces together, studying them intently. But the meaning of the strange characters continued to elude him.

Though the tablet intrigued her, Halime glimpsed it only briefly if she happened to be around when Galip had it out on his desk. She was extremely busy during the school year, racing about with little spare time. However, one day as she passed through the archaeologist's office, Galip was standing by a bookshelf riffling the pages of a large and dusty volume on ancient languages. Halime stopped short, surprised at the unusual clutter on Galip's desk. Books and scraps of paper filled with scribbled notes covered the surface. The tablet lay at an off-angle to Halime's view, but her eyes were automatically drawn to it by the gleam of polished gold. The tablet's unusual angle presented the characters in a different aspect. Like invisible ink under heat, one hieroglyphic magically materialized into a crude hippopotamus. She bent to examine the character.

It was plain; the symbol was definitely a hippo, and two small dots had been impressed next to the hippo's body. Halime studied the tablet. Though some hieroglyphics were faint or appeared distorted, she was able to make out two dots in juxtaposition to many of them. Some characters had different accompanying marks, but it seemed they had a common pattern or theme. She almost said something to Dr. Yaldiz, but he was engrossed in his search, and she didn't want to disturb him. Anyway, he surely had seen the same thing.

She decided not to mention her theory until a more opportune moment.

Chapter 58

The underground city, where centuries earlier Gregori the monk secreted the tablets, had seven entrances, each hidden within an uninhabited house. Amid the surface clutter of shops and homes, those "gateway" houses were indistinguishable from other buildings. Sealed from below, the underground maze was virtually impenetrable. With multiple wells and packed warehouses at their disposal, those who fled underground in times of siege could survive for years.

Waves of crusaders came and went. When the Fourth Crusade–a Crusade for Christ in name only–looted and virtually destroyed Constantinople, the Byzantine Empire reeled in a downward spiral. It left rural monasteries without central leadership.

The Ottomans eventually conquered the entire continent of Asia Minor. Constantinople, by then a dying metropolis, was left until last. The magnificent city's end finally came at the hand of the determined and clever Mehmet II, leader of the Ottoman Turks. The Ottoman Empire gradually absorbed the Seljuks.

When the Moslems migrated to Cappadocia and the Hidden Valley, they destroyed any exposed painted faces. According to the Qur'an, those were "forbidden images." Collapsed or inaccessible chapels, such as Gregori's Tile Chapel with its glorious portrait of Najila as Mary, escaped damage.

At first, the Ottomans let other religions coexist with their Islamic beliefs. People no longer had to seek refuge from persecution underground. However, on a torrid summer day, the corridors and caves below the surface offered relief from the heat. Locals continued to use parts of the upper levels as dwellings to stable their stock and for storage. Few people ventured beyond the fourth level to the lower underground passages and caverns that did remain accessible.

The Hidden Valley remained inhabited until the mid-twentieth century. As the underground city's tufa ceilings and walls rotted and collapsed, many lives were lost. In the 1960s, the Turkish government evicted everyone for their own safety.

* * *

Cappadocia Province, Turkey, 1968

With a new season upon them, Galip and Morgan threw themselves into their work. Logistics occupied them, and they had little time to think about the broken tablet. After Turkey's worst winter in thirty years, the weather mellowed at last. The deep snowpacks retreated; Anatolian villagers no longer had to protect themselves and their livestock from starving mountain wolves.

The team's primary task was to prepare a field laboratory and campsite for the students and amateur archaeologists who would help that summer. Arianna looked forward to working in her own specialty, in what she most enjoyed—potsherd archaeology. Halime had worked with Arianna during the survey but now held her customary post as administrative aide to Galip.

Galip's policy was for every team member, no matter what rank or title, to spend time every day in the field with a brush or trowel. Although Halime remained Galip's aide, she and Arianna jointly supervised the excavation of side-by-side grids in a large underground room. Arianna and Halime believed this room to have once been the dwelling of an important person. They hired Mohammed, a young man from the nearby village, to perform the heaviest digging and to haul the exhumed debris to the surface for screening.

Mohammed, a wiry lad of seventeen, proved to be eager and bright. He and Arianna got along well, but because of her limited Turkish, Arianna often had to call on Halime or Refah to translate. Mohammed tried to teach Arianna the words they most often used, but his rural accent, quite different from that of someone from Ankara or Istanbul, made it difficult for Arianna to understand. Her frustration often showed. Consequently, Mohammed felt sorry for her and grew protective.

As Refah's assistant and official photographer, Morgan recorded the team's daily progress. He was at the site early every morning and again at day's end. Between photo sessions he did book work, sometimes at the motel, sometimes at the dig.

Refah seemed to be everywhere at once, and Ahmet, the Turkish labor foreman, was always at his side. Arianna disliked Ahmet from the day Refah first introduced him to the team. Ahmet looked right through her, as though she wasn't there at all, as though she didn't exist. Initially, she thought he might be shy. In time, she changed her mind. The man made her skin crawl, though she couldn't define anything concrete that caused her unease.

During the past winter, Refah had contracted a Turkish electrician to wire the excavation site. Bare light bulbs hanging from wires strung along the ceilings now illuminated the underground city where they worked. Everywhere else, particularly down in the lowest levels, it was total darkness. A person going into an unlit section had to carry a powerful, long-lasting flashlight or lantern.

A favorite pastime of Arianna's, during her off hours, was the exploration of the subterranean city's unmapped areas. Sometimes Morgan went with her, sometimes Halime or Refah went along.

One day, Arianna decided to reexamine a large room at the deepest level. Refah believed the huge cavern might have been a common area for celebrations and meetings. Because of the room's size and its considerable distance from every entrance to the underground city, Arianna argued that it was a refuge in case of attack. She hoped to find evidence that would lend credence to her theory.

No one was free to accompany her on her investigation. Halime and Refah were off working in another place. Morgan was still at the hotel, scheduled to come to the site later in the dolmuş.

"Mohammed, I'm going below for a while." Arianna shoved a geologist's pick into her belt and lit a lantern. Pointing toward the dark opening that led to the next level down, she said, "If Halime comes, tell her where I am."

Not wholly comprehending Arianna's words, Mohammed merely grinned. As Arianna left, he returned to his digging.

Arianna carefully made her way through centuries-old rock debris not yet cleared from the narrow passages. The section she wanted to explore lay four levels down and half a mile east of the active site. It took her twenty minutes to reach the sixth level.

At the far end of the gloomy passageway to the Great Room lay a steep flight of rough, hand-cut steps. Lifting her lantern high, Arianna cautiously started down. The rubble-strewn steps were not uniform and, in the lantern's flickering light, she had difficulty seeing where she was going.

Precisely positioning each foot as she descended, Arianna was about two-thirds of the way down when she heard the sound of something moving behind her. Startled, she turned to see what it was and lost her concentration. Instead of landing squarely on a flat surface, her foot hit the step's beveled edge and slid off. Her ankle turned and she plummeted, head first, into the blackness below.

Arianna had no idea how long she had been unconscious. Because she could see nothing, she thought she was dead. Then waves of nauseating pain pulsated in her head, arm, and foot. *One was not supposed to hurt in heaven.* She lay on her left side in absolute darkness. She vaguely remembered falling. When she tried to get up, she screamed as pain seared through her body. Her right ankle was useless, perhaps broken. Her right elbow and arm hurt the worst, and she could not move the limb without crying out. The fingers of her left hand tentatively probed her throbbing head; they found sticky gobs of blood matting the hair over her right ear. Lying absolutely motionless to let the pain and nausea subside, Arianna began to realize her predicament.

Dear God, how long have I been here? Injured and alone, she couldn't even see. Then she remembered the lantern. Groaning, she turned onto her stomach and groped in the thick layer of choking dust. The effort made her almost faint, but she kept searching. Her fingers closed on cold metal. As she dragged the lantern closer, she heard the tinkle of broken glass, and felt that the metal was wet with oil. She weakly shook what remained of the lantern. It was empty.

* * *

Mohammed continued to dig and haul loads to the screeners until it was time to quit. Halime had not come by, and he briefly wondered why Matmazel Arista had not returned, but team personnel was not his responsibility.* Besides, he knew by reputation that American women cared for themselves. At day's end, Mohammed left for his village without telling anyone that Arianna had gone off by herself.

No one missed Arianna until Morgan returned from Niğde to photograph the day's work and to transport the team to the hotel. When he arrived at the site, Morgan followed his usual procedure of shooting the day's finds. He finished, then waited in the dolmuş for the rest of the team. Refah soon joined him. They were deep in discussion about a strangely-shaped pot discovered that day when Halime threw her rucksack on the middle seat and climbed in after it.

"Where is Arianna?" Refah asked her.

"I have not seen her since lunch," Halime answered.

An alarm sounded in Morgan's brain. "I haven't seen her since this morning." He thought a moment. "Mohammed was working with her. Has he gone home?"

Just then, Ahmet strutted by, but did not look over at them.

"I will ask Ahmet if he has seen Miss Arista." Refah jumped out of the dolmuş closely followed by Morgan. Refah shouted at Ahmet, stopping the foreman in his tracks. Morgan stood by while Refah questioned Ahmet in Turkish. Refah turned to Morgan. "Ahmet says no one is underground. He saw Mohammed heading toward the village."

Matmazel means *mademoiselle* (French). The Turkish language contains many French words and phrases.

Morgan grabbed Refah's arm and pulled him toward the entrance to the underground city. "Let's go inside. Arianna might be locked in."

Refah shook his head. "I think we should go to the village to ask Mohammed about Miss Arista. He works with her; he must have seen her last."

"She may have gone back to Niğde," Morgan said hopefully.

"I do not believe she had reason to go there. Please, Morgan Bey, let us find Mohammed. It will save much time," Refah urged.

"Okay, but tell Ahmet to come with us. We may need him."

Refah said something to Ahmet and the foreman jumped into the dolmuş front passenger seat. Morgan and Refah took the second seat.

It took twenty-five minutes to drive to the village and locate Mohammed. Refah translated for Morgan while he and Ahmet questioned the boy. "Mohammed claims Miss Arista went down to a lower level by herself," Refah said. He looked worried.

Without warning, Ahmet suddenly balled his fist and hit Mohammed. The blow skidded along the side of Mohammed's head, and he sank to the ground, blood spurting from his ear. Before Morgan and Refah could react, Ahmet straddled Mohammed and pummeled the hapless boy.

Refah and Morgan leaped to Mohammed's rescue. Morgan yanked Ahmet to his feet. Drawing back his fist, he was about to hit Ahmet when Refah grabbed Morgan's arm. "I will take care of him."

Refah spoke to the foreman in clipped, angry Turkish. Ahmet's black eyes glittered and his mouth tightened. He answered Refah's questions in an imperious tone. Refah repeated the conversation to Morgan. "Ahmet says Mohammed was negligent. That is why he punished him. Ahmet also says he will help us search for Miss Arista, but he is not happy to delay his evening meal." Refah's tone betrayed his disgust.

The atmosphere in the crowded dolmuş was thick with tension as they sped back to the underground city. Despite Refah's repeated rebukes, Ahmet continued to belabor Mohammed's perceived negligence. Pale and shaken, poor Mohammed sat in silence, clasping a bloody cloth over his injured ear. With each curse the foreman hurled at him, he shrank farther into the van's corner.

Arianna's teeth chattered not only from shock but from cold. The thick wool sweater she always wore when underground was not enough to protect her from the cavern's icy air and chilly floor. She knew she could not remain inactive much longer in the frigid temperature; she had to have help. Using her good arm and foot, she propelled her body forward like a baby learning to crawl. Her fingers groped for the stone staircase. She hoped she was headed in the right direction.

It seemed she crawled a hundred yards before she finally touched the bottom step. Dragging herself upward, she nearly passed out when she accidentally bumped her injured arm on the broken edge of a step. At last, her grasping fingers clawed at the groove that held the round stone gate. Knowing she had to be at the corridor entrance, she sobbed with relief. She reached out expecting to find space—the passageway opening. Instead, her hand hit solid stone.

Confused, Arianna lay still for a moment. Then it hit her. Somehow the massive wheel door had rolled across the opening, sealing her in. "Jesus, please help me!" she screamed into the black void.

CHAPTER 59

They stood just outside the underground city's entrance. Mohammed shook with apprehension. "I do not know where Matmazel Arista went." He was almost crying. "I do not know when she left. I think after the noon meal."

Morgan interrupted Refah's relentless interrogation of the boy. "He's told us everything he can, Refah." Picturing a worst case scenario, Morgan insisted, "We have to go down there and look for Arianna. She might have fallen; she might be unconscious or bleeding. Tell Ahmet to unlock the gate."

Ahmet, who had hidden his considerable knowledge of the English language from everyone, including Refah, understood what Morgan said but pretended not to. Morgan had already turned away; he did not see Ahmet's change of expression. However, Refah happened to glance at Ahmet at that instant. He saw the hate in Ahmet's eyes. Ahmet's unwarranted hostility puzzled Refah. What grievance did his foreman have against Morgan? The rest of his fellow Turks liked the big American.

"Open the gate, Ahmet Bey," Refah said quietly.

Slowly, deliberately, Ahmet retrieved a rusty iron key from his pocket and inserted it into the old-fashioned lock. The lock refused to release, though Ahmet twisted the key back and forth.

Morgan shouldered Ahmet aside. Grabbing the key, he disengaged the lock with one hard rotation. Holding up the key, he turned and faced the foreman with a questioning stare. His expression sullen, Ahmet merely shrugged.

Morgan was the first through the heavy metal gate, followed by the rest of the team, including Halime. When Refah pulled the switch for the central electric distribution unit that controlled the underground city's lighting, nothing happened.

Refah flipped the switch twice more. "The power is out again. Allah curse the Russians who make defective generators such as this one. We must use lanterns."

As they advanced through the silent corridors like ghosts of the underground city's long-dead inhabitants, their feet stirred up the powdery dust. It drifted in lazy tendrils, carried on the draft that always swirled through the passages whenever the entrance gate stood open.

"Why would Arianna have gone below by herself?" Morgan asked Halime. "She knows the rules. No one should go alone into the unworked sections."

Halime appeared pale and stricken. "Arianna did not tell me she wanted to go down there today. I would have gone with her."

"She did not say anything to me," Refah said.

They had descended to the excavation site where Arianna last worked. Morgan adjusted his lantern flame higher. "No sign of her here. Refah, ask Mohammed if he has any idea in which direction she may have gone."

Refah briefly spoke to Mohammed. Pointing to a narrow opening in the limestone, he said, "Mohammed remembers Arianna entered that tunnel."

Morgan started for the opening, then stopped. "Refah, why don't you have Ahmet search another area just in case we're heading in the wrong direction?"

Refah nodded. "That is a good idea."

When Refah told Ahmet to search the passage opposite the one Morgan and the rest of them were about to enter, Ahmet argued loudly in staccato Turkish. The two Turks debated a moment, then Ahmet shrugged and sullenly went into the other passage.

"What was all that about?" Morgan asked Refah.

Refah thrust up his chin, clucking his tongue. "Ahmet says he does not like to go into that area. He believes it contains bad spirits. I told him there is no proof of anything in there, and I personally wanted him to go that way." Refah shot Morgan a wry grin. "Ahmet does not wish to lose his fine-paying job." Refah shook Morgan's arm sympathetically. "Now, let us seek Miss Arista, my friend."

Followed by Morgan and Halime, Refah entered the same passage Arianna had taken. Refah had been in that particular passageway several times and was familiar with its twists and turns. He walked swiftly, holding his lantern low to see his way across the debris-strewn floor.

Morgan and Halime were soon left behind. When Refah went around a bend in the passage, they lost sight of him and saw only the glow of his lantern. Suddenly, they heard a shout. Refah's words were unintelligible, muffled by distance and bad acoustics, but the urgency in his voice caused Morgan and Halime to break into a trot despite the dangerous footing.

They found Refah standing in front of a massive round stone. He frowned. "Someone rolled it shut. It was open when I checked this corridor two days ago."

Morgan examined the huge wheel. "I haven't been down here before. I'm scheduled to photograph this area next week." He knew the ancient occupants of the underground city fashioned immense stone wheels to close off strategic passages in case of attack from above. When not closed, the wheels rested in deep notches chiseled into the wall. The groove in which a wheel laid slanted downward toward the far wall. The gentle slope allowed one man to easily roll the wheel shut. Once in position, the wheel-door effectively sealed the city's inhabitants in and the invaders out. Gravity made it difficult to roll the wheel back up the ramp. With the wheel closed and a wedge lodged behind it, no enemy could penetrate that particular passageway without smashing the great stone.

Clearly upset, Refah demanded of Halime, "Who closed this? Dr. Yaldiz does not want anything disturbed before Morgan photographs it."

"I, too, heard Dr. Yaldiz tell the workers not to move the wheels. This was open when Arianna and I were here last year—long before you came down here," Halime said, miffed by Refah's accusing tone. Refah and Morgan then tried to heave the huge stone wheel aside, but they discovered that both of them using their combined strength could not move it one inch.

* * *

Arianna fought the hypothermia that numbed the pain but dulled her senses. "Dear God, please do something; please, please help me," she whispered through chattering teeth into the dark. Praying did not come easy, even on this desperate occasion. She was not yet sure that God answered personal prayers anyway. But talking to anyone—even a distant deity—in the vacuumlike silence comforted her. She tried to remember the Lord's Prayer. "Our Father, who art in . . ." She stopped. Had she really heard voices from the other side of the thick stone?

Pounding her fist on the unyielding rock, Arianna screamed, "I'm here! I'm in here!"

* * *

Halime heard Arianna's faint call first. "That is Arianna!" she cried.

"Praise be to Allah," Refah breathed.

Morgan put his mouth close to the fine crack between the wheel and the wall. "We hear you, Arianna! How are you?"

Morgan! Oh, thank you, God. "My arm and ankle are broken, and I'm freezing. Please get me out. Please hurry!" Arianna sobbed.

"Refah and Halime are with me. We'll try to roll the wheel open. Can you help from that side?" Morgan asked. "We'll do it on the count of *three.*"

"I'll try." Arianna willed her lethargic body to obey, but she was too weak to help them. "I can't," she moaned.

"Don't hurt yourself any more. We'll manage somehow," Morgan told her.

Refah stooped in front of the wheel to examine the stone trough that held it in place. "We need a wedge to get it started."

Swinging his lantern back and forth to light every crack and cranny, Morgan searched the passage around them. "Nothing here that would work."

"There are shovels and picks where Arianna was working. I could get them," Halime suggested.

Refah agreed. "That is a good idea. We need two shovels and one pick. Morgan, you go with Halime. It is too much for her to carry. I will stay here and plan what we will do."

"Let's go, then," Morgan shouted to Halime. Grabbing their lamps, they tore down the passage, retracing their steps to the site where Arianna and Mohammed worked. They returned in ten minutes with the shovels and pick.

When new, the wheel and its frame had exactly matched. Some ancient engineer had created a perfect seal with no vulnerable fissures. Fortunately, erosion had softened the contours of both wheel and opening, and the fit was no longer precise. Refah inserted a shovel blade into the fine crevice, between the frame and the wheel's edge. As he pried at it, the wheel moved a little. "*Çok güzel.* Very good," he grunted. "Morgan, when I make a space, wedge your shovel blade into the opening. Halime, when it is large enough for Arianna to come through, set the pick crosswise into it to keep the wheel from rolling back down the ramp."

Refah threw his weight against the shovel handle. It bent and creaked, but did not break. Slowly, the wheel edged upward toward the notch in the wall. When there was room, Morgan worked his own blade into the opening, and the two men pried together.

The gap widened to four inches. From her side Arianna managed to force a rock into it. When the gap was wide enough, Halime jammed the pick lengthwise into the groove, between the wheel and the wall.

Refah and Morgan hesitated before removing their shovels; they did not want the wheel to roll back and crush Arianna as she came through. Satisfied that the steel pick would hold the wheel safely, Morgan reached into the opening. Arianna held out her hand to him. He grasped her wrist and dragged her through. During the rough maneuver, she cried out in agony, but, now safe and sobbing with relief, she threw her good arm around Morgan's neck as he bent over her. "I didn't think you'd find me; I thought I was going to die in there."

As he carried Arianna the half mile to the surface, Morgan was profoundly aware of her smooth skin against his. He paused to tenderly kiss her cheek.

Arianna said nothing, but tucked her chin more firmly into the curve under his jaw. Despite her intense pain, she was fully aware of the strong but gentle support of Morgan's arms.

When they reached the third level, Refah and Morgan called to Ahmet. He did not answer and there was no sign of the foreman. They did not pause to consider his strange behavior. Even if he remained inside, they had no choice but to lock the entrance to the underground city behind them. That done, they left for Niğde to find a doctor for Arianna.

CHAPTER 60

Refah stood just inside the underground city's entrance, holding a clipboard with a list of Turkish laborers. Running the point of his pencil down the list, Refah told Morgan, "Everyone reported for work, Ahmet included." As he said this, Refah penciled a check next to Ahmet's name.

"Ahmet deserted us yesterday, Refah. What if we had needed him to help get Arianna out?"

"I am angry, too," Refah agreed. "I have known Ahmet many years, yet I now discover he is a stranger."

Morgan's mouth tightened. "I don't care for the man; I can't help it."

"He is a good foreman; things would not go well without him."

The American nodded. "True enough. Guess there's no choice but to work with him. However, I *would* like to know why he skipped. And if he was down there, how did he get out after we locked the gate?"

"I am told there are a hundred passages leading underground. We have blocked some entrances. Others, the local people have kept secret." Refah slipped his pencil into his shirt pocket. "This morning, I must make the long trip to Adana to buy supplies. I cannot confront Ahmet until tomorrow afternoon."

"If you learn more, clue me in right away, won't you? We have to get to the bottom of this."

In Adana, Refah purchased fresh fruit and vegetables, then entered a shop that resembled a general store of the type common around the turn of the century in midwestern America. The little shop had almost everything a rural Turk might need. A jumble of rusted farm tools and plastic housewares dangled from the ceiling and walls. Cardboard boxes of seed, nails, and miscellaneous household fixtures lined part of one wall. A stack of brightly colored carpets woven by the local women lay on the floor in the middle of the shop.

Refah searched until he found the thing he wanted buried under a pile of miscellaneous clutter in a remote corner of the store.

Arianna was too stiff and sore to work at the site. As it turned out, her ankle was badly sprained not broken; a cast and sling supported her broken arm. She tried to help Halime clean and classify, but the task proved too much, so she volunteered to sort the staggering pile of paperwork. It released a grateful Halime of the onerous chore.

On his return from Adana, Refah found Arianna frowning over a stack of invoices. He held something behind his back. "I have brought you help."

Her expression sour, Arianna looked around the room. "Who?"

"Not who. What." Refah held out a handcrafted, T-shaped object made of wood. "I purchased this in Adana."

Arianna's expression immediately softened. "Oh, Refah, what a thoughtful gift." She reached for the crude crutch. Placing it under her good arm, she awkwardly rose to her feet, saying, "It's wonderful! I thank you from the depths of my soul, Refah. You'll never know how grateful I am. Now I can escape this awful paperwork and go below again."

Refah grinned. "Not until you get used to it."

The crutch hurt Arianna's underarm at first, but after Halime taped a doubled towel around the horizontal portion of the *T*, it no longer irritated her. Four days after her entrapment, Arianna returned to work below ground.

Meanwhile, Galip and Refah thoroughly questioned everyone involved with the site, from Morgan and Halime to the least significant of the part-time laborers. No one admitted to having seen anything unusual.

"The stone door couldn't possibly have rolled down the incline by itself, could it?" Morgan asked Refah. Though he knew the answer, he had to ask.

"I do not think so. It has been in place for decades, and it would take a strong man to move it. The laborers were told their first day on the job not to touch anything without permission."

"How about visitors?"

"I have checked. No tourists or unauthorized persons visited the site that day."

Morgan looked disappointed. "Then, we still know nothing?"

"Correct."

Hearing of Arianna's accident and on summer vacation, Beverly drove to Niğde. She found Arianna unusually quiet and introspective. When they had a chance to talk that night, Arianna told Beverly, "At the time I was too terrified for it to register, but thinking about it now, I felt God—or something—was nearby when I was trapped down there. I couldn't see anything in the dark, but my impression was of a palpable presence. I know I didn't imagine it."

"The Holy Spirit! It had to be."

Arianna shivered. "I wish I knew. It was eerie."

Beverly, sensing that Arianna was at last ready, that same night led her friend to Christ.

Within a few days, Beverly went home to Ankara. Despite himself, Morgan wanted to learn more. Because he had no Bible of his own and could not readily obtain one, he asked Arianna if they could study together when they both were free. This Sunday evening was one of those rare opportunities. They sat on a sagging divan in the motel lobby. Arianna's Bible lay open on the cushion between them.

Morgan took Arianna's good hand in his. "Promise me you won't ever again go off alone."

Arianna laid her cheek against Morgan's shoulder. "It will kill me, but I promise."

"It is your cussed independence that will kill you." Morgan patted her hand. Arianna had changed. Much of what now attracted him to her was what had attracted him to Kwan Mei. Why? The common denominator, he reluctantly admitted to himself, was that both were Christians. *I'm a rotten cad, but I fall for decent women,* he concluded. He lightly kissed the top of

Arianna's head and thought, *Maybe she can tame me as she has tamed herself.* He did not yet realize that it was the Holy Spirit who had tamed her.

Halime's respect for Refah steadily grew, especially since Arianna's rescue. She saw he was liked by everyone, though he often had to mediate heated labor disputes among the workers. Often, when he was nearby, she caught herself covertly watching him.

Arianna and Halime sat at a table in Arianna's motel room sorting shards uncovered that day in Halime's grid. They used soft damp cloths to clean the chaotic collection, then tried to match the pieces as if working a giant jigsaw puzzle.

Halime held out a jagged shard the size of her palm for Arianna's inspection. "This reminds me of the markings on Dr. Yaldiz's big artifact—the gold one." She pushed the fragment across the table to Arianna.

The unknown potter had sketched a dog-type animal with ochre slip, a yellow colored, liquid clay. Only the front half of the body remained.

"Did you ever really study Dr. Galip's tablet, Arianna? It shows many animal-like signs that are similar to this."

Head bent, eyes focused on sorting, Arianna merely shook her head.

Halime rested her chin on the heel of her hand. "It had animals and numbers; I am sure of it." She glanced at her watch and jumped up. "Dr. Yaldiz is still awake. Let us go see him."

Arianna yawned and stretched her good arm. She had half-heard what Halime said. "I need a break anyway." She rose and adjusted the crutch. "Say that again. I apologize; I wasn't really listening."

CHAPTER 61

It was Galip's habit to leave his door ajar until he went to bed in case someone wanted to evaluate the day's work with him. He was reading an archaeological magazine when Halime and Arianna paused at the threshold.

Halime spoke first. "Dr. Yaldiz, may Arianna and I come in?"

The archaeologist put down the magazine. "Yes, yes, come in." He waved an empty glass. "I am ready for another tea. Will my most favorite young ladies join me?"

When Arianna and Halime agreed, Galip phoned the desk to order a samovar and additional glasses.

"Sit! Sit!"

The women sat on spare camp stools that were always on hand in Galip's room. Galip settled in his desk chair, crossed his legs, and lit a cigarette. He puffed clouds of foul smoke at the ceiling until Arianna choked and had to repress a cough. Galip never noticed.

"Halime and Arianna, you look uncommonly elated."

"Forgive me, Arianna," Halime apologized, "but I can explain my ideas to Dr. Yaldiz better in my own language." She began to speak to Galip in Turkish. "Dr. Yaldiz, you once said you found your mysterious tablet near Büyük Ağri Daği. Is that not so?"

Her question surprised Galip; Halime had never shown much interest in the artifact. "That is true," he answered. "I was a young soldier in the army. Why do you ask, Halime Bayan?"

"Tonight, a thought came to me, Dr. Yaldiz. Could the hieroglyphics on the tablet be a *müfredat-cetveli*?"

"A detailed list? List of what?"

"Of animals. The English have a word . . ." Switching to English, Halime turned to Arianna. "There is an English word for the record a store uses to keep track of what it has."

Arianna thought a minute. "A stock list?" she offered. Halime shook her head. "I'm sorry, Halime. I'm not sure what you mean."

Just then, Morgan rapped on the side of the door frame. "Is this a private conference or may I join you?"

Galip waved him in. "Come, Morgan Bey. I sadly lack chairs. You will have to sit on the bed."

Morgan sat on the faded spread. Turning to Halime, he said, "I happened to overhear your question. Is *inventory* the word you're looking for?"

Halime's face lit up. "It is exactly the right word. Thank you, Morgan Bey." She turned to Galip. "I believe the tablet is an inventory."

Galip thought a moment. "It is possible," he said at last.

"Didn't the ancients usually write their inventories on stone, clay, or animal skins?" Arianna asked. "Has anyone ever found anything that old on metal, Dr. Yaldiz?"

"I myself have not seen such a thing."

"There might be something to what Halime says, Dr. Yaldiz," Morgan broke in. "You and I have had little time to discuss the tablet. Where did you find it, anyway?"

"I just asked Dr. Yaldiz the same question," Halime remarked.

Suddenly, a tiny spark flickered within Galip Yaldiz's mind. When Morgan uttered the word *inventory*, then asked about the tablet's origin, the spark burst into a flame that threatened to consume Galip. The others' animated conversation became a dull roar in his ears, and he feared his middle-aged heart would pound itself to bits. In a hoarse monotone, he said, "Morgan Bey, I found it at the foot of Mt. Ararat."

There was a pregnant silence. Halime's hands started shaking, so she tightly clasped them together. Her voice trembled with emotion as she said, "The story of Noah is in our Koran, as it is in the Christian and Jewish sacred books. Perhaps the tablet is from the ark."

Not truly recognizing the impact of Halime's statement, Arianna cuffed Morgan's shoulder. "Think of it, you and Dr. Yaldiz may have discovered the sole surviving artifact of Noah's ark."

Barely recovered from his initial shock, Galip said, "It would not be the *only* object remaining from the ark. You forget the hand-tooled wood retrieved by Fernand Navarra in 1955, and wood recovered by the team he guided in 1969."

"I'm not denigrating Navarra's discovery, but his find was only wood," Arianna argued. "Also, was it even authenticated?"

"It is from a species of tree nonexistent today," Galip said.

"Nothing proves it's a part of the ark, and carbon dating isn't always accurate on items that old. The tablet, on the other hand, has legible characters on it," Arianna countered, but her professional objectivity was rapidly deteriorating. "Noah's signature, or any signature from his era, could be indisputable proof, could it not?"

"Always there are those who would debate its authenticity, Miss Arista," was Galip's ironic reply.

Morgan had a sobering thought. "Presuming we have an inventory of some sort, can it be translated?"

Galip laughed, then said wistfully, "If the Czech genius Bedrich Hrozny still lived, there would be no doubt. However, he is long dead. Therefore, tomorrow, I will phone a Dutch philologist colleague."

Galip gazed at Halime, a hint of moisture in his eyes. "Halime Bayan, you are the one to whom Morgan and I should give the credit, should we learn what the golden tablet has to say." Galip took Halime's hand and gently lifted it to his lips. *"Teşekkür ederum,* we both thank you." Ignoring a Turkish taboo against such intimacy, Galip kissed his assistant's fingers.

CHAPTER 62

Galip's home study looked nothing like his neat museum office. Randomly stacked books and magazines filled the shelves and bookcases that lined the walls. Galip sat behind a cluttered desk sorting through old Byzantine coins he had purchased the day before.

Galip's wife entered the room. "There is a long-distance telephone call for you from Amsterdam."

Galip dropped the coin he had been examining and leapt to his feet. Racing to the phone, which was in another room, he picked up the receiver.

"Hello, Galip my friend!" The Dutch philologist spoke in heavily accented English, the only language common to both men.

Galip strained to make sense out of the awkward words, a feat made doubly difficult by transcontinental static.

"The characters represent a list . . . animals," the Dutchman was saying, ". . . two marks above a hieroglyph. A pair . . . species . . . characters show two marks . . . symbol above. I think it is a *Zeven.*"

"A what?" To Galip, the last word had sounded like "saben," with a long *A*.

The long-distance connection was suddenly clear, and Galip heard the philologist laugh.

"*Seven,* . . . the number seven."

Galip hid his exultation with difficulty. If his suspicions were confirmed, he doubted that the world, even Turkey, was ready for such a disclosure. He had to be careful, go slowly, not give too much away, particularly to a fellow professional who might let this important information slip to the press. His country would not welcome an inundation of scientists and the world press streaming to the sensitive Mount Ararat region near the Russian border. He remembered the trouble that previous ark expeditions had experienced, especially with the Turkish authorities.

Of course, he would tell Morgan, because Morgan had the matching piece. And he would also tell Refah, Halime, and Arianna; they all deserved an update. He trusted their loyalty and discretion.

Calming his voice as much as possible, Galip asked, "Were you able to decipher all I sent you?"

The telephone connection worsened. "I finished . . . copies . . . assume . . . others," came the crackling reply.

"I sent you a copy of everything," Galip shouted, frustrated.

"It is not . . . have . . . partial list." The Dutchman's next sentence was brilliantly clear, as was the rest of the transmission. "Do you believe, as I do, that the tablet could be from Noah's ark?"

Galip's heart skipped a beat; he could not think of a safe answer.

The philologist suggested, "Read Genesis, the first book in the Christian Bible."

"I am familiar with the tale," Galip croaked.

"According to the Bible, Noah's ark contained more animals than this tablet records," the philologist continued.

Galip didn't dare admit that he, too, believed the artifact was from the ark. But what was this about *more*? Cautiously, he asked, "This may not be the only tablet, then?"

"I am sure there were others."

Every nerve in Galip's body hummed. A wave of exhilaration flooded his mind's remotest corners, teasing and titillating. He wanted to drop the receiver and dance around the room—to shout praises to Allah. Instead, controlling his emotional high, he calmly asked, "Can you determine the script's author?"

"Dr. Galip Yaldiz, my dear friend, if you want for me to say Father Noah made the tablet, I cannot. It is sorry I am, but, there is nothing to prove he wrote the inscriptions."

Galip sighed, relieved, yet disappointed.

The Dutchman continued. "Your tablet appears very old. Do you think it a hoax, Galip?"

"I have no doubt as to its age. A cursory carbon dating of microscopic biological ash in the clay shows it was created at least six thousand years ago."

The philologist sighed. "To see the original, a year of my life I would give."

Galip caught the Dutchman's wistful tone and decided to reveal a bit more. "I found the larger piece years ago. An American staff member has the matching corner. My assistant was the first to propose that the artifact might be an inventory. She and my team anthropologist drew the copies you have."

The Dutchman then asked the dreaded question. "When will you release your discovery to the world?"

Galip shuddered and hedged. "I do not know. Nothing has been proven, but be assured, I will give you credit for the translation. Thank you for doing it for me. Now, I must say goodbye, my good friend." Before the Dutchman could ask another question, Galip hung up.

Galip left the next day for Cappadocia where the team, now in its third season, had been working since late spring. He couldn't wait to let his staff in on the great news.

This year, their second season at the present level, they had reached the site of Arianna's entrapment. The entire underground city was now wired and lighted. The project was on schedule, but it was not easy to maintain it. Minor annoyances had continually plagued them; something was always going wrong.

Arianna and Halime had spent three days laboriously sectioning the great room into grids. The morning before Galip returned from Ankara, they descended into the underground city to find their stakes pulled and the cords broken and tangled. It meant they had to remeasure and mark the squares.

Halime and her new helper, Mohammed's younger brother, were reconfiguring the grids nearest the cave's east wall. The boy was called Pire, a nickname meaning "flea." Arianna and Mohammed worked at the cavern's opposite end.

Arianna had decided to move one square to a more promising location. Pire stretched the measuring tape, while Arianna hammered in the pegs. Holding the fourth and final stake firmly in her left hand, she dealt it a hefty blow with her right. She almost fell forward, when the stake suddenly disappeared into what she had thought was rock-hard ash.

Arianna easily slipped the stake out and shifted it six inches to the left. She tried to set it. The same thing happened again; the stake went all the way in. Trying for a solid spot that would hold the rod in place, she finally threw the hammer to the side. Repeatedly thrusting the stake's pointed end into the surface, she discovered that she had at her feet a debris-filled depression in the rough shape of a circle, a little more than a meter in diameter. She straightened, and, brushing the dust from her knees, cried, "Halime, I think we've found our first well!"

CHAPTER 63

Because it had been Arianna's find, and the square in which it stood originally assigned to her, Galip insisted she be the one to further explore the well.

Centuries of accumulation—a mix of nature's debris and human discard—had to be removed. The bore's diameter was too small for more than one worker at a time, so employing a big, battery-powered mechanic's light, Arianna personally performed the excavating. As she dug deeper, Mohammed manipulated a winch and bucket so that it acted as an elevator for her to go up and down in, and lifted rubbish to the top. So far, they had cleared the hole to about fifty feet.

Descending, Arianna sat on the bucket's uncomfortable rim, her arms and legs wrapped around the rope. The once bright kerchief, which she wore wrapped across her nose and mouth like a peasant woman's, was filthy. It barely filtered out the choking dust that periodically doubled her over in a fit of coughing. If the well went much deeper, she'd have to call for a pump to clear the air.

"Easy does it, Mohammed," Arianna's muffled shout echoed from the pit. As her toes contacted the bottom, she signaled him with two jerks of the rope. Mohammed shifted his hands to get a better grip on the winch handle, stopping her descent. The rope slackened and Arianna disentangled herself from it and the bucket.

For the past month, the few bits of pottery Arianna had found dated from the nineteenth century near the well's surface to the thirteenth century farther down. Yesterday, she had come across a twelfth-century coin, the most important object the well had yet produced.

This morning, spurred by her exciting find the day before, Arianna had difficulty disciplining herself to work the next layer of debris slowly and methodically, but her training prevailed. She conscientiously troweled through the packed earth and rock, wrapping small pieces that interested her in tissue, then dropping them into a cloth bag tied to her belt. The loosened earth and rock she put into the bucket. Placing any large objects on top, she secured the entire load with a net. When the bucket was full, she tugged the rope twice, signaling Mohammed to haul it up.

At the top, Mohammed set the individual artifacts aside for later study at the laboratory. He then disengaged the bucket and carried it to the other side of the cavern, where eager young students from Western Europe and the United States waited to sort its contents. Using a metal screen stretched across a wooden frame, the students scrupulously sifted the bucket's contents looking for anything Arianna might have missed.

Down in the well, Arianna stopped digging when her trowel blade rasped against a sizable piece of pottery. Exchanging the trowel for a soft house-painting brush, she dusted the dirt away from what turned out to be the conical bottom of a large storage amphora. She sighed with disgust; the team had already uncovered a multitude of such amphorae in the underground city. She lifted the shard from its centuries-old bed. Beneath the dome of pottery, half exposed within a nest of decomposed leather fragments that disintegrated at even her delicate touch, lay a gold coin.

Feeling that her effort and discomfort might finally be worth something, Arianna fished a pair of tweezers from her shirt pocket and freed the coin. Gently rubbing the metal between her fingers, she peered at it, trying to identify its source. The coin had two heads on it; they looked to be Roman or Greek, but numismatics was not her forte. She wrapped the coin in a tissue, which she dropped into the bag at her waist. With the tweezers, she painstakingly retrieved a few flakes of the crumbled leather. These, she carefully placed into a clear plastic specimen box. At that moment, Refah shouted down the hole that it was time to quit. Relieved that she would soon breathe fresh, pure air instead of dust, Arianna straightened. She groaned as her stiff knees snapped and cracked.

That night, during the evening meal, Arianna handed Galip the tissue-wrapped coin. "I found this today. What do you make of it? It doesn't fit in the time period we've excavated so far."

Galip unwrapped the coin and examined it. Laying it on the table, he said, "This is a fourth-century solidus. The portraits are of Emperor Heraclius and his son. Though it is not especially rare, this one is in excellent condition."

Arianna held forth the specimen box that contained the leather fragments. "It looks as if it had been in some kind of purse."

"Yes, it may have been. . . . It is a mystery, Miss Arista. Perhaps it was accidentally dropped into the well or hidden there."

* * *

The next day, Arianna resumed her excavation. She had just begun to free and box the rest of the purse fragments when the tip of her tweezers grazed metal. At first, she thought she had uncovered the black, oxidized edge of another silver coin. When she brushed the debris away from the object and saw its size and form, her eyes widened. She squealed with surprised delight. Instead of the expected coin, she retrieved a huge cross fashioned of filigreed silver and set with precious jewels and amber. Moistening the corner of a tissue with her tongue, she wiped off some of the dirt. Closely squinting at the cross, she was able to make out an insect of some kind preserved in the ancient amber. She could not wait for evening to show the cross to Dr. Yaldiz and the team. Clambering into the bucket and yanking at the rope, she screamed, "Mohammed, pull me up! *Çabuk!* Hurry!"

The excitement in Arianna's voice stimulated Mohammed to hoist her up at record speed.

CHAPTER 64

The farther into the bore hole Arianna went, the more fruitful her efforts. Just before she found the silver cross, she had steadily unearthed artifacts from the late Byzantine era, mostly pottery and discarded household items. Two days after finding the cross, however, she began to uncover beautifully wrought gold and silver religious artifacts that were encrusted with precious and semiprecious jewels. Some were adorned with glass instead of jewels, and she remembered that glass once was valued equally with, or more highly than, gemstones.

Though Galip tried to prevent knowledge of Arianna's find from leaking to the public, the news spread as swiftly as an Anatolian grass fire. The world press, throngs of curious Turks, and self-seeking opportunists descended upon the area. Refah was forced to station guards at the hotel, the lab, and at the entrances to the underground city. He made three phone calls to the authorities to gain permission, then closed the upper levels to everyone but the team.

* * *

It was near quitting time. Arianna's legs ached from hours of kneeling on the deep well's icy floor. Finding glamorous and valuable relics is every archaeologist's dream. However, during the weeks on site, she had uncovered so much treasure that the gleam of more gold protruding from the rubble no longer greatly excited her. But when she exposed an object larger than anything she had previously come upon, her jaded interest instantly flared anew. She briskly whisked dirt from it using a squirrel-hair watercolor brush. Suddenly, she was no longer tired. Her knees didn't hurt; nor did her stressed wrist and finger joints.

Before her, its gold shining in the lantern light, lay a large tablet inscribed with tiny, indecipherable characters. Brushing along the tablet's side, she revealed what appeared to be another tablet beneath it. Arianna stared at the artifacts. An image instantly came to her mind—Dr. Yaldiz's tablet with its missing corner, and Morgan's piece that fit that corner.

A short time later, Arianna knelt at the rim of the well watching Morgan ride the bucket to the bottom. He carried a camera with a strobe flash mounted on a tripod. His photographs would show the great golden tablets as she had found them, one on top of the other. That accomplished, they could be removed from the well.

Reaching bottom, Morgan stooped over the tablets and blew off dirt that had fallen during Arianna's ascent and his descent. "These look exactly like the one Dr. Yaldiz and I have!" he shouted up to her, his tone incredulous.

"Didn't I tell you so?" came Arianna's answering shout.

She patiently waited while Morgan shot his stills. When he finished and Mohammed had hauled him up, Morgan laid his equipment down, clasped Arianna around the waist, and swung her in a circle.

"What a find! You're going to be famous." He set Arianna on her feet, and they performed a few steps of the "swim" while a mystified Mohammed gawked at their strange antics. Morgan abruptly stopped. Laughing, he gave Arianna a brief hug. "I'm getting too old for this."

Arianna quickly stepped away from Morgan and primly pulled down her sweater. "Dr. Yaldiz doesn't arrive from Ankara until after midnight, so he won't be available before tomorrow. What shall we do with the tablets in the meantime?" Arianna mused, more to herself than to Morgan. "I guess I'd better ask Refah." She started toward the passageway leading out. Morgan followed close behind. When they were out of Mohammed's sight, Morgan caught Arianna's shoulder and spun her around.

"I've waited a long time to do this." He drew her to him and, tilting her face with both hands, he lightly kissed her. When she didn't pull away, he kissed her again, this time with definite ardor.

At first, Arianna stood motionless and stiff in Morgan's embrace. He had caught her by surprise. Well, sort of by surprise; since her accident, she had half expected him to make some kind of move toward her. Now, by habit, she began to resist, not to give in, but her body automatically reacted to their mutual desire. Leaning hard against him, she returned his third kiss with equal passion. And it felt good.

Morgan gently pushed her away. "We'd better find Refah." Holding her hand, he led her up the passage.

Peering into the well, Refah said, "I want Dr. Yaldiz to see the tablets as you found them, Arianna. They will give him much pleasure." He spoke in rapid Turkish to Mohammed, then changed to English. "Mohammed will personally guard them during the night, but he needs his evening meal. Arianna, would you get something for him from the mess tent, and take it to him? Morgan and I have to plan tomorrow's work."

While Arianna went for a tray of food for Mohammed, Refah handed Morgan the key to the entrance gate, saying, "I have my own car here. You can see there are guards at the main entrance, and at the other entrances we know about. I must drive to Ankara tonight to fulfill a speaking engagement at an international meeting of archaeologists Tuesday morning. You and Arianna will have to take the dolmuş back to Niğde without me."

"I can't remember if the hieroglyphics are the same, but the three tablets are related; I'm sure of it," Morgan declared on the way to Niğde.

"I can't wait to see the expression on Dr. Yaldiz's face when he sees the two I found. What do you think he'll do?"

Morgan shrugged. "Who knows? Especially since there are three now, and one of them is his. These last two belong to the Turkish government, of course. The follow-up should be interesting."

They couldn't wait until the next day to tell Dr. Yaldiz their exciting news; they unanimously decided to stay up until he arrived. When he came, just after midnight, his eyes were bloodshot from the drive, but he did not appear otherwise tired. Quite the opposite in fact; his step was light and he sported a big grin. Between sips of strong Turkish coffee, Galip told his team that the Dutch philologist had succeeded in translating the writing on the original tablet. However, Galip deliberately did not mention his discussion with the philologist regarding Noah. It was too soon.

Refah waited until Galip finished telling them his news, then winked at Morgan and began. "Yesterday, Arianna uncovered two similar tablets in the well. We think they may be from the same source as yours."

Galip blanched and clutched at his chest. Alarmed, Morgan and Refah jumped to their feet. They rushed to the archaeologist. "What is wrong, Dr. Yaldiz?" Morgan asked.

Galip opened his eyes and blankly gazed into space. Shuddering, he at last focused on Morgan. "I am not ill, only overwhelmed. Where are the two tablets now?"

"Still in the well."

His hands shaking, the archaeologist lit a cigarette. "My Dutch friend thinks the piece that he translated is part of a set." Galip's arduous nighttime trip from Ankara was now affecting him—he constantly blinked and rubbed his eyes—but he insisted, "We will go to the underground city at once; I must see them."

Morgan had no intention of returning to the dig that night. "You're tired from the drive, Dr. Yaldiz. The tablets will be there in the morning."

"I agree with Morgan," Refah said. "The entrances are secured, and Mohammed is guarding the site."

Giving in to the younger team members, Galip dropped into his chair and sighed. "Yes, you are right; I do tire more easily these days. We will wait until tomorrow."

Chapter 65

The next morning, Galip, Halime, and the two Americans arrived at the underground city before anyone else. Refah had already taken off for Ankara. Nobody had rested well the previous night, except for the road-weary Galip, who immediately sank into a deep, dreamless sleep.

Morgan unlocked the gate. On entering, he pulled the main switch handle that was supposed to turn on the lights. Nothing happened.

Choosing a lantern from the supply underneath the fuse box, Morgan lit it. He handed it to Arianna. "Here, hold this up for me while I check the box." He opened the box and swore. "Someone's ripped off the fuses."

"Who could have done it?" Galip asked.

Morgan swore again. "I have no idea. The lights were working when we left."

"Morgan turned them out himself," Arianna added.

"And I personally locked the gate." Morgan slammed the box door shut. "Maybe Mohammed took the fuses for some reason." Determined to instantly solve the mystery he shouted, "Mohammed, are you in there?"

"You know he can't hear you," Arianna declared.

Morgan gave her an exasperated look and lit three more lanterns. He handed one each to Halime and Galip, keeping one for himself.

"Come on, then. If Mohammed won't come to us, we'll go to Mohammed."

No one so much as smiled at Morgan's lame attempt at humor.

At the well, they found everything as Arianna and Refah had left it the night before. Mohammed was nowhere in sight.

"I guess being alone down here frightened him; he must have gone home." Arianna tried not to reveal the surprise and disappointment she felt at Mohammed's desertion.

Morgan looked puzzled. "Mohammed couldn't have left through a locked gate."

"He must have gone out another way familiar to the locals. He disappeared just like Ahmet," Arianna grumbled as she walked over to the well and peered into the black hole. Even though she lowered her lantern below the well's rim, she couldn't see the bottom.

"Dr. Yaldiz, do you want to go down? I'll work the winch," Morgan offered.

The archaeologist nodded. "Yes, I would like to see the tablets as Arianna found them."

Morgan placed his lantern on the ground next to the winch and grasped the handle with both hands.

Holding his lantern in one hand, Galip curled his free arm around the hoist rope, put one foot into the bucket, and wrapped the other leg around the rope.

Arianna and Halime watched while Morgan slowly lowered the archaeologist into the well. As the bucket twisted and swayed, Galip's shadow leaped on the curved walls of the shaft. Still descending, Galip scrutinized the gloom below; he thought he saw a glint of gold.

Ten feet lower, Galip suddenly cried out in dismay. Mohammed's contorted body lay sprawled at the bottom of the well. The yellow glint Galip had seen came, not from precious golden artifacts, but from a gold-capped tooth in the dead boy's gaping mouth.

Chapter 66

Turkish officials immediately sealed off the underground city. No one, including the archaeologists, was allowed in during the investigation of Mohammed's death. Their above-ground work at a halt, there was little to occupy the team.

Arianna rarely cried; it was not her nature to show emotion other than anger, but she had broken down and wept when they found Mohammed's pitiful corpse. She was weeping now as she and Morgan sat on the hotel terrace shaded by an ancient olive tree. "Why did it have to happen to such a sweet boy?"

Morgan pulled her close and breathed in the exotic scent of Shalimar, Arianna's favorite perfume. "It's a tough one, for sure. It's hard to believe that he accidentally fell into the well; he was too familiar with the site."

Arianna looked up at him, her eyes and cheeks shiny with tears. "His lantern was still at the top, though it was shattered. He must have dropped it, then stumbled into the hole in the dark."

"That's probably what happened." Morgan gently brushed the tears from her cheeks. "Can you handle going back to the well site—that is, when the Turkish police allow us in?"

"I'll have to. Those plaques, tablets, or whatever they are, are still down there. It's funny the police didn't mention them; they won't answer a question about anything unless it refers to Mohammed. I wish they'd let us go back down." She ducked her head into Morgan's chest. "I'm ashamed to admit it, but I *am* anxious to get the things above ground into sunlight where we can really see them." Her body jerked with a sob. "Who'll work the winch for me now?"

Morgan gave her a comforting hug. "The whole business is strange. Something just doesn't feel right."

A week later, when the officials finally let the team back into the underground city, Arianna could hardly bring herself to go down into the old well. But when Morgan offered to work the winch until another operator could be found, she felt better about it.

As Morgan turned the handle, Arianna slowly dropped into the formidable hole. She became increasingly puzzled the closer to bottom she descended. No light reflected off metal. She didn't wait for the bucket to get all the way down before she jumped to the bottom. Frantically, she dug into the dirt and rubble with her bare hands. There was nothing there; the tablets were gone.

* * *

That evening, Galip, his expression grim, gathered the team at the underground city's main entrance. "The tablets found by Miss Arista are missing, and Refah brings alarming news from the police." He beckoned to Refah. "Refah?"

Refah stepped forward. He hesitated, then spoke softly. "The police do not think Mohammed died accidentally; they say he was murdered."

"What makes them think so?" Morgan asked.

"The police say the fall did not cause all of Mohammed's bruises."

The team, individually and collectively, recalled the annoying incidents that had plagued them since the first week of excavation: tools had been mysteriously damaged or had disappeared; not easily accessed sites had been vandalized; the lighting system had consistently and unexplainably failed. Refah had dismissed the occurrences as mischief performed by boys from the local village. He had repeatedly entreated the *muhtar,* the village alderman, to reprimand the youths, and the *muhtar* dutifully lectured the boys, who proclaimed their innocence. Nevertheless, the harassment had continued.

Refah had always believed that the frequent power outages bedeviling the project were due to faulty equipment. For the first time, he asked himself whether sabotage was involved. He took Arianna aside. "Do not go anywhere alone. I am now sure someone rolled the wheel door shut to trap you."

"You don't think someone tried to kill me too, do you, Refah? What possible good would that have done?"

"I do not know, but I wish everyone, especially you and Halime, to be very cautious."

After their evening meal, Morgan and Arianna often sat on the hotel terrace to escape the cigarette smoke that always filled the lobby and dining room at mealtime. Because reading matter was scarce, and because they usually wound up in heated discussions about the Bible—about which neither knew more than the other—Arianna began to bring the little Bible Beverly had given her. From then on, Morgan and Arianna took turns reading aloud from it, comparing it with the King James version Beverly had brought with her. One night, Arianna, reading from the King James quoted 1 Samuel 2:7, "The Lord maketh poor, and maketh rich: He bringeth low, and lifteth up."

"God wrote that verse just for me," she commented. "Finding the tablets made me rich and losing them brought me low." Atypically shy, not looking at Morgan, she murmured, "*You* 'lifteth' me up, Morgan McCauley."

He said nothing but brought her hand to his lips and kissed it. Tears flooded her eyes; tears came more easily these days.

"Material things are expendable," she went on, speaking softly. "I don't feel as bad about the loss of the tablets as I do about Mohammed's awful death. The whole thing is a horrible nightmare."

"Mohammed didn't deserve to die." Morgan set his tea glass on its saucer with such force, Arianna wondered why it didn't shatter. His fingers curled into a fist. "I wish I could get my hands around the murderer's neck."

Arianna shook her head. "Jesus said we're supposed to have mercy for our enemies, but, no matter how I try, I can't forgive the person who killed Mohammed. And if the tablets are what we think they are, and they *did* come from Noah's ark, then they're vital to the very history of mankind. How could someone steal something so dear to the world's three greatest religions?"

Glaring under thunderous brows, Morgan slammed his fist on the table. "Ha! I wouldn't be surprised to discover that a fanatic *from* one of those great religions stole the tablets to prevent the other two from getting their hands on them."

Arianna blurted, "You don't suppose the thief is going to strip off the gold and melt it down?" The thought of such a catastrophic deed was almost too much. She began to cry again.

Morgan slid his chair over next to hers and put an arm around her shoulders. "Maybe the tablets will turn up in a private collection someday."

"That's better than destruction," she said and sighed. "But it wouldn't bring Mohammed back."

Morgan rose from his chair. Taking her hand, he pulled her to her feet. "Let's get out of here and go for a walk or something."

CHAPTER 67

Morgan and Arianna walked hand-in-hand on Niğde's main street. Morgan peered at the sky. "The moon is a perfect crescent; if there were a star between its points, it could be the emblem on the Turkish flag."

Arianna frowned. "Isn't it backward, though?"

"You're right, it is backward." He smiled and squeezed her hand.

The squeeze felt wonderful. "I've made the same mistake," Arianna giggled. "I can never remember in which direction the crescent faces."

"I'll never forget again."

"Wanna bet?"

"Nope."

Arianna gazed at the moon. "I came across an interesting fact about the Turkish flag in a recipe book, of all places. To commemorate Vienna's stand against the Turks in 1683, Viennese bakers shaped bread into croissants for the first time. You know, crescents?"

"I love you," Morgan said, impressed.

What would I do without Morgan? A shaft of sweet pain flashed in Arianna's breast. *Am I falling for him?* The thought was not unpleasant.

They strolled along the dusty street in companionable silence until they came to a brightly lit café. Throbbing strains of Turkish folk music blasted from the café's open doorway. Four men played the traditional trictrac at a table under the café canopy.

Morgan and Arianna stopped to watch the game. Arianna flinched when one player, a very old man with a mean expression, threw his marker at the man across from him. As he clumsily tried to lift himself from his chair, the two Americans could see that the old man's right leg was twisted and misshapen.

Arianna could never have imagined that the old man was her grandmother Ylenah's twin brother, Ephraim, Arianna's granduncle.

At age eighty-nine, Ephraim Trajian, or Ephraim Cesur, as the locals knew him, had only one pleasure left in life—trictrac. The game wasn't yet over, but his hip and leg ached so much, he couldn't concentrate. Calling for his grandson, who was inside the café, Ephraim shakily reached for a battered pair of crutches. Suddenly, his rheumy eyes fell on Arianna, who stood in the shadows. Peering into the dark, confused by the mists of time, he thought he was seeing his twin sister, Ylenah—the young Ylenah, as he had last seen her half a century before. "Ylenah?" he croaked.

But no one heard his feeble voice. His attention was diverted when his opponent shouted an insult. Of course, Ephraim, being Ephraim, had to respond in turn.

From where they stood, Morgan and Arianna could see into the café. Every rickety chair contained a man in the worker's common uniform—black suit and black cap. The clickity-click of a half-dozen trictrac games sounded during lulls in the music.

"Don't they ever sleep?" Arianna asked out of the side of her mouth.

Morgan chuckled. "Have you ever noticed how many of the men, especially the old guys, sit around snoozing during the day?"

"I guess I have at that. Hey, look, there's Ahmet."

"So it is. We haven't seen much of him lately. I wonder what he's up to."

The foreman sat at a table near the back of the café. Across from him sat a stout, middle-aged man who, in an expensive light-gray suit and no hat, looked out of place among the locals. His head was slightly bald, his graying moustache and hair neatly trimmed.

Something jabbed at Morgan's memory. Try as he might, he couldn't remember if he really had seen the man before. He shrugged off the vague notion; the stranger merely resembled every Turk of his general description who wore a moustache.

"What could that awful Ahmet and such a sophisticated-looking individual possibly have in common?" Arianna whispered.

"Beats me, but they sure are going at it."

Obviously in the middle of a heated argument, ignoring the babble surrounding them, Ahmet and his companion leaned across the table toward one another. Ahmet shook his fist while the other man stared at him with taut lips.

"You've never liked Ahmet, have you?" Morgan asked.

"No."

"Any particular reason?"

"I don't trust a man, or a woman, who can't look you in the eye," Arianna said. "Ahmet gives me the cold shoulder or gazes over my head whenever I talk to him."

"I wouldn't let it bother you."

"Well, it *does* bother me," Arianna snapped.

At that moment, Ahmet pushed a large cloth sack lying on the floor by his chair toward the other man. After furtively glancing around the crowded café, Ahmet spread open the sack's mouth. The fat man impatiently yanked at the sack and the cloth fell away. He quickly resealed the opening, but not before Morgan and Arianna saw what the sack contained.

Morgan swore under his breath. "He's got the tablets!" Arianna started to rush into the café. Morgan grabbed her arm, restraining her.

Arianna clawed at his hand. "What are you doing? We have to get the tablets."

"No, we have to get the police."

"Ahmet will escape," she protested.

Even as Arianna spoke, Ahmet and his companion left their table. Morgan pulled Arianna into the shadowed entryway of an abandoned shop. "Shh," he hissed. "Let's see what they do."

The portly man exited the café first. Ahmet closely followed with the sack slung over his shoulder. As they passed old Ephraim, Ahmet's companion helped Ephraim to his feet and partially supported him. They headed toward a light-blue

Mercedes Benz sedan parked under a brightly lit billboard sign advertising a prominent Turkish insurance company.

Ahmet waited while the older man helped Ephraim into the car, then opened the trunk. Ahmet hoisted the sack into the trunk and slammed the trunk lid shut. He remained there, his flattened palm extended to the other man. Even over the loud music, Morgan and Arianna could hear the fat man's derisive guffaw. Reaching into his breast pocket, he extracted a wad of bills, peeled several off, and tossed them on the ground at Ahmet's feet. Still laughing, the fat man climbed into the car. The Mercedes sped down the road, leaving Ahmet choking in a swirl of dust.

Arianna screamed, "Do something, Morgan! He's got the tablets."

"Go for the police. Hurry! I'll get Ahmet."

Morgan raced across the street and grabbed hold of Ahmet's shoulder. Surprised, the foreman wrenched free and tried to run, but Morgan tackled him, throwing him to the ground.

Arianna ran the half block to the *polis-karakolu,* the police station. Though a light shone in the window, the building was locked. She pounded on the door and shouted for help. When there was no response, she ran back to Morgan.

Ahmet had gotten to his feet, but Morgan, who was a head taller, had the foreman's arms pinned behind him. Every time Ahmet moved, Morgan jerked them painfully upward.

Arianna nervously circled Morgan and Ahmet. "No one is in the station. What'll we do now?"

"We'll take him to the hotel where he can be watched until we can get hold of a policeman."

Morgan manhandled Ahmet, pushing him toward the hotel, while Arianna dashed ahead to alert Refah and Galip.

On being awakened, Galip immediately sent a hotel employee for the police. Arianna and Halime waited in the lobby while Galip and Refah interrogated Ahmet in Galip's room. At first, Ahmet refused to talk; but when Galip's soft voice grew harsh and Refah grabbed a hank of Ahmet's hair, the foreman decided to answer their questions.

"Ask him the identity of the man who took the tablets," Morgan urged.

Galip snarled something at Ahmet in Turkish.

"He says he knows him only as Muhsin Bey, *The Benefactor,* a dealer in antiquities."

Later, when the police had taken Ahmet, Refah and Galip repeated Ahmet's confession to Arianna and Halime.

Muhsin Bey had learned of the newly discovered tablets through an underground source. He demanded that Ahmet, a member of Muhsin Bey's Communist cell—and frequent trictrac opponent of Ephraim, Muhsin's father—acquire the artifacts for him. Ahmet, believing there was a cash reward and that his status in Muhsin's eyes would rise, eagerly accepted the challenge. The night of Mohammed's murder, to avoid the entrance guards, Ahmet had stayed in the underground city.

Waiting until Mohammed fell asleep, Ahmet quietly slid down the rope into the well. He could barely manage one tablet and climb back up the rope; he left the first one on the well's rim. As he reached the top with the second tablet, Mohammed awakened. During the ensuing scuffle, Ahmet shoved Mohammed over the edge. The boy instantly died when he hit bottom.

As far as Ahmet knew, Muhsin Bey was headed that night for a hotel in Ürgüp, intending to leave in the morning for the south coast.

Galip motioned toward the door. "Morgan, Refah, and I will try to catch Muhsin Bey."

Arianna kissed Morgan's cheek. "I'll worry every minute you're gone."

Morgan laughed it off. "I'll reciprocate in spades when we return."

As the three men walked out, Arianna and Halime stood mute, both wearing troubled frowns.

CHAPTER 68

At that late hour of night, the eleven-kilometer drive over the well-maintained gravel road to Ürgüp did not take long. When the men arrived in the small town, Morgan and Refah stayed in the car while Galip looked for the single hotel's manager.

Galip discovered they were too late; their man had already checked out. "Did Muhsin Bey say where he was going?" Galip asked the sleep-drugged manager.

The manager thought a moment. "He asked me about the road to Karaman." The manager yawned. "I hope I have been of help to you, Professor Doctor."

"You have. But tell me another thing: Is the road to Karaman still inferior? I have driven it, but not recently."

"It is a rough road yet, but if one is going to Silifke, the way through Karaman is shorter than it is traveling through Mersin."

Galip left the manager with a few liras for his trouble. Trotting to his battered Anadolu, where Morgan and Refah waited, he told them, "I think Muhsin Bey is heading for the south coast, perhaps to Taşugu. The hotel manager thinks our man is on his way to Silifke by way of Karaman."

Galip motioned Refah out of the passenger seat and slid into it. "Refah, it is your turn to take the wheel. I am too tired to drive."

As Refah worked to start the car, Galip said, "Though the southern route to Silifke through Mersin is half the distance, the shorter road from Niğde to Karaman is very bad. If we take the shorter route, we must go back to Niğde for the Cadillac dolmuş. The Anadolu's engine gives much trouble."

Refah said, "If we take the shorter route, we might reach Karaman before Muhsin Bey."

When the men returned to Niğde, Arianna informed them that the police wanted them in the station at eight the next morning for questioning.

Galip and Refah conferred in Turkish, then Galip called the police and had a short, crisp discussion with someone on the other end. When he hung up, he looked smug. "It is late. There is but one man on duty. When I told him we were going after Muhsin Bey tonight, he did not like it, but he does not have the authority to stop us."

"Good!" Morgan said. "We may catch him yet."

Seeing that Arianna and Halime looked disappointed, Morgan asked Galip, "Can the ladies come along? There's plenty of room in the dolmuş." Best to have Arianna close where he could keep an eye on her.

Reluctant to expose them to danger and hoping they would decline, Galip asked the women, "Do you wish to come with us?" But Arianna and Halime eagerly accepted.

"We are all fatigued," Refah cautioned. "Shall I ask Onur to drive?"

"Yes. Awaken him," Galip said.

Refah returned in a few minutes followed by the confused Onur, who appeared half asleep. Galip explained to the driver why they needed him. By the time the archaeologist had finished, Onur was wide awake and ready to start.

"Let us go on to Karaman," Morgan proposed. "Instinct tells me Muhsin Bey is in a big hurry. If he is, he will not take the long way through Mersin."

Galip wanted to stay as close to the mysterious "Benefactor" as possible. "Onur has had the most sleep. Let us go on to Karaman. We can sleep while he drives."

* * *

Galip's assessment of the road to Karaman, like Onur's faith in the old Cadillac's ability to withstand the road's rotten condition, proved significantly inaccurate. The road was little more than a dirt track mainly used by the railroad to service the raised rail bed that ran alongside it. The Cadillac lurched over ruts and pits like a drunken Brahman bull.

A horseshoe nail—the chief menace to every driver in Turkey—caused their first flat tire. When Onur opened the Cadillac's trunk to get the jack, Morgan stared in amazement at three spare wheels all nestled within the spacious compartment.

"So that's why Onur didn't put our baggage in there—why he lashes everything to the roof rack at the mercy of the elements."

Refah chuckled. "There is more, Morgan. Have you seen Onur's wonderful engine?"

"No. What's special about it?"

"Onur, may we see your engine?" Refah asked the driver in Turkish. At Onur's upward nod, Refah released and lifted the hood.

Morgan peered in at the immaculate motor. "Now I've seen everything," he laughed. The block had been neatly sliced in half, and the Cadillac was running on only four cylinders.

"We Turks are masters at mechanics, no?" Refah said, grinning wickedly.

"I can't believe it." Morgan hunched under the hood in order to examine more closely the remarkable innovation. "No wonder we couldn't catch up to a Mercedes. We're running with equal power, instead of having the advantage of eight cylinders." He waved at Arianna, who sat with Halime on the railroad embankment. "Come see this, Arianna."

Rising, Arianna walked to the front of the car. "I don't know much about motors. How can it run cut in half like that?"

"It's working on the remaining four cylinders."

"Oh, I see," she said, not seeing at all.

Riding in the rear seat of the dolmuş upset Halime's stomach; she felt terribly nauseous.

"In the front seat you will not become ill," Refah assured Halime.

When they were on the road once more, Halime sat between Onur and Refah. She began to feel better almost immediately. She could look straight ahead, thus avoiding the side window vision that had caused her distress. Refah's nearness, rather than disturbing or irritating her, proved soothing. Eventually, she fell asleep, her head resting on his shoulder. Refah's lips lightly brushed her forehead. Not fully awakening at his gentle caress, Halime purred a faint "mm" and cuddled closer.

The second incident occurred when Onur turned his head to speak to Galip, who sat behind him. The big dolmuş hit a pothole at sixty miles an hour. As he struggled to hold the bucking steering wheel, Onur shouted a torrent of Turkish profanities. Finally gaining control, he stopped the car. Onur's hands shook, but he quickly removed the badly bent wheel, deftly replacing it with one of his spares from the trunk.

Though he had several hours' head start, Muhsin Bey had also suffered a flat tire and damaged wheel. And while the Mercedes carried a spare wheel, the overweight man's poor physical condition slowed the wheel's replacement; he barely got it on. Also, his spare was low on air, forcing him to creep at less than twenty-five miles per hour the rest of the way. When he reached Karaman it was before dawn, and he had to wait for a gas station to open. After many delays while he served other customers, the British Petroleum attendant tightened the last nut on the Mercedes' repaired wheel.

Refah was the first to spot the Mercedes. "Hey, there is our man," he cried.

Onur slowed the dolmuş to a crawl, saying something to Galip, who translated for the Americans. "Onur says we must stop for petrol."

"Oh no!" Arianna cried. "He'll get too far ahead of us."

But Onur swung the Cadillac into the BP station Muhsin Bey had just vacated. While the car's big tank was being filled, the four watched helplessly as Muhsin Bey disappeared west toward the Ankara-Silifke highway.

Twenty minutes later, they were again in pursuit. They did not catch up with the Mercedes until they arrived at the town of Mut, nearly seventy-five kilometers south of Karaman. The Mercedes, its hood raised, sat next to the gas pumps at another BP station, but its driver was not in sight.

"Stop here, Onur, where he cannot see us," Refah said when the Cadillac was a block away.

Morgan leaned his elbows on the back of Onur's seat and peered through the windshield. "Something must have delayed the guy, otherwise we could not have caught up with him."

"Steam comes from the Mercedes radiator," Galip pointed out.

"It looks like our friend has more trouble than a flat," Morgan gloated.

"What are we going to do now?" Arianna asked.

"I suggest we contact the local authorities," Galip said.

Morgan disagreed. "Ordinarily, I think that would be our next move. But we don't know if he'll remain here, and it might take too long to explain to the Mut police why we want him arrested. Even so, it wouldn't guarantee they'd do it. Meanwhile, this Muhsin character gets away again."

Refah added his voice to Morgan's. "We cannot let the criminal escape with the tablets."

"Now, my two young friends, we will see what happens next." Galip leaned back against his seat, folded his arms across his chest, and closed his eyes. "I will sleep until our man appears."

Everyone in the Cadillac was exhausted. Their only consolation? Muhsin Bey, without the relief of a second driver, likely had even less sleep than any of them.

"There he is," Arianna suddenly exclaimed. Carrying a soft drink bottle and a pastry, Muhsin Bey was striding toward the Mercedes.

"Ah ha, our man is mortal; he has to have nourishment." At the thought of food, Morgan hungered, too. "How about it; dare we stop to eat?"

"I'm too tired to eat, Morgan," Arianna said. "I wouldn't mind a Frukos, though."

Refah and Galip wanted to continue the pursuit.

"Guess breakfast will have to wait," Morgan sighed, vainly envisioning a generous plate of bacon and eggs, unheard of in rural Turkey.

The BP attendant had hosed the Mercedes's radiator, cooling it; the steam had subsided. When Muhsin Bey climbed into the seat of the blue vehicle, Onur started the Cadillac's engine. Gripping the steering wheel, he prepared to speed after the other car.

Muhsin seemed unaware of his pursuers. He did not hurry, and his poor driving showed his fatigue. At times, the Mercedes swayed almost to the other side of the road.

Onur kept the Cadillac a discreet kilometer behind, waiting for the chance to safely overtake and confront Muhsin Bey.

Both vehicles slowed as the road ascended the Taurus Mountain range via a deep gorge cut by the turbulent Göksu River. Eventually the narrow canyon spread to a broad valley, and the Göksu River widened.

"Man, will you look at that!" Morgan exclaimed. He had just seen his first giant water wheel eerily turning in the river's sluggish current.

The rest of the Cadillac's passengers, all of whom, including Arianna, had previously traveled to southern Turkey, were familiar with the Ferris wheel-like contraptions; but Morgan marveled at every one they passed.

Suddenly, Onur braked the dolmuş and steered it to a wide spot in the road. Galip had been dozing in the corner of his seat. The rocking of the Cadillac, as it bumped across the edge of the macadam and onto the shoulder, abruptly awakened him. "What is happening?" he cried.

"He has stopped," Onur replied.

They silently watched Muhsin Bey open the engine compartment and then jump backward when the car's radiator spouted a plume of steam.

"Our man has a serious problem," Galip chortled.

"Let's hope so," Arianna added.

Muhsin had parked the Mercedes on the shoulder high above a water wheel that had been erected in a manmade channel parallel to the river. The diversion channel's current turned the majestic wheel in slow motion.

Morgan's patience had grown short and he craved action. "He doesn't know any of us. Let's offer him our help."

Galip was not sure he wanted to tangle with their quarry, though they outnumbered the mystery man by four. "Morgan Bey, you and Arianna saw Muhsin put the tablets in the boot of his car. Now that we have caught up with him, what is your plan to retrieve them?"

"How do we know if he still has the tablets?" Halime asked, sounding worried.

"We don't, but we should find out." Morgan tapped Onur's shoulder. "Let's go . . . before he has a chance to drive off."

Gravel shot from beneath the Cadillac's wheels as Onur floored the accelerator pedal.

CHAPTER 69

At the sound of the big Cadillac pulling to a stop on the shoulder behind the Mercedes, Muhsin Bey looked up. Though he believed the Cadillac was simply a dolmuş, he tensed, thrusting a hand under his coat.

"Refah," Morgan grinned, "let's give him our aid."

Maintaining expressions of compassion, Morgan and Refah casually strolled toward the Mercedes. They could see their quarry was weary. His shoulders sagged and dark shadows lay beneath his eyes. A bad scar disfigured one eye, which was nearly opaque and appeared to be blind. Refah did the talking. "Perhaps we can be of help?" he offered.

Morgan's stretch in Korea had taught him to read the enemy's body language. He did not like what he saw. They were dealing with a really cool character, he decided. And, once again, something about the man prodded Morgan's memory—that same sense of familiarity he had experienced when he and Arianna first saw Muhsin Bey at the café in Niğde.

While Refah and Muhsin Bey had their heads under the hood, Morgan nonchalantly leaned against the driver's door of the Mercedes. Scanning the unkempt interior, he almost shouted in triumph. There, in plain sight on the front seat, was a dirty cloth bag—the very same bag that he and Arianna had seen Ahmet hand over to Muhsin! By the bag's shape, it was evident the tablets were still within it. Somehow, without informing the thief, Morgan had to let Refah know the tablets were on the seat, not in the car's trunk.

"We have extra water," Refah was saying in Turkish, "and a container to carry more from the river."

"Allah, curse this worthless vehicle," Muhsin Bey swore. "It has been nothing but trouble. There is not a mechanic this side of Istanbul fit to repair it," he sniveled, ignoring the fact that he sadly neglected his automobile, ordinarily one of the finest and most reliable in the world.

"You are on a business trip?" Refah ventured.

Muhsin's eyes became guarded. "I travel much for business." He glanced suspiciously at the white Cadillac. He could see dimly four occupants: two women, a man, and the driver. It was curious that a dolmuş, filled with fares, would stop to help a stranger in so remote a place. It especially puzzled him that the passengers, not the driver, came to his aid. To cover his unease, he said, "Do you tour the coast? The southern sea is most pleasant this time of year."

"Yes," Refah replied, as he fiddled with a filthy spark plug.

"The tall one is an American?" Muhsin Bey asked, examining Morgan with unveiled contempt.

"Yes," Refah answered without further explanation. He straightened. "Come, let us get water for your engine."

The two Turks, followed by Morgan, started to walk toward the Cadillac. Morgan wracked his brain for a way to let Refah know about the tablets. He was unaware that Refah had also seen the cloth bag.

Galip had exited the Cadillac. He now stood at its left side on the shoulder at the road's edge. As the three men approached, despite the intervening years, Galip recognized their quarry.

"Tuhaf Cesur!" Galip exclaimed, not really believing it.

Ignoring the fact that the man who now called himself Muhsin Bey had once tried to kill him, Galip embraced him and kissed both his cheeks. "You have changed little since our days in the military, Tuhaf."

Suddenly, Morgan knew where he had seen Muhsin; he recalled the photograph on Galip's desk—a photograph of Galip, standing next to a round-faced young man, both of them in uniform.

Today, instead of a uniform, Tuhaf, alias Muhsin, wore an expensive silk suit. His suave appearance was marred by the livid scar that ran from his hairline diagonally down his forehead, and continued across his left brow. His left eyelid sagged, and the eye was indeed blind.

"Galip Bey, my old friend, how pleasant it is to see you! It has been many long years since we were boys together in the army."

Masking his shock—and burning hatred—Tuhaf returned Galip's embrace. Tuhaf was not naive; meeting the archaeologist in this remote place was scarcely coincidence. He was sure he knew why the archaeologist was there. Galip was after the tablets. Furthermore, he had not forgotten; it was Galip who had disfigured him, scarred him for life. But how could Galip possibly know he had the tablets?

Galip stepped back to examine Tuhaf. "The years have treated you well, Tuhaf."

"I am known as Muhsin," Tuhaf corrected, in a voice that did not conceal his bitter hostility.

Galip stifled a laugh. "Yes, Muhsin *is* preferable to Tuhaf, 'The Comical One.' Your father did you an injustice when he named you so."

Tuhaf spat in the dust at Galip's feet. "My father was a fool." *So are you, my old army buddy,* he thought, hiding a smirk with much effort.

CHAPTER 70

From the day he had watched Galip brush the grime off its gold sheathing, Tuhaf had been obsessed by his memory of the tablet. He spent fifteen years in prison for his assault on Galip—fifteen years of his prime forever lost, fifteen years to plan revenge.

Upon his release, Tuhaf formulated a plan to steal the precious tablet. Tracing Galip to Ankara University, Tuhaf began to follow him. It was Tuhaf, skulking in the shadows outside the archaeologist's home, who Morgan spotted the night of the team's first briefing.

Galip's residence had every window barred by wrought iron, and wrought-iron outer doors protected the two entrances. Tuhaf had once peered through a brightly lit window when the Yaldiz family was absent from the room. It happened to be the very window next to the cabinet that once contained the tablet. Tuhaf saw it—so close, so golden, so inaccessible. Standing outside, barred from the treasure for which he lusted, Tuhaf raged with frustration.

Unable to get to the tablet, Tuhaf sought revenge in other ways. The newspaper *Hurriyet* published an article about Galip's pending exploration of an underground city near Tuhaf's Cappadocia home. Tuhaf set out to sabotage Galip's operation.

Long a Communist sympathizer, Tuhaf attended a cell meeting in Niğde, where he encountered Ahmet. Ahmet boasted of his position at the site. Like others of his ilk, Ahmet was willing to do anything for money. Under Tuhaf's expert tutelage, he managed to continually disrupt the excavation.

When Arianna uncovered the two tablets in the well, Ahmet immediately informed Tuhaf, who by then called himself Muhsin Bey. It was Tuhaf who ordered Ahmet to steal the artifacts before they were removed and shipped somewhere else. Young Mohammed unwittingly became the plot's innocent victim.

* * *

Driving as fast as possible on the poor roads, Tuhaf had feared time was growing short. He envisioned the cabin cruiser, anchored off the Silifke coast. The ship would take him and the tablets to the Black Sea port of Odessa, at the easternmost fringe of the Soviet Union. In Odessa, he planned to build his very own *dacha* after selling one tablet on the black market. The second tablet he would keep for himself—to fondle, to enjoy, to gloat over. He knew the cruiser's captain would not wait for him if he arrived late.

Morgan saw the rancor in Tuhaf's eyes. Still, he was unprepared when Tuhaf thrust his hand inside his coat and pulled out a handgun.

Onur, who had remained in the driver's seat of the Cadillac, was closest to Tuhaf. He instantly reacted, flinging open the massive steel door. It slammed Tuhaf broadside with such force, it nearly knocked him off his feet. Momentarily, Tuhaf stumbled and reeled, but he managed to maintain his balance. Before Onur or Morgan could stop him, Tuhaf shot Onur in the face. Onur crumpled, his upper body sliding to the gravel, his legs wedged between the seat and the door frame.

Forgetting that age slows the reflexes, Galip lunged instinctively at Tuhaf. Tuhaf fired again. The bullet pierced Galip's breast, and the archaeologist collapsed beside Onur, one arm across the driver's neck.

Tuhaf briefly aimed the pistol at Morgan. To Morgan's relief, instead of firing, the Turk whirled and ran toward the Mercedes. He had to get away.

Morgan shouted to Arianna and Halime. "Help Onur and Dr. Yaldiz." He cuffed Refah's arm. "Come on, Refah, let's nab that . . ."

Sliding into the Mercedes, Tuhaf again attempted to start its engine. Though the starter growled, the motor refused to turn over. Grabbing the sack with the tablets, Tuhaf leapt from the car and scurried over the embankment. As he stumbled through the swampy field toward the river, the heavy sack hampered his headway. Breathless, he paused at the water-wheel millrace. He turned and saw Morgan and Refah crossing the field; they were already too close. With the slowly revolving wheel hypnotically luring him on, Tuhaf plunged into the waist-high water.

Morgan and Refah came to the millrace just as Tuhaf tripped on a hidden waterlogged root. Tuhaf fell and completely disappeared underwater. Morgan launched himself into the current. Half swimming, half wading, he approached Tuhaf, where Tuhaf floundered beneath the huge wheel.

Sputtering and choking, Tuhaf surfaced only to see Morgan bearing down on him. The Turk—desperate to escape the big American yet save the tablets—heaved the cumbersome bundle onto one of the five-gallon tins lashed to the wheel. As the wheel slowly lifted the tin above his head, Tuhaf fought to get to the opposite end of the race before the bucket tipped and dumped the sack in the water.

Refah splashed up to Morgan and stood beside him, dripping. They gawked at the water wheel, mesmerized, as the tin with the tablets rose to the top.

"Why did he do that?" Refah panted.

Morgan snorted water from his mouth and nose. "Who knows? He must have slipped a cog. Do we go after him or after the tablets?"

Refah did not hesitate. "Let us recover the tablets; the authorities can handle Muhsin Bey."

As Tuhaf labored ahead of them in the millrace, the sticky mud sucked at his feet until his forward movement almost ceased.

"If we leave the water and go by land to the far end of the wheel, we'll get there first," Morgan suggested. When Refah agreed, they climbed out of the millrace and trotted south along its bank. A slime-lined irrigation ditch filled with murky water blocked their path. The ditch was too wide to leap, too foul to swim, and appeared much too deep to wade. They had a choice of either returning to the beginning of the race or of going back to the road and crossing the irrigation ditch at the culvert. They decided to use the same route as Tuhaf, though it meant that the thief would beat them to the tablets.

By the time Morgan and Refah had reached the near end of the water wheel and stepped into the water, Tuhaf was at the wheel's descending side. When the sack was within arms' length, Tuhaf tugged at it. He had wrenched it half out of the tin when the loosely woven cloth hooked on the can's sharp edge; it ripped, releasing both tablets. One tablet crashed onto the cement collection trough. The artifact's ceramic core shattered, and segments of fired clay and gold sheathing flew in all directions. Most of the pieces landed in the Göksu River, where the current carried them off or they sank to the bottom.

Horrified, Tuhaf frantically scrabbled to hold on to the remaining tablet. When he had it, he grasped it firmly against his chest. Shocked, he stood and stared at the spot in the river where the other tablet pieces had disappeared.

The sound of Morgan and Refah splashing through the water behind him alerted Tuhaf to his predicament. Using the trough's rim for leverage, he clambered from the millrace and staggered across the field to the road.

"Refah, he's heading for Arianna and Halime!" Morgan shouted. The two men struggled onward and out of the race. They were three-quarters of the way across the field as Tuhaf gained the road. Huffing to the steep embankment, Morgan and Refah started to ascend it, then abruptly stopped. Tuhaf loomed on the shoulder above them.

"Down! He still has the gun," Morgan warned. The American dropped, dragging Refah to the ground.

Tuhaf squeezed the trigger, but nothing happened. Mud and water had saturated the weapon. He started to hurl the useless pistol to the dirt, but changed his mind and ran to the dolmuş.

Arianna and Halime bent over Galip. The archaeologist lay

moaning, his hands clasped to his bleeding chest wound. Onur had not stirred. Neither woman saw Tuhaf until he rounded the front of the vehicle, his gun pointed at them.

Before Arianna or Halime could react, Tuhaf threw the tablet onto the driver's seat and yanked Arianna to her feet. "In!" he hissed, shoving her through the open driver's door.

Maneuvering across Onur's legs and the tablet, Arianna slid to the passenger side. Tuhaf kicked Onur's legs free and, sliding the tablet to the middle of the seat, scrambled into the car.

Arianna made a daring, final effort to thwart Tuhaf. As he bent to turn the key in the ignition switch, she tried to jerk the key free. Tuhaf backhanded her with his right arm. The savage blow knocked her sideways, and her head struck the sill of the window. It was the last thing she remembered.

Tuhaf steered the accelerating Cadillac at Morgan and Refah, who were coming at a run along the shoulder. To escape the juggernaut that roared at them, both men dived off the road. They crouched below the embankment edge watching helplessly as Tuhaf sped away with the unconscious Arianna.

CHAPTER 71

Morgan and Refah ran to Halime and the two injured men as a massive cross-country freight truck sped down the road toward them. Waving his arms, Morgan ran to the tarmac's domed center. The monster tractor's brakes screamed. Dust clouded the air as the rig slid to a twisting, grinding halt, half on, half off, the shoulder. The driver had all he could do to keep the trailer from jack-knifing behind him. Red-faced, the driver flung himself from his cab and spewed a volley of angry Turkish. With a physique like Hercules, he came at Morgan like a huge steam engine.

Morgan stepped backward with his hands up, fingers spread. Shrugging, as if helpless, he pointed to Refah. Refah hurriedly broke in, stepping between the two men. After waving Morgan away and having had a short conversation with the truck driver, Refah informed Morgan, "He almost did not stop; he is afraid of hijackers."

"Be sure to tell him how grateful we are," Morgan said.

"I have already done so. I told him a Communist shot Onur and Dr. Yaldiz. He does not like Communists."

Morgan pressed Onur's jugular. "Nothing we can do for Onur; he's dead." He examined Galip, who lay barely conscious.

Saddened, Refah said, "It will be hard on Dr. Yaldiz. Onur has been his driver for many years."

"Dr. Yaldiz looks pretty bad, Refah. We need to get him to a doctor. And we need to get Arianna away from Muhsin. I'm afraid he's already had too much of a head start."

Refah looked grim. "I do not know of a hospital that is near here."

"Ask the trucker if he has a CB," Morgan suggested.

Looking blank, Refah asked. "What is CB?"

"A citizens' band radio, a two-way radio. Don't your cross-country haulers carry them?"

"I do not know."

Refah and the truck driver exchanged a few words.

"He does not have a radio, but he will stop the next vehicle that comes by. He will tell the driver to send the police and an ambulance," Refah explained.

"Good! I hope someone comes along soon."

"He also says he will stay here until the police arrive. Halime wants to stay, too."

Morgan glanced over at Halime, who tended to Galip. "Are you sure about this guy, Refah?"

"I have heard my uncle who lives in Afyon speak of him. When he does not drive a truck, he is one of Turkey's best-known wrestlers."

"But I still hate to leave Halime alone with only him and a badly injured man."

Refah asked Halime, "Are you sure you will be all right?"

"I will be fine, Refah. Go! Find Arianna."

Morgan started for the Mercedes. "I think I can fix his car."

Steam no longer shot from the Mercedes' engine, and the block was cool enough to touch. Morgan gave the radiator and hoses a cursory check, but he couldn't find a leak. He inspected the water pump and found it in working condition.

"I'll have to crawl under; there may be a hole where I can't see it from above. Watch for cars, Refah. I don't want someone running over my feet."

Morgan slid under the front end of the Mercedes, his long legs jutting into the road. Minutes later he emerged, exultant.

"I've found the leak. There's a pinhead-size hole in the radiator hose where it connects to the engine block. Ask the trucker if he has any electrical tape."

Refah ran back to where the truck driver was watching Halime administer to Dr. Yaldiz. The driver's arms were stretched at a forty-five-degree angle from his body as he shaded Galip and Halime with a tattered gray blanket. The man's powerful muscles glistened with sweat from heat radiating off the pavement.

Refah briefly spoke to the truck driver, then rummaged

behind the truck cab seat. Returning to the Mercedes, he handed Morgan a roll of tape.

"Can you fix the hose with this?"

"It's exactly what I need."

It took Morgan less than five minutes to mend the leak. He slithered from under the Mercedes.

Refah jangled a set of keys. "Our friend, Muhsin Bey, left these behind."

After they refilled the radiator with water from the river, they went back to check on Galip's condition. The archaeologist was conscious, but weakened from loss of blood.

Morgan knelt down by the injured man. "Muhsin has Arianna. I've repaired his car, and we're going after him. Meanwhile, Halime and this man will stay with you until someone arrives to help."

As Morgan and Refah trotted to the Mercedes, Morgan growled, "I'll drive." His nerves were raw from lack of sleep and anxiety over Arianna. He had to have physical action or explode. Seeing he had stung Refah with the sharpness of his tone, he amended, "You can take the wheel later."

"That is fine, Morgan. It is not too far to the coast. Let us hope we find the mangy son of a donkey."

CHAPTER 72

They did not catch up with Tuhaf, who had too long a lead. But hours later, when the setting sun lolled just above the western horizon, they came to the Cadillac dolmuş. It had been abandoned on the road that paralleled the Mediterranean coast. Neither Tuhaf nor Arianna was in sight. By this time, Refah was behind the wheel of the Mercedes. He skidded to a stop, and he and Morgan jumped out.

A ruined fort or castle hunched on a rise at the extreme eastern end of the deserted strand. Fire thistles surrounded the castle ramparts. Morgan stared at the foreboding, thistle-guarded ruin. "Do you think he took Arianna into *that?*"

"I think maybe Tuhaf has taken her to the ship," Refah said, pointing to a white yacht anchored just beyond a tiny island. The island, about a mile offshore, contained another ruined castle.

Morgan peered from beneath his hand at the distant ship. "They must have used the dingy that's tied to the yacht to get across the water. How are we going to get out there?"

Refah nudged Morgan and pointed to a tumble-down, weather-beaten shack on the beach. "Let us see if someone is in there."

They headed to the ramshackle hut that had been built of driftwood and flotsam gleaned from the sea. As they neared it, they saw an old rowboat, bottom-side-up, on the sand next to the hut.

Refah called out. When no one responded, the two men entered. At first, in the rapidly fading light, they did not see the man working on nets by a small, flyspecked window.

"We wish to rent a boat," Refah said in Turkish to the fisherman. "We wish to surprise our friends on the ship that is anchored on the other side of the island."

The old fisherman dropped the net he was mending to the

packed sand floor. Jabbing his curved needle into a ball of cord, he stood up complaining, "Why do you come here to bother me? Can you not see I am busy?"

Refah realized the fisherman was nearly deaf. Shouting, he repeated what he had said before entering.

The old man snapped, "Why do all you people suddenly ask to go to a mysterious boat I have never before seen? My brother was forced to take a foul-mouthed Anatolian and his woman out there a few hours ago. *Tamam*. It is finished."

The fisherman glared at Morgan and Refah with rheumy eyes. True, his brother had been well paid for rowing the couple out. But something suspicious was going on. Neither he nor his brother had liked the fat one, who was rude and pushy. And the pretty foreign girl looked frightened. These two looked desperate. Perhaps he could earn a few liras for himself.

"I do not rent my boat, but I will personally take you beyond the island, if it is worth my trouble." Extending his flattened palm, the old man grimaced a sly, toothless grin.

After paying the fisherman a generous sum and plying him with more questions, Refah turned to Morgan. "He says that it is low tide and the sandbar, spanning the entrance to the bay, is exposed. He insists the yacht cannot leave until midnight, when the tide is at its highest."

Morgan sighed with relief. "That gives us the opportunity to rescue Arianna—and the tablet—before high tide." Knowing they had more time, Morgan could think better. He soon developed a plan. After dark, they would take the rowboat to the island, then swim from the island to the cabin cruiser.

"It will be dangerous." Morgan said. "Whoever is on board is probably armed. We don't know if Tuhaf has more men out there, either, so we'll have to use caution in approaching the boat. How does that sound to you, Refah?"

When Refah hesitated, then bleakly nodded, Morgan added, "Ask our fisherman friend if there are sharks in the bay."

Refah did not answer.

"Refah?"

"I cannot swim," Refah announced, looking at once ashamed and sorrowful.

Refah's disclosure stunned Morgan, but he immediately rationalized that few Turks born on the steppes of Anatolia would know how to swim. As for himself, he had been a member of the Bakersfield High swim team, and he swam like a fish.

Morgan would not have Refah's help directly, but Refah revealed a plan of his own. "I will drive to Silifke and contact the authorities for help. It is a short distance; it will not take me long."

"I'm still going out there as soon as it's dark."

"I do not think it is wise for you to rescue Arianna by yourself, Morgan." But Refah could not talk Morgan out of it.

"You should get started," Morgan said curtly, "though I sure wish you were going with me. Hurry back; I may have trouble."

In the diminishing twilight, the oar blades cut powerfully into the water; the little rowboat hissed through the wavelets. The fisherman rowed, but not facing the stern as Morgan had learned to when a child on vacation at Lake Isabella. Instead, the old man faced the prow as he rowed. Morgan marveled at the wiry Turk's deft manipulation of the odd-looking oars, which had large, bulbous shanks that resembled Popeye's plump forearms.

As they approached the island's lee shore, Morgan tapped the Turk's shoulder and motioned for him to cease rowing. When the skiff glided to a stop, the fisherman sank a cement-filled five-gallon can into the shallow water to serve as an anchor. They waited there until the sky was completely dark, then Morgan had the Turk row to the other side of the island to a position far enough from the cabin cruiser to avoid being seen by anyone on board.

The night was moonless so far, but lights in the ship's cabin and on the rear deck sparkled on the surrounding sea. When the lights gradually blinked out and the only illumination came from the cabin portholes, Morgan stripped to his shorts and slid into the sea. His skin barely felt the tepid water until he began silently breast stroking toward the cruiser. Then, as he swam, the water brushed along his body like delicate feathers. At another time or place, he would have thoroughly enjoyed his first dip in the Mediterranean.

The cabin cruiser was about half a mile out. As Morgan neared it, the incoming tide and a rising wind made it more difficult to swim. Finally attaining the ship, Morgan clutched the anchor chain. He remained afloat, with his nose just above the water's surface.

Shafts of light still slashed from the portholes. The yacht was old, and its brass fittings were green with corrosion. Dingy white paint peeled from the planks like skin off a bad sunburn. Morgan's unprotected toes recoiled from clusters of knife-sharp barnacles that clung to the hull below the waterline.

Boisterous voices, the words slurred, revealed to Morgan that more than one man was on board, and that they were drinking. Arianna was in more danger than he at first believed. He quietly stroked along the side of the yacht. Reaching the stern, he spied a rope boarding ladder dangling from the rail. *The creep has made it easy for me*, he thought, relieved.

Careful not to rock the rolling cabin cruiser out of synch with the swells, Morgan slowly climbed the ladder until his eyes were just above the rail. Now he had a clear view of the deck and cabin. There was no one in sight. He hauled himself over the rail and crouched on the filthy deck. The stench of diesel oil and putrefying fish seared his nostrils.

Making his way forward along the rail, past the open cockpit to a cabin porthole, he cautiously scanned the interior.

What once was a luxurious yacht was now a disreputable trawler. Ragged, greasy curtains flapped in the breeze filtering through the open door and portholes. The fine mahogany cabinets were gouged and salt stained.

Tuhaf sat with two men at a long table, which was strewn with the remnants of a meal. He had removed his coat and tie, but still wore the same trousers and shirt, now rumpled and stained. The other men dressed as common fishermen.

When Morgan saw Arianna, he stifled a groan. A large bruise colored her swollen jaw. However, she appeared to have no other injuries. He wanted to burst into the cabin to maim— to kill—the man who had hurt her.

It took all Morgan's self-control to wait for his chance to attack.

CHAPTER 73

Arianna slumped on a bunk in a corner of the yacht's cabin. Pretending to sleep, she covertly watched the tipsy men through half-closed lids. Though she was unbound, she didn't dare twitch a muscle. She found it difficult to keep from rubbing her aching temple—the one slammed against the Cadillac's window frame when Tuhaf backhanded her. Nausea caused by pain and by the rough sea made it hard to think. *Oh, please, please, Lord God, don't let me throw up in front of them.* But she needn't have feared; her stomach was empty. *Dear God, let Morgan find me,* she silently prayed. *I'm so afraid.*

Morgan backed away from the porthole and squatted on the deck. He had to get Arianna out of there somehow, but he couldn't do it without a weapon of some sort. He rose and crept aft. Stealthily searching through the junk that littered the deck, his probing fingers curled around cold, hard metal.

Hallelujah, a crowbar. Exactly what I need, he exulted.

He swung the bar above his head to test its balance. Morgan grinned wickedly; it would do just fine. But he had to know how drunk the men would get. He returned to the porthole.

Tuhaf nursed only one glassful, while the other two men kept filling theirs. Twenty minutes later, Morgan saw Tuhaf impatiently shove away the hand of a sodden crewman who tried to give him more liquor. Ten more minutes and the crewman slumped on the table, his face buried in his arms.

One down, and two to go.

Tuhaf was not drunk enough to be dismissed as a threat. Neither was the third man, who wore a filthy captain's cap that once was white. When the latter left the cabin and stumbled to the rail to relieve himself, Morgan curled into a tight ball. Before the man could turn around, Morgan hit the back of his head with the crowbar, an inch below the rim of his cap. The man doubled over without a sound and slipped forward across the rail and into the water. The act sickened Morgan. Korea was long ago—he thought his killing of men was over.

He went back to his place at the porthole. The crewman who lay across the table had not changed position. Tuhaf restlessly paced the cabin. Morgan had a sudden thought. Had Tuhaf overhauled his pistol since it misfired earlier that day? If so, he could not chance bullets flying around the tiny cabin with Arianna in it; he had to distract the Turk, had to disarm him somehow.

Moving aft again, Morgan stood out of sight beside the cabin door. He held the crowbar horizontally, like a medieval halberd in front of his chest. His leg muscles tautened in preparation for the dash into the cabin. But before he could make his move, Tuhaf loudly called out in Turkish. Morgan froze.

Tuhaf shouted again. When there was no answer from the man Morgan had knocked overboard, Tuhaf bulled up the cabin steps and out the door. Before Morgan could strike, the Turk saw him and ducked down the steps, back into the cabin. A shot sounded and a bullet rang against an iron bait box behind Morgan.

Guess that answers my question, Morgan thought grimly. *He's cleaned his gun.*

Tuhaf reached up from where he knelt on the cabin floor and flipped a switch. The interior lights went out. A crescent moon had risen above the horizon, and its meager light shining through drifting clouds was all that illuminated the pitching vessel. When his eyes adjusted to the dark, Tuhaf crept over to Arianna who lay curled in the bunk corner, her face buried in a pillow with her hands over her ears.

Tuhaf manhandled Arianna into the ship's prow storage compartment and locked the door. The darkness was absolute; she could not see a thing. Arianna's teeth rattled with dread. She began to pray in the only way she knew how—simply, sincerely. Suddenly, she felt a presence. Calm and an assurance of rescue replaced her fear.

With Arianna contained, Tuhaf crawled to the top of the cabin stairs and peered out. He could see someone—a man—

crouched in the shadows halfway across the deck. There was no sign of the captain.

The moon emerged from the clouds and, by its light, Tuhaf recognized his adversary as the tall American from the dolmuş.

Morgan tensed as Tuhaf braced his gun barrel on the door frame and aimed. Confident, sneering, Tuhaf curled his index finger around the trigger and slowly squeezed.

A split second before the gun fired, a four-foot swell—actually a small tsunami, the result of an earthquake deep under the Cyclades earlier that evening—surged beneath the boat with the action of a pneumatic jack. The cabin cruiser rocked and abruptly rose straight up, then dropped the same distance. Tuhaf was thrown down the stairs, his arms and legs flailing like a windmill. The bullet intended for Morgan buried itself in the cabin ceiling.

The wave's elevatorlike action first flattened Morgan, then the deck dropped away, suspending him in air. When he came down, it was onto a pile of nets. It would have been funny had the situation not been so treacherous.

Tuhaf quickly recovered and stumbled to his feet. From a belt sheath he drew the same knife with which he had slashed Galip decades earlier. He was too late. Morgan cleared the stairs and was onto him; his fist smashed Tuhaf's Adam's apple. Gagging, Tuhaf collapsed into a nonthreatening heap. Morgan hesitated only a moment, then tapped Tuhaf on the head with the crowbar. Muhsin Bey no longer moved.

"Arianna, where are you?" Morgan shouted.

"I'm locked in here."

Morgan strode to the storage compartment and raised his foot. "Get back and shield your face; I'm going to kick the door in."

"Go ahead, I'm ready."

The door shattered under the impact of Morgan's size thirteen boot. Arianna flew into his arms and her icy lips pressed his. He returned the kiss until he felt her lips warm, then he gently pushed her away. "Let's go before Tuhaf or the sot flopped on the table come to."

"What about the tablet? It's here somewhere." She started to search the cabin.

"Forget the tablet, Arianna. Your life is more important than any relic. Let's get out of here."

"We can't leave it behind!"

"We have to." That said, Morgan grabbed Arianna's arm and dragged her out of the cabin and up the stairs. Tuhaf never stirred as they hopped over his supine form.

Morgan led her to the yacht's stern. To his dismay, he saw that the yacht's dingy was gone. Apparently its rope had been too loosely tied and it had drifted off. "Do you feel up to a swim?"

"You mean you're going to let that awful man have my tablet just like that?" Arianna screamed at Morgan.

"This is no time to argue, woman. Its weight would sink who-ever carried it." With that, Morgan picked Arianna up and threw her overboard, then jumped in after her. Arianna snorted and hacked water from her lungs, but Morgan heard no further protest from her. Swimming with a smooth Australian crawl, he headed toward the skiff.

That Morgan might leave her behind terrified Arianna. Though a strong swimmer herself, she had to work to keep up with him. Staying enough ahead to motivate Arianna into try-ing her utmost, Morgan managed to keep an eye on her in case she got into trouble.

When they reached the island, the old fisherman helped them into the rowboat. He had just picked up the oddly-shaped oars when the cabin cruiser's engine coughed to life.

"Şimdi! Şimdi! Get going, effendi," Morgan shouted.

The old man merely sat stupefied by all the excitement. Morgan pushed him aside, took up the oars, and frantically rowed for shore.

"He's coming after us," Arianna screeched.

Morgan looked back to the cruiser in time to see a spotlight blink on. The spot's bright circle skimmed back and forth over the swells, searching. Morgan could not row fast enough to escape the shaft of light that skewered them. Gathering speed, the cabin cruiser turned and moved in their direction.

Arianna howled, "He's going to run us down."

The spotlight held them in its beam, guiding the cabin cruiser closer and closer. As it gained speed, the ship's bow lifted ominously.

Suddenly, over the sound of the sea and the yacht's engine, they heard the muted *pop-pop-pop* of a helicopter coming from the east.

"It must be the Turkish Coast Guard," Morgan cried.

Tuhaf had also heard the helicopter and doused the spotlight. The yacht swerved and sped away, the throb of its engine fading as it headed seaward.

Morgan shouted over the helicopter's noise, "He can't make it across the sandbar; the tide's not high enough." At that instant, a tremendous detonation pummeled their ears. An enormous fireball, mushroom-shaped like an atom bomb cloud, broiled skyward. Burning wreckage, glowing like fireworks from a Roman candle, splashed into the sea around them.

"He hit the bar. He must have had explosives or munitions aboard," Morgan shouted above the din.

Arianna huddled against Morgan for protection. They watched the remains of the cabin cruiser burn and sink, carrying to the Mediterranean floor Tuhaf—and the priceless gold-sheathed tablet.

* * *

Morgan and Arianna sat on the sofa in front of Morgan's penthouse fireplace. The fall air hadn't yet turned chilly, but despite his vow not to use precious wood unnecessarily, Morgan had built a fire for Arianna. She still shivered with horror when she remembered how narrowly she had escaped injury or death.

Shimmering in the firelight, the last surviving tablet's golden corner lay on the coffee table in front of them. Morgan picked it up. "I'm going to give this to Dr. Yaldiz; it holds only bad memories for me."

Arianna gently took it from him. "It really belongs to Turkey anyway," she said.

The two of them fell silent. Each recalled the series of events that brought them together. Arianna unconsciously rubbed her thumb over the gold sheathing. Frowning, she studied the artifact.

"This character stands by itself, and it's larger. Look!" She pointed to what looked like a rectangle with four slashes over it. "This is the lower left corner of the tablet, right?"

"Yes. Why?"

"Most ancient languages read from right to left, instead of left to right like English."

"So?" Morgan pulled a magnifying glass from the coffee table drawer and examined the character Arianna had indicated. It resembled a boxlike ship and rain. "This reminds me of a *chop*," he said.

"What's a chop?"

"It's a Chinese seal or signature. They also used it in India and . . ." Morgan stopped. Coming to the same conclusion, they stared at one another.

"If the tablets are authentic, and this is Noah's signature, why did God let all but one be destroyed?" Arianna wondered.

"Maybe this isn't His time to reveal Noah's ark."

"Why not destroy them all, then?" She sounded bitter. Morgan put down the glass. "It doesn't matter if all or none are left. I don't want anything more to do with any of them; this piece has brought me enough grief." He took Arianna into his arms. "You are all that is important to me now; I don't want to lose you, too."

Epilogue

Galip sat in his favorite chair at the team's season-end reception. He fondly watched the young people as they laughed and talked. Knowing this team had been the best, he hated to see it break up and the members disperse.

Refah was speaking. "Ahmet did not know that Tuhaf, alias Muhsin Bey, merely used him. Ahmet expected Tuhaf to help him rise to an important position in the Communist Party." Halime sat next to Refah, her gaze lingering lovingly on his face.

"Tuhaf Cesur also used Ahmet in his plan for revenge against me," Galip said. "I believe Ahmet thought what he was doing was for the good of Turkey. He must have learned Tuhaf planned to take the tablets out of the country—to Russia."

Morgan nodded. "That could have been what Arianna and I saw them arguing about in the café."

"Yet Ahmet willingly gave the tablets to Tuhaf. We saw him do it," Arianna interjected.

"Tuhaf paid Ahmet a good sum for a common laborer," Galip added. "But when Tuhaf promised to increase the ante, Ahmet's greed overcame his ideology."

"I'm glad Ahmet will be in prison for many years." Halime sighed. "He disappointed us all."

Arianna looked around Galip's living room at the others, saying, "I don't know if I'll ever get over losing poor Mohammed, then both tablets."

"The loss of Mohammed and my driver, Onur, is sad for us and for their family and friends; the loss of the tablets is a loss for the world," Galip said.

Morgan had his arm around Arianna and sympathetically squeezed her shoulder. She reached up to hold his hand. He turned to Galip. "There are still the tablet pieces you have, Dr. Yaldiz. By the way, where are they?"

Galip smiled. "Locked in the museum vault along with the beautiful cross and other objects from the well. The museum director and I are the only persons who know the combination. You may have your piece whenever you wish, Morgan, but I would like to keep it for a while."

"Dr. Yaldiz, the corner is yours; I no longer need it." What Morgan did not say was that he no longer needed the searing pain of Kwan Mei's memory.

"Will the remaining tablet prove the existence of Noah's ark?" Refah asked.

"I personally believe Noah, or a member of his family, made the tablets," Galip declared. "But what we have left, even a possible signature, is not enough scientific proof."

"Centuries ago people wrote that the ark was on the mountain then," Refah said.

"Well, Dr. Yaldiz, I too am convinced the tablets are authentic." Arianna lifted her face to Morgan and their gaze met and held. "Someday I'm going to search for more evidence. Maybe go after the tablet that went down with that Muhsin character."

Morgan laughed. "What makes you so sure the tablets were really from Noah's ark?"

No longer afraid of revealing her heritage, Arianna spoke deliberately. "My Armenian grandmother told how the priests made regular trips up Mt. Ararat to visit the ark. In fact, my grandmother thinks she may have found a piece of something from it when she was thirteen."

Arianna's friend Beverly had been invited to the reception and now joined in the conversation. "I guess the secular and scientific communities have to have physical evidence," she said. "But as often as God gives the human race proof of His Word, people still refuse to believe it. Jesus is the best example; though He performed miracles and was even resurrected, they didn't believe in Him either. I think that the ark will be revealed someday—in God's time, not ours. We just have to have faith that every word in the Bible is true, including the story of Noah's ark and the Great Flood."

"The Qur'an tells the same story." Wincing, Galip leaned forward in his chair. Though his wound still hurt, the bullet had merely glanced off his ribs and he was rapidly recovering. "Yes, someday Allah will show the ark to the world," he said. "And, my young friends, someday I will organize a search for the tablet that went down with Tuhaf."

Halime then thought of something everyone seemed to have forgotten. "Could it possibly have escaped damage?" she asked.

Galip chuckled. "We'll never know until we find it, will we?"